Crazy Horse and Chief Red Cloud

Warrior Chiefs - Teton Oglalas

Ed McGaa, J.D., Eagle Man

With Dr. John Bryde and
John McGaa, M.S., OST 40960

Editors: Diane Elliott and Linda Stevenson

Cover illustrated by Marie Buchfink

D0965041

Four Directions Publishing, Minneapolis

Four Directions Publishing

For information, address:
P.O. Box 24671, Minneapolis, MN 55424
Eagleman4@aol.com or Pahaeagle@rap.midco.net

First Edition

Cover illustration by Marie Buchfink
Art Direction by Kimberlea A. Weeks

ISBN 0-9645173-3-7

Contents

Acknowledgements

To the Thunder Valley Sun Dancers.

To Crazy Horse Mountain.

To Korzcak* and Ruth.

To Anne and Jedwiga Ziolkowski.

To Lula Red Cloud and Harry Burk.

To loyal and supportive Dave Strain, Dakota Books.

To loyal and supportive Angela Wozniak.

To my 'Striper' Carolina fishing buddy, Gerry Hayes.

To my Iowa Pheasant buddy, John Jacobson.

To old Rex* for saving my life in a blizzard.

To Connie Bowen.*

To Mary Dohm.

*deceased.

Capt. McGaa, son John and
Marine Phantom F4B

Foreword

Catlin's Creed:

I love a people who have always made me welcome
    to the best they had.
I love a people who are honest without laws,
    who have no jails and no poorhouses.
I love a people who keep the commandments without ever
    having read them or heard them preached from the pulpit.
I love a people who never swear, who never take
    the name of God in vain.
I love a people who love their neighbors as they love themselves.
I love a people who worship God without a bible,
    for I believe that God loves them also.
I love a people whose religion is all the same, and who
    are free from religious animosities.
I love a people who have never raised a hand against me, or stolen
    my property, where there was no law to punish for either.
I love a people who have never fought a battle with white men,
    except on their own ground.
I love and don't fear mankind where God has made and
    left them, for there they are children.
I love a people who live and keep what is their own
    without locks and keys.
I love all people who do the best they can.
And oh, how I love a people who don't live for the love of money!

— George Catlin (1796-1872)

George Catlin, Artist, who lived for eight years among Native American tribes, said in 1841: "Nowhere, to my knowledge, have they stolen a six-pence worth of my property, though in their countries there are no laws to punish for theft. I have visited forty-eight different tribes, and I feel authorized to say that the North American Indian in his native state is honest, faithful, brave...and an honorable and religious being."[1]

Contributors

Dr. John Bryde — Sioux History

Dr. Bryde is a personal friend. I used to fly him from the University to his extension classes throughout South Dakota. He was once a Jesuit missionary on the Sioux reservation, where I was born, the Oglalas. He would point below and tell me of my people. Upon crossing the Missouri, he once said, "Now there is where your people first crossed over." He would point upstream and add, "Now there is where a large Arikara encampment was located. Your people had to get past them before crossing over." Rich history was passed on, as we flew.

A deep scholar of Sioux history: He is one of those rare historians who spoke our language rather fluently. This allowed him to receive valuable information from the old time Sioux who could reach way back while he was yet, a young Jesuit priest and intensely interested in Oglala history, especially from our point of view. Often there is a huge difference.

He was there at a time when the elders personally knew the great chiefs and of the many battles, skirmishes, raids and war parties against other tribes, and not just against the Army alone. The old timers had much to talk about; much to tell; in their own language for their past held wondrous adventure. Siouxs, especially Teton Oglalas were never in awe of a white man, especially a pompous one. They were loaded with the rich Sioux humor as well and many an academic earned himself a bundle of derisive jokes in Lakota at his own expense. The more pompous and superior, the more the old warriors would have a grand time playing the fool who thought he was so important yet had nary a single coup nor had braved the many dangers his subjects had faced numerous times. It was impossible for them to obsequiously relate to one who had never exposed himself to the tests of the battlefield, crept silently toward a guarded horse herd, touched an enemy, fought hand to hand, danced the grueling sun dance or braved a blizzard to bring back food for the people. Their value system was not based on how much a man could accumulate or a puny degree he claimed.

Larry McMurtry, the noted author of Lonesome Dove had this to say in his book, Crazy Horse, regarding Sioux language. "There is also — rarely mentioned but critical — the huge problem of translation. The old men who were looking back across the years and yielding up their memories of Crazy Horse did so in the Sioux language, a language seldom easily or accurately brought into English."[1]

Dr. Bryde spoke Lakota at a time when many of the old Sioux would not convey their rich past unless they could tell it in Lakota. They were much more comfortable (and accurate, in my opinion) speaking their own language. Doctor Bryde personally knew many of the historians who descended onto the reservation. Hotels and boarding houses did not exist on the Pine Ridge and often, the only place to stay was the Jesuit, Holy Rosary Mission during the summers when anthropologists, historians and related academics came to dig in droves for the past. 'Doc' was quite familiar with their studies and aware of their findings and views. Much of what 'Doc' has to relate is not found in modern history books, however, because historians with limited time and schedule did not have the access, productive setting, congenial atmosphere, established 'Indian' credentials and Time; which John Bryde managed to be so privileged with. It was no question to the Sioux either, 'Father Bryde' was highly respected by the people. He had the 'heart' behind his many interviews which were devoid of academic formality. This the people appreciated and hence they were more conducive to reach back into that past when they fought for their freedom upon the Great Plains.

Doctor Bryde is retired in Vermillion, South Dakota where he once taught at the University. He is 85 years at the time of this writing and came to the Oglalas in 1945. He told me to bring his words back alive from his earlier writings, long out of print. I have taken the liberty to also include much of what he has personally taught me.

John McGaa, Oglala Sioux, Wayzhazha sub-band
Fictional History of Crazy Horse

Little is known of Chief Crazy Horse's personal life. No authentic picture exists either of this famous chief whereas photographs of Chief Red Cloud and Sitting Bull are numerous. Away from the battle field or planning the war party he would return to his reclusive role. He even shunned council meetings unrelated to the major issue of his time — defending the tribe. His grave remains unknown. Most of Chief Crazy Horse's biography comes from fictional biographers. So-called 'fiction' can often be dead centered as to a subject however, for it can convey the 'Spirit' of a person but that 'Spirit' can not truthfully be brought forth unless the author has a truthful, respecting attitude. At least that is how a Sioux would believe. The old timers would respect an Indian author who has a sweat lodge in his own back yard, as son John has. We Sioux believe in the word 'Spirit' deeply. We also respect one's blood. 'The Spirits can speak through one's blood,' is one of our beliefs. Maybe John has that access. We would not think of claiming direct lineage to the great chief as he had no progeny that lived to mate and reproduce. But we are of the Oglala, the Wayzhazha sub-band, to be specific, who were exceptionally loyal to Crazy Horse's band. All the way with him to the end, they loyally rode. Of the Oglalas, they were the last to come in. In our way of thinking, we are connected to our Spirits. We shall see.

About the Author

Ed (Eagle Man) McGaa, J.D. is a registered Teton Oglala, born on the Pine Ridge reservation. Following his childhood ambition, he became a Marine Fighter Pilot and flew 110 combat missions in Vietnam. He holds a law degree from the University of South Dakota and is the author of seven books; including *Mother Earth Spirituality* (Harper & Row Publishers), *Nature's Way* (Harper/Collins) and *Native Wisdom* (Council Oak Books). Eagle Man participated six times in six years as a sun dancer under the tutelage of the holy men Chief Eagle Feather, Chief Fool's Crow and Ben Black Elk.

Introduction

Crazy Horse and Chief Red Cloud is an attempt to portray two great men of the same tribe and to dispel the white man's constant attempts to create a rivalry and animosity between the two, hence to dilute and downgrade the magnificent Sioux culture. Sadly, in my opinion: Too many white writers, had their Sioux martyr, Crazy Horse, Sitting Bull or Spotted Tail, all of whom did not live long after the Custer Battle; and hence; proceeded to wrongfully and errantly negate the one who lived, the great chief of many battles, by weapon and word: Chief Red Cloud.

This book will also focus on early history and religion as well for it is the core from where these great men were shaped. Odd, that earlier writings have refused to offer, in depth, such rich ingredients.

"Sioux Wipe Out Custer!"

These headlines once read; ranging far and wide across the land and on into Europe. Chief Crazy Horse and Chief Sitting Bull both fought in this attack by the notorious 'Pehin Zizi' (Yellow Hair), Lt. Col. George Armstrong Custer.

Modern academics now prefer; Lakota or Dakota vs the term Sioux, which dates back to Capt. Jonathan Carver, early 18th century explorer who transmitted the Chippewa/French identification, Nadeswesous, or Nadoswessioux, meaning enemies. Natives to the western reservations in these modern times, at least those who are older or have not gone on to college, refer to themselves simply, as 'Sioux.' Being of the older generation myself, I stubbornly prefer to be called a Sioux. Didn't those headlines above notarize the fierce resistance of a strong willed people against overwhelming odds? Yes indeed, we were capable enemies. To the entire **Indian** world at that time, being a Sioux was indeed a people you respected. Without intention to belittle or downplay but there was little battle strategy needed in that encounter, except for a hasty flanking movement cutting off higher ground by Crazy Horse. The encamped Sioux simply grabbed up their guns to return a hail of fire, stopping the astonished U.S. Cavalry cold. Pinning the Army down, they then worked their way in closer. The Army, shot their horses and dug in behind them, attempting to return fire. Maybe the whole encounter lasted an hour. One survivor, a horse named Comanche, remained of the initial attacking side. The combat conditioned warriors were well armed and with plenty of ammunition, which metal detectors would prove in later years. Where did those arms and their ammunition come from? Why did they have such a supply of ammunition and the firearms to deliver such an adequate reply? How was the entire tribe able to move so suddenly, their belongings on travois?

Chief Red Cloud, the great military strategist, did not fight in that battle for he was not there. Much of the modern weaponry, however, in the hands of the retaliating Sioux existed due to this venerable general of the plains; to wit: his repeated success in earlier battles; many battles. Horses do not spring up and multiply overnight nor is there some gullible tribe out on the plains just waiting to give away their horses. Indians did not pan Black Hills gold either and then travel to some horse auction or gun show. It took a century to build up the vast herds and the arsenal the Sioux wound up with. Many raids and skirmishes, many close encounters with other tribes and then the blue coats, the Army, brought guns. To experience 80 coups as Chief Red Cloud held, you had to be a determined and gifted warrior. The Spirit World surely had to be watching out for such a one. Without Red Cloud's initial success, especially the capture of enemy horses and weaponry, Custer would have destroyed a primitively armed force encamped along the Greasy Grass (Little Big Horn River) that fateful day no different than the murderous Chivington wiped out a lightly armed Cheyenne encampment. The study of Red Cloud's combat track record, will be explored in this essay, for he, indeed was the equal of any Sioux chief but then we are getting ahead of our story.

Errant Misrepresentation

The great Lakota (Oglala) chief was errantly misrepresented in a television depiction over a century later, by Ted Turner Enterprises which was woefully deceptive to a national audience. Turner followed the old Hollywood recipe; create false stereotypes and pit Indian against Indian, this time it was two great chiefs, and nothing could have been further from the truth. To me, the deception Turner projected was akin to a Marine Colonel, deceiving a successful Marine General, akin to Lt. General Chesty Puller's reputation, one who had come up through the ranks with a long string of successful battle field conduct and experienced campaigns including the severe mauling of six Chinese divisions out of the Chosen reservoir and the colonel getting away with it through official Marine Corps channels. It isn't done in the U.S.M.C. and it certainly was not acceptable conduct back in the days of the plains warriors who regarded warrior hood as up close to their religion. Honor, Bravery, Courage, Generosity, and plain Truth were not mere words to these people whose solemn dignity bespoke the highest regard for the word Truth. They gave little quarter as their latest enemy taught them coup was not honored. Truth to a plains warrior was the deepest ingredient of their circle. Yes, life was a circle to the Sioux, for to them, a life without truth, was no life at all. As we progress, I hope this writing will convey that appreciation viewed from the eyes of the plains warrior as he rode ever so free upon what was a seemingly endless plain.

Sioux culture and customs alone will prove Turner's enormous error. No doubt, this was the initial impetus, the catalyst why I endeavored to write this book. Mari Sandoz began to surface in the likes of Ted Turner as I began to explore, especially in her attitude toward Chief Red Cloud, the only prominent Lakota warrior chief besides Gall who lived onward. Maybe, it was the Spirits within my Wayzhazha blood or was it Alice and James W. Red Cloud who sheltered my Mother and Father during those Great Depression times and whose son I was named after?

There are many Crazy Horse and Red Cloud books out there, but most do not cover this serious misunderstanding and worse, none will tell you in depth about what made **both** these men, truly great! Some are derogatory in part; especially the older books when writers were so locked into their Euro-centric, false sense of superiority and/or just could not imagine a presentation that did not play off one against the other. 'The only good Indian is a dead Indian?' Or is that the one, the old time writer could actually like?

Speaking of a crucial interview devoted to the last 15 months of Chief Crazy Horse's life with He Dog, Author McMurtry states, "Except for one or two incidents, the other thirty-five years of his life are barely touched on; and the interview, all told, is only about fifteen pages long, questions included. Mari Sandoz then wrote a biography which is 428 pages long, many of them purely speculative. Stephen Ambrose, a professional, historian, writing in the mid-seventies, devotes about half of a 538 page book to Crazy Horse, and, like Sandoz doesn't seem to mind putting words in the mouth of this man of few words."[1]

"If the word "record" is to mean anything, one would have to say that for much of Crazy Horse's life, there is no record."[2]

Great Presidents

As honest, respectful historical models, of which no American president could compare, other than possibly, Washington, Jefferson and Abraham Lincoln, in my opinion, many Sioux leaders rose to a high zenith of exemplary man. Before we proceed further, I think these three presidents need some clarification as to my claims on their behalf:

Washington: Our first president can easily be acclaimed to such a high degree. George Washington, General of the Continental Army, could have been our emerging country's first dictator; such was the dependence the early colonists entrusted to him. Instead, to a bickering, fledgling Congress, he served his term as President and then simply stepped down, retiring to his beloved Mount Vernon. He had out fought a better equipped British Army complete with Hessian mercenaries and a more powerful and numerous shipped, supplying Royal Navy. At the time, people were not used to the idea of a leader being elected by the people except for what they had learned from the Indian tribes all around them. Yet Washington placed the idea of an elected leader far above what history had shown in the world's governments in those times.

Jefferson: It is my personal opinion that Jefferson was strongly influenced by another great leader, Benjamin Franklin. Franklin knew the depth of true democracy when he was sent as an emissary, along with Thomas Paine to woo the Iroquois away from the British as supportive allies in the early days of the War for Independence. Both men were deeply moved at the freedoms the Iroquois enjoyed, Freedom of Assembly, Freedom of Speech, Freedom of Ownership, Freedom of Elected Leaders and so many more basic freedoms that the early colonists had never experienced. A book by Jack Weatherford, *Indian Givers*, would come forth several centuries later extolling the many gifts the earliest inhabitants of this land would pass on to the entire planet. My opinion is that the greatest gift from man to man or a people to other peoples would indeed be true Democracy. It is regrettable that so many of this land's population have no idea that Democracy came right out of this continent and from the Iroquoian Confederacy. I cite Jefferson, strongly influenced by Franklin, as being better positioned to carry on these early principles of democratic government into a written Constitution, a Bill of Rights and further; the actions and conduct of a selfless leader in elected office. Jefferson had the bravery and courage to break away from the established mold of barony and nobility to create a society governed essentially by popular vote.

Lincoln: He freed the slaves! Our nation was not a true Democracy until the coming of the man who was reared in a log cabin and had to fight a civil war. He gave his life before slavery's abolishment. Slavery can never be an ingredient of Democracy if we truly respect the reality of real, natural Truth when we attempt to debate the merits of this great discovery or invention, whichever-Democracy! The animal brothers and sisters have basically democratic lives and they do not have slaves!

What of the early Greeks and the Romans and their reputed Democracy? Southern historians cloud the raw facts that these early institutions were slave states and only a privileged few could actually vote whereas Iroquoian women had the right to vote with the added power of the right to recall through the Iroquoian word 'caucus.' A 'caucus' of women would consult with each other and vote out an Iroquoian Confederacy leader who was inept or derelict of his duties. I guess that we can call Iroquoian Democracy as 'Democracy Plus!'

Crazy Horse Mountain

At present a mountain in the Black Hills is being carved in the likeness of the younger chief, Crazy Horse, who is sitting upon a spirited horse; left arm rests across his steed; *Tahshuunka Wakan* (horse). His fist pointing: His unspoken words proclaiming: "My lands are where my dead lie buried."

Tah Shuunka Wakan means 'big dog holy' the early Sioux word for horse because when the people first saw the horse a man was riding it. They proclaimed that such an animal at first sight was a big dog and that a man could ride upon it, therefore it was of course 'Wakan' (wah kahn, holy) because the man could make it go obediently to where he wanted it to go. It was friendly, like a dog is to man. Surely it was a great gift from Creator, 'Wakan Tanka' (wah kahn tahn kah, Great Spirit, Great Holy), and in time the entire Sioux Nation would be mounted, hunting the buffalo very effectively upon the Great Plains.

Tah shuunka Wakan — In this writing, Siouan words will be spelled phonetically as the white man spells his words. Yes, phonetically and contrary to the practice of Academia, both non-Indian and Indian scholars who still won't cross the line and sit at the lunch counter or move up to the vacant spaces at the front of the bus, so to archaically speak! For example: The commonly spelled word; Wasicu which means white man and oft mispronounced as 'Wha See coo.' It is pronounced in Lakota/Dakota as wha shi chu (wha shee chu). Older pronunciation was wha shee eeh chu glu ble ahtah, or; 'always reaches for the fat' or 'he always reaches for (takes) the biggest pieces' (at a serving). Hence, it will be spelled as whashichu: Because that is the way it sounds! Tankasila (Grandfather) is another word that has most of our non-native speaking youth mispronouncing as Tahnk ah see lah. Taunk-ahh-shi lah is the pronunciation utilized by my mentors, Chief Eagle Feather and Chief Fools Crow. Above, I purposely place an extra 'u' in Tahshuunka, in an attempt to save a mis-speaker from a high degree of embarrassment, especially before a Sioux audience. Shuunka, is one word that you do not want to mis-pronounce especially with the preceding word Tah, which means big or large. Enough said. One can always blame their embarrassing error on the Academics. Lastly, I too have a high degree in Academics, and therefore (Iktomilah) qualify myself to call 'Academics' — 'Academics.' My knowledge base however is more reliant on my earned association with the true old-timers and of course many of my resultant direct experiences due to their tutelage. Oddly, many Academics seem to have difficulty with such a fortunate background that provided direct observation as well.

Masters of our Own Visions

One of the Hurons explained to Baron Lahontan, a French ethnographer who lived with the Huron tribe back in the colonial period. The Hurons deplored the European obsession with money which compelled European women to sell their bodies to lonely men and compelled European men to sell their lives to the armies of greedy men to enslave more people. "We are born free and united brothers, each as much a great lord as the other, while you are all the slaves of one sole man. I am the master of my body, I dispose of myself, I do what I wish, I am the first and last of my nation...subject only to the Great Spirit."[3] Author, Jack Weatherford goes on to state that

Lahontan's writings rested on a solid base of ethnographic fact: the Hurons lived without social classes, without a government separate from their kinship system, and without private property.

Writing from Within

I will attempt to write 'from within' of two Sioux leaders but also of the people's values as expressed by the Huron's above. Maybe the knowledge of my teachers and their profound experiences can reach where some historians could not. I always thought that an experienced sun dancer could convey the depth of such a powerful ceremony far more deeply than a white man who had never endured the grueling yet deeply beautiful event despite the white man's degrees and credits from some supporting institution. Yet, most all books centralizing on the demanding Sun Dance are written by inexperienced white men, all of whom are academics. Worse, none of them believe as we Indians believe! One has written three books on the subject and never personally knew any of the holy men conducting the event nor has he personally exposed himself to his subject matter other than as a very brief onlooker, yet there they are three volumes in the nation's book stores.[4] See Eurocentrism and Native Americans. An interesting Book Review.

No wonder Academics hide behind their university presses and despise those few who expose them. It is a pretty serious spiritual world for a sun dance pledger beginning with the lonely thirst filled Vision Quest lasting for days. I also think that if one believed in the Way, a more accurate account of traditional tribal based history and cultural aspects could be arrived at from an experienced writer. Yet, most academics will no doubt attempt to subvert this assertion, even some native scholars who have had to spend four long years or more in the white man's institutions learning what Indians are all about! One famous Indian writer/scholar from my age bracket, and a Sioux at that but not a Teton, wrote a book on Native Spirituality and never included one Medicine person of Native background that he personally knew! He describes Sun Dance and Vision Quest from a narration by a white woman who had absolutely no spiritual respect for her subject. Worse, he does not include any personal information regarding his own participation, which seems highly unlikely. He is an Academic. He did manage to include a few Black Elk quotes. I strongly suspect that he did not personally know any real Sioux medicine men and yet he proceeded boldly to tell us academically about Sioux Spirituality! One academic named Julian Rice went so far as to complain in his writings that I and another Native writer have capitalized on our writings. I allowed my books for sale...as he did his and as have all the rest of the academics writing on Native peoples including the Indian academics! I have to subsist in this world no different than he does and do not have a university supporting salary. I do not write to a specific group. I write! What a ridiculous, weird, racist assertion.

Since the Sioux were dedicated combat warriors, maybe even that role, close-fire-in-your-face combat, experienced by an author; should or could be of some help — for we are dealing with two leaders who saw a lifetime of deadly combat — we shall see. Sheer, terror filled combat: As the two great warrior chiefs experienced! A rare few of the academics are combat experienced. They spend too much time deploring the military, in my opinion. Universities are hot-beds of insults for our dedicated military yet many of them clamor to write about the real warriors. What have they experienced? Long and lonely tours overseas? Months at sea for some, the long wait before the fight. Numbing cold, torrid heat, insect infested nights. The dread of POW/MIA! Seeing your wounded! The Dead! Agent Orange, crawling snakes, probing rats, and now suicide bombers out of nowhere. The hunt, risk and sacrifice for the wounded and those behind. Does this teach one anything? It certainly projects vividly in the mind. These experiences are not the experiences of most Academics, my opinion. I have been exposed eight years in Academia, and I say this from what I have observed. I will let the reader make their own minds up.

Returning for Your Own

The Marines go after their wounded and their dead as well, little different than the Sioux. Crazy Horse made this one of his 'trade marks' so to speak. Red Cloud too, for he was so rescued after an arrow was buried deep into his torso and was found missing. His comrades risked a fatal attack when they placed him on a slow travois.

I remember an entire day, and a long night, never leaving my plane. Flying five missions back to back to rescue two helicopter loads of Marines who were trapped on a high ridge, little different than what Red Cloud experienced. Half never made it out. They just disappeared including the pilots into an enemy battalion: Never showed up on POW roles either: Just disappeared. But the Marines fought on to get the other load out. We fought long into that night and later under flares which is a dreadful experience, especially in the mountains under a black deadly sky. You had to know your terrain for often you would be pulling out in a canyon with enemy infested mountains on each side alternating your approach and pull out because of enemy fire. A box canyon could be fatal. An AD, several gun ships, and an A-4 as I can remember were shot down. Our two F-4s made pass after pass for we carried the most ordnance, 12 big shots (500 pounders) and could stay on station much longer except for the Spad which did not last long because of his risky slow speed (compared to ours) on pull out. The first three missions, I do not remember dropping more than one piece of ordnance per pass. Each explosion kept the battalion warily back. To buy time, we often made false passes (no drops). It was touchy bombing as you had to be damned careful for your own men so close. We two pilots had to go back repeatedly because we knew the area and it was getting dark and our speed allowed us to get back- quickly, by combat standards. Such a marvel was the Phantom in that era. We were the major source for protecting those below. It would have been suicide to send in new pilots. It was getting dark after the third run.

I was sitting in the revetments reloading and refueled. I munched on a hamburger and a 'loaded' malt, from the squadron's flight surgeon, which kept one from going to the bathroom except for urinating after you unstrapped and walked to the end of the broad aircraft and relieved into the kerosene exhaust. One engine whined at idle while ordnance crews scurried beneath the plane. "Chief, you have to go back out. I can't send fresh pilots. They won't be able to handle it." My Skipper (squadron commander) implored. Marines, like Red Cloud and Crazy Horse, go back after their warriors. After the fourth mission on a black night by then, he again asked. It is all in my log book in case would be detractors seek verification. My officer's record book repeats my experience by my commander in recommending me for a high medal. I never got it although the other pilot did. I was getting out for law school. Maybe that was why because we both experienced the same circumstances on those missions. Upon my return, my tribal chairman, Enos Poor Bear, publicly presented me with an Eagle Feather at our Sun Dance. I should be more than satisfied, I know. I have one nagging request, however. I want that high medal pinned on my pillow when I'm gone. Since the other pilot got one, as well (Major Tom Duffy — KIA on a later mission). I earned it! Early the next morning, after my fifth mission, two helicopters extracted the survivors of that battle. We brought out our own!

Similar Experience

Does a combat warrior whom has had similar experiences as the subjects he has dedicated his involvement to; does this background aid him to project into the 'true Real' of his subjects whom also faced death more than a few times (at least 80 coups each) upon a battle field? Does a sun dance experience or several afford deeper understanding to offer future readers? Does being of 'the blood' alter one's projection? From what I have read so far, about my people, I would answer that question in the reverse. I think it has 'altered' the writings of many writers, whom **are not** of 'the blood!' There are exceptions however, such in depth writers as Dr. Bryde, John Neihardt, J. Epes Brown, Vinson Brown, Tom Brown and, of course, Jack Weatherford are among my favorites. Maybe that is why I so admire the writings of Thor Heyerdahl. He lived his writings! Scholarship and research is never to be downplayed, but neither should related experience and especially when unusual circumstances favor access. One circumstance for this writing was Dr. Bryde's honing of a new language. This diligence brought forth a bounty of material. He was also blessed with simply being 'There' and earning respect. 'Being of the Blood' can be bountiful too.

Carolinas

Earliest Mythology

I do not consider mythology, when I write about the Sioux, as anything more than passing information. Such information is not offered as a historic happening. Charlotte Black Elk, an Oglala, along with many supporting Lakota/Dakota, claims that we Sioux evolved from Wind Cave in the Black Hills. The original opening was but a small aperture, smaller than the torso of a human being by far. Wind from the fist size opening allegedly blew the hat off a bypassing cowboy; thus, it was discovered. According to her theory we were confined there, within the void, for quite sometime. Eventually, the early Sioux emerged out of this cave and therefore the Black Hills is our birthplace. Again, I personally hold this concept as mythology, although many Sioux consider Wind Cave as the birthplace of the Lakota/Dakota people. It is a free country and I have no objection to what people choose to believe, as long as they do not get over zealous and attempt to cast harm on those who will not join in their views. Superstition has killed millions down through time along with unimaginable mental and social suffering fostered against the non-superstitious. When I enter the Spirit World, I want to proudly look back and reflect that I allowed few superstitions to guide my trail. What I can directly observe from my surroundings and/or become influenced from plausible scientific theories is the basis of my belief s and that includes origin as well.

Siouan speaking tribes of the Carolina's were the Wacama, the Catawba and the Biloxi. The Biloxi moved as far south as South Carolina, yet never left the East with the main body of migrating Sioux. The Wacama remained in North Carolina and have a creation or origin myth that a comet, or some space entity, crashed in nearby Lake Wakama. This is where the Sioux came from, in their own mythological viewpoint. Some Sioux think we come from the star group Pleiades, often visible in late summer. Sure seems like a long journey in my personal opinion. I visited the Wacama tribe several decades ago. I made a trip: a sort of "Roots" trip, if one reflects back to Alex Haley's cinematic work on the African slaves coming to America. I did not have to cross an ocean however; instead, I had a talk with the tribal chairwoman of the Wacamas. She said that the last Siouan speaker, an old Grandmother, had died some thirty years before. This was in the 1980's. The tribe seemed to know nothing of their culture during my visit. "We are all Christians," she admitted, "we know little of the past as your tribe does."

The National Geographic Supplement, September, 2005,[1] suggests the Sioux as being from the Ohio area and negates the possibility of the three remaining tribes staying in the Carolinas, but also negates the added clue offered by the medicine bundles of the Siouan speaking Kansa and Arkansa tribes. In the early 1800's, the chiefs of these two tribes stated that they were from the tciyeta (ocean) which is at Nyu Yak (New York), (the land where the Sun comes up from the water); known to us as the Atlantic Ocean. Their medicine bundles were analyzed and the sea shells therein did indeed come from the east coast, precisely the bay that the chiefs described. The Kansa and Arkansa evidence suggests that the Sioux may have once been in Iroquois territory, but were finally driven out once the Iroquois formed their strong confederacy of five tribes. This theory would have the Sioux as once coastal dwellers at one time and another strongly supporting and related (coastal dwellers) factor will be brought out later. This theory is yet another riddle to be solved, possibly for those who believe in a Spirit World, wherein we may all go some day. Any historical puzzles will be answered, hopefully there, should such an entity (Spirit World) exist.

The Sioux – Since the 1500's

The history of the Sioux during the past five hundred years can be traced from their origins in the Piedmont area of the Carolinas. To their North were the Iroquois, the most powerful of the North American tribes. The Iroquois were a united confederacy, made up of five organized tribes. The next most powerful tribe in North America was the Cherokee. Their domain lay south and southwesterly of the Piedmont where they enjoyed lush agricultural lands. European ships were passing up and down the Atlantic coast by this time. For it was a century since Columbus and the first newcomers brought their fatal diseases, wiping out or severely decimating many coastal tribes. The Shawnee were most likely already west of the soon-to-be-migrating Sioux. The Sioux were called Lakota or Dakota in those times. They regarded themselves as the Friendly People of the Seven Council Fires. Later, they would pick up their "Sioux" name from the French explorers on their journey westward. At the time that Columbus landed on a few islands south of Florida, I believe someone entering into the piedmont — of what would later become the Carolinas — would have heard the term, 'Hau Kola,' which means "Hello friend" in Sioux.

We can imagine the Sioux living quite comfortably in the piedmont area that provided adequate soil for tilling and planting. Meat supplemented their diet: primarily deer and wild turkeys, which foraged in abundance all the way to the Mississippi River. Their houses were not the conical buffalo-hide covered dwellings that came later, they were square or rectangular frame structures made of sturdy saplings and covered with bark and thatch from lesser branches — often with leaves for insulation. Winters were milder than the climates of the northern United States. Overall, they were quite peaceful, as were many of the agricultural tribes who had little need or desire for pursuing another tribe's possessions. Their diet consisted of corn, squash, beans, potatoes, tomatoes, and the rich array of wild game the land offered. Fish also supplemented their diet. Journeys to the nearby Atlantic coast brought them succulent seafood as well. Truly, they lived in a virtual paradise. It remains a mystery why they would up and vacate such choice living conditions and head westward. No one has yet to come up with an adequate explanation for that mystery.

The Westward Move

Some scholars believe it was the constant raids by the powerful Iroquois to the North. If this was the case, then why did they continue to move so far away from their adversaries — two thousand miles in all? The Cherokees to their South were considerably more peaceful than the Iroquois. No doubt, the Cherokees appreciated having the Sioux as a buffer between them and the powerful Iroquois.

The westward move soon became a mass migration, and very few stayed behind; only the Catawbas, Biloxis, and Wacamas primarily. They would soon be swallowed up by the European tide of immigrants fleeing their own homelands. Europe was not a particularly choice land to live in at the time the Sioux were leaving their productive lands in the Carolinas. Europeans were barely removed from serfdom, brutalized by a harsh church that was still in the throes of the Inquisitions. The Europeans had two masters: the church hierarchy and the land owning nobility of barons and earls. They knew nothing of the Democracy the American Indians were enjoying at the time Columbus was making his journey and even later, when the Pilgrims landed.

Raleigh's First Colony – 1585-86

History offers evidence regarding the seagoing vessels that were now beginning to appear more frequently after Columbus' voyage. A discourse on Sir Walter Raleigh's unsuccessful settlements on Roanoke Island and the Pilgrims should prove to be of interest and bears such evidence. Sir Walter Raleigh, under the blessings of Queen Elizabeth, sent a colony of 108 persons to Roanoke Island. The expedition sailed in seven ships from Plymouth, England, April, 1585. Included in the group of sailors and colonists were two American Indians: interpreters Wanchese and Manteo, just then returning to America after an earlier exploration which brought them to England. The first attempt at colonization proved unsuccessful and all but 15 men returned, primarily because of the mistreatment of the at-first friendly Indians of the outer bank islands. The Indians were initially of great assistance, but the egotistical superiority of the English was too much for the Indians and open warfare broke out. A second attempt in 1587 resulted in the lost colony of Roanoke Island. The English-Spanish war, and the invasion of the Spanish Armada, prevented the re-supply for the second wave of colonizers. The Indians simply overpowered and destroyed the entire settlement. No one was found when the English finally returned.

Pilgrims – 1620

On Sept. 6, 1620, the Pilgrims set sail for the New World on a ship called the Mayflower. They sailed from Plymouth, England with 110 people aboard. The long trip was cold and damp and took 65 days. Since there was the danger of fire on the wooden ship, the food had to be eaten cold. Many passengers became sick and one person died by the time land was sighted on November 10.

Plymouth, which was named by Captain John Smith six years earlier, offered an excellent harbor, with a large brook. The bay itself, provided a resource for fish and shellfish. The Pilgrims biggest concern was attack by the local native Indians. But the Plymouth Bay area Indians proved to be a peaceful group, as were most of the coastal Indians in comparison to the far more warlike Europeans, and did not prove to be a threat. The Europeans had a history of constant wars up to this time, but were loathe to admit it. Instead, even the peaceful Indians who would teach them to survive would be branded as warlike savages and hostiles. They were seen as pagans because of their religion: a creator based spirituality, which taught them to be kind to strangers regardless of their color and differing beliefs.

Over half of the Pilgrims died during the long first winter. In the Spring of 1621 an Indian walked into the Pilgrims camp bearing the words "Welcome." His name was Samoset. He had learned English from the captains of fishing boats that had sailed off the coast. He returned with another Indian named Squanto, a Patuxet Indian who spoke even better English. Squanto told the Pilgrims of his voyages across the ocean and of his visits to England and Spain. It was in England where he had learned to speak so well. But when he returned to his homeland, he discovered that his tribe had been wiped out by the white-man's diseases. He was the last of the Patuxets.

Squanto's importance to the Pilgrims was enormous, and it can be said that they would not have survived without his help. It was Squanto who taught the Pilgrims how to tap the maple trees for sap. He taught them which plants were poisonous and which had medicinal powers. He taught them how to plant the Indian corn by heaping the earth into low mounds with several seeds and fish in each mound. The decaying fish fertilized the corn. He also taught them to plant other crops with the corn. Beans and squash for example, mutually benefited each other, as well as the corn plant. The harvest in the following October was very successful. The Pilgrims found themselves with enough food to put away for the winter. There were fruits and vegetables, fish to be packed in salt, and meat to be cured over smoky fires. The Indians annually held tribal Thanksgivings to their Higher Power. Obviously, the Pilgrims were influenced by this acknowledging conduct and held a Thanksgiving for their survival and appreciation, which has grown into a national holiday. Chief Massahoit of the Wamponoag tribe arrived with over 50 braves and helped the Pilgrims to celebrate the event.[2] Sadly, the Native originators receive little credit for this event.

The Move Westward

By the 1600's, they were already on their great move westward. The Iroquois were mentioned as a possible reason for the Sioux's sudden migration from their comfortable surroundings. One would wonder as to what significant event would drive out an entire tribe — other than another, more powerful, invading tribe. If that were the case, the Sioux would have been severely mauled, and the victor would have picked up an enormous line of captives. But this was not the case. Could it have been the deadly diseases that the early ships had brought to the coastal tribes, as in the case of the Patuxets? This scenario is indeed a more plausible theory than attacks by another tribe. Again, I offer the nagging question, why did they migrate two thousand miles: to distance themselves from such fatal diseases? I have a third theory, which I will go into at a later time after the reader becomes a bit more acclimated to Native culture. It too is but theory and speculation, but could prove plausible and at very least…interesting.

Exodus

Down the Ohio River Valley, the Sioux moved on. Not in one mass but gradually, band by band and in varied sizes. Possibly, bands joined for security to minimize resistance of the other tribes along the way. Eventually, they congregated in the Midwest and would soon encounter the Chippewa and Cree farther north as early as the 1600's. The Shawnee were the largest tribe to be confronted along the way. They seemed to have smoked the peace pipe with the Sioux bands, granting them unrestricted passage. As stated earlier, it was not one mass movement. It may have taken the Sioux a century to reach the Mississippi, sometimes settling on their journey, but gradually heading westward and turning upstream when they reached the Mississippi.

When the main body of Sioux reached the Mississippi some bands broke off and crossed the great river. The Mandan eventually crossed to settle far upstream. The Arkansa, and more likely the Kansa, may have crossed the great river near the Missouri confluence. Joe Medicine Crow, tribal historian of the Crow Indians in Montana, states that the Crow broke off from the main body of Sioux on their upstream journey at the mouth of the Wisconsin River. The Crow then wandered for a century toward the shores of Lake Superior and eventually crossed westward over the Great Plains, finally settling in Montana where they remain today. They would scout for the U.S. Army, and in time, against their former relatives the Sioux.

After the main body of Sioux congregated near the headwaters of the Mississippi, fierce opposition from the Chippewa sprang forth. Then, as the Sioux moved even further north, the allies of the Chippewa, the Cree, waged battles with the newcomers. Fighting was quite primitive by modern standards. Flint knives, stone axes, bows and arrows were the warrior's tools. At first the Sioux got the best of their foes as they traveled northward against both opponents. It was during this time that the name "Sioux" was first placed upon the invading Lakota/Dakota, allies or friends, which they preferred to call themselves.

Nadowessi

The adventurous Captain Jonathan Carver, an early American explorer and writer who fought in the French and Indian War, brings us to an early contact with the Sioux in the 18th century. Carver was instrumental in the transmittal of the naming of the Dakota/Lakota as 'Sioux.' The Sioux, possibly the Santee group, had reached into Wisconsin by as early as the 17th century. Wisconsin and Minnesota were considered the wild, western territories in those times; Ouisconsin and Minne-ahtah. Minne-ahtah means much water. Ouisconsin is not a Dakota/Lakota word. Neighboring tribes primarily to the north - Objibway, Chippewa and Cree — referred to the Dakota/Lakota as Nadowessi, which meant lesser enemies as compared to the bigger enemies to the east; the Iroquois, the powerful confederacy who pushed them westward. Faced with an endless stream of European immigrants, the Iroquois moved west and northwest up the Hudson valley and consequently drove the Chippewa (Ojibwas) out of their ancestral lands surrounding the St. Lawrence Seaway. The newcomers moving up the Mississippi south and east of the three northern tribes initially proved themselves as deadly and aggressive enemies on the move. The French, as was there custom, came along and added x or ioux to the Chippewa/Cree term and we have Nadowessioux. That term was soon shortened to the word Sioux, a combination of French and Chippewa.

Although the term "Sioux" is a practical name — which combines the Lakota/Dakota designation — some college educated Indians and many academics (Indian and non-Indian) in particular disapprove of the term "Sioux". However, a sign on a tribal building wall, back on my home reservation, simply reads "Oglala Sioux Tribal Council." The Tribal Council stationery also reads "Oglala Sioux Tribal Council." On the adjoining reservation less than a hundred miles east, their signs reveal "Rosebud Sioux Tribal Council." If it bothers an academic that we are "incorrect," they should first complain to the Tribal Councils instead of employing academic circles to change our name, which we have grown quite used to.

Any name can be a source of pride and respect when we have dignity and a proven Track Record of fighting successfully in many battles. I suppose I can qualify as an academic if degrees are a prime qualification and which I disagree with of course. I have a Doctorate of Jurisprudence but it was my experience and initial fortitude — common sense actually — to be with the real old-time holy men and other great teachers, like Ben Black Elk and Hilda Neihardt (daughter of John Neihardt, author of Black Elk Speaks). This is where I received a considerable amount of my knowledge, along with Doctor John Bryde's influence, where it pertains to tribal history. Dr. Bryde speaks fluent Lakota. As I have mentioned, he spent many years among the Oglalas as a Jesuit missionary. Add to this mix another mentor, Dr. James Howard. I flew both men throughout the state of South Dakota as a commercial pilot, while working my way through three years of law school. Both were teachers at the University. Dr. Howard also had two adopted Indian children whom he raised. Long hours in the cockpit sitting close to two knowledgeable scholars revealed much of my tribe's history as the Dakota landscape passed beneath us. Participation in the ceremonies, especially at the time when they were being revived by the old-time medicine people, was a god send. So revealing, that I must simply credit fate or the Forces for giving me the opportunity to acquire such valuable information. A truly traditional Indian would credit the Spirit Forces, who to us still abound upon the land. They placed me in those times, according to my belief system, the moment, and the place; which was more than coincidental — Just my opinion.

Bear in mind, this was a time when a majority of Indians — even Siouxs — were brainwashed in the boarding schools to deny their heritage when it came down to the spiritual or religious side. I recall, as a law student about to speak at an event at one of the South Dakota colleges. My theme was "Go back to your culture." Russell Means was also a speaker. The then reigning Mrs. South Dakota, an attractive Yankton wife of a successful basketball coach — both of Sioux extraction — publicly stated to the news media she would turn down her speaking request because of the presence of myself and of course Russ Means. We were "persona non grata" because we advocated our spirituality as worthy of going back to.

Very few Indians back then rallied to support us: we who were bound and determined to bring back the old way. I was not at the forefront but I did join them. The old traditionalists led then: mainly the holy men, well before others, and — I note — the absence of the Indian academics back then. That is why so few of them can honestly quote the old time medicine people as their close advisors. Look at their books! I look at these academic authors who write about our spirituality and especially our Sun Dance; none of them have ever been in the demanding and grueling (deeply moving event) Sun Dance! Only one Academic do I know, a so-called, full-fledged academic (if degrees are the requisite), Dr. Chuck Ross. He is a Santee Sioux, who has been in more sun dances than I have and now conducts the beautiful, fulfilling ceremony in the Black Hills. Chuck is an author whose books I have recommended ever since they were published. I will take experience any day over Academia when writing of a people's deepest beliefs and their resultant culture. Enough said! Once again, I proudly quote those historical newspaper headlines, "Sioux Wipe Out Custer!" We will not be undermined by the labels of Dominant Society, or anyone else who wants to label us without our express permission.

While we are on the subject of names; what about the term Indian or Native American; which is constantly brought before us? Dr. Beatrice Medicine, a Sihasapa, Teton Sioux and a noted anthropologist has this information to pass on to us:

"The term Native Americans, the most recent gloss for North American aborigines, is now in disfavor with many tribal groups and individuals. The National Congress of American Indians, a powerful self-interest group, has passed a resolution (1978) opposing its use at their last convention. Throughout the historic

Indian-white interface, such names as 'North American Indians,' 'American Indians,' 'Amerindian,' 'Indian American,' and 'First Americans' have been in vogue at various times. In this essay I use Native American and American Indian interchangeably. As for the focus of the essay, the Lakota who are often labeled 'Sioux,' 'Teton Sioux,' 'Western Lakota,' and 'Dakota' in the anthropological literature, I use the term 'Lakota,' for I am referring to the Western Sioux who speak the Lakota dialect of the Siouan language. I also use designations such as 'Rosebud Sioux' to indicate the reservation as a social system to which one assigns oneself. This is accepted procedure by most Lakota Sioux."[3]

Dr. Bea, is my "Indian Aunt," another of my teachers and always a strong supporter. Pilamiya Oh Tun win, Pilamiya.

In the summer time on various Sioux reservations, there will usually be some old-timers sitting around discussing yesterday. If you get the chance, ask them what tribe they are from. They will reply that they are Sioux. If you ask them what particular band they are from, one will point to himself and say, "I am an Oglala Sioux." He may point to another and state, "He is a Sichangu Sioux from over there on the Rosebud." Then, ask them if they are Lakotas or Dakotas. They will respond that they are Lakotas. Perhaps one will remark, "We are Lakotas, the Dakotas are far to the east; but, we are all Sioux."

Sioux Held their Culture – Others Did Not

Indeed, the Dakota were considered enemies by those who came across their path, and offered resistance to the many groups on their westward journey out of the East. I have often made the statement that the Sioux are the last of the large tribes to be reined in from their natural, Creator given freedom; and hence, this is the major reason why they have kept so much of their culture compared to the other tribes who have spent much longer with the dominating white man and his "melt-all" culture and concepts. The Sioux have only been "in" for a mere hundred years. This was a blessing for us and is the major reason why we still speak and retain our language, and why we have kept our religion intact. It is simple math; less time with the dominant culture and you retain more of your own culture. The majority of America's once prolific tribes have lost their language and know nothing of their religion. It is not their fault however. Time, along with geography, has had a lot to do with their loss. A tribe spending two hundred years with Dominant Society can easily lose their roots. Four hundred years with the white man's destructive methods for rooting out native culture and it is a miracle that some cultural roots manage to survive. The Navajo and Pueblo suffered under the brutal Spanish occupation and, their equally destructive, Spanish church: which made slaves of the people, digging for silver and gold in the many mines dotting the southwest. Geography protected the tribes to some degree (especially the vast spaces of the West); yet, the Pueblo, Zunni and Navajo religious concepts differ considerably from the Northern tribes. In my own opinion, the Spanish church influenced their religion over the 400 long years they suffered under brutal rule, until Congress finally passed the freedom of religion act in 1978. To this day, missionary churches still hold the most prominent sites within the Pueblos.

The Wacama Sioux tribe of the Carolina's, has lost their old language and culture. Now, however, we have recording machines, video cameras and compact disks that they can use to regain the old ways. They are able to regain their language, customs and culture (possibly at least, the old spiritual ways) as many tribes in the same situation are attempting to do across the land. Indian language courses are very popular, and the sweat lodge itself is becoming a prominent ceremony far and wide across America. Those who respect and utilize the sweat lodge, typically learn many Sioux songs.

The same situation that happened to the Wacama, the loss of language and customs, would probably have developed for the main body of Sioux had they not exited to the west. As a large tribe they would have undergone their own Trail of Tears — as did the Cherokee tribe — had they not left on their own. More than likely, they would have been exterminated. The less exposure to Dominant Society, the more cultural retention a tribe will maintain. This is not a difficult formula to understand. This explains why the Sioux are probably a more reliable North American tribe to study in relationship to understanding what Nature-based people believed in. Choosing, like wolves, to migrate away from overwhelming threat; they were the last of the large tribes to come in from their freedom on the Great Plains.

Religious Aside...

Yes, we admit that we have never seen Creator, but we do believe in its existence; because, we can readily see everyday what It has created for us. It would be an insult to Creator, in our opinion, if we attempted to deny that what we observe was not made by such a certain and great entity. It would also be a gross insult to Creator if we ever attempted to deny that it made all of what we can behold, without a deep sense of appreciation, recognition and thankfulness. That is why it has always been difficult for us to believe that the white man's devil/Satan exists. We have never seen it! The white man can never produce it for us when we ask him to. Instead, it has been our experience that he becomes extremely angry at us when we query him on it. So, it is probably best just to avoid that subject when we are in his midst. What is Mystery, if it causes arguments, is probably better to just leave alone; otherwise, nothing gets settled. We will always be the first to admit that we do not know exactly who Creator really is. We cannot lie about that statement, however, just to please the white man. We once were forced to be his way, and it resulted in dire results. Even as an author of a book that will be primarily read by a white audience, I will not lie and try to be pleasingly exact when it comes to that which is Mystery. I just cannot do it. It is too vast for us to try and pin down with an accurate description. We are quite content to continue onward with this attitude. We have been doing so for years.

I believe the reader is starting to realize that the Northern Plains Indians thinking and beliefs are indeed different, as were the thoughts and beliefs of the two great Chiefs we want to know more about. I believe it was the tribe that heavily influenced both men, who they would become — so to speak — and of course their own inner fortitude. The customs, culture, codes; their historical knowledge, lessons, lore, legends, winter counts; all had their impressions as both men grew from childhood.

Physical Comparisons

I have observed that the Sioux and Iroquoians are not similar in looks compared to most of the other tribes. The once-bordering Cherokees may be grouped in with the Sioux, since they are certainly the lightest complexioned, Caucasian-featured people of any North American tribe I have ever seen. The Mandans (whose main reservation is far north along the Missouri in North Dakota) are almost as light as many Cherokees, but they have more Indian features than the Cherokee's. I am speaking about Mandan individuals whose blood is over half Mandan. Contrary to many Europeans: they do not have the features of a receding hair line just above the brow, no monks-spots (pre-mature balding at the top of the skull), and in general, are not "hairy." Instead, as with most Plains Indians, they are fairly to totally without hair on the chest, back and extremities. The Mandans are tall and heavy-boned people like the Northern Europeans, but have a "commonality" in their facial appearance; whereas just about every Cherokee I have met (who was not enrolled from the Oklahoma reservation based in Tahlequah, Oklahoma) seemed to have differing, unrelated, Caucasian dominant features.

The Hunkpapa Sioux in areas of central North and South Dakota are large people in general. The Hunkpapa are slightly darker than the Mandans, but similar in appearance and relatively hairless — with little or no facial hair. Most Siouan people have a heavy head of hair where it counts — on top of the head — and do not go bald, even in senior age. Their hair may thin, but I have yet to see a full-blooded Sioux that went bald (unless some sickness caused it). The hair also stays black much longer it seems. I can personally attest to that claim. Over two decades ago at my high school class reunion, white hair and/or baldness was already making its appearance among my non-Indian classmates, and was almost totally encompassing among the majority at our recent, last gathering except for me and a few other Indian blooded classmates.

Mississippi Headwaters and Further West

In the early 17th century, driven by the Iroquois, the Chippewa were being confronted on a new front by the Sioux. According to Dr. John Bryde, (Modern Indian Psychology) the Sioux won the initial battles; as they had grown accustomed to doing on their migration trail westward from the Carolinas. They had previously swept through the Shawnees, the related tribes west of the Carolinas and those settled in the fertile Ohio River Valley. They quickly gathered a reputation for being fierce fighters. When they came into the Minne-ahtah (Land of much water) region, the Sioux were made up of three groups or divisions: the Tetons; the Yanktons, including the Yanktonai; and the Santees, who were made up of four tribes. The Santees encompassed the Mdewakanton, Wahpeton, Wahpekute, and the Sisseton. All Santees spoke the "D" dialect of the tribe's language and referred to themselves as the Dakota. The Santee tribes may have been the earliest portion of the great Sioux migration; for they ranged far into Wisconsin.

Westward

As mentioned earlier, the main body of Sioux explored the headwaters of the Mississippi. Despite some earlier battles, the Yanktonai tribe made peace with the Crees who lived to the north of the Sioux while the Cree allies, the Chippewa, were further east.

With the peace, came intermarriage between the Yanktonais and the Crees; even when the rest of the Sioux were vigorously attacking the Crees. Before 1660, the Sioux were winning most of the battles; in 1658 the Sioux won a bloody fight according to Radisson an early French explorer. In 1670, however, the Crees and their Algonquin-speaking allies traded in their furs for French guns from the Hudson Bay Company. They angrily retaliated against the Sioux for the earlier battles. In 1674, the Crees attacked and killed Sioux envoys at Sault Ste. Marie. The flash of gunpowder and smoke from many yards away — with it's accompanying loud "Bang" — would soon send shivers through even the most stalwart of the Sioux warriors, who were still inexperienced with gun fire. The loud sound accompanying each firing, and resultant death or wound, was a terrible experience to behold. Guns were such superior weapons that the Sioux had little choice but to "up and move." For the Chippewa, with their Cree allies and French guns, the tide changed: the Dakota/Nadowessioux advance into what is now Northern Minnesota became a retreat down from the headwaters of the Mississippi to the Minnesota River valley and the area of present day Minneapolis. A Sioux named body of water, Lake Minnetonka (Great Water or Big Water) lies just west of Minneapolis. In a matter of 10 years, an eyewink in historical terms, most of the Chippewas southern enemies had vacated out of northern Minnesota.

The migrating people realized that the land of Minne-ahtah was also a cold, inhospitable place to live. Far fewer artifacts are found within this region, a fact that suggests that most tribes avoided the area to some extent. Several artifact collectors I have known, related that an unusually long warm period accounted for most of their collections. Deep snows, cold winters can indeed be fatal. Further south-east, in the Kentucky area for example, numerous artifacts — stone axes, arrowheads and spear points — are still found to this day by collectors. This simple fact illustrates that the more conducive the land was for productive agriculture, the more population the land attracted and sustained. Productive agriculture typically does not grow as abundantly where the winters are long and the summers are short. Being comfortable was another main reason tribes would be drawn to an area. Extreme cold, dangerous deep winter snows and a shorter agricultural season were generally avoided; unless, a smaller tribe was being crowded by potential enemies and did not have a choice. Often these tribe's settlements would be only temporary: until better locales were scouted or they joined together with another smaller tribe for mutual survival and movement onward.

The Sioux, as I refer to as the general mass of individual migrating bands, would send out scouts and were always looking for what lied beyond the next bluff or river. The majority of the Dakota/Lakota were soon heading westward. The Yanktons and Yanktonai were the first to move. They drifted southward and came to the great elbow bend of the Minnesota River in the Swan Lake district. The Yanktons crossed the Minnesota River, separating from their tribal cousins, the Yanktonai, and settling in an area between what is now Blue Earth, Minnesota and the famous Pipestone Quarries near the Western edge of Minnesota. The Yanktonais went up the Minnesota River. Later the Oglalas and Brules (Sichangu) would cross the same area and occupy the Blue Earth River prairies westward, placing them west of the Yanktons. They would parallel the Yanktons and push on further west, gradually leaving the Yanktons behind them.

The Cheyennes were in front of the Teton Siouxs, and were eventually pushed back to the Black Hills but not until later. First, the lead tribes — the Oglala and their close associates the Sichangu (would later be called Brules) — would have to get past the powerful Arikara. The Arikara were settled comfortably in bastion like earthen structured barricades: Indian forts along the Missouri. It was a perplexing situation for the Siouxs. Twenty thousand Arikara, including several thousand warriors and some mounted, were a bit much for the Oglalas who could not muster more than five hundred warriors, all of whom were on foot. A particular grouping of Teton bands, the Saones, would go up the Minnesota River, taking them further north. This group included the Hunkpapas, whose chief would eventually be Sitting Bull. They too, were blocked by the Arikara at the Missouri river. It would be a half century (around 1825) before the Saones would reunite again with their Teton relatives to the south (Oglala and Sichangu): to camp once again together during the annual Sioux Nation sun dance.

The last of the Sioux tribes to move would be the Santees, some of them settling down in Eastern Minnesota and the Twin Cities area (the Mdewakanton), where they remain to this day. The Santees were the last to leave the Wisconsin woodlands, and were possibly who Captain Carver wrote of when he projected the new name, Nadowessioux (or Sioux) upon the wandering People of the Seven Campfires. Of the Santees, the Sissetons would move the farthest west, settling in northeast South Dakota.

New Tribes

All the tribes would face opposition and have to fight as they moved westward. The Iowa (Eeh oh wahs) and the Otoes claimed the Blue Earth River lands. The fierce fighting reputation the Tetons commanded sent the two tribes running southwest to join up with the Omahas. The Omahas had once held the Pipestone Quarries but the Yanktons had driven them out. Eventually the Omahas settled at the mouth of the Big Sioux River where it emptied into the Missouri. The Sioux had spent nearly a hundred years in Minnesota and now they would spend nearly a hundred years in western Minnesota and eastern South Dakota. We shall leave the Sioux as they progress westward toward what would later become the Dakotas.

French Guns

In retrospect the French guns (along with the cold weather), which drove the Sioux westward out of Minne-ahtah, were a great blessing from a cultural standpoint. The Chippewa would spend at least a century more in close contact with the Europeans and hence lost much more of their culture than the Sioux. Up to the date of this writing, the Sioux have but a century of contact with the white man, whereas the Chippewa have at least two centuries of contact and resulting cultural disintegration. Many modern day Chippewa, who now prefer to be called Anishanabe (Ah nish ah nah bay), have embarked on a great effort of preserving their past and incorporating their ancestral roots into their daily lives. A majority of the Sioux, eastern tribes primarily and the post war generation, were also thoroughly indoctrinated into the white man's beliefs. Nowadays, many language programs are underway and the old religion is being practiced openly. The Canadian Chippewa have been successful in maintaining their language connection and fewer have succumbed to the white man's religion. They are of great value for ongoing language programs and the retention of the old ceremonies and spiritual ways. The Sioux, like the Canadian Chippewa, were aided by the shorter duration under the white man's rule, his missionaries and the missionary influenced government Indian agents. The Sioux's geography also became a blessing, as the Sioux reservations are vast. The Pine Ridge Reservation is close to one hundred miles square in size; an area larger than some states. The Standing Rock and Cheyenne River Sioux reservations are also vast. The two adjoin one another, their combined land reaching into both the Dakotas.

Tetons

The Tetons were one of the original Seven Council Fires of the Sioux. They increased significantly in population when they found the horse and the vast buffalo herds in the Dakotas and what now part of Nebraska is. They evolved into the seven sub tribes or seven bands of the Teton Sioux. Chief Sitting Bull, Chief Gall, Chief Red Cloud and Chief Crazy Horse would soon become their leaders; all would speak the L dialect. They were all members of the Teton Lakota Nation. Historically, three of these tribes stand out and are listed first below. (If we refer to the Sioux as a Nation, then we can confer tribal status on the seven tribes. If one refers to the Sioux as a Tribe we would name each of the seven as bands.) They are:
1. The Oglala (Red Cloud, Black Elk, Crazy Horse).
2. The Sichangu (Spotted Tail).
3. The Hunkpapa (Sitting Bull and Gall).

4. Minicoujou.
5. Sihasapa (Blackfeet).
6. Oohenumpa (Two Kettles).
7. Itazipco (No Bows).

The last five representatives of the Tetons, including the Hunkpapa, would be referred to as the Saones. The Tetons would soon be the most numerous of the Sioux, more numerous than the other two divisions put together.

Exodus West

To refresh our memory, the Sioux migrated down the Ohio River Valley to a once pristine Mississippi. The Kansa and Arkansa were among the migrating Sioux and broke off when the tribe came to the confluence of the broad Missouri and Mississippi Rivers. The Arkansa and Kansa generally remained in this area, although some Kansa and Arkansa headed across the river and southward. The main Sioux group started upstream to the head-waters of the Mississippi. On the northward journey other Siouan-speaking bands broke off. The Mandan left to cross the big river and eventually head up the Missouri. The Crow soon parted at the mouth of the Wisconsin River and headed northeastward toward Lake Superior. The Sioux were in three major groups while in the Wisconsin/Minnesota lands. The Tetons, partic-ularly the Oglalas, would emerge as the principal leaders in the expansion westward.

Oglalas

The westernmost Sioux had spent approximately a hundred years in Minnesota and Wisconsin and now the Tetons would enter western Minnesota and eastern South Dakota. The Sioux progressed westward around the mid-1700's toward what would later become the Dakotas. By now the Sioux would be trading with the French fur companies. As the Chippewa and Cree did to the Sioux, the Sioux began using their new guns on the tribes they encountered; especially those tribes encamped along the Missouri River.

* * * *

Teton Oglalas

The Sioux had spent at least a hundred years in Minnesota and Wisconsin and now the Tetons would enter western Minnesota and eastern South Dakota. Of the three divisions, only the Tetons would cross the wide Missouri with the exception of some Yankton.

Arikara

The Arikara were a formidable obstacle to further expansion. The whole Sioux nation could not muster as many warriors. The Arikaras had log and earthen villages, large villages up and down the Missouri strongly fortified with ditches, earthen walls and cedar log stockades. Some of these forts were tremendous in their size. One great fortress, about seven miles south of Pierre was built on a high plateau. The Arikaras lived mostly by corn planting and raising other vegetables and had hundreds of acres under cultivation growing a variety of crops. Since they had horses, they would also supplement their diet with buffalo hunts. The Sioux who had spent some years near the James River were about to face some troubled times and initially accepted charity from the Arikaras. In the ancient Indian tradition of sharing, they had no hesitation to beg from the Arikaras, who gave them food and even a few horses; other accounts say it was the Cheyennes. In the beginning the Sioux were on fairly good terms with the Arikara and would visit with them in their villages. To the rear of the Tetons were the Yanktons. Feeling hemmed in they feared crossing the Missouri however for there were too many mounted Arikara warriors carrying Spanish saber blades tipping their long buffalo spears. On the open plains they could easily ride down and kill any bands that were on foot, as the Sioux were. Their westward drifting movement was essentially stopped for at least 25 years. The Tetons balanced this threat by periodically getting up large war parties of several hundred men and driving the Arikaras into their fortified villages, so well fortified that the attackers could not storm them. After taking a few scalps and maybe a few horses, the Tetons would plunder their corn patches and go back home. Then disaster struck the Arikaras that changed everything. Between 1772 and 1780, three great epidemics of small pox hit the Arikara. Their population was reduced from 20,000 to 4,000. The strong fortified villages on the east bank of the Missouri could no longer hold out and were destroyed. As a result the Arikara withdrew to the west bank and consolidated all of their people in four to five villages just below the mouth of the Cheyenne River.

Pushing Westward

The way was now open for the Tetons to cross over and push westward. The Oglalas led the way. They were the first of the Sioux to pass over the Missouri, the first to reach the Black Hills and the first to turn south to reach the Platte River in Nebraska. It was the year 1775. Far to the east a new nation was about to declare its independence. The American colonists were desiring freedom and control of their own destiny. The Declaration of Independence would bring a new era of freedoms unknown in Europe.

The next 100 years saw an incredible expansion in territory and an explosion in population that would make the Sioux the most powerful tribe on the Great Plains. The strength for this expansion came not only from physical strength and endurance but also from an inner spiritual strength that gave them supreme confidence and pride in themselves and a conviction that they couldn't lose. It would seem that this inner spiritual strength came from their intense awareness of their union with the Great Spirit, with themselves and with this Creator's Nature. There was a thrust to the people that made them recognize no odds. This same strength gave them the force to adapt to anything in changing their way of making a living because they were about to change from a food gathering and planting people to a people constantly on the move, hunting the buffalo for a living. Adaptability was a key word for the success of the Sioux, especially the Oglalas and their almost constant partners the Sichangu (Brules).

From a small band of foot traveling rovers that straggled to the Missouri between 1750 and 1775, carrying their belongings mostly on their backs and begging food and horses from the Arikara, in just a few years, they were to be swarming over the plains from the Missouri to the Rocky Mountains and from the northern border of Kansas to the Canadian border. The very name Sioux, not as much the terms Lakota or Dakota, but Sioux, would strike terror in the hearts of other Indians and non-Indians alike. Obviously they retained their identification as Lakota or Dakota but as the Tetons went westward and became more successful the other tribes, especially those who were in front of them and had to fight or flee from the advancing Oglalas, they were referred to by opposing tribes as Sioux. The name obviously stuck and in time, even the Tetons got used to it.

Horses and Leadership

Essential to the southern Tetons expansion at that time were two ingredients: horses and leadership. They were soon to have both. Accounts vary as to how the Tetons first got their horses. Some accounts state that they received their first horses from the Arikara and some accounts hold that they got them from the Cheyenne. They did not get them all at once however. Early raids saw them picking up a few horses here and there but not in huge numbers all at once.

As to the actual crossing of the Missouri, the following is one of the traditional stories of the Tetons. One day the Oglalas were traveling along the Missouri right below the great bend in the river, some say Crow Creek and others say near Platte Creek. There were about 30 to 40 lodges in the group and they were afoot and nearly starving. It was wintertime and the Missouri was frozen. Suddenly the Eyapaha, the camp crier, called on the men to go after buffalo that had been spotted out on the frozen Missouri. Instantly the whole camp got involved hunting down and killing as many buffalo as possible. Since the buffalo could not run on the ice very well and kept falling down and thrashing around, the people were able to kill a great number of them. When the slaughter was over they found themselves much closer to the west bank than they were to the east bank (from where they had come from). They set up camp on the west bank and began skinning, cutting and preparing the meat which took them a number of days and before they were finished, a warm wind came up and melted the ice on the river, leaving them stranded on the west bank.

Buffalo Meat

An interesting note on buffalo meat: Scientists have had a difficult time growing cancer cells in it and cancer was a rare disease among the buffalo dieting Sioux. Modern dieticians consider it a prime nutrition source especially for those afflicted with diabetes. Many tribes, most all of the western Sioux, are now raising their own buffalo herds and the reservation inhabitants readily proclaim the merits of buffalo meat. Long ago, diabetes was almost an unknown disease among the early Sioux. Now it runs rampant among most of the western tribes. It is so prevalent that conferences are being held and the buffalo diet is seriously being discussed along with other safer foods which lead back to the old traditional fare basically and away from the modern diets and canned soft drinks which are referred to as 'junk foods.'

First Horses

One day, the stranded Oglalas saw two scouts approaching on horses. They turned out to be Cheyenne and fortunately were friendly. Since the Cheyennes had horses to drag their long tipi poles, their tipis were very tall and impressive. The Cheyennes took in the Oglalas and treated them fine. At the end of their visit, the Cheyennes gave the Oglalas a number of horses, which, according to this account, was the beginning of the vast herds that the Tetons were going to have.

With horses now, although still only a few in number, the Tetons began an amazing development. They gradually acquired more horses and it was not long before they were ranging far and wide, hunting the buffalo and fighting other tribes on all sides. The very year that they crossed the Missouri, 1775, one of the great leaders, Standing Bull, got up a war party that went westward far enough to discover the Black Hills. They came back with glowing reports of this beautiful country that was surrounded by buffalo and this, in turn, caused the Tetons eyes to keep turning farther westward.

The horse was the catalyst that released the tremendous energies of the Sioux. In a few hours now they could travel distances that took them days to travel when they were afoot. For one thing, this meant game and buffalo could be spotted, run down and killed, all within a few hours. Before, when they were afoot, it would take days to organize such a hunt and to bring it off and this only with all the people in on the hunt. Now, a few hunters on horses could do in a few hours that which it took all the people many days to do. As a result of this increase of food, the people grew stronger and more vigorous. Babies that would have lost their lives by the constant travel and shortage of food were now being saved, and the people increased in number. Daring leaders were not lacking to get up exploratory parties and war parties to increase the range of their territories.

One result of these early successes was that other Tetons and some Yanktons, still on the east side of the Missouri, heard about these exploits and came to join the Oglalas, bringing their families. This increase of people made the people stronger than ever and gave added force to their expansion. The Oglalas became so numerous and strong that it was not very long before they, in turn, had to divide up into seven sub-bands, as they swept the western prairies as far west as the Powder River in

Wyoming. The "powder" that made up this explosion of people and territory was made up of:

a. daring leadership.
b. the horse.
c. the tremendous inner spirit and pride of the people themselves.

Although the Indian values had been operating in the people for centuries, it was during this period for about the next hundred years that these values can be seen most clearly, propelling the people to greatness and generating the immediate historical forces that shaped the behavior of the Indian people living today.

The noted Indian value of sharing and generosity, for instance, is seen most clearly in the two areas in which they shared: food and shelter, and praise and shame. Now that they had horses to bring game, this meant fewer hunters could bring in even more game. Yet, although fewer were doing the actual getting of the game, the whole group still shared in the more game that was brought in. Whatever a few did, they did for the whole group.

Other Tribes

This great expansion of territory caused, of course, conflict with other tribes, which required other tribes to move. People in those days moved either because they were looking for better places to live in order to eat better, or they moved because they were pushed out by other bands of superior size and force. It is hard for us today to realize that the peoples in those days saw no particular injustice in this practice and accepted it as one of the laws of life. They saw all the land in the whole world as belonging to everyone. As to who roamed over this particular territory at this time depended upon this particular tribe's size and strength. This was a law of life that they all accepted. Again and again, one sees examples in Indian history in which a given tribe would be pushed out by another larger tribe. Some years later, the pushed out tribe, now grown larger than the tribe that pushed them out, would come back and push out the original "pusher-outers." Throughout Indian history, there was a constant shuffling of territories. For instance, one can find a given tribe on a map from a certain period and when one looks at the map again a hundred years later, that tribe is not there, but hundreds of miles away in another direction. When a strong tribe would push out a small tribe, the smaller tribe would, in turn, push out someone smaller yet, and so it would go down the line, causing another reshuffling of the territory. As we said, this was one of the laws of life in those days, and everyone accepted it.

What is remarkable about this in the case of the Oglala is that such a vast territory could be taken over by a people who were so small in number in the beginning. After the first 25 years since crossing the Missouri, when they were gradually acquiring horses, they still had the incredibly small number of only around 500 people. This was the estimate of Lewis and Clark in 1804. Only twenty years later, in 1825, this number had quadrupled, i.e., made the amazing increase of four times its original number. This quadruple increase brought the number of the people up to around 1,500, with about 500 warriors. This increase was not all birth rate, however. This increase was caused, as was mentioned earlier, by other Tetons and some Yankton people coming to join the Oglalas.

The Brules were soon to follow. Farther north, on the eastern side of the Missouri, the other bands of Tetons — the Saones — were held up for about another 20 years (about 1795) because the remaining Arikaras had gathered themselves together and in this way, resisted for this length of time the westward movement of the Teton Saones. The Hunkpapas and the Blackfeet Sioux were held up until about 1825 and were the last to come across.

Bad River

When people traveled in those days, they had to stay close to water, usually following rivers. As the Oglalas headed westward, they followed the Bad River which flowed directly from the Black Hills. The farther west they went, the flatter, drier and hotter the land became, especially from about the end of June onward. The buffalo was plentiful, however, and the Oglalas didn't care how a land looked as long as there was plenty to eat. Indeed, the Oglalas soon learned to love their new homes with its high, dry and windy plains. In the words of George Hyde, it was "a hard country where men had to be fully alive to avoid perishing." This was a land to test their mettle and the Oglalas, being a rugged people, thrived on it.

Farther south, the Brules followed the White River westward. Here, the land was greener and living conditions were congenial, and it was not long before the Brules were roaming it as far as Wyoming and as far south as the Niobrara River.

It was said that this expansion of territory caused conflicts with the other tribes and, from the time that the Tetons crossed the Missouri, small in number though they were, they were soon engaged in fighting other tribes on all sides. When they ranged as far west as the Black Hills, this was the area in which the Kiowas were living at that time. They immediately started attacking the Kiowas and Kiowa tradition has much to say about Teton attacks at this time.

Kiowas and Omahas

An entire division of Kiowas were destroyed by the Sioux in one battle and the attacks became so numerous that the Kiowas gave up their old custom of traveling to the Missouri River to trade with the Arikaras. The next tribes to receive the attention of the Tetons were the Poncas and the Omahas. About 25 years before, they had been driven out of their homelands by the Tetons and had settled in northeastern Nebraska. Since that time, they had been getting guns and ammunition from the Sacs and Foxes of the Mississippi and were building up a revenge attack on the Sioux. About 1778, three years after the Tetons crossed the Missouri; the Poncas made peace with the Oglalas, then came back with a heavy war party and made a surprise attack on their camp. The Poncas were beaten off and lost sixty of their warriors in that fight. The Omahas also had been building up with guns and ammunition in order to get back at the Tetons. Around 1784, about 10 years after the Tetons crossed the Missouri, the Omahas, led by their great chief, Blackbird, began attacking both the Oglalas and the Brules. Fighting went on at regular intervals for about the next seven years, when peace was temporarily established. We say temporarily because, although two tribes would fight with each other and would be almost traditional enemies, there would be times of peace from time to time when they would trade with each other — as the Tetons did with the Arikaras in the winter of 1792-1793, although the Oglalas and the Brules had been fighting with them just the year before.

In the year 1780, however, the Oglalas and the Brules were fighting the Arikaras, who, as was said, were occupying the west bank of the Missouri around the present town of Pierre, South Dakota. At the same time, they were fighting the Kiowas and the Crows among some other tribes in the Black Hills country to the west. The serious fighting with the Crows started in 1785-1786 when Bear's Ears, a Brule, was visiting in an Oglala camp. He and a famous Oglala warrior named Broken Leg Duck decided to relieve the Crows of some of their horses in a routine horse stealing foray. Leaving their own horses some miles away, they crept up on the Crow horse herd, crawling on their bellies and hiding in the tall grass now defenseless without their horses. The Crow horses spooked, however, and the alert guards spotted them. They were run down and killed before they could get back to their horses. This aroused the Oglalas so much that they attacked the Crows so frequently and successfully that the Crows, who had occupied the country from the Black Hills northward, centering along the Little Missouri, were finally forced to retire westward to Montana.

Cheyennes and Crows

Farther to the south of the Black Hills where they were living at this time, the Cheyennes were the next to receive the attention of the expanding Oglalas and Brules. Since the Brules had followed the White River and settled in southwestern South Dakota, it was there where they encountered the Cheyennes and who began the hostilities. One of the great Brule war leaders, Owner of the Flute, led a war party against the Cheyennes about 1793. The Cheyennes spotted them coming, however, laid a trap for the party and killed not only Owner of the Flute, but most of his warriors. Immediately the war pipe went out from the Brules to their Oglala relatives inviting them for reprisals against the Cheyennes. The Oglalas, never ones to turn down a fight, came whooping to join the fray.

The next year, in 1794, the Brules and Oglalas made up a huge war party and went looking for the Cheyennes south of the Black Hills. This time, proceeding with more caution, they surprised a huge Cheyenne camp, killed many of the people and captured the whole camp with all its contents. The Tetons, particularly the Brules and the Oglalas, were unpredictable as to how they would treat their enemies. Some enemies, such as the Kiowas and the Crows, they drove out for good and kept up a running fight with them for years. To other enemies, such as the Cheyennes and the Arikaras, they would extend peace from time to time. In the case of the Cheyennes at this time, they soon made peace with them and let them return to the country south of the Black Hills.

Teton Saones

This removal of the Arikaras in 1799, from their old home near the mouth of the Cheyenne River to their new homes farther south near the Grand River is an important date for the Tetons. The way was now open for the Tetons — Saones to cross the river and move west ward. The Minicoujous led the way westward up the Cheyenne River, followed by the Itazipcos (Itazipza, No Bows) and the Two Kettles. The rest of the Saones, the Hunkpapas and the Blackfoot Sioux were to follow about 1825. The date is important because now the Minicoujous, No Bows and Two Kettles were closer to the Oglala relatives and could strengthen them in their ventures. It made the Oglalas stronger than ever and gave more power to their thrusts for more territory. About forty years from this point in time — about 1840, perhaps — a full half of all the people who called themselves Oglalas were of Saone blood. This, as was mentioned before, was because the daring leadership and successes of the Oglala leaders drew these Teton Saones to the Oglalas and made the people stronger.

You will recall that sometime around 1785 the Oglalas had driven the Crows out of the land north of the Black Hills and had forced them to retire as far west as the Powder River country in Wyoming. Here, far away from the Tetons, the Crows were not much troubled by them. Once in a while the Tetons would get up a horse stealing party to invade the Crow territory, but there were no battles on a large scale. Also, during this time (about 1785-1800) the Crows liked to come eastward to trade with the Mandan and Hidatsa villages on the Missouri River, near the mouth of Knife River. Sometimes the Tetons would catch them on the trail and attack them. This was the only way that the Tetons kept up their occasional contacts with the Crows.

Lewis and Clark

At the time of the coming of Lewis and Clark, however (early1800's), the Tetons were engaged in a new war with the Crows. According to the winter counts, it was about 1801, that a large war party of Tetons had invaded the Crow territory around the Powder River country. The Crows, however, because of the frequent, small horse stealing forays of the Tetons, had been long trained to keep a sharp eye out for them and spotted them coming. Near the mouth of the Powder River the Crows laid an ambush for the Tetons and succeeded in killing around 30 of their warriors. This, of course, was a great disaster and called for the traditional retaliatory blow.

In those days, the loss of many warriors or even of one great man did not cause the Tetons to turn tail and run. It caused just the opposite — a great gathering of warriors to strike back and balance things out. The manner in which they did this was fixed by custom and the Tetons and Cheyennes followed pretty much the same fixed method. First of all, they did not gather immediately and strike back. The people would wait for one winter (a year) and during this time the relatives of the dead men would take the war pipe around to as many sub-bands and other tribes as possible.

During these visits, they would publicly mourn their dead and ask the other sub-bands and tribes to join them in a war against the enemy that had caused these losses. In each camp the leading man would hold councils and help the chiefs decide whether to accept the pipe or reject it. The chief — especially the Teton chiefs usually decided to accept the pipe because the Tetons were never ones to pass up a fight; also, they had long memories and there was hardly a tribe on the plains with which they had not been in conflict at one time or another and were ever ready to renew old grudges. Once the pipe was accepted and smoked by the chiefs, the camp was pledged to take part in the forthcoming war. A place and time was set for the gathering and, in the following summer, those who had accepted the pipe all met at the assigned place and moved as quickly and quietly as they could into the enemy territory.

Crows

The traditional plan of attack was to try and take the enemy camp at dawn which was the best time for the attackers. They had the advantage of light (which a night attack would not give them) and the sleepy, disorganized condition of the enemy. These types of attacks were usually successful and generally resulted in a large number of enemy warriors killed, many women and children captured and the entire content of the village taken. Thus it was that when the Tetons lost their 30 warriors in the ambush by the Crows at the mouth of the Powder River, they followed the above described custom and spent the whole year in sending the war pipe around. This resulted, the following year in a huge gathering of Oglalas, Brules, Minicoujous, and Cheyennes. They met at the assigned time and place and moved into Crow territory. The expedition was a complete success because they surprised and captured an entire Crow camp.

The Crows also, however, had long memories and when, twenty years later (about 1820), they surprised a war party of Cheyenne Bow String warriors on the Tongue River. They killed every man in the party. This time, it was the Cheyennes turn to send around the war pipe and the first ones to whom they sent it was the Oglalas and some other Teton subbands. The Tetons quickly smoked the war pipe in acceptance and, a year later, came running to the appointed place. The assembled Cheyennes and Tetons moved quickly and quietly westward into Crow territory on the Tongue River. They discovered a huge Crow village of over a hundred lodges and, following the traditional manner of attack at daybreak, captured the entire village.

Sun Dance

Besides the above described occasions for conducting war with large forces, the Tetons also had another method. Every summer they would hold their annual Sun Dance after the summer buffalo hunt was over. Immediately after the Sun Dance, they would get up a war party of several hundred men (which was a tremendous force in those days), decide which enemy to attack, then move into that territory and strike a heavy blow. Even while they were in Minnesota and still afoot, the Tetons employed this method, going as far as the Missouri to attack the Omahas, Mandans or Arikaras.

It was during this period, 1800 to 1825, that the Oglalas developed a regular beat, traveling back and forth between the Black Hills and the mouth of the Bad River on the Missouri. For fifteen to twenty years after they first crossed the Missouri, they would go back to the Missouri, sometimes even east of it, in order to make winter camp. From about 1805 on, however, they began to spend their winters on the eastern edge of the Black Hills, usually near Bear Butte. When spring broke and the grass was up, they would make their way down the Bad River, hunting as they went along. On arriving at the Missouri, they would be reunited after the winter's separation with their Brule and Saone relatives. They would then take part with them in one of their favorite pastimes: stopping traders coming up the Missouri to trade with the Arikaras and Mandans, either robbing them or trading with them — at prices that the Teton chiefs themselves would decide.

Traders and Trappers

The Tetons did not do all of their trading in this fashion, of course. Ever since the coming of the French traders and trappers back in their Minnesota days, trading had become an important part of their lives. It was from the traders that they would get the most precious things they needed, which were guns and ammunition. After these items were acquired, they then wanted metal knives and the iron kettles that made cooking so much easier, as well as the metal products from which they could make better tools and better arrowheads and lance heads. Next in line came blankets, ready-made clothing and the bright beads that they liked so much for clothing decorations. In order to get as many of these things as possible, they had developed the habit of saving and tanning as beautifully as possible as many furs as they could get.

It is important to know where these trading posts were because their locations were largely responsible for the travel movements of the Sioux at this time. You will recall that, when the Oglalas and Brules crossed the Missouri, the Oglalas made their way westward along Bad River and the Brules along the White River. When the Oglalas returned to the Missouri periodically, they would follow roughly the same route along the Bad River; the traders knew this and set up a trading post on Cedar Island, right where the Bad River flows into the Missouri. This trading post was called Fort Teton for many years and was the principal trading post for all the Tetons for many years after crossing the Missouri. From the beginning, it was the French traders from St. Louis with whom they were quite friendly. From 1800 to 1817, the Teton trade was almost exclusively in the hands of these French from St. Louis at the trading post on the mouth of Bad River.

After 1817, American companies entered into the fur trade and competition became keen among the various trading companies. It was during this time of the early competition among these companies that the traders resorted to dirty tricks to get fur from the Indians as cheaply as possible. They began for the first time to bring in whisky in large quantities as items of trade. It is almost impossible for us today to realize what this did to the Indian people. The Sioux had never seen hard liquor before and were not told how it would affect them, nor were they instructed in the proper method of drinking — such as a little bit at a time. Not being told how to drink it nor how much to drink at a time, they drank it like any other liquid, such as you would drink a light drink today. Since they were not taught how to handle it, they would rapidly become intoxicated and trade off their furs for ridiculously small prices. Losing their furs for small prices was not the greatest harm that came from drinking. The worst thing that resulted, as we shall see later, was that they would fight and kill one another, their own people, when they were out of their heads with liquor. For an Indian, this was unthinkable in a sober state because every life was precious in order to keep the people strong. One great man that was lost at this time from the drinking was the father of Red Cloud because, later on, Red Cloud said many times that his father died of drink. This does not mean that he became an alcoholic and drank himself to death as some people do today. It probably means that on an occasion he drank too much of the bad or rotten kind of liquor that the traders often used. At any rate, the improper use of liquor — from not knowing how to use it — was going to cause great harm to the Indian people later on.

From about 1825 to 1835, the American Fur Company had practically a monopoly on the trade with the Tetons. The old Fort Teton at the mouth of the Bad River had been abandoned and a new post, called Fort

Tecumseh, was erected at the same place. Up to this time, the Tetons kept coming in to the Missouri River country to do their trading. After 1825, however, this same company decided to move closer to the Tetons and set up branch posts in order to get their trade more quickly by saving the Tetons long trips across South Dakota to the Missouri River. In 1829, an Oglala post was established near the Black Hills at the mouth of Rapid Creek near Bear Butte, and the Oglalas traded here until about 1834. About the same time, another branch post for the Brules was established on the White River near the present town of Pine Ridge. The immediate effect of this trading post on the Oglalas was that it kept them fairly close to the Black Hills for five or six years, from 1829 to 1835.

Having their own private trading post, however, did not mean that the Oglalas had to stay in one spot. They were too wild and accustomed to roaming to be tied down to one spot, and they still made occasional trips back to the Missouri. It was on one such trip, in 1823, that they arrived at the Missouri just in time to join up by invitation with some other Indians for a fight with their old enemies, the Arikaras. The Tetons, naturally, eagerly joined. In this fight, we find the Tetons in a very strange combination: they were going to be fighting alongside the U.S. Army against the Arikaras.

You will recall that the Arikaras, about 1799, had pulled themselves into three strongly fortified villages on the west bank of the Missouri, not far north of where the Grand River runs into the Missouri. By 1810, these three villages had been reduced to only two in number, but they were so strongly fortified that not even their strongest enemies, the Tetons, could break into them. The only things the Arikaras needed to hold out against the Tetons were guns and ammunition, all they had to do to get them was stay in the good graces of the traders who came up the Missouri periodically to trade with them.

General Ashley

According to some authorities, the Arikaras tired of the cheating practices of the traders and in an effort to gain control of the trade decided to do away with these enemies. During the years, 1822 to 1823, they began a series of attacks on the traders. These attacks came to a head in 1823 when a trader named General Ashley was arriving with a large party of trappers to trade with Arikaras for horses. Suddenly the Arikaras attacked him and his party at a spot not far from the Arikara village. Ashley managed to get his men out of the trap, but lost thirteen of them in the fight. He fled down the river for about eight miles and made camp. From his camp, he sent calls out in all directions for help — from other Indians friendly to him, from trappers in the area and from the army, which was some miles down the river.

The traders out in the fields quickly responded and urged all the Tetons they could find to come with them. The Tetons didn't need any urging and, smelling a fight, came in a hurry. The army was much slower, however, and it was several weeks before a small force of infantry and riflemen arrived under command of Colonel Henry Leavenworth. The Tetons were there in great numbers waiting impatiently: Oglalas, Minicoujous, Saones, and some Brules and Yanktons. The Tetons regarded the soldiers with great curiosity and were anxious to see them in action because they had heard much about their fighting ability from the traders they knew.

Sioux and U.S. Army – Allies

Colonel Leavenworth took command of the entire fighting force of the Indians, soldiers and trappers, and when he finally started moving up the river toward the Arikaras camp, he had a total fighting force of about 1,100 men, which was almost twice the number that the Arikaras had. Arriving at the Arikara camp, Colonel Leavenworth was surprised to see that the Arikara warriors had come out on horseback and were lined up in front of their fortified villages. While Colonel Leavenworth was deciding how to arrange his men, the Tetons solved the whole maneuver for him. With war whoops of delight at seeing their old enemies, the Tetons pushed everyone aside and rushed straight at the Arikaras. After a short, hard fight, they drove the Arikaras back into their villages. After thus acquitting themselves so handsomely and, knowing from long experience that they couldn't tear down the walls of the fortified villages, the Tetons now drew back to watch the white soldiers blow out the walls with their cannon. Colonel Leavenworth, however, was a cautious man and making no move to attack, became involved in long discussions with his officers. This disgusted the Tetons so much that they finally withdrew and headed for the corn patches of the Arikaras where they spent the rest of the day feasting. The winter counts of that year record, 'Helped the white soldiers and got plenty Arikara corn.' This feasting and resting went on for the rest of the day while Colonel Leavenworth was trying to make up his mind what to do.

The next day, the Colonel again drew his men up in line for battle. From the corn patches, where they had kept the pots boiling, the Tetons kept a watchful eye on the proceedings and waited patiently for the white soldiers to drive the Arikaras out into the open where they could get at them. But again, the Colonel was slow to act. He drew his men up in one position for assault, then shifted them all to another position. A few cannon shots were fired into the walls by the artillery, but did not do enough damage to shake the Arikaras. This went on for most of the day until late in the afternoon. By this time most of the trappers and traders and even some of the soldiers were so hungry that they came over to join the Tetons in the corn patches. This was too much for the Tetons because they liked to get their fighting over with quickly and go home. With considerable disgust at the fighting ability of the white soldiers, they loaded their ponies with as much corn as they could carry and started home — taking with them eight of Colonel Leavenworth's horses, as 'just' compensation for their services.

Happy Years

The years from 1800 to 1825, were very happy years for the western Tetons. By now, they had asserted their supremacy over the tribes that they had encountered on first coming out on the western plains — the Kiowas, Crows, Cheyennes, and, farther back east, the Omahas, Poncas and Arikaras. The great high plains belonged to them and they felt safe and at home. At this time, they were untroubled by the intrusion of non-Indians, and there were no powerful enemies to fear. Buffalo and other game were plentiful and there was usually enough to eat. Camping frequently within sight of the Black Hills, their eyes turned often to the mysterious land which they now regarded as their own. Instead of returning to the Missouri River to winter, they often now made their winter camps near sheltered streams on the eastern edge of the Black Hills. How long they would have stayed in this area, no one knows, but something happened down in southern Wyoming in 1834 that drew them down there. It was this new country that was to be the base of their operations until the reservation days would begin. It came about in this way: someone started a new trading post there and simply invited them down. They went, liked it and stayed. It was in this country in Wyoming that they would spend their finest days and rise to their greatest triumphs. This is the land where Red Cloud and his Tetons would win their war against the U.S. Government and make that government accept Red Cloud's terms.

You will recall that the Tetons, especially the Oglalas, after crossing the Missouri and going west, settled east of the Black Hills. They made periodic trips back to the Missouri to trade and visit relatives. During the period from 1825 to 1835, a company known as the American Fur Company had practically a monopoly on trade with the Tetons and it was this company that the Tetons usually returned to the Missouri to trade with.

Around 1824, General Ashley decided to try to get furs in a way faster than dealing with the Indians. Sometimes the wandering bands were hard to find and at other times, they would come to the meeting place late, or they might miss them altogether. General Ashley's plan was simple; send large numbers of trappers into Indian Territory and have the trappers themselves get the furs. These trappers got along well with the Sioux. Since they were small in number, the Sioux weren't worried about their running the game out. Also, these trappers frequently married Indian women and this gave them relationship ties with many bands.

General Ashley's plan was very successful, and this group became known as the Rocky Mountain Company. These trappers brought in so many furs that the American Fur Company decided to imitate them and send their own trappers into the field. Competition between the two companies was very hot.

Traders set up a trading post at a Wyoming location close to the Nebraska border. It would later be called Fort Laramie. Bull Bear, a famous Oglala Chief, like all good Tetons, was always eager to look over a new situation and promptly came down with about 100 lodges. He liked it so well that he spent the winter there and sent the good word to the rest of the Oglalas, who also promptly came. In 1835, there were over 200 lodges on the Platte, numbering about 1,000 to 1,200 Oglalas.

Although the Oglalas had been in that territory before, the presence of a new trading post gave them a new reason to stay in touch with that part of the country. The Rocky Mountain Company soon sold out to the American Fur Company and the Oglala found themselves trading with their old friends again, but in a different place.

Pawnees

While ranging the "new" territory, the Oglalas being good Tetons, and the best fighters on the plains, were always sniffing the breeze for the possibility of new enemies to try out. Shortly before they had come to the Laramie area, the Pawnees had been fighting the Cheyennes, and, around 1830, had wiped out an entire war party of Cheyennes. The Cheyennes sent around the war pipe and a large body of Arapahoes and Sioux (mostly Brules) answered the invitation to war on the Pawnees. The battle turned out badly for the Cheyennes because they lost their sacred Medicine Arrows in the fight. At any rate, this brought the Pawnees to the attention of the rest of the Tetons and they settled down to some serious fighting.

The Brules would attack the Pawnees in the earth lodge villages on the Loup Fork in eastern Nebraska, and the Oglalas would lie in wait for them when they came westward on their semi-annual buffalo hunts. By 1832, the Pawnees had been so badly beaten by the Brules in their homes on the Loup Fork that they fled to the south bank of the Platte. After a few years, the government persuaded them to go back to their original home. It was here in June of 1845, while rebuilding their new villages, that they were attacked by the Sioux and completely routed. Over seventy Pawnees, including a head chief named Middle Chief, were killed, thirty lodges destroyed and a large number of horses taken.

For the next twenty years, the Sioux continued to fight with the Pawnees whenever they met them. During the winter of 1837-1838, an Oglala named Paints-His-Cheeks-Red and all his family, along with a cousin of Red Cloud's (also named Red Cloud) were killed by the Pawnees on the North Platte. The war pipe went around and in 1838, a war party descended upon the Pawnees, killing many and taking a large number of horses.

Bull Bear

The following summer, 1839, the Sioux and their allies surprised a large hunting party of Pawnees on the hunting grounds near the branches of the Kansas River. Eighty Pawnees were killed and the Sioux lost only one man. The Oglala Chief, Bull Bear, led this war party. It was on the return home from this fight that the German traveler, Wislizenus, met Bull Bear and his Oglalas. Wislizenus described him as 'rather aged, and of a squat, thick figure.'

Whatever his appearances, Bull Bear was the great chief of the Oglalas at this time and the one force holding them together. He was somewhat a dictator and he ruled with an iron hand. He was tough and fearless, with a violent temper when angry. If some Oglala opposed him and he could not shout him down, he would slip a knife into him and kill him on the spot. He seems to have ruled wisely, though, and was usually on good terms with the Whites.

Around 1840, Bull Bear and the Oglalas who followed him decided to hunt even farther west than the Laramie Fork. They went into the Laramie Plains near the extreme head of the North Platte. The result of this shift of hunting grounds immediately brought them into conflict with the Snake Indians who lived in this western area and who had fine herds of horses. Instantly the Oglalas were interested and in no time at all they were raiding the Snakes. They soon found that this territory was crossed by war parties of several tribes and that this country was a brewing pot of all kinds of troubles. Ever eager for a fight, this only delighted the Oglalas and they soon found themselves carrying on three different fights at once. Naturally, the Snakes fought back during the first fight that shaped up. While fighting the Snakes off and on, the Sioux discovered that their favorite enemies, the Crows, also raided this territory for Snake horses. They promptly took up their old fight against the Crows whom they had not fought in ten years. The third source of trouble was the white trappers who had either wintered with or were living with the Snakes and Crows.

While fighting the Snakes and Crows, the Sioux saw these white trappers fighting with their enemies and, when they suffered heavy losses, put the blame on the trappers. Word of this soon got around to the Oglala sub-bands who, in turn, quickly developed the same dislike for these trappers. Although this dislike was first directed to the trappers, it soon spread to all white men in that area and it was not long before the Oglalas and other Indians on the upper Platte were talking of killing or driving out of the country all the whites except a few favored traders. This, in turn, angered the whites and they were soon sniping at the Oglalas which made a running, three cornered fight.

Whiskey

It was at this time the bitter competition between the two fur companies, the Rocky Mountain Company and the American Fur Company, became worse. It was also about this time that other companies moved into the area and competition became hotter than ever. It was not long before they all resorted to using more and more bad whiskey as one of their main means of getting furs cheaply in order to beat their opposition. As was mentioned before, however, losing their furs at cheap prices was not the worst thing that happened to the Sioux. The worst thing that happened was that, drinking the liquor like water, they would fight among themselves and kill one another. It was almost unheard of that a Sioux would kill another Sioux. Yet, after the coming of the liquor, instead of riding off and living with other relatives when he got in an argument, they fell to fighting and killed one another. This had happened once before to them, in 1822, when they were trading on the upper Missouri and they had seen scores of their tribesmen killed in drunken brawls. The wiser chiefs and older people did not want liquor around. When trouble developed among themselves because of liquor, they blamed the white traders who had urged them to take it.

The list of killings at this time recorded in the winter counts and by other sources is almost unbelievable. It is no wonder, then, that this type of liquor supplying white person became a target for many of the Sioux.

Chief Smoke and Bull Bear

It was during this period of liquor trading that the trouble between Chief Smoke and Chief Bull Bear came to a head. Chief Smoke was a genial, rather plump and good-natured leader of a sub-band of Oglalas who, because of the chief's name, were called the Smoke people. Chief Smoke was not out to out rival Bull Bear but, since Bull Bear could not stand any other rival, he regarded Smoke as a danger to his position and was always jealous of him. When the traders suggested to Smoke that he put himself up as the chief of all the Oglalas, Smoke had not the slightest intention of doing so. This so enraged Bull Bear, however, that he roared into Smoke's camp and challenged him to come out to fight.

When old Smoke would not come out, Bull Bear stabbed Smoke's favorite horse and stomped back to his camp in a high rage. Although Smoke did nothing about this, the young warriors who followed Smoke, including an up and coming young warrior named Red Cloud, were angry and decided to wait and look for a chance to kill Bull Bear. It was not long before Bull Bear himself forced the occasion upon them.

Bad Faces

In 1841, one of Smoke's followers, a Bad Face, stole a woman belonging to Bull Bear's group. Bull Bear had disliked this man for a long time. It also happened just at this time that one of the fur trading companies had just traded a lot of whiskey with Bull Bear's band. Fortified by the cheap liquor, Bull Bear gathered some warriors together and came roaring into the Bad Face camp. The invading force shot the father of the young man who had stolen the girl and then prepared to wipe out the entire village. At this time, the young followers of Smoke who had been waiting for this trouble charged at Bull Bear and his group. A bullet struck Bull Bear in the leg and he fell to the ground. It was Red Cloud who was quickest and dashed in to kill Bull Bear. He shot him through the head and he died instantly. Since it was Bull Bear who had attacked the Smoke group, it would seem that Red Cloud's killing him was simply in self-defense. In the long run, if Bull Bear had not been drinking, the whole thing would probably never have happened. One account also says that six warriors were killed and among the dead was a brother of Red Cloud, a chief named Yellow Lodge.

The followers of Smoke became angry at the followers of Bull Bear and they separated and drifted apart. The Smoke people and the Bear people, as they were called, carried this dislike for one another for years. The death of Bull Bear had a bad effect on the Oglalas which caused them not to work together for some years. Bull Bear had held a number of the bands together and had imposed a unity of action upon them. After his death, the bands wandered around without any strong leadership. A prominent Oglala at this time, Eagle Feather, said that since the death of Bull Bear, the Oglalas had been like children who did not know their own minds. For some years, the individual bands would wander their own ways, rarely united in purpose. At this time Red Cloud was still too young to take over the leadership but his time would come.

Non-unity

It was during these several years of non-unity that another disaster struck the Tetons in this area. Epidemics of cholera and smallpox began to run through the bands and many of the Indians died. They felt that this had come from the white immigrant and this made them dislike the immigrants all the more. To escape the sickness, they fled from the South Platte country to the North Platte, many dying on the way. Captain Stanbury's party came up the Platte that summer and discovered the cholera in all the Sioux camps. Near Ash Hollow he found five deserted lodges filled with the dead Sioux. A little farther along the road, he found other camps with cholera raging in them and sent his own doctor to help the sick Indians. The Sioux swallowed the medicines eagerly because they believed that, since the sickness came from the whites, the whites would have the medicine to cure it. What they did not realize was that as many white people were dying of it as were Indians. This epidemic lasted for about a year and a half and was another cause for the growing resentment against the whites among the Sioux.

It was at this time, around 1850, that the superintendent of Indian Affairs lived in St. Louis, many hundred miles away from Indian Territory. He was not a superintendent in the sense that we know today. He was simply the man appointed by the U.S. Government to make deals with all the Indian tribes. Reports to him at this time showed the growing restlessness and resentment of all the Indian tribes and he felt that trouble was brewing. He urged the government to give money for a great council in which he hoped to calm down the Indians and create peace among them. This council was to be for peace among the Indian tribes themselves (persuade the tribes, Snakes, Sioux, etc., to stop fighting each other) as well as for peace between all the Indian tribes and with the whites.

Great Council

Early in 1851, messengers were sent throughout the west to all the tribes to come to a great meeting on Horse Creek, near the Upper Platte, some miles east of Fort Laramie. Fine presents were described and promised to all who would attend. This was Sioux territory and many of the old enemies of the Sioux were terrified at the idea and refused to come. The messengers begged and coaxed them and finally most of them promised to come. They all came except the group who feared the Sioux most at this time, the Pawnees. They did not come.

The entire Oglala band was there and most of the Brules. For two weeks they feasted free of charge on government food and visited relatives and friends. Finally at the urging of the government, they said they would keep peace among themselves as well as toward the whites. Surrounded and guarded by white soldiers during this time, there was little chance for the tribes to quarrel among themselves, and it is little wonder that they said they would be peaceful.

The government hailed this peace council as a great success and went back to St. Louis. The tribes broke up and went home fighting contentedly on the way with one another. The 'peace' lasted only during the two weeks of the camp, and it was hardly over before the Sioux were busy fighting the Crows again, as well as the Pawnees. This was the second 'peace' council, which, like the first in 1829, on the Missouri River below the Big Bend, was of little profit.

For one thing, little did the government realize the system for making peace that the Indians had among themselves. Tribes would war for awhile, then when it was mutually advantageous for both sides to have peace (e.g., too cold to fight; not enough food, etc.) they would arrange peace. No outside agency or power could impose peace among them if they were not mutually ready for it. The Sioux had the same attitude toward the government and the whites in general. In their minds, they would keep peace as long as it was helpful to both sides. When it was helpful to either side not to have peace, then it was natural to go back to fighting. Not knowing this, the government for the next year was spreading the good news back east of the new peace in the west, unaware that the old fights were still going on in the west as happily as ever.

* * * *

Rise of Red Cloud

Rise of Red Cloud 1821 or 1822-1909 (86 or 87 years.)

In the years shortly preceding and following 1850, there was trouble brewing in the area above the North Platte. Both the non-Indians and the Indians had their problems. The main problem of the non-Indians was the growing restlessness and hostility of the tribes in that area, especially that of the Sioux, who never took anything sitting down. The resentment on the part of the Sioux had grown from several causes.

The first and most obvious cause of resentment was the gradual decrease in the number of buffalo. Long accustomed to thinking that the supply of buffalo from Mother Earth was inexhaustible, it came as a shock to them, when checking with other bands, to find that there were actually fewer buffalo around, and that bands had to travel farther and farther to find them. Since the Indians had been living on the buffalo for centuries and had apparently never made a dent in the vast herds, the only cause of the decrease was the large number of non-Indians coming through their land and settling near it.

The Sioux, in their first contacts with the non-Indians, were, for the most part, favorable and friendly, and they readily traded with them. Many French had settled down with the Sioux and had married their women. Rarely had there been any fighting between the Sioux and the non-Indian traders. Thus, it came as somewhat of a shock to them when they were fighting the Snakes and the Crows in the years following 1840, to find that the non-Indian trappers who had intermarried into those tribes were fighting back at the Sioux along with their Snake and Crow friends and relatives. When things went badly in a fight, the Sioux blamed much of it on these non-Indians. Their dislike for these non-Indians who were living with their enemies quickly spread to non-Indians in general and this, joined to their blaming the disappearance of the buffalo also on the non-Indians, made them angrier every time they thought about it.

Finally, the fact that the non-Indians' liquor was the occasion for the death of many Sioux at the hands of their own brothers, saddened and angered the wiser among the people and this, again, deepened their resentment against the non-Indians.

Wagon Trains

In 1841, the Sioux curiously watched settlers pass through on their way to California. At that time, there were only around 100 per year traveling through, which would be one or two wagon trains at the most — hardly enough to cause more thian a passing glance from the Sioux. However, nine years later, in 1850, there were 50,000 traveling through, and all of them ate the buffalo and other game as they passed.

Whereas, formerly the Sioux had seen only one or two wagon trains a year going through, now they were suddenly seeing on an average of one or two a day. This was too much, and something had to be done. Before they could do anything, however, this was their problem: they had no leadership to unite them.

You will recall that, since the death of Bull Bear, there had been no real strong leadership among the Sioux. Each band and sub-band went its separate way, and there was no one strong enough to gather warriors and sub-bands into a large and strong force under central leadership. They felt they had to do something and to do it on a large scale, in order to be effective. How could they do it without a strong leader?

Uniting Leader

It was at this time that Red Cloud appeared as the answer to their problem of leadership and union.

Since it was during the 1860's that so many of the Oglalas began to focus on Red Cloud for leadership, and since he did not just pop out of the ranks by accident, it will be necessary to go back a few years to understand how he rose to leadership. You will recall that not just anyone could be a chief, but that he had to rise from the ranks of the warriors. When a young man started out, he was just another warrior, but when he proved himself in battle, others would begin to follow him. As he continued to become more successful in battle, his following would gradually become larger and larger until, eventually, he would be a great chief. His becoming a great chief was always determined by his ability as a warrior and the number of his followers. This was the history of Red Cloud.

Birth

A great deal has been written about the whereabouts of Red Cloud's birth, when he was born, and how he got his name.

There has been some dispute among the authorities as to when Red Cloud was born. Sioux winter counts seem to place the date of his birth in 1822. Red Cloud himself, however, told his long-standing friend, Charles W. Allen, that he was born in 1821. If there is one thing in a man's life that he should remember it is his birth date. Taking the authority of Red Cloud himself, then, 1821 seems to be the date of his birth.

It is less clear where he was born. Red Cloud himself always insisted that he was born on the banks of the Blue Water Creek near the spot where it empties into the Platte. In 1870, he told officials of the Department of the Interior that he was born near the forks of the Platte and, twenty seven years later, in 1897, he told the Senate Committee on Indian Affairs the same thing. Hyde, the famous historian of the Sioux, says that Red Cloud was born somewhere east of the Black Hills, and that Red Cloud only said that he was born near the Platte to show the government that the Sioux had a right to the lands in that area. This seems to be a rather unfounded assertion on Hyde's part, and one is compelled to believe either Hyde or Red Cloud himself. The choice seems rather clear.

Scarlet Warriors

As to how Red Cloud got his name, all kinds of explanations have been offered. The most common story written is that Red Cloud was born on the night that a giant meteorite swept across the sky (September 20, 1822) and lit up the whole night from Minnesota to South Dakota. This meteorite was seen at Fort Snelling in Minnesota and by tribes far out on the plains; in fact, it was recorded in a number of winter counts. This version claims that in commemoration of this unusual happening, the baby born that night was named Red Cloud, because the sky was lit up like a great red cloud. There is no proof at all that this was how Red Cloud got his name, although many still believe this.

Another version is that of Agent McGillycuddy who, around 1890, only passed on what he had heard from others. "Red Cloud," McGillycuddy said, "referred to the way in which his scarlet blanketed warriors covered the hillsides like a red cloud." It must be said that very few believe this account of this origin of his name. For one thing, he would have had to have been a great warrior by then to have so many warriors following him and, logically, he must have had his name before then.

The simplest explanation seems to be that Red Cloud was named after his father as well as his grandfather; both of whom, it seems, were called Red Cloud. An old Oglala chief named American Horse, who lived at the same time as Red Cloud, said this, as well as did Allen. It must be remembered that Charles W. Allen, who was postmaster in Pine Ridge in the 1890's, was a close friend of the old chief, then around seventy years of age. He persuaded Red Cloud to tell him the story of his life, and much that we know about Red Cloud came through Allen as the source. American Horse and Allen, therefore, having lived at the same time as Red Cloud, would seem to know what they were talking about. Although sons would frequently have different names than their fathers, it was also common for the sons to receive the name of their father, especially if it was a great name and the father was well known. Captain James H. Cook, a famous frontiersman, and one of Red Cloud's closest friends, said that Red Cloud's father was a "big chief," although he did not give the name of the father.

Little is known of Red Cloud's boyhood. In order to become the great warrior that he became, though, he must have excelled in the routine training of boys and men of that time; learning to ride so that he and the horse were practically one being; learning to hunt — to shoot with bow and arrow and the rifle; and learning to fight. All of these skills would have been useless; however, without the fighting heart behind them, and that he had such a heart, Red Cloud soon proved.

First War Party

During the winter of 1837-1838, the Pawnees killed an Oglala named Paints-His-Cheeks-Red and his whole family, along with a relative of Red Cloud's who was only 26 years old at the time. The usual punishing party was organized and the war pipe went out. Although he was only sixteen years old at the time, Red Cloud was eager to go, not only for the fight, but also to avenge the family honor in the loss of his cousin. A young man on his first war party was not expected to distinguish himself in any special way. He was out to learn by watching the others and to help in any way he could. His coming back alive was sufficient cause for celebration on his return from his first war trip.

Red Cloud, however, was outstanding from the beginning of his warrior's life. Instead of hanging back and watching, he leapt right into the fray. On his first trip out, he got his scalp, the first of many to come (some say eighty). After that, he was always eager to go out and always had his ear to the ground for any kind of a fight. He was at least six feet tall, as described by an army wife and stating that he looked very impressive. Lula Red Cloud, was told by her Grandfather that Chief Red Cloud was well over six feet and taller than the grandfather who was over six feet. There were many photographs of Red Cloud but most if not all of these were never taken when he was in his younger days as a fearless and ferocious warrior. In his pictures he stands a degree taller than most who stood beside him, including white men. He also appears solidly built. Six feet was a tall man back in those days. In hand to hand combat and especially the way the Sioux fought on the open plains and most always commencing from a mounted attack, being taller, with but just a few inches reach on your opponent, was a tremendous advantage. Siouxs were generally taller than the Europeans they came across in the 1800's. Walk through a British museum if you are so fortunate to travel. Compare the size of the armor that the English knights wore. They were quite small men by modern standards. The American Indian ate much more meat and protein than did the early Europeans whose basic diet was gruel and little meat in comparison. Chief Crazy Horse, however, was considerably smaller than Chief Red Cloud.

Horse Stealing

Horse stealing was one of the most dangerous and brave things a person could do. Horses, considered as the greatest wealth, were kept close to the camps, and to crawl on one's belly without benefit of a horse for escape, was extremely dangerous. It was not very long after the raid on the Pawnees that Red Cloud went on a horse stealing trip against their old enemies, the Crows. It was Red Cloud who crept in, sneaked up behind and killed the one guarding the horses and made off with fifty of them. Naturally, the Crows, after they rounded up the rest of their stampeded horses, started to chase the Sioux. The next day, when they caught up with the Sioux (who couldn't travel very fast while driving fifty head of horses), the Sioux turned to fight, and it was Red Cloud who killed the chief of the pursuing Crows.

On another trip deep into Pawnee territory, Red Cloud was not content with one scalp. With his own hand, he killed four of the Pawnees. His reputation was growing fast; when Red Cloud went out, things really moved. Any party he was on always came back victorious.

Utes

The Pawnees, the Crows, and the Snakes were not the only ones receiving the attention of the Oglalas at this time. The Oglalas were quite impartial about with whom they fought, and the Utes also came in for their share of the competition.

In one battle against the Utes, the Oglalas were fighting them vigorously near a creek. A Ute, trying to escape by crossing the stream on a wounded horse, was about to drown. Red Cloud, never willing to lose a scalp, splashed out on his own horse, grabbed the man by his hair, and dragged him in to the shore. On reaching land, Red Cloud pulled out his knife, cut off the Ute's scalp, and then let him fall to the ground. He had a trophy he wanted. Captain Cook, who in later years was a great friend of Red Cloud's, said that Red Cloud "was a terror in war with other tribes." His fame was growing so that his very name struck fear into other tribes.

Close Combat

To the average reader, the taking of an opponent's scalp in battle must seem blood curdling but it was a common custom among most northern tribes. Some authors claim this method was introduced by the French, others blame the English (probably French authors). Regardless, there existed far more 'blood curdling' methods of human cruelty based out of Europe during the centuries long Great Inquisitions. They were so grisly that I will not go into detail. A book, Malleus Malificarum; was written by two Dominican priests and published close to when the time Columbus sailed. It includes a papal bull from Innocent VIII sanctioning their authority as papal appointed Inquisitors (1481) with unlimited powers to stamp out alleged heresy. The books primary emphasis was the torture of humans, mostly women to bring forth confessions from a multitude of suspects accused of heresy. Most were falsely accused, mainly in Northern Germany. It held wide spread influence, for Inquisitors through out Europe utilized it as the 'Bible' to extort various 'confessions.' It was the best seller throughout Europe receiving re-publication down through the following centuries.[1]

Red Cloud's killing of Bull Bear in self defense, however, drew the attention of the people as a whole to Red Cloud and lifted him up most as a great fighter. As has been said, though, he was still too young to assume the leadership that Bull Bear had held. Nevertheless, he came out of the fight with his reputation greatly enhanced. Shortly after this, he led his first war party, which was the sure sign of his importance and the proof that he was on his way up.

War Party

It was this important war party, the first that he had ever led, that came close to being his last. Red Cloud and his warriors thought that it would be just a routine run against their old enemies, the Pawnees, who were then camped on the Middle Loup River. The Oglalas, however, underestimated their old foes, and barely escaped getting wiped out themselves. For quite awhile after the fight, Red Cloud's warriors thought that he was dead, because they were unable to find him. Sometime later, however, they found him badly wounded by an arrow that had penetrated through his body right below his ribs. One of the older men broke the arrow, pulled it out, and stopped the flow of blood before Red Cloud bled to death. He spent a bad night, but he was able to eat a little the next morning. His men made a travois and carried him from behind a horse. They expected the Pawnees to chase them and to renew the fight. This would have been disastrous for them. The Pawnee, however, remembering previous beatings from the Oglalas, considered one fight enough and had decided not to press their luck. The war party finally got home safely, but Red Cloud was not out of danger yet. For two months, he was very sick, swinging between life and death but, after that, he gradually began to regain his full strength and vigor. This wound, however, was to bother him for the rest of his life, and he lived to be close to ninety. That it never slowed him down in the least, we shall see shortly.

On his recovery, Red Cloud took to the warpath more vigorously than ever, as though to make up for the two months he had lost in recovering. Some years later, Captain Cook wrote that the old Oglalas who had fought by Red Cloud's side as young men proudly and loudly recounted his exploits to anyone who would listen. His size no doubt accounts for his ability to survive over 80 coups and/or taking of enemy scalps. He was deemed ruthless but it was a ruthless time. No longer would the counting of coup be practiced once the Army was encountered, at least not in the heat of battle for attempting to touch a saber swinging cavalry man or one carrying a pistol or both would result in too many losses which a besieged people could not afford.

In the beginning of this section, we said that in the years shortly preceding and following 1850, trouble was brewing in the area above the North Platte. Restlessness and hostility were growing not only among the Sioux, but also among the other tribes stemming from the decrease of buffalo, the increase of immigrants, death causing diseases caught from the immigrant non-Indians, and the evil caused in their midst by the non-Indians' liquor.

Red Cloud did not emerge as the uniting leader against the non-Indians until the 1860's. From the 1840's to the 1860's, while Red Cloud's star was rising, several important things happened that caused a stiffening resistance among the Indians which finally found their focus on Red Cloud as the one best qualified to represent all their grievances and anger.

You will recall that in 1841, the Sioux saw only about one or two wagon trains a year going west through their country, and that by 1849, a year after the discovery of gold in California, this trickle had built up to over 50,000 a year. During the middle years of this buildup in traffic, the government felt the restlessness of the tribes and, in 1845, felt that something should be done to pacify them. The first plan was to talk to them nicely, offer them lots of presents, and to ask them to be peaceful.

Col. Kearney

Thus it was that in 1845, Colonel Stephen Kearney rolled into the American Fur Company's post at Laramie with seventeen wagonloads of presents and provisions, and accompanied by five companies of well equipped and well mounted cavalry. Here he met with over a thousand Sioux. He paraded his seventeen wagons full of presents in front of the Sioux, gathered them in close, and delivered the speech that he had come to give.

He told them that the Great White Father in Washington was deeply concerned with their welfare and that, as he was also the father of all the non-Indians coming through, he wanted everyone to get along nicely together. He told them to stay away from the non-Indians' whiskey which they could get so easily from traders. His main point was that the travels of the immigrants should not be disturbed, and, therefore, the Indians should peacefully allow them to pass through. The Sioux, paying more attention to the wagonloads of gifts than to the words of Kearney's speech and with a growing impatience for him to finish, quickly promised that they would let the travelers go through, suggesting in addition that he get to the business at hand, that is, to the dividing up of the gifts — blankets, cloth, knives, beads, and tobacco. Kearney, pleased with the willingness of the Sioux to cooperate, passed out the gifts, gave them a warm farewell, and rode off highly pleased with himself that his mission had been such a great success. There would, he thought to himself, be no more trouble on the immigrant trail.

Kearney, however, had hardly disappeared down his homeward trail, when the Sioux realized that the gifts did little to relieve their rising anxiety, nor were they any kind of a substitute or exchange for the decreasing number of buffalo. Their restlessness and hostility, far from dying down, grew greater. For this reason, advice went to Washington from experienced men in the West that what the Indians needed to keep them 'peaceful' was not gifts and in 1849, only four years after Kearney's effort, the little fur trading post to which Bull Bear and his many lodges had been originally invited, now owned by the American Fur Company, and which was so pleasantly familiar to the Sioux, was bought by the Government, made into a fort, and staffed with some soldiers. It was now called Fort Laramie. This immediately caused further hostility among the Sioux. Traders were one thing, but soldiers were something else. Soldiers, to their way of thinking, came into a country for one purpose, and that was to fight. When and where they didn't know, but it did mean that a fight was coming and they braced themselves in preparation for it.

Soldiers

You will recall that one type of non-Indian that the Indians always liked was the trader. Since he had to make his living from the Indians, he was always pleasant and friendly with them, giving them gifts from time to time and always inviting them to come in. Coming in to the trading post was always like a pleasant holiday for the Sioux — something like "going to town" occasionally for country people. They looked forward to seeing the new articles the traders would have, meeting old friends, receiving gifts and shopping around in what to them would be like a supermarket today. Hence, it was a pleasure for them to come in to the trading posts because of what was waiting for them at the end of the trip — friendship and gifts. To come in now and to find soldiers in the place of friendship and gifts was a severe shock to them. Soldiers always meant trouble. It is true that the first soldiers at Fort Laramie were very few in number and could not have done much at all against any organized resistance on the part of the Indian tribes; however, to the Indian way of thinking, a few soldiers on the scene always meant that more were coming, and it was the thought of their increasing numbers and the inevitable trouble that would follow that stiffened the resistance of the tribes to all non-Indians in general. Word immediately spread through all the tribes, and the original feeling of general friendliness toward the non-Indians was replaced by a feeling of hostility and a readiness to fight. The fact that these soldiers, along with the passing immigrants, were practically in the middle of their hunting grounds at this time, only added to their rising anger. The suspicions of the Indians were all too correct, for trouble was coming.

After the governmental purchase of Fort Laramie, now fortified by the presence of soldiers, it took only about a year for word to get around to all the tribes and for hostile feelings to reach a new height. The anger and hostility of the tribes became so great that the government decided to try another "gift giving" meeting coupled with more peace talks. It was thought that the combination of gifts and talks plus the presence of the soldiers might work in calming down the anxious tribes. Thus it was that a great meeting was planned in 1851, and messengers were sent out a year ahead of time to all the tribes on the northern plains. Lavish gifts were promised and much feasting was guaranteed.

This was the gathering to which we referred earlier, when all the tribes except the Pawnees (for fear of the Sioux) showed up and feasted royally for eighteen days, said they would be friendly with everyone — Indians and non-Indians alike — and then resumed their customary fighting on the way home from the council.

Although there was much feasting and gift giving, it is interesting to note that the government for the first time was demanding more than just promises of peace. It was at this meeting, the Fort Laramie Treaty of 1851, that the government Insisted that the Indians agree to the following conditions:

a. That each tribe stay within its own "territory" and not go into the territory of another tribe.
b. That the tribes stop warring on one another.
c. That the tribes not bother the immigrants coming through.
d. That, if a tribe harmed another tribe or immigrants coming through, they would make up for the damages and punish the offenders.
e. That the tribes recognize the right of the government to establish roads and military posts as well as other posts through this Indian territory.

If the government had known enough about Indians and their values, they would have seen that the conditions laid down at the meeting were impossible from the beginning.

In the first place, the Indian value of Adjustment to Nature motivates them to get along with people. Disagreeing with someone in matters not vitally important is a form of not getting along with another, because it might upset him. Consequently, you give him the answer you think he wants to hear in order to get along with him, rather than to upset him. You don't upset him until you are forced to, such as when you are threatened with the loss of your life or property. Thus, the tribes would readily agree to almost anything, and this is the basis for their agreement to the provisions of the treaty.

'Territory'

In the second place, in their total experience, it was unheard of that one tribe stay strictly within one area and never wander into the 'territory' of another tribe. For centuries, they had been moving one another around, and it was taken for granted that, if one tribe moved into another tribe's territory, this was because the tribe was:

    a.   stronger, and

    b.   had special need or liking for that territory.

A weaker tribe, having been forced out, would then move in on another tribe that was weaker than they, and so forth. This, to their way of thinking, is what decided what territory belonged to whom at any particular time.

Therefore, the conditions demanded by the government were clearly impossible according to the Indian way of thinking, and they couldn't imagine that the government could be serious about their adhering to these impossible conditions. It wasn't long before it dawned upon the tribes that, impossible as these conditions seemed, the government was serious about them and intended to use force to prove it. This only made the Indians more determined to use their own force to resist this threat to their lives and to their property. It was clear that a battle was lining up between these opposing forces, but several more things happened before this came about, making the Sioux angrier and forcing them to search for a leader to unify them in their rising opposition.

Mormon Cow

The first of these incidents that further stirred up the Sioux was the famous case of the Mormon cow. Just three years after the Fort Laramie Treaty, in 1854, during which time the new Fort was slowly filling up with soldiers, a party of Mormons on their way to Utah was camped near Fort Laramie. Also camped near the Fort was a group of Brule Sioux. Their Chief was Conquering Bear, more commonly known as simply The Bear. A cow belonging to the Mormons strayed away while grazing and wandered into the Brule camp. For these people, who were accustomed to riding for miles at breakneck speed to kill an animal this size (such as a buffalo), to have such an animal walk right into their midst was a clear gift from heaven. What's more, to the Indian way of closely guarding their stock (horses), any animal loose like that was fair game for the first one to capture it.

Consequently, the Brules, with joyful and grateful hearts, immediately fell upon the Mormon cow, butchered it, divided it up, and promptly ate it, rejoicing in their good fortune. When the Mormons found out what had happened to their cow, they went immediately into Fort Laramie, only a short distance away, and reported the incident to the commanding officer.

Lt. Grattan

The commanding officer sent a brash, hotheaded, young officer named Lt. Grattan with 29 men out to the Brule camp. Lt. Grattan was only twenty-one years old and just out of West Point Military School. Looking down upon the Indians, he thought the only way to handle them was to act tough and fast. To old Conquering Bear, this young man was just a "puppy," and the old Chief tried to reason with him as an adult reasons with a child. Conquering Bear tried to explain what had happened, but, since Lt. Grattan couldn't speak Sioux and Conquering Bear couldn't speak English, the conversation had to be carried on through an interpreter who was drunk, at the time. This didn't help the situation any, and the impatient, young lieutenant withdrew his men from the camp and began to shoot at the Bear and his people. During the first round of shots, Conquering Bear was killed. Immediately, his people were aroused. They returned the fire and wiped out Lt. Grattan and his entire force of 29 men.

Word of this immediately spread through both the Indian and non-Indian sides. The Indians were moved to attack the immigrants on the Platte Valley Trail, and the non-Indians were moved to send out more soldiers. Just a year later Brigadier General William S. Harney left Fort Leavenworth in Kansas with a force of 1,200 men with orders to make peace by force on the immigrant trail. In August of 1855, General Harney with his 1,200 men came upon Little Thunder and his band of Brules. Harney immediately engaged the Brules and, with his superior force, killed 136 of them, put chains on the rest, and dragged them to Fort Laramie. A month or so later, he set out for Fort Pierre on the Missouri River where he spent the winter. Without any government authorization, he gathered together the Sioux camping around Fort Pierre and forced them to agree to permit immigrant travel along the Platte Valley trail and to allow a military road from Fort Laramie to Fort Pierre.

Little Thunder Band

The fate of Little Thunder and his band at the hands of Harney and his huge force struck terror into the Oglalas around the Fort Laramie area. Living in small groups, no match for such a superior force, and with no leadership to unify them, they temporarily scattered. The Bear people, Bull Bear's old group, went south of the Platte and hunted along the Republican River, while the people of old Chief Smoke, the Smoke people, went north to the Powder River country. This spreading out of the Oglalas to the north and the south left the trail along the Platte undisturbed by the Sioux for several years.

Gold

Although the Oglalas, after Harney, had scattered north and south of the Platte for awhile, something happened about six years later, in 1862, that caused them to begin uniting; not only among themselves, but with other tribes as well. Gold was discovered in Montana in 1862. This meant that a new trail would be made and this new trail, called the Bozeman Trail, went right through the heart of Sioux country. You will recall that the discovery of gold in California in 1848 had caused the buildup of immigrant traffic on the trail along the Platte. Now, that traffic was increased, and a lot of it was going up the new trail through Indian Territory. First there was the trail through Indian country along the Platte in the 1830's. Secondly, there was the trail demanded by Harney from Fort Laramie to Fort Pierre in 1855 through Teton country. Now, a third trail through the extreme western part of Sioux territory, the Bozeman, made the Indians feel that they were truly surrounded and that they were headed for a last ditch fight for survival.

It was during this very year, 1862, when the Tetons were feeling the pinch in the extreme western part of Sioux territory that, at the very opposite side of the territory in the extreme eastern part, Minnesota, violence broke out between the Sioux and the non-Indians which was to send its shock waves throughout the whole Sioux nation. This was the famous Minnesota Uprising. It was a short-lived event, leaving the Santees to small reservations in Minnesota. The Sissetons were established in the northeastern corner of what would become South Dakota. The western Sioux were too far distant to offer aid yet some Santees and Yanktons managed to escape to the western tribes and did engage in some battles with the Army.

* * * *

Red Cloud's War

Red Cloud's War

> *They made us many promises, more than I can remember.*
> *But they kept but one – They promised to take our land...and they took it.*
> — *Chief Red Cloud*

The Sioux were now entering upon the stormiest period of their history. The old things were fast giving place to new. The young men, for the first time engaging in serious and destructive warfare with the neighboring tribes, armed with the deadly weapons furnished by the white man, began to realize that they must soon enter upon a desperate struggle for their ancestral hunting grounds. The old men had been innocently cultivating the friendship of the stranger, saying among themselves, "Surely there is land enough for all!"

Red Cloud's Rise to Leadership

Red Cloud was a modest and little known man of about twenty-eight years, when General Harney called all the western bands of Sioux together at Fort Laramie, Wyoming, for the purpose of securing an agreement and right of way through their territory. The Oglalas held aloof from this proposal, but Bull Bear, remember, the Oglala chief, after having been plied with whisky, undertook to dictate submission to the rest of the clan, namely threatening the chief of the Bad Faces, Chief Smoke. Calmly, without uttering a word, Red Cloud faced the bully chief, Bull Bear and his son, who attempted to defend his father, and shot them both. He did what he believed to be his duty, and the whole band sustained him. Indeed, the tragedy gave the young man at once a certain standing, as one who not only defended his people against enemies from without, but against injustice and aggression within the tribe. From this time on he was a recognized leader.

Man-Afraid-of-His-Horse, then head chief of the Oglalas, took council with Red Cloud in all important matters, and the young warrior rapidly advanced in authority and influence. In 1854, when he was barely thirty-five years old, the various bands were again encamped near Fort Laramie. The Mormon immigrant train, moving westward, left their footsore cow behind, as mentioned earlier and the young men killed her for food. The next day, to their astonishment, the brash lieutenant with twenty-nine men appeared at the Indian camp and demanded of old Conquering Bear that they be given up. The chief in vain protested that it was all a mistake and offered to make reparation. It would seem that either the officer was under the influence of liquor, or else had a mind to bully the Indians, for he would accept neither explanation nor payment, but demanded point-blank that the young men who had killed the cow be delivered up to summary punishment. The old chief refused to be intimidated and was shot dead on the spot. Not one soldier ever reached the gate of Fort Laramie! Here Red Cloud led the young Oglalas, and so intense was the feeling that they even killed the half-breed interpreter.

In 1862, a grave outbreak was precipitated by the eastern Sioux in Minnesota under Little Crow, in which the western bands took no part. Yet this event ushered in a new period for their race. The surveyors of the Union Pacific were laying out the proposed road right through the heart of the southern buffalo country, the rendezvous of Oglalas, Brules, Arapahoes, Comanches, and Pawnees, who followed the buffalo as a means of livelihood. To be sure, most of these tribes were at war with one another, yet during the summer months they met often to proclaim a truce and hold joint councils and festivities, which were now largely turned into discussions of the common enemy. It became evident, however, that some of the smaller and weaker tribes were inclined to welcome the new order of things, recognizing that it was the policy of the government to put an end to tribal warfare.

Red Cloud's position was uncompromisingly against submission. He made some noted speeches regarding this issue.

"Friends," said Red Cloud, "it has been our misfortune to welcome the white man. We have been deceived. He brought with him some shining things that pleased our eyes; he brought weapons more effective than our own: above all, he brought the spirit water that makes one forget for a time old age, weakness, and sorrow. But I wish to say to you that if you would possess these things for yourselves, you must begin anew and put away the wisdom of your fathers. You must lay up food, and forget the hungry. When your house is built, your storeroom filled, then look around for a neighbor whom you can take at a disadvantage, and seize all that he has! Give away only what you do not want; or rather, do not part with any of your possessions unless in exchange for another's.

"My countrymen, shall the glittering trinkets of this rich man, his deceitful drink that overcomes the mind, shall these things tempt us to give up our homes, our hunting grounds, and the honorable teaching of our old men? Shall we permit ourselves to be driven to and fro — to be herded like the cattle of the white man?" His next speech that has been remembered was made in 1866, just before the attack on Fort Phil Kearny. The tension of feeling against the invaders had now reached its height. There was no dissenting voice in the council upon the Powder River, when it was decided to oppose to the uttermost the evident purpose of the government. Red Cloud was not altogether ignorant of the numerical strength and the resourcefulness of the white man, but he was determined to face the odds of those times rather than submit.

"Hear ye, Dakotas!" he exclaimed. "When the Great Father at Washington sent us his chief soldier [General Harney] to ask for a path through our hunting grounds, a way for his iron road to the mountains and the western sea, we were told that they wished merely to pass through our country, not to tarry among us, but to seek for gold in the far west. Our old chiefs thought to show their friendship and good will, when they allowed this dangerous snake in our midst. They promised to protect the wayfarers.

"Yet before the ashes of the council fire are cold, the Great Father is building his forts among us. You have heard the sound of the white soldier's ax upon the Little Piney. His presence here is an insult and a threat. It is an insult to the spirits of our ancestors. Are we then to give up their sacred graves to be plowed for corn? Dakotas, I am for war!"

A favorite ploy the Sioux used against the army was to utilize the strength of their horses which were daily exercised and conditioned, in contrast to the Cavalry's horses which were often enclosed within hastily built and confining stockades. A select group of Sioux riders would ride before the forts just out of rifle range and tantalize the troops inside. The Army would often respond by saddling up their horses and weighing them down with rations and ammunition. Out the gates the Army troops would charge, bugles blowing on poorly conditioned horses. The Indians would flee down a pre-designated route where the main band of warriors would be concealed in gullies and draws close to where their leaders would estimate that the Army horses would become winded. The Sioux would hit the army with spirited mounts at the time the cavalry horses were too winded to maneuver effectively. Historians may argue otherwise, but how else could the Sioux capture so many weapons and an abundance of ammunition? They were well-armed when they defeated Colonel Custer at the Battle of the Little Big Horn. Metal detectors in recent times have proven how well armed the Sioux really were.

News of the Minnesota Uprising, in 1862, and of its disastrous consequences for the Santees spread immediately throughout the West and caused further fear and tension among all the western tribes. Although the western Sioux refused to join Little Crow in hitting back at the settlers and the army in Minnesota country on the grounds that it was not their fight, nevertheless, they kept a wary eye to the east for the possible appearance of more soldiers from that direction. They had learned from bitter experience that, when the army came to hit back, the soldiers made little distinction between bands and tribes. Indians were Indians, and they frequently hit the first band that they saw when on a punishing expedition. This, for example, was borne out in the case of Brigadier General Alfred Sully in the Spring of 1864, following the opening of the Bozeman Trail. Sent out to clear the road to the Montana gold fields with a huge force of 4,000 cavalry and 800 mounted infantry, he attacked anything that moved. Encountering the Sioux at Killdeer Mountain with his superior forces, he chased them south in a three day running battle.

It was while they were still looking over their shoulders toward the east that a blow struck on the far western part of the plains that made not only the Sioux, but all the plains tribes tight with apprehension and more ready than ever to fight at the mere sight of soldiers. This was the Sand Creek Massacre at Sand Creek, Colorado Territory in August of 1864, just two years after the Minnesota Uprising.

You will recall that the opening of the Bozeman Trail through the heart of Sioux Territory was the final sting that the Sioux needed to engage them in a fight. Like a swarm of angry bees, they and their allies were aroused and they showed it by launching attacks on stage stations, immigrant trains, ranches, and farms all the way from the Little Blue Valley in eastern Nebraska to Denver. Travel in the Platte Valley came to a standstill and recent settlers fled places in eastern Nebraska. The outbreak was so widespread and so mobile that the army could not pin down any one band for effective retaliation. Even during these military strikes, however, the government continued to make constant pleas to individual bands to come in and to be peaceful.

One of the bands who accepted the invitation of the government to come in was a band of 250 lodges of Cheyennes (around a thousand people) under the leadership of two Cheyenne chiefs, White Antelope, and Black Kettle. They were assured by the commandant at Fort Lyon, Colorado, that, if they came in and camped close to the Fort, they would be safe and protected. They came in, pulled in all the guards and lookouts, and settled down to a peaceful existence while the war blazed around them.

Chivington

It was during this time that Colonel H. M. Chivington, working out of Denver with the Colorado volunteers, was out looking for hostile Indians to punish for the current trouble along the Platte Valley. He came upon these peaceful Cheyennes, surrounded them, and attacked them without asking any questions, or checking with the army at Fort Lyon. White Antelope, making no effort to fight whatsoever, was one of the first to be killed in the village and over half of the people, men, women, and children, were killed. Their entire horse herd was captured and their village was destroyed. Those who managed to escape on foot made their way in the bitterly cold weather to a Cheyenne camp on the head of the Smoky Hill Fork. Black Kettle, who was one of the survivors, was rejected by his own people for leading them into a trap. It is difficult to emphasize how much this stirred up all the plains tribes. War pipes were sent out to the Northern and Southern Arapahoes, the Northern and Southern Cheyennes, the Oglalas, and the Brule Sioux. All tribes accepted and the war was on in earnest.

In the meantime, the commandant at Fort Lyon as well as the agent for the Cheyennes, Samuel G. Colley, were in despair over this terrible action of Chivington. They were the ones who had persuaded the Cheyennes to come in and now they had been betrayed by Chivington. They saw that all hope of peace was lost and they complained bitterly about Chivington to Washington. As a result, Chivington was investigated and disciplined by army authorities, but the damage had already been done.

The tribes had been pushed to the limit and could no longer be contained. All they needed was leadership, and by now, the leadership was at hand. It was time for Red Cloud — and Red Cloud was ready.

Right after the end of the Civil War, when the forces of war in the far West were gathering that would bring Red Cloud to the fore, groups of humanitarians, church groups, and idealists gained much influence in Congress to do something about bettering the lot of slaves just freed by the Civil War. This interest in minorities who were having a hard time quickly spread to the Indians, and now, with the war over, more attention could be given to Indian policy in the West. These people decided that the way to deal with the Indians was to treat them kindly.

Peace Commission

Thus it was that in May 1865, when the military was straining every muscle in preparing for an all-out war against the tribes of the far West, that Senator J. R. Doolittle obtained an order suspending movements of troops against the southern plains tribes, and then had a peace commission appointed to make peace with the Indians. The soldiers in the far West, surrounded by and watching the tribes around the Powder River and the Upper Missouri who were angry as hornets and about to break out in a fight at any moment, could not figure this out, but they had to sit in silent frustration and wait for the peace commission to act.

The peace commission did act, but not in the area of the country that needed it. The trouble was in the far West, and, when the peace commission came out, they went up the Missouri, gathered in all the friendly chiefs who had been living along the Missouri, and coaxed them into signing a peace treaty. To members of the peace commission, it would seem that an Indian was an Indian and one band the same as another no matter where the band lived — whether along the Missouri or 600 miles to the west, where the real trouble was. It would seem this way, were it not for the fact that the heads of the commission, General Curtis (the one who had sent Colonel Chivington against the Cheyennes) and Newton Edmunds, had been dealing with the hostiles in the far West for several years and knew the distinction of bands, the various chiefs, and who was hostile and who was not. At any rate, the friendly chiefs along the Missouri River were given gifts and they readily signed the peace treaty. In the meantime, 600 miles to the west, Sitting Bull was very influential with about 2,000 lodges of angry Sioux along the Little Missouri. Along the Powder River, there were an additional 2,000 unfriendly Sioux.

The thorn in the treaty was the insistence on the part of the government that it had the right to establish roads and to build forts in the Sioux country, including the touchy Bozeman Trail area. At the moment when the 'tame chiefs' (mostly Yanktons and Saones) along the Missouri were agreeing to the establishment of roads and forts through country 600 miles to the west of them, the rightful owners of that territory, Tetons and other western tribes, were fully determined that no non-Indians were going to enter their country.

During October 1865, this peace commission contently went back home, confident that they had made peace with the hostiles. They told everyone that the trouble was over. The problem was that no one had told the military commanders in the West, nor the hostile Tetons — who were watching one another warily — that there was "peace" between them, and that it was the friendly Yanktons and some Saones on the Missouri who had agreed to permit the establishment of roads and forts through the far western, hostile territory.

It finally occurred to someone that a peace treaty involving the land of hostile Tetons should include the assent of these Tetons also. At the end of October, a copy of the treaty was hastily sent to Fort Laramie and the commander there was instructed to bring in the Teton chiefs and to have them sign. However, things were so touchy that no trader, or even a mixed-blood was willing to take the risk of going out and inviting in the hostile chiefs. Thus it was that the commander, Colonel Henry E. Maynadier, sat for three months with the peace treaty in his hands without seeing an Indian. Finally, a few "friendlies" who had been forced into the hostile camps by mistreatment of the military came by about the middle of January and signed, but these were not the real hostiles. Early in March, Spotted Tail came in to bury his daughter beside the grave of Old Smoke, which was located just west of the Fort, and he complained bitterly about the treatment that his people had received from the soldiers. He spoke vaguely of the Oglalas coming in, but nothing happened until the summer of 1866.

Because of the delay in getting any action in signing from the hostiles (October of 1865 to the summer of 1866), Mr. E. B. Taylor came out from the Indian Office with a document appointing himself and Colonel Maynadier as peace commissioners to deal with the hostile Sioux. He persuaded messengers to go out to the hostiles, promising rich presents and even ammunition, and then sat back to wait. His boldness paid off. About a month later, the Sioux came down from the Powder River area in full force, and Taylor finally found himself face to face with the real force behind the hostilities; Red Cloud had come. With him were Man Afraid of His Horse, and the other important chiefs of the hostiles.

This was a momentous meeting. From this moment on, it would be a contest between Red Cloud and the full military might of the West.

The first thing that Red Cloud and the other chiefs demanded was that the treaty be read carefully to them. When the treaty reading came to the part about building roads and forts through the Powder River country, Red Cloud and the other chiefs rose to their feet and emphatically and angrily said "No!" They had seen their land cut through by trail after trail, and this far western land, except for the hated Bozeman Trail, was the last uncut land that they had. Here they would take a stand and fight to the death, if necessary, and they told Taylor this.

Taylor was really in a bind. Because of the so-called peace treaty signed by the eastern chiefs had been spread around, immigrants were actually on their way — only a few weeks behind Taylor on the trail — assured ahead of time that it would be safe to go through the Bozeman Trail and Powder River countries. Red Cloud was equally determined that no non-Indian was going to set foot on the Bozeman Trail and he had told Taylor this. Taylor was determined that nothing should prevent the signing of this treaty, and, in his desperate efforts to please the Sioux, he assured them solemnly that no new roads would be opened and no forts built.

It was while Taylor was emphasizing, apparently very sincerely, this very point of no new roads and no forts, that 700 soldiers with 226 wagons of road and fort construction equipment under the command of Colonel H. B. Carrington marched into Fort Laramie. The Sioux might have been on the verge of believing Taylor, but, when they found out that these approaching men had come to guard the Bozeman Trail and to build new forts — the very thing that Taylor had assured them would not happen, Red Cloud flew into a rage and told Taylor that he was now aware of having been deceived. He angrily stomped out of the meeting, shouting to his people to break up their camp, to go home, and to prepare for war. His last words to Taylor were that if anyone set foot on the Bozeman Trail or tried to build forts there, he would battle them to the death.

Taylor did a very foolish thing. He sent word back East that the treaty was a success, that the road was open and that only a few unimportant chiefs such as Red Cloud and Man Afraid of His Horse had not signed — but they didn't matter anyway. Because of Taylor's announcement, there occurred the shocking spectacle of the government's permitting immigrants to go unsuspectingly into what the immigrants thought was peaceful country and which in reality was boiling with angry Sioux, Cheyennes, and Arapahoes. Chief Red Cloud was fully determined to cut down the first thing that moved.

Col. Carrington

The very first parties on the Trail were instantly attacked. Yet, the government refused to face the fact that a full-scale war was shaping up in the last great hunting grounds of the Sioux. The government remained confident that this first skirmish was just the work of a few soreheads and refused to worry about it. The center of this shaping, full- scale war was Colonel Carrington with his 700 soldiers and 226 wagons of construction equipment — tools, saw-mills, forges, hardware — in short, everything that they needed to build forts. Right after the Laramie meeting from which Red Cloud had left in a rage, promising a fight, Colonel Carrington pulled out of Laramie with his wagons and soldiers and headed up the Bozeman Trail. From that moment on, he was never out of the sight of the Sioux scouts. Day and night, his movements were watched, as the Sioux waited for their chance to put the promise of Red Cloud to work. Carrington's plan was simple and clear-cut:

    a.   To keep the Bozeman Trail open, and
    b.   To build two more forts along it, making a total of three.

Red Cloud's plan was also simple and clear-cut:
    a.   To close the Bozeman Trail, and
    b.   To remove the three forts.

Colonel Carrington was not a fighting officer. He was an engineer by training, given to fussing about details, and during the time on the

Bozeman Trail, he seemed to regard the Sioux as though they were a bunch of angry bees swarming around who would soon go away. On June 28, 1866, Carrington reached Fort Reno. He planned to rest there a few days and then go up the Bozeman Trail about forty miles to build a fort which was to be called Fort Kearney. Fort F.C. Smith, to be built up at the top of the Bozeman Trail, would make a total of three forts that would guard the Trail nicely and keep the Sioux under control. Carrington, however, hadn't reckoned on Red Cloud.

Two days after he had arrived at Fort Reno, seven Sioux warriors ran off some stolen horses within two miles of Fort Reno. Carrington, under close guard, left Fort Reno on July 10 and three days later arrived at the spot where he planned to build Fort Kearney. The very next day, a group of friendly Cheyennes came in to see Carrington and told him that Red Cloud had 500 warriors, as did Man Afraid of His Horse, and that they were going to fight him. Carrington did not seem too concerned and set about building his fort. At the same time, he sent two companies on up the Bozeman Trail to build the last fort, Fort F.C. Smith.

The Sioux immediately began raiding all along the road. Wagon trains barely set out when they were attacked. The Sioux boldly raided close in to the new forts, running off stock and attacking any group of soldiers that they met. Yet, with his nose in his blueprints, Carrington seemed hardly aware of what was going on. On August 28, just a month later, he sent in an optimistic report saying that everything was going nicely. In the same report, however, he stated that 33 non-Indian men had been killed along the new road in the past five weeks, that the Sioux were making daily attacks, and that seventy head of government animals has been stolen near Fort Kearney alone.

During July and August, Carrington was busily building Fort Kearney. His troops could not go a mile outside of the camp without being attacked. On July 17, the Sioux coolly dashed up within sight of his soldiers, ran off 174 mules, killed two men, and wounded two others. The same war party killed six non-Indians within a few miles of Carrington's camp. So angry were the Sioux by now that they decided to lay off their favorite enemies, the Crows, and invited them in to be friends for a while and to help them fight the immigrants and the soldiers on the Trail. Red Cloud himself and Man Afraid of His Horse even visited the Crow camps, and the visits were returned. Red Cloud had his camp of over 500 of similar size on the Powder River. The more hostile bands of Cheyennes had joined Red Cloud, and Medicine Man, an Arapaho chief, brought his whole group in.

Toward the end of that summer of 1866, Red Cloud eased up a bit for two reasons:

1.   He wanted to get in a supply of meat by way of the annual buffalo hunt, and
2.   It was time to retire for the annual Sun Dance. It was about this time that Jim Bridger, the famous mountain man, was employed by Colonel Carrington. Even Jim Bridger couldn't get close to the angry Sioux, so he tried to find out their plans through the Crows. From the Crows, he found out where the main camps of the Sioux were, as described above. He also reported something very interesting that he learned from the Crows. He told Carrington that Man Afraid of His Horse had told the Crows that he had been receiving tobacco from the soldiers at Fort Laramie. Sending tobacco always meant an invitation to come in and talk. Man Afraid of His Horse said that he intended to go and that the forces of the Bozeman Trail would have to wait until he returned. This indicates that Man Afraid of His Horse was still considering signing the treaty. It also indicates that the only force holding the Sioux together in order to fight was Red Cloud. Man Afraid of His Horse apparently changed his mind, however, because when the fighting started again, he was in the thick of it.

With their tipis filled with dried meat from the buffalo hunt and their spirits renewed by the celebration of the Sun Dance, Red Cloud and his warriors returned to the fighting in earnest. To show how angry and determined Red Cloud was, one has only to consider that he decided to fight during the winter. This was very unusual because all the plains tribes usually let up on their warring during the winter time. Warring during the spring, summer, or fall — their usual times, was dangerous enough, but to risk sudden blizzards, to risk losing their precious horses by way of starvation on snow-covered, grassless prairies, and to risk the easy detection of their tracks in the snow — all were too much when added to the already great risks of war in itself. War in the wintertime, therefore, was usually out, but not this winter for Red Cloud. The fact that he was able to stir up the other bands and tribes and to get them out of their warm, winter lodges in order to fight indicates the force of his leadership.

Fetterman

It was right at the beginning of winter toward the end of November, when the Sioux were warming up for the winter war and laying their strategy that a new officer arrived at the fort. His name was Captain Fetterman — a name which was soon to become famous. Unlike Colonel

Carrington, he was a professional soldier (this meant that he intended to spend his life in the army) and he came directly from the Civil War with a fine war record. He had volunteered for Fort Kearney, knowing that he would see plenty of action and hoping to better his record and rise rapidly in rank with some brilliant fighting against the Sioux, who, he thought, would be pushovers.

About a week after he arrived, he got his first chance to tangle with the Sioux. About the middle of the afternoon on December 6th, the lookout at the fort signaled that the wood-chopping party that had been sent out to gather wood was being attacked by Indians. Captain Fetterman was delighted to be ordered out with forty cavalrymen to rescue the wood-gathering party. Colonel Carrington also went out with another group of cavalrymen. The plan was that Fetterman should go directly for the Indians, so that Carrington could circle around behind them and try to catch them from the rear while they were occupied with Fetterman.

Fetterman directed his men straight toward the firing at a dead gallop. He came upon the Indians who were riding in circles around the wood train and he charged straight at them. The Indians held their ground until Fetterman and his men came within rifle range, then turned, and to Fetterman's way of thinking, ran like rabbits. Fetterman was delighted and was surer than ever that the Sioux were pushovers; that is, he thought, if they would ever stand still and fight. The small Sioux war party that he was happily chasing swung around a large hill and immediately obliged Fetterman by standing still and fighting. The reason that they stopped and turned to fight was that there was a large body of Sioux warriors waiting for them to lead Fetterman into the trap. Both groups of Sioux, now outnumbering Fetterman, turned and charged him. Fetterman, with only 25 men, dug in to fight. Just when it seemed that Fetterman would be overrun and wiped out, his luck held out, and Colonel Carrington suddenly appeared with his men, and the Sioux withdrew.

On returning to camp, Fetterman didn't seem to realize that he had had a very close call and that he was saved from being completely wiped out only by the arrival of Colonel Carrington. All he could remember was how those Sioux ran from him like scared rabbits and he thought it was only an accident that he and his men had run into the larger body of Sioux. Apparently, he hadn't realized that he had fallen for the oldest trick in the world: that of using a decoy party to lead the pursuing enemy right into the arms of a larger force waiting for them. Delighted by the memory of the running Sioux (not yet realizing that he had fallen for the trick), he loudly boasted, "Give me eighty men and I'll ride through the whole Sioux nation." It was just two weeks later that Fetterman had his second chance to tangle with the Sioux.

On December 20, 1866, Colonel Carrington was fussing around the fort with his usual love of detail. He rode out, looked at the wood-hauling detail, made some slight changes, ordered a bridge to be built over a small creek, and returned to the fort quite satisfied that all was going so well and that the annoying Indians were frozen in for the winter. Little did he know that these annoying Indians were, at this very moment, gathering around him like angry clouds before a storm.

Just a few miles from the fort at the mouth of Prairie Dog Creek, they came drifting in as silently as the recently fallen snow. Red Cloud and his Bad Faces were there. The Minicoujous with their great war chief, High Back Bone, were there in numbers and were going to have a major part in the fighting. Crazy Horse, at this time about twenty-four years old, was there with his Oglala sub-band, his Wazhashas (Wha zha zhas) along with He Dog and Short Bull who were also famous fighters. Old Two Moon of the Northern Cheyennes was there and, to complete the picture, the Arapahoes were there in force. Their plans were made and they were about to make their first major strike.

Around eleven o'clock in the morning, the word came to the fort that the wood train was again under attack. Colonel Carrington immediately ordered Captain James Powell to take some men and to go out and rescue the wood train. When Captain Fetterman heard this, he came panting up, begging to be sent out in charge of the rescue party in place of Captain Powell. He pointed out to Carrington that he had seniority over Captain Powell — had been in the army longer — and, therefore, from the viewpoint of greater experience, he should be Carrington's first choice. Carrington knew that Fetterman was a reckless and headstrong man and he was reluctant to send him, especially after the close call that he had had in this first fight with the Sioux. He finally gave in, however, to Fetterman's pleadings, but, in order to keep him from doing anything reckless, he gave two strict orders: 1) rescue the wood train, and 2) don't chase the Indians beyond Lodge Trail Ridge. Fetterman readily agreed, ran for his horse, and led his men out to meet the Sioux again. As he rode out of the fort, a strange thing was happening. Whether Fetterman was aware of it or not, he had exactly eighty men.

The wood train with the attacking Sioux was so close to the fort that Colonel Carrington and the others could watch the rescuing action. Suddenly Carrington froze with fear as he watched Fetterman. Fetterman did not go directly toward the Sioux as he was ordered to do. Instead, he headed for the hills in a circling motion and his intention was clear. He was not intending to simply drive off the Sioux but was trying to get behind them in order to engage them in a fight to the finish. Right on the top of Lodge Trail Ridge, beyond which he had been told not to go, he ran into a band of ten warriors. Little did he realize that this was a decoy trick. Most writers today say that the young Crazy Horse was the leader of the decoy group and that he did his job well. The decoy group immediately turned and ran and Fetterman thought again how they resembled rabbits as, without hesitation, he spurred his men after the ten warriors. Fetterman didn't know it, but just beyond Lodge Trail Ridge, there awaited two thousand Sioux, Arapaho, and Cheyenne warriors.

When the ten decoys reached a certain point, they separated into two groups, crisscrossing each other's paths. This was the signal to the other waiting warriors and the trap was sprung. Yelling their war cries, the two thousand hiding warriors charged and completely surrounded Fetterman. It was so sudden that many of the warriors charged all the way through Fetterman's astonished troops. Gunfire came from all sides and the sky was filled with arrows. The winter cold was so intense that, when a man was wounded, his blood froze to his body. Fetterman's men fired their one shots from their old fashioned muzzle loading rifles and before they had a chance to reload the angry Indians were all over them. There was a fury of hand-to-hand fighting with war clubs, tomahawks, and knives.

The fight was fast, furious, and over in a very short time. Fetterman realized his mistake too late. Seeing his men quickly wiped out, he kept firing his revolver until he had one shot left. As the swarming Indians closed in on him, he placed the revolver with its one remaining shot against his temple, pulled the trigger, and took his own life. His entire command of eighty men was wiped out. Red Cloud was showing that he meant business.

Let us stop at this moment. Who was in command? Chief Red Cloud, right? Whom did the warrior chief pick as one of his main battle warriors? Crazy Horse, right? It would seem to me that the older chief was deeply impressed with this young warrior who was 22 or 24 years old approximately since there is some disagreement as to his birth date. Crazy Horse, no doubt had much respect for Chief Red Cloud at that time and no doubt was deeply appreciative of the trust the older chief displayed as to his personal selection for specific combat duty. These thoughts would last a long time, maybe a life time as I hold my thoughts for my squadron commander, who sent me out mission after mission that long day and night to rescue the entrapped Marines and then honored me in my record jacket. This is a deep portion of being a warrior, since I speak from a bit of considerable combat experience more so than my academic counter parts especially those who would pit the younger warrior against the older one, as has been displayed in some of their writings. Warriors in heavy combat and repeatedly facing danger, most often carry on their mutual respect for a lifetime has been my experience. Had I not understood the depth of proven warrior-hood which is deeply bonding, maybe I could have succumbed to being misled by ego or a false sense of superiority but such is not the case in my experience.

That night, the temperature fell to thirty below zero and the wind kept rising. Even so, Carrington, completely shaken now, thought that the Sioux would attack again during the night. Great drifts of snow kept piling up against the walls of the fort and Carrington kept men shoveling the snow away in the bitter cold throughout the night. If the snow had been permitted to drift, it would have become so high that the Indians could have used it to come over the walls. Desperate for help, Carrington asked for a volunteer to ride through the blizzard to Fort Laramie for help. A civilian named John Phillips volunteered to go. Colonel Carrington loaned the courageous man his own horse, a Kentucky thoroughbred. Through the deep snow and bitter cold, Phillips rode the 236 miles to Fort Laramie in two days and two nights. On arriving at the fort, the horse collapsed and died on the parade grounds and it was weeks before Phillips recovered from the punishing ordeal. Before Phillips himself passed out, however, he gasped out the words that were going to be fateful to the Sioux. "Those people at the fort need reinforcements. Most of all, they need modern rifles." He was referring to the need for replacing the old muzzle loading, one shot rifles against which the Indians could attack while they were being reloaded.

When news of the loss of Fetterman and his eighty men got to army headquarters and to the newspapers back East, the public began screaming for blood and demanding to know who was responsible for this loss. They had to blame somebody. We already know that the one to blame was Fetterman himself for disobeying orders, but there always has to be a scapegoat. The scapegoat in this case was Colonel Carrington. He was relieved of his command almost immediately and Colonel H.W. Wessles was sent out to take his place.

Wessles intended to take out after the Indians right away, but in the bitter cold and the deep snow his infantry could not get around and he had to call off the pursuit. Red Cloud, although he continued to attack anything that moved on the trail, was compelled to ease off also because of a lack of ammunition, but the government was not aware of this.

In February of the second year of the war, 1867, another one of the interminable commissions was appointed to investigate the Fetterman disaster and to try again to negotiate with the Indians. This was called the Sanborn-Sully commission and it reached Fort Laramie in April of that year. Right away, the friendly chiefs, most of them from south of the Platte, came in, signed, and collected around $4,000.00 in supplies. These friendlies were told that the agency was being moved to North Platte and that they should go there from now on for their supplies. This pleased most of the friendlies with the exception of the Loafer Band who were so used to living immediately around Fort Laramie that they didn't want to move.

On June 12th, the commission was delighted to see Man Afraid of His Horse, Red Cloud, and Iron Shell come in for a talk. The enthusiasm of the commission, however, quickly disappeared when they discovered that the main thing that these chiefs wanted to talk about was ammunition. With this on their minds, it was rather clear to the commission that the chiefs meant to continue the war. After this Laramie meeting, some of the followers of Red Cloud and Man Afraid of His Horse quarreled and broke up, and some of them moved south of the Platte. These were mostly southern Oglalas under Little Wound and Pawnee Killer who had gone north to join Red Cloud back in 1865.

Custer

It was about this time that Custer entered the Sioux scene. As Pawnee Killer peacefully worked his way south, Custer convinced General Sherman that Pawnee Killer was a suspicious character who would bear watching and General Sherman permitted Custer to do just that. Wherever Pawnee Killer and his band went, they found Custer and his regiment lurking around and watching them from over the nearest hill. After a while, this annoyed the Oglalas because they liked their privacy and, what's more, Custer and his soldiers were scaring the buffalo.

Although Pawnee Killer had little ammunition and was outnumbered by Custer, he decided to force Custer to show his hand. He took his warriors out for a skirmish with Custer. He actually tried the old decoy trick and Custer fell for it, sending Captain Hamilton and twenty men straight into the trap. Because of his superior numbers, however, Custer was able to send a rescue party and Pawnee Killer had to withdraw.

Shortly after this, these Oglalas came upon a group of soldiers coming up from Fort McPherson with orders for Custer. They ambushed the soldiers, killing all of them. With these troops was Red Drops, a sub-chief of Man Afraid of His Horse's band, who had unwisely consented to serve as guide for these troops. During the battle, Red Drops kept shouting out to the Sioux that he was an Oglala and that they should stop shooting at him. His mere presence with the soldiers, however, so angered the Sioux that they paid no attention and killed him along with all the soldiers.

The presence of Custer and the fighting of Pawnee Killer set off some of the other friendlies south of the Platte and, before they knew it, the settlers in that area were annoyed to see that the distant war up north on the Power River had apparently spread down to them in the south. It was in this country that the southern route of the Union Pacific Railroad was being built. The peacefulness of this area permitted such a project, but now, with this sudden rousing of the friendlies, time that would have been spent in building was now spent in beating off Indians. One chief, seeing the rails for the first time, was curious as to what would happen if he piled some ties on the tracks. He found out, as he watched the train go into the ditch. The Sioux broke into the cars and collected the finest stock of groceries, hardware, and dry goods that they had ever seen. They loaded their ponies as high as they could and got out before the troops could arrive.

The anger of the settlers in the formerly peaceful country south of the Platte moved the government to send out another peace commission. The Sioux were always delighted to see peace commissions come out because this always meant presents and supplies for them. This time the commission was made up of J.B. Sanborn, General W.S. Harney, and N.G. Taylor.

The commission sent out word that a great council was to be held at Fort Laramie on September 13 and that the richest presents that the Indians had ever seen would be handed out. At this time, North Platte marked the end of the new Union Pacific Railroad. Here the commission got off and found Spotted Tail and Man Afraid of His Horse waiting for them, eager to talk. The commission noted in its report that a difference of opinion had arisen for awhile but that the meeting ended in perfect agreement. The difference of opinion was that the chiefs had angrily demanded ammunition and, after displaying some very bad humor at the prospect of not getting it, the commission gave in and let them have the ammunition over the loud protests of the military. It was well known to the military that the Indians used their bows and arrows for hunting and saved their ammunition to shoot back at them, the military.

From this 'victory' at North Platte, the commission hurried to Fort Laramie fully expecting Red Cloud and all his hostiles to be waiting for them. They found no Indians there, but a message from Red Cloud was waiting for them. Red Cloud said that he was too busy to come down at present but that he might be able to see them later possibly next year. When Red Cloud said he was too busy to come down just then, he meant that he was so busy attacking the three forts and everything that moved on the Bozeman Trail that he couldn't afford to take a day off and come down.

By now, during the summer of 1867, the forts were so closely and constantly blockaded that even the wood trains frequently had to fight their way out of the forts and anyone who dared to move along the Bozeman Trail had to do so under heavy guard. Dog Hawk, a chief from the Powder River country, wandered into Fort Laramie at this time with the news that Red Cloud and his band were determined to make this summer more active than the last. As early as May of this summer, word had come in that Fort F.C. Smith was in desperate straits. There were only 200 men at the fort and all of the horses were either dead or run off by the Sioux. They needed food and provisions right away. It was fortunate for these people at the fort that the Sioux withdrew for their annual Sun Dance at this time. A relief party was able to sneak through unmolested.

It is a strange fact that the government was still insisting that there was no war. Yet, by now, the Bozeman Trail had been abandoned for use by both immigrants and freighters. The only ones using it were military supply groups who had to fight their way to the forts. The posts protected themselves and nothing more. The road that they were supposed to be protecting had been deserted by the public.

After the Sun Dance, Red Cloud's Sioux and their Cheyenne allies began to lay plans for attacking the forts, but they could not agree. As so often happened in Indian discussions like this, the group split up as a result and each group went where it wanted to go. Most of the Cheyennes headed north to attack Fort F. C. Smith, while Red Cloud and about 1,000 of his warriors went down to attack Fort Kearney. This was to be the occasion of the famous Wagon Box Fight.

Springfield-Allen Rifle

On August 2, 1867, Captain Powell, the man whose place Fetterman had begged to take on that fateful day, was assigned to guard the wood-cutting detail going out from Fort Kearney. For some time, Powell had been trying to figure out a way to surprise the Indians. His chance came when, about the middle of the summer, the government sent out a new 'secret weapon.' These were the new breech loading rifles, 1866 Springfield-Allen model, with a cartridge shell which could be ejected after firing and reloaded much faster. The old rifles that they had been using and which the Indians were using would only fire one bullet and it took about a minute to reload by way of a four stage operation. After firing, a man would have to put the butt of his rifle on the ground. He would then drop a firing cap down the barrel of the gun from the open end which would make the powder go off. Next, he put in the powder and tamped it down. Finally, the bullet went in and he was ready to shoot again. The Springfield ejected the spent shell and was quickly reloaded with a fresh one.

In a battle, the ones attacking knew of this time lag, of course. The usual strategy was to provoke the enemy to fire and then, before he could reload, to rush him. Captain Powell knew that the Indians would be expecting this time lag and with his new rapid firing rifles he felt he would surprise them and do great damage.

Along with this new rapid firing rifle, Captain Powell had another trick planned. Usually, when the wood-cutting parties went out, they took the wagon beds off the wagons and left them at the fort. The cut down trees were stacked, therefore, only on the running gear of the wagons on top of the two sets of wheels. On the morning of August 2, Powell ordered his men to take the wagon beds along, after holes, just big enough to stick a rifle barrel through, were drilled into them. Since a wood-gathering party always attracted Indians as certain as honey attracts bees, he felt reasonably certain that the Sioux would show up. On arriving at the tree cutting spot, Powell had some of his soldiers surround the wood cutters to protect them and ordered the others to take the wagon beds off and to prop them up on their sides in the shape of a small fort. He then settled down to wait.

He didn't have to wait long because about 1,000 Sioux were slipping silently toward him. They were mainly Oglalas, Minicoujous, and Sans Arcs under Red Cloud, High Back Bone, and other young chiefs, as well as young Crazy Horse. The Sioux had planned to use the old decoy trick but, as so often happened, some of the young warriors, more eager for glory than team action, rushed out ahead of time and stampeded the herd of horses and mules belonging to the fort. Crazy Horse's party swung around to attack the wood-cutting camp and the rest of the warriors joined them.

The Sioux rushed in, expecting the first firing to be followed by the long pause which would be the time to over run the little fort. As they rushed in during what they thought would be the pause, the new breech loading rifles kept on firing, causing heavy losses among the Sioux. They began circling the wagon box fort for another rush and again lost heavily. Next, they abandoned their horses and tried to work in on foot, but the steady firing was too much for them. The chiefs ordered a withdrawal and the fight was over.

Much has been written about the Wagon Box Fight because of early rumors that had gotten into the newspapers. Actually, the Sioux rode away regarding this fight as a victory. They had captured a great many horses and mules and only six warriors had been killed and six wounded. According to George Hyde, they had inflicted heavier losses on the non-Indians, killing several workmen, one officer, and five men in Powell's force. White Bull, a Lakota, stated that his people rarely tolerated losses over 1 or 2 percent if given the time or chance to withdraw from an unfavorable fight. His people could not afford high casualties. What appeared in the newspapers, though, and in early books were wild stories of every variety. One early account said that 3,000 Indians attacked and that 1,137 were killed. Another account was supposed to have quoted Red Cloud saying that he lost over 600 men. Still another account said that Red Cloud went into battle with 3,000 men and lost over half of them. Even Captain Powell who was the one who was under attack didn't report as wild figures as the above. He estimated Indian losses around 60 dead and 120 severely wounded, but these figures are too high, as we saw above.

It is interesting to note that in his old age, Red Cloud, when asked about the losses, had been in so many fights that he said he didn't even remember it!

The important aftermath of the Wagon Box Fight was that the government finally opened its eyes and realized that Red Cloud was not merely a chief of a small group of discontented Indians, but that he was the leading force behind several thousand highly skilled fighters. After the Wagon Box Fight, Superintendent H.B. Denman of the Indian Office reported that the display of strength shown by Red Cloud indicated that the government must either make peace with the Indians, or else flood their country with troops and fight a long and costly war. The long and costly war was out and only one other alternative faced them: agree to Red Cloud's original demands — abandon the forts, the Trail, and get out. This they finally decided to do. Red Cloud had won his war.

Toward the end of 1867, the officials in Washington decided to offer the Indians a new treaty. This was the famous treaty of 1868. As far as the Tetons were concerned, this treaty specified that all of the State of South Dakota west of the Missouri would be Indian land and that the Powder River and Big Horn countries would be recognized as Indian Territory into which no non-Indian person could go. Thus, after two years of struggle, Red Cloud and his allies had won their fight. It took the rest of 1867, to draw up the treaty and during the first part of that year the leaders of the new peace commission came out to gather up the chiefs again for the grand signing.

Fort Laramie Treaty of 1868

Arriving at Fort Laramie in April, the peace commission expected to find large numbers of Indians waiting to sign. The usual number of friendlies came in to sign and to receive the gifts, but none of the hostiles who had caused the trouble in the Bozeman Trail country came in. The commission waited for some weeks — all the time sending word to the hostiles that the commission would agree to their terms of abandoning the forts and the Trail. Red Cloud sent word down about the middle of the summer saying that he was too busy to come down and that he was going up to the Rosebud to hunt buffalo. Furthermore, he stated that he was not going to sign the treaty until the troops got out of the Bozeman Trail country **first**.

A great council was held at Fort Rice for the Upper Missouri Sioux on July 2. It took an entire day just to distribute the presents to the assembled chiefs. Red Cloud and his comrades, other warrior chiefs, refused to attend.

These chiefs stubbornly held to their demands: get the troops out and abandon the forts and the trail first, then they would sign.

The government finally gave in and toward the end of the summer of 1868 orders came to the military in the three forts to withdraw and abandon them. Captain Powell was still at Fort Kearney when the orders came to withdraw. As company after company marched out of the gates, Red Cloud and his warriors sat on their ponies not far off and watched in grim satisfaction. When the last soldier had left the fort, the Sioux swarmed down upon it and burned it to the ground. Fort F.C. Smith and Fort Reno were also abandoned, and now Red Cloud had truly won his war.

Instead of rushing right down to Fort Laramie to sign, Red Cloud waited around for a couple of months just to make sure that the soldiers were not coming back. Finally, at the beginning of November, he rode to Fort Laramie. On November 6, he finally signed and a new era of relationships with the government began. The Senate ratified the Treaty in 1869 in the Spring.

As we travel on, Chief Red Cloud will walk the political trail and be condemned by the whites and his own people as well, because of a deep inner code which championed a regard for Natural Truth. He simply would not go back on an oath he had taken and his main goal was to keep the Treaty of 1868, the treaty his warriors and leadership had won for as long as the grass will grow, as long as the rivers will flow and as long as our dead lie buried. Chief Crazy Horse, who was stabbed and died at a young age for a leader, knew well the meaning of that treaty. Chief Sitting Bull was killed not long after he returned from Canada in 1890. Red Cloud had at least 80 coups and Crazy Horse is reputed to have had more. The warrior who stands fearless in the heat of battle is the true warrior and who can calmly lead with victorious results. Among the Sioux, this warrior gathers a following. There are even those great warriors who lost a battle but against overwhelming odds, these too can be just as great as the victorious. History is generally portrayed only through the eyes and later recording of the victor however and the vanquished seldom receive their honor…at least in this world.

Had Red Cloud been mortally wounded in battle, in my opinion, he would have been the one exalted and would have been declared as the greatest warrior but such was not his lot and his people had to live in a state of captivity and despair as he lived on. White authors had their two martyrs in Crazy Horse and Sitting Bull, even Spotted Tail of the Brules was killed, by a tribesman, no less, now they could take out their animosity for the Indian on the warrior chief that lived. How do I regard Crazy Horse as comparing to Red Cloud? In my opinion it was a matter of who was born first actually. I think either man was as brave as the other. As a combat experienced author, I look in awe at their personal 80 some coup experiences. They were most certainly — combat tested! Their society was spiritually based, but yet was not controlled by a self-perpetuating religious hierarchy. This form of society, in my opinion, produced better leaders relative to being truly concerned for the welfare of the people they led than what we experience today through this materialistic accumulation requirement cursed on us by modern political governing parties. Rarely does a combat veteran get elected anymore. Simply count the 100 senators we have today.

The two Sioux leaders we are studying were as great as the other, in my opinion and in that group I will also include Chief Sitting Bull. Who was greater, General Patton or the Marine's General Chesty Puller? It is foolish to attempt to make these decisions. Both were great men as well as was General MacArthur, who experienced combat in WWI as well and later won the Medal of Honor.

Patton's decisions in WWII were brilliant and he was known to not exhibit fear when in direct exposure to artillery or German air raids. Ask his men! Chesty Puller was heavily experienced in direct combat. Letters to his wife, revealed his sheer lack of fear when he was surrounded by Chinese divisions. The by-passing of the huge Japanese garrison at Rabaul, in WWII was a brilliant call by MacArthur. Here, he wisely saved thousands of G.I.s by simply avoiding a combat landing. Not a shot was fired when ships entered the Rabaul harbor at the end of the war. The starved Japanese troops who had to subsist mainly on fishing, boarded the ships peacefully for their homeward trip.

As 'Shogun of Japan' General MacArthur's rising ego blinded his basic military duty, however, and kept him too comfortably entrenched in his Imperial Palace. He never went back out in the field to his command until it was a bit late. The Eighth Army was woefully inadequate prior to the Korean invasion as a consequence of the Supreme Commander Far East, never inspecting his troops and hence realizing the severe inadequacy of equipment while in garrison. The grandeur of the Imperial Palace had mesmerized him into forgetting he was still a soldier, and even a brilliant soldier has his duties. In Korea, he made the daring Inchon invasion decision against one of the world's sharpest tidal drops which could leave a fleet stranded in mud. This brilliant move, countered by objecting admirals, broke the North Korean invasion and simmered congressional criticism of being woefully unprepared. He relied too heavily however, on an old hand of the 'Palace Guard' serving him since the WWII Philippines retreat. A stubborn Chief of Staff, named Major General Charles Willoughby, gravely erred regarding the North Korean invasion and later the Chinese entry into Korea, which warnings he foolishly ignored despite a plethora of evidence from varied intelligence gathering sources. Not foreseeing the mass deployment of Chinese divisions against approaching U. N. troops so close to their border was MacArthur's undoing and his ensuing fall from his military throne was occasioned by President Truman; of 'The buck stops here.' Great heroes can err, like most ordinary humans, especially when deviated or separated from their primary mission by human ego and the sudden enjoyment of extreme materialism.

George Hyde Summary:

Red Cloud's War is summed up in the words of Author, George Hyde, *Red Cloud's Folk:*

In recent years, a tendency has developed among some authors of books on Indians to deprive Red Cloud of all credit for having led in the war of 1866-1867. If he did not lead, who did? Neither Sitting Bull nor any of the chiefs of his northern group of Sioux hostiles appear to have taken much interest in this struggle; indeed, Sitting Bull, who is supposed to have been so wise and far-seeing, had no thought of uniting with Red Cloud, but waited placidly until his own hunting grounds were invaded before he took any real action. Red Cloud put himself at the head of the opposition to white encroachments on the Sioux lands at the Fort Laramie council in the spring of 1866 and he held firmly to his position until the last soldier had left Powder River. The years 1866 and 1867, were Red Cloud's day and the struggle that took place in the Powder River country in those years will always be known as Red Cloud's War.

* * * *

Black Elk's Vision

Religious concepts versus Spirituality

The Indians followed the buffalo and often the buffalo followed a great circle of their own. The Greasy Grass wandered and meandered, bound by Creator's gravity, dribbling its course eventually toward the sea. But a few years later a great battle by two-legged (human) would be fought by those who respected the teeming herds which grazed its meadows and those two-legged in blue who did not. Newspapers would soon make this river as historically immortal as Bastogne, Kasserine Pass, Guadalcanal, and the Chosen Reservoir. Maybe some of Caesar's and Alexander's battles as well. The Battle of the Little Big Horn would echo worldwide. But for the moment, the winter counts would term the slow paced river as the Greasy Grass. A young boy named Black Elk, a Teton Oglala, had a powerful vision here on its banks as would a great chief named Sitting Bull, but a few years later. His vision, Sitting Bull's, however was for the moment; the men in blue would be falling, helplessly head first, down, into a great Sioux, Cheyenne, and Arapahoe camp and they would be swallowed up. Maybe this Greasy Grass like Bear Butte Mountain or the Pipestone Quarries is a special place for those who quest. I would have to consider the boy's vision as the more profound however. Maybe one could claim that it held more of a world view. For Sitting Bull, his vision or dream soon bore truth. The soldiers did 'fall' fatally for them, into the Sioux camp and it was easy to understand as well for most to believe its truth. Black Elk's vision is indeed puzzling, yet millions have become aware of what the boy experienced, after he journeyed into a strange Spirit World. The boy was innocent and it would have been difficult for him to make up such a vivid portrayal. His life long actions following this great event insured this vision as the river's journey would end at the sea.

McMurtry states that writers or historians on Chief Crazy Horse "have convinced many readers and certainly not this reader — that they have an accurate grip on the deeds, much less on the soul, of the Sioux warrior we call Crazy Horse."[1]

So let us probe the soul of Crazy Horse and Red Cloud as well, for they were both Teton Oglalas with spiritual concepts quite varied from Dominant Society's.

Do Indians have religious prophets? I would consider the Oglala named Black Elk as more of a visionary than as a prophet upon which the white man both the Christian and the Islamic seem to place a greater reliance upon. Indians I have known, mostly Sioux, shy away from all-knowing prophecy because they truthfully admit that when dealing with Mystery there are simply too many unknowns. I say that, not looking for argument. It is simply the way and how we have observed upon our own life journeys. It is all that we can offer; what we have experienced and are too respectful, even now, to try and embellish and change its direction.

From my experience with the white man's proclamations, most seem to be more in error than they are right on. We constantly hear the doomsday predictions which never occasion. I personally shy away from so-called prophecy other than what is scientifically obvious such as real facts on over population and the disasters it can bring and evidentiary disclosures such as what happened to the folks who over populated Easter Island for example. Thor Heyerdahl impregnated my mind years ago with his description of Motane Island, a ghost island that once held abundant life but man had literally killed and he too had to flee for his survival.

A Once Lush Island in the South Pacific

Motane was once a thriving island. Before World War II, Thor Heyerdahl wrote of his observations in the book *Fatu-Hiva, Back to Nature.* [2]

The island (Motane) was where modern man had beaten nature. He had entered this south sea paradise intent on improving conditions for himself and his uncivilized local host. Through bringing plants and domestic animals, he had also upset the whole balance of a life lived in accord with local conditions. "Failing in his effort to help the islanders in order to benefit from them, white man withdrew from the island as soon as he confronted his own shadow, and the encroaching jungle followed at his heels, often right down to the island shore, until everything it had lost was re-conquered."

Captain Cook estimated a local Polynesian population of one hundred thousand when he ran into the island group in 1773. After him came European settlers, whalers, and missionaries. A good century later, in 1883, the total census was 4,865. By 1920, the population was down to 3,000, mainly due to European germs and living conditions. On Motane, the death rate was so high that not a single survivor had remained to tell the story of what had long since become a ghost island.

The Europeans brought a different living system and they brought disease. "On Motane, local history ended. Perhaps the last surviving Polynesian died on the family's pandanus mat on just this paepae where we were sitting. Perhaps the last desperate family embarked in their canoe to escape to Hivaoa, whose mountain crests could be seen in clear weather. Or perhaps the last survivor was a child left alone between the trees and the animals. We shall never know."

With no humans, the domestic animals ran wild and the sheep were the survivors. With flesh-eating man gone, the sheep of Motane multiplied. Hordes of wild sheep consumed all within reach, and when famine hit them, they devoured the roots of the grass and the bark of the trees turning Motane into a desert. "Motane's biological clockwork had not only stopped, but was set in backward motion, until the hands showed a visitor pretty much what our planet looked like before life emerged from the sea. If the Moana's crew managed to catch the last of the scraggy sheep, then the miniature world we saw from our hilltop would more or less match Planet Earth, in the period when life was confined to the ocean and the air: the remote era when eroding rock had liberated the first salts and minerals ashore, which, dissolved in water, had combined with sunlight to fill first the ocean and then the air with creatures swimming and flying around the lifeless coasts. But if all the world were reduced like Motane, how many million years would we have to sit alone on our hilltop paepae waiting for algae to be washed ashore and develop into grass and trees once more, or for fish to jump ashore and acquire lungs and legs and fur a second time? The tiny fish we had seen jumping in the surf area on the cliffs of Fatu-Hiva had certainly jumped like that for hundreds of thousands of years, and not one of them was as yet ready to take the first leap on the long road toward kangaroo or monkey. Better to take care of the world we had. It would take a long time to get a new one."

Planetary heating is now getting some startling proclamations from leading scientists based on real, measured and observed factual data which is convincing to me and yet the white man's religious leaders seem unmoved and many oppose the scientists. According to Bill Moyers in a startling speech to the Center for Health and the Global Environment, Harvard Medical School, they smugly declare that biblical prophecy is being fulfilled and many are out rightly pleased with the downward environmental spiral of the planet despite the fatal outcome for two-legged which can result.[3] I do wish I had their confidence…if they are right! They could possibly be! For not long ago, the Indians indeed thought that the Benevolent Creator had blessed the wahshichu immensely. No doubt that is why so many tribes readily embraced the white man's religion. They had a more powerful God, obviously as we were constantly beaten back; as simple as that. The buffalo have all but vanished and look at how productive the lands are now! Yes, the white man can offer many convincing counter arguments. It would be a lie, would it not, **to not** allow his view; his accomplishments? The Oklahoma tribes had little problem changing their spiritual view.

Native Worldview

There is a big difference between Native worldview and White man's worldview when one compares the influences of each others religion. If we wish to understand Crazy Horse and Red Cloud is there some man-made rule which states we should not at least attempt to understand their spiritual worldview? I have combined the information offered from old Black Elk with that of his son, Ben Black Elk, the interpreter of every word of the book, *Black Elk Speaks*. Ben was a personal friend and influenced me beginning when I was a child. Even when I was a Marine pilot I would stop and see him when he worked at Mt. Rushmore after I would land a military machine at the Ellsworth Air Force base near Rapid City. As military pilots we had to take cross-country flights as part of our training. I would always choose my hometown which had the convenient military field nearby. At the University of South Dakota I helped bring Ben to the campus wherein he offered several lectures. My close friend by then, beautiful Connie Bowen saw to it that Ben was always comfortably housed. Ben Black Elk was most appreciative. As mentioned earlier, Ben was the interpreter between his father, Nick Black Elk and the writer, John Neihardt who authored the book *Black Elk Speaks* back in the thirties when this great revelation was written.[4] The book has gone on to many millions of readers and has been printed in numerous languages.

The Vision

In a time when the tribe enjoyed the freedom of the Great Plains, a powerful vision took place. This event occurred several years before the famous Custer battle, no doubt in the very camp of Oglalas under Chief Crazy Horse's command. A boy named Black Elk was a young boy when he had such an open, understandable vision as it pertained to all of Creator's Nature which surrounds us. It began with the Wamaskaskan, the animal creations, finned, flying and four legged, all in a myriad of gracious display. His vision took him into a Rainbow Covered Lodge of the Six Powers of the World.

Two spirit men carried this young boy upward to the spirit world. On a cloudy plain, thunder beings leaped and flashed. A bay horse appeared and spoke: "Behold me!" The boy walked on toward a cloud that changed into a tipi with a rainbow for an open door. Within, he saw six old men sitting in a row. He was invited to go through the rainbow covered lodge door and told not be fearful.

He went in and stood before the six old men and discovered that they were not old men but were the Six Powers of the World. Of the powers, the West Power, Wiyopeyata, (pronounced with a guttural — we yoke-pee ahh tah) spoke first. When the West Power spoke of understanding, the rainbow leaped with flames of many colors over Black Elk. The West Power gave him a wooden cup filled with water and spoke. "Take this, it is the power to make live." The West Power gave him a bow and spoke. "Take this, it is the power to destroy." The West Power then left and changed to a black horse but the horse was gaunt and sick. This is the way the Vision is best described and for deeply interested readers regarding the spiritual, I suggest any of my previous books and of course *Black Elk Speaks* or *The Sacred Pipe* by J. Epes Brown. Each Power spoke in the above manner.

I will not go into much detail as to the Vision as most readers are no doubt centered on our two main subjects and an Indian's view thus regarding their lives. Their Spirituality, however, was based on Nature and the following may offer an indication as to where their beliefs were centered.

The Six Powers [5]

West Power. We acknowledge the life-giving rains as the power to make live. The thunder and the lightning are the power to destroy but we realize more life than death transpires with each rain. As the sun goes down in the west, darkness comes to the land. The color for the west is black.

North Power. The cold north has Mother Earth rest beneath the white mantle of snow. She sleeps and gathers up her strength for the bounty of springtime. When the snows melt, the earth is made clean. When native people wintered over, often confined to a small area for a lengthy time while they waited for the spring thaw, they learned to be extremely polite, to be truthful and honest with each other. They kept clean by using the sweat lodge to take winter baths and to beseech to the spirit world. The cleansing white wing emphasizes endurance and cleanliness.

East Power. The third power brought him the red pipe of peace. To have peace, one must first become aware of knowledge, which comes forth out of the red dawn, the east, with each new day. When you have knowledge and it is discussed and considered, it can become wisdom. Others share their thoughts, their observations and their needs. The red dawn rises to bring a bright new day in which we can add knowledge to our lives on a daily basis as long as we walk this planet.

South Power. Medicine from roots, stems, herbs and fruits are associated with the south power. The sun rises higher and higher as the South Power advances with summer. Plants such as corn and wheat will bring forth yellow or golden kernels that will sustain much life through the long winter. Abundance is the primary gift from this power, for it makes all things grow and we are allowed to take that which grows. To be thankful for what you receive adds strength to your search for your bounty; sustenance, provisions and shelter.

Sky Power. Father Sky spoke and said the things of the air would be with Black Elk to help him in his struggle. Could these "things of the air" also be the open space of communication which now can transcend across the globe? Can it also be the satellites — "things of the air," beaming back video and radio waves so we may see and talk directly across the skies? If so, Truth will be more difficult to distort. Now we have modern communication that is allowed by the mystery of the radio waves, the television waves and other mysterious gifts. The computer stores vast information and transmits volumes in an eye wink. None of this could so perform were it not allowed by a Powerful Vastness! These communicative forces, created for our use, fosters optimism that our planet can be saved from past practices of destruction.

I perceive that what the Sky Power said could be closely associated with the advance of more communicative people upon the earth because the things of the air are helping to promote peace and harmony. It is happening right before us.

Earth Power. Mother Earth, the Sixth Power, spoke and took Black Elk to the danger that was confronting the earth. This danger was the Blue Man of greed and deception that was already harming the living things in more ways than just drought which the rains could cure as always, down through time. This Blue Man symbolizes the corruption, insensitivity, greed and ignorance which are upon the Earth. The Blue Man would wreak great destruction using lies and untruths and would have to be addressed or else all creatures including two leggeds would perish: Perish through their greed and over consumption.

Untruth is the Blue Man. Everyday we observe much deception by those who lobby our political leaders in Washington with disregard for the environment and the ongoing dilemma. As the situation worsens, more eyes will be opened and eventually the old ways of Nature's Truth will have to be accepted in order to finally destroy the Blue Man. Hopefully, it will be in time for the planet to have a chance to regain the old harmony which was there in the first place. Traditional Siouxs insist that two leggeds will discover that there is no other choice. Religious fundamentalists will hold to their beliefs and no doubt keep on praying and waiting for miracles. It would be extremely convenient if their beliefs work out as they vehemently proclaim. The movies, tales, and fiction literature most often have satisfying endings. Scientific proclamations do not always paint a rosy rainbow covered ending or bear chocolate covered results. Being told one has cancer is not a pleasant revelation. Barring some miracle by Creator, if Creator is so inclined, the realistic and workable solution will be to return to the values that actually worked. The ozone layer, water depletion and the population spiral will not wait for miraculous curing, it seems. Some tragic consequences will be learned along the way. As I have said earlier and aside from Black Elk, I hope that the hopes of Dominant Society come through but in my own opinion, I consider that highly questionable if I am to remain honest. It is still a Democracy and one should be allowed their views, should they not?

The colors to be remembered as representing the four directions are; black (west) and following clockwise, white (north), red (east), and yellow (south). Blue, for the life giving rains, often represented the west also. These are Black Elk's colors. So many tribes, including Sioux bands, know nothing about this arrangement or ignore it.

Black Elk intended that the world should know of his vision. Several writers had earlier attempted to secure Black Elk's story but he was not satisfied with them. When John Neihardt came to his cabin, he told Neihardt that he was the one he was waiting for. It was in the fall. Black Elk said that it was too late that year to relate his vision. "You come back when the grass is so high," the holy man held out his hand to indicate the height of spring grass, "and I will tell you my story."

Ben Black Elk interpreted between Neihardt and the holy man, Black Elk. Ben was well satisfied with the finished writing, *Black Elk Speaks*. His satisfaction should dispel the false accusations which have been heaped on John Neihardt as self composing. Here we have the interpreter being very satisfied. Wouldn't one who had ordinary common sense and a bit of intelligence easily discern that a son is generally, usually going to know which are his father's words and which are those of someone else? Especially when he interpreted a long conversation both ways — in English and Lakota! Ben always spoke glowingly of the finished work as, "My Father's book!" It was published in 1932 but at that time there existed so much prejudice and ignorance that it went into remainder and copies were sold for 45 cents a piece. It wasn't until thirty years later that the importance of such a profound vision would be rediscovered, thanks to the interest of Carl Jung and Dick Cavett. The book has now sold well over a million copies and has been printed in many languages, including Japanese.

The reservation missionaries made a strong attempt to dislodge Black Elk's vision and were almost successful. Why? All that I can surmise on their behalf is that it intruded on their belief system. It was also quite convincing if one would rely on direct observance of what all surrounded us. Many Sioux know little about it, or they believe the detracting dogma perpetuated against it. That is their loss, my opinion. I harbor little remorse for those who deny direct observation. Hopefully, there exists a Spirit World in which we can be with our own kind. That categorization, also hopefully, will not be a separation by race or worldly accomplishment but one of how well we utilized our mind while here upon this journey. How much did we place into this greatest of gifts which Benevolent Creator has designed specifically just for us! However, there are many from all walks who are taking a serious look at this vision. Joseph Campbell's remark that this vision is the best example of spiritual imagery is very appropriate. There are many people who have discovered the visible Six Powers of this earth and who are now relating these daily entities in balance, acknowledgement and kinship to their everyday lifestyle. Black Elk lived at a time when both Chief Crazy Horse and Chief Red Cloud were alive and in power. I believe that both of the two leaders we will be studying were spiritually respectful men who believed that it was the Six Powers (Shakopeh Ouyea) who regulated the known world to the Sioux under the laws, actions and powers of the Creator, Wakan Tanka, as both men understood it.

Canton Asylum

The Canton Indian Insane Asylum was created in 1902 while Red Cloud was in his eighties; a time when the United States' official Indian policy was assimilation. The Federal Canton Indian Insane Asylum was built out of brick at Canton, South Dakota, in the eastern part, south of Sioux Falls, the largest South Dakota town. I even have a picture of it sent to me by a Canton township person. It demonstrates how brutal and primitive the mindset of the government officials was as well as the church people who lobbied for it. Leonard Bruguier says whatever the intent behind the asylum; it was a convenient tool for reservation agents. Bruguier is a member of the Yankton Sioux and Director of the Institute of American Indian studies at the University of South Dakota.

Many Indians who went into Canton, simply disappeared. A large graveyard is now part of the Canton golf course. 121 bodies, former patients, are buried between the 4th and 5th fairways.[6]

Bruguier: So in order for the agent to feel more comfortable being surrounded by yes-people, it would be very easy for him to say "This person's insane," and have him shipped to Canton to be administered by a whole different set of rules. Basically you'd just be able to get rid of 'em." It is alleged that medicine men were also incarcerated with no symptoms whatsoever of 'insanity.' This too was a method to wipe out the old religion.

Black Elk's 'Conversion'

After the Custer battle Black Elk settled on the Red Cloud Agency. He was a part of the short-lived Ghost Dance and had been in Europe with Buffalo Bill Cody's 'Wild West' shows. Returning to the reservations he took up his call once he found that he had strong healing power. His reputation grew and he had many Tetons coming to him for various afflictions.

In 1902, Black Elk had an experience with a Jesuit missionary. Father Aloysius Bosch, who came upon Black Elk innocently doing a healing ceremony and was promptly set upon by the angry priest from Holy Rosary Mission. The yet young visionary and practicing medicine man had his altar dismantled and sacred objects (peace pipe) thrown on the ground. The burly priest yelled at the Indians in attendance and told them to go back to their camps. This account is partially recorded by Raymond DeMallie and the negative portions (from an Indian's point of view) have been excluded or told not according to Neihardt's notes.[7] Hilda Neihardt told me personally she was quite set out against DeMallie whom she had given permission to see her father's notes and primarily by this omission to offer the full story. She was extremely disappointed that he omitted key materials in the so-called 'conversion' controversy that modern academics are constantly bringing up regarding Black Elk.

What was omitted was that Aloysius Bosch returned to the mission, and under a clear blue sky, lightning hit the priest's horse and he was thrown from it and died. The Indians naturally believed that the priest should not have been so disrespectful to the Native Way and went on happily with their healing ceremonies. Within a few years, along came Father Lindebner and did the same thing. Black Elk was grasped by the neck and yelled at, "Satan Get Out!" Black Elk was a slight man and not a typical Sioux warrior whom a priest would have a hard time in so subduing. He was also in the throes of despair at the time. After thrown physically into a wagon by the overre-acting Lindebner, S.J. and hauled to the Holy Rosary Mission to be exorcized by one Father Joseph Zimmerman, S.J.; Black Elk was converted. He was issued a pass for his compliance and now could travel freely upon the reservation. In time, as long as he did the bidding of the missionaries, he could travel to other reservations as well, which he did.

Canton Asylum was in full operation at the time and the Sioux 'Grape Vine' certainly knew of it. Numerous books clamor regarding this superioristic 'conversion,' egotistically championed by the likes of Raymond DeMallie, Clyde Holler, and the Jesuit writers, Steltenkamp and Steinmetz. Oddly these men offer little focus on the profoundness of the Vision despite the reference to it from Joseph Campbell to Bill Moyers; **"the best example of Spiritual Imagery!"** Also, none of these academics mention in their writings; the foreboding asylum which waited for medicine people who would not toe the missionary line. More than one holy man was 'converted' to avoid this horrid place and more than one medicine man who would not comply, was forever doomed behind the restrictive bars at Canton.

Vine Deloria, well-known Yankton Sioux writer, never mentions it (Canton) in his extolling of the 'Big Four,' Episcopal breed missionaries, one of whom was his Grandfather. His Great Grandfather had to kill four Sioux; the white man's God told him so, regarding conversion and the book is thus dedicated. I have to be honest however, and admit that his first and last of these killings, the victims definitely deserved their fate. The breed priests, Lambert, Deloria, Ross and Walker; their pictures are in his book, *Singing for a Spirit*, and are dressed in their missionary finery wearing those 'Mickey Mouse' hats that we also saw the Diocesan Catholic priests wear. That is what we Indian youth used to call them. By 1900, '12,000 (Indians) were converted,' he proudly states. Evidently the 12,000 disappeared for the Wakpala mission became a ghost church. Chief Eagle Feather and I used its abandoned basement over a quarter century ago to hold a *Yuwipi* Spirit ceremony heavily attended by spiritually hungry Hunkpapa. DeMallie disrespectfully refers to the *Yuwipi* as a 'conjuring' ceremony. If my Great Spirit told me to go out and kill four Indians to join some new religion, I doubt if I could do it although I have to respect, the great-grand father, Saswe, as I said, for taking out the two who definitely deserved their fate.

The following is an interesting note. I was reading a book of Vine's father's the well-known missionary in South Dakota. At the very end, I was totally surprised in finding my name. Vine Sr., stated that he wanted his ashes flown over a particular Dakota area by none other than me, the Sioux pilot, Ed McGaa. Maybe, my strong return to my people's old ways as well as my championing of the Return disparaged the fulfillment of Vine, Senior's specific request, by relatives, as I was never contacted. At the time, however, Vine, Senior, was well aware of my sun dance return and public championing of the Old Way. Deep down in, despite being a converted churchman, he obviously respected my stand to issue such a personally important request.

I can't help but think of the old traditionals however, bleakly attempting to hold onto the old Sioux Way at that time or the ones doomed at Canton Asylum. Reservation missionaries, mostly white ones, had strong influence on the government agents. Yes, it is interesting how some so-called scholars can omit some hard-core evidence that does not support their egotistical, religious superiority.

I must remind the reader: **'My spirituality is my choice for MYSELF, but I do not hold it out as superior for YOUR needs or your MINDSET'.** I know that sounds highly unusual in this proselytizing, I-know-everything world. My tribe is still intact. Possibly, that is the reason it works for me. Most readers are not specifically from a tribe. Nature will take care of everything, eventually, one way or another, is my reassurance. Simply carry on, care for your offspring, appreciate and be good citizens. If you increase your knowledge base as you are presently attempting to do, then that is well and good, (wasteh aloh) my opinion. Leave it at that. Mystery is mystery and we should definitely not be fighting or arguing over it. Wah- steay- ah- loh!; spoken firmly, it is a very pretty word, and we use it often to compliment.

Prior to Canton being investigated and soon afterwards shut down, Black Elk boldly told of his powerful vision, Standing Bear standing beside him to verify; every word passing through his interpreter son, Ben, while Enid Neihardt, John Neihardt's daughter served as stenographer. John Neihardt listened to every word and often broke into the old man's running conversation to ask a question to verify a particular point. The old man would frequently lapse off into a deep nap, revive, and continue on. The missionaries were greatly disturbed when they discovered they had been omitted from the telling and demanded from Neihardt a copy of his manuscript.

When asked, by Neihardt, "On what grounds do you make such a demand?" The Jesuits replied that they indeed had a right to such information since Black Elk was now, 'one of theirs.' They also believed that they could then 'edit' on behalf of Black Elk. John Neihardt not being of any particular white man's faith, simply scoffed and refused to deliver. The Jesuits were highly incensed and not used to being rebuffed on what was 'their Sioux reservation' but little could they do about it. Such was the accustomed pomposity of the reservation missionaries over the Sioux. Later, the writers previously mentioned, came along to seriously distract from this simple yet deep discourse given beside a log cabin in far out Manderson, South Dakota. Julian Rice should also be added to the list of 'conversion squabblers.' All have neglected to explore what I presume to be the major issue of Black Elk- his Vision! The academic writers however, have tied themselves in knots as to what degree Black Elk agreed or did not agree to be converted! I will guarantee an interesting evening, should some

University include me in an open meeting or discourse with these writers.[8] See; Review of Clyde Holler's Sun Dance Books and related commentary on other writers by Dr. Dale Stover.

I had the fortunate opportunity to view Susan Zucotti, *Under His Very Windows*, the renowned Jewish scholar debate some Academics. I think the Universities owe the same favor to the experienced traditional supporting Indian writers. Notice, I use the term experienced and will also add — connected; such as; personally knowing tribal medicine people. Dr. Bryde would be an excellent partner as he enters mid-eighties. I do have that Juris Doctorate so should qualify academic wise.

Shouldn't a religion stand for God's ultimate objective; that we sincerely cultivate and practice Truth? I mean, real, real sincerely as if the Creator was right before you and you were about to divulge what you genuinely observed with no alteration, no ulterior motive or just to please some one. Wouldn't a man, about to tell a powerful happening held up inside of him for decades and along with much supporting evidence and a personal friend right there to help verify, and your very own son, to serve as an interpreter: wouldn't this be sufficient enough evidence to pass on to a narrator or a recorder who has the immediate opportunity to question or have repeated what he did not at first comprehend or understand fully? Why would religious outsiders be needed to further the truth of the relating? Why would they want to "edit" this work? Is that how organized religious history has been explained or verified down through time? Is this what they call the 'sanitation process' or 'political correctness' in order that the control of the people comes first? This thought process is what the Indians faced when they had to deal with the treaties to a high degree, is my opinion. The white world and the Indian world indeed were very separate when it came to basic human understanding and carrying out the full meaning of the word — Truth!

As I have said repeatedly in many of my works; I firmly believe that Mother Nature is about to deliver some very ultimate Truths. Why? Because human has allowed himself to be so misguided by some ultimate untruths which are highly incompatible with Mother Nature's environment. It is as simple as that. Time will certainly tell.

In Oklahoma, few of the tribes kept their language, fewer kept their religion, the old spirituality of their forefathers. One tribe even referred to itself as a civilized tribe whatever meaning that meant. For we Sioux, we were always an extremely 'civilized' tribe, in my opinion.

The reservation boarding schools were used to make the Indian children into white children. Hair was cut. Long hair meant manhood to the Indian men. And one day Red Cloud found his own daughter scrubbing a floor with a white woman threatening her. This and other episodes turned him against education for a while. These were not the promises promised in the Treaty of 1868.

Toward his last days he did praise education and saw it as the major means to adjust to the demands of the dominant world surrounding his people. Half the day the students labored in the fields, or scrubbing, cleaning and maintaining the boarding schools. Far too much time was spent on religion in the Christian boarding schools. In the end, the Indian student received very little 'formal' education as was received by the white students off reservation. When it came time to compete for college they were ill prepared and not until after WWII, was there hardly any enrollment into the colleges and universities.

I had six brothers and six sisters. I was the last. The old traditional Sioux family was much smaller in size than what the reservation families had after the missionaries spread their influence. My parents, both Oglalas with some Cheyenne blood as well which was not recorded on the tribal rolls; both went to boarding school — to the 6th grade; my mother and 8th grade, my father, respectively. Our Oglala blood line was registered or as some say, enrolled. Neither parent ever learned to drive a car but certainly knew horses. All of my brothers and sisters, except the one sister next to me, went to reservation boarding schools. None ever walked into a college except when a few sisters attended my graduation from a Catholic men's University, years later. My father did not own a suit so was too reluctant to attend. I attended a public school when my family moved off the reservation due to the War Department confiscating the northern end of the Pine Ridge reservation for an aerial machine gun and bombing range for WWII training. We had 30 days to vacate our property and were fortunate to get jobs at the new military air base being hastily built in Rapid City. In those days there was no such thing as protest. A World War was on and we actually were proud that our land was helping fight the war in an indirect way. Five of my brothers saw combat. My father worked at the military base. Prejudice existed in Rapid City but the war effort was first and foremost. Every one hated the 'Germans and the Japs' during that conflict. Since so many Indian men were in the service and most volunteering for front line units, prejudice abated considerably. Had I not gone to public school, I seriously believe I would never have had the confidence and mainly the preparation to pursue a higher education after high school. Few of my age group went on to graduate from college.

Beseechment

Beseechment or Ceremony will offer us a yet even deeper look into the Sioux mindset. Ceremony is merely human's attempt at some form of communication into a Spirit World, so to speak or an attempt to express respect, appreciation and communication to one's concept of his or her Higher Power. When Christians or Islamic go to their Churches or Mosques, a Sioux presumes that these folks are going to attempt to communicate to their Higher Power concepts. Religion, basically is the same all over the world. Too bad, human's ego can so quickly make lethal, resources consuming wars, out of it.

The primary ceremony for the Sioux was the annual Sun Dance which is mentioned by most all past writers in regard to Chief Red Cloud and Chief Crazy Horse but I do not believe any of them went in and explored why this was such an important event to stop fighting their campaigns. Something this important would certainly bear some scrutiny, some curiosity, some probing; would not one think? Did Chief Crazy Horse or Red Cloud go into the Sun Dance before their Creator concept? Did they ask Wakan Tanka to spare them one more time, one more battle, feed them one more winter, bring the Wahshichu to the treaty table? Would not these issues be heavy on their minds? Several of my books go into greater depth regarding the ceremonies practiced while the tribe was free on the Great Plains. I have participated as a Sun Dance Pledger in six sun dances. Many sun dancers have taken part in many more sun dances than I but as a writer, I believe I have taken part in at least six more sun dances than all the rest of the related subject writers except Dr. Chuck Ross and Manny Two Feathers.

Ceremonies help the individual to grow in their life's quest. Since we are not gifted like an Orca or a Dolphin as to the murky waters of life, I believe ceremony also can become a tool — so to speak — to hone one's intuitive abilities. These animals can find their way about in the dark oceans of the world for their food besides having an uncanny ability to suspect quite accurately when danger is near. Ceremony can enable you to be more sure of your perspectives toward truth. Many ceremonies are universal. I hope the universal ceremonies can be rescued from some erroneous designed form of ownership in order that all creeds and tribes may rightfully enjoy the blessing of our common ceremonies. It is my belief, however, that some ceremonies are tribal, and maybe not meant for everyone. Vision Quest and Sweat Lodge however are not 'owned' by anyone. Down through time, both have been practiced throughout the planet.

The Pipe

It is the use of the pipe in ceremony, that I believe Chief Arvol Looking Horse, Keeper of the Pipe, objects mostly to. Therefore I recommend that you use a wotai stone (wotahwe) as your beseechment item should you be non-tribal and wish to beseech in the Natural Way.

The hills and streams are full of them and you will be surprised that a special stone is out there somewhere waiting for you to find it. Use that! I no longer use a peace pipe and gave both of mine away, since controversy presently reigns regarding their use. What few ceremonies I still do, I am quite satisfied with the Spirit connection that faithfully occurs regardless that I use one of the two wotai stones I possess instead of utilizing the peace pipe of which I am quite familiar.

Sun Dance – Wiwanyang Wachipi

Chiefs Crazy Horse and Red Cloud devoted their time and energy to the annual sun dance obviously according to past writings although little or no detail was ever submitted. Except for a very few individuals in these modern times most will never experience this ceremony as it is a tribal thanksgiving. Most are not of a tribe but it is important knowledge to have, as it helps one to further understand the spiritual depth of the old traditionals. Even a closed ceremony gives us insight into the development of intuition when we hear or read the stories of those ceremonies.

There are many, many summer sun dances now held on the reservations in the Dakotas and especially on the Rosebud and Pine Ridge Reservations (Tetons naturally!) because the youth especially are seriously returning to the old ways. As the Tetons led in the past when they crossed the Missouri, so it is today in the spiritual. When I was younger, there was but one Sioux Tribal Sun Dance held at Pine Ridge Reservation. This ceremony was banned by the government in the early 1880's. Sporadically it was done in secret out in lonely areas of the reservations by brave and stubborn holy people. It did not return in public form until the 1950's after the old prophet Black Elk died. Chief Eagle Feather, the true Sun Dance Warrior of modern times, said he was going to bring back the Sun Dance, "Out in the open," and Chief Fools Crow said, "I will pierce him." How a young half-breed boy that was only a mere pow wow dancer the night before that famous event, could be at that first modern era, public sun dance is indeed more than coincidence, but I was there and sitting beside my step-grandmother. It was a pitiful crowd but it was out in the open, defiant and the beginning of the Great Return. Oddly, missionaries and government authorities paid us little attention. They were so used to winning that a couple of old futile holy men to them were considered harmless. The small crowd proved that.

Frank Fools Crow was the Sun Dance Chief for the six sun dances in which I took part in the later sixties and early seventies. My first Sun Dance I was not pierced since I had just returned from war. The next four Sun Dances held at Pine Ridge, I was pierced and my last Sun Dance was way up at Green Grass on the Hunkpapa reservation where the sacred pipe resides and at that Sun Dance all of we dancers did not pierce. Russ Means was there and I believe both the Bellecourt brothers who were Chippewa. Dennis Banks was also there, if my failing memory serves me right. Both Russ and I had to give speeches since Fools Crow told us so. Chief Fools Crow and Chief Eagle Feather both officiated at that ceremony.

In my time tribal Indians only took part in the piercing ceremony and I believe that all of the participants were Sioux, Oglala, Sichangu, Hunkpapa, or Minicoujou. Maybe a few of the other Sioux were also represented among the pledgers as one in my limited capacity did not go about asking for credentials. My mother warned me that I might not be allowed to dance as I was not a full-blood and only half-Indian. A friend, Sonny Larive, also a half-breed had danced the year before so I didn't quite believe my mother who would have been relieved had I been rejected as the missionaries were pressuring her to somehow forbid me to dance. They were fearful that we younger ones and me as a combat warrior would set an example for the young to return to the old way. They were right! At my last piercing Sun Dance, the arena was vibrant with many young Sun Dance pledgers. Fools Crow had to have help from other holy men to pierce all of us. The once pitiful crowd almost two decades before had grown to a huge throng that swelled to the periphery of the arena.

Now it is a different world in regard to Sun Dance. No longer is there one Sun Dance on one reservation as in my time. It grew as it would have to. No longer could one Sun Dance manage the thousands of pledgers now coming from many reservations and off-reservation as well. Throughout Sioux country and even out to the Nation it spread.

You can go to some Sioux reservations and see Sun Dances ranging from wide open (meaning non-Indians can participate as pledgers) to closed Sun Dances that require you to show a tribal enrollment card before you are admitted to watch or participate. Some of these Sun Dances are so strict that your non-tribal spouse, if you have one, cannot be admitted with you even if you are an enrolled tribal member. One of the most beautiful and respectful Sun Dances I have seen in years was such a closed Sun Dance conducted by an honorable Oglala holy person, Rick Two Dogs, on the Pine Ridge Reservation. Those of Indian descent, 1/4th, 1/8th and 1/16th and enrolled tribal members are finding themselves most welcome at many of the so-called "closed" Sun Dances. Dr. Charles Ross, an enrolled Mdewakantonwan Sioux, also holds a deeply spiritual sun dance in the Black Hills. My Nephew, (1/4th) and his son (1/8th) just finished their first two Sun Dances on the Pine Ridge Reservation in which there were over 100 participants (dancers/pledgers). They are pledged to dance at least four sun dances at Thunder Valley near Rockyford which takes up a four year span. As this writing is being finished, both are making preparations for their third endurance. My Nephew is in his 50's. The Thunder Valley Sun Dance is one of the most arduous and testing of bravery of all the sun dances. I call it the "Marine Corps" or "Army Airborne" of all the Sun Dances. No drinking of alcohol or consuming of any drugs vows including all forms of hallucinogen rejection such as Peyote are vowed for a four full years and adhered to faithfully by the Thunder Valley pledgers. Often these vows of abstinence last a lifetime. As I said, it is definitely a strict and demanding Sun Dance and yet hundreds participate.

Chief Fools Crow's Sun Dance

My description of the Sun Dance is based on what I viewed under Chief Eagle Feather's and Chief Fools Crow's direction. The Sun Dance is a time when the people thank the Great Spirit, publicly and out in the open as a tribe. It is also a time, that certain men can and will fulfill their Sun Dance vows, usually for a favor or a request that was made in time of need. A desperate hunter might take a vow to be pierced in the forthcoming Sun Dance if he would see a winter deer to bring back to hungry people. I personally took a vow to pierce in the Sun Dance if I would come back from the war in Vietnam. No one forced me to take this vow and the pain that I endured was of my own choosing much like a woman who gives birth to a baby. She chooses her own pain so that the people might live. A Sioux woman can also dance in the sun dance, but she does not pierce because she has given her pain when she bears children. Such is the depth and recognition of woman in Sioux ceremony.

Around the Sun Dance tree, placed earlier in the center of the tribal arena, the sun dancer would dance. Singers are gathered around a large drum to sing old tribal songs. For me, these songs are hauntingly beautiful. Four days the dancers would fast and pray around the tree and sleep in isolated tents away from the on-looking spectators usually in a small tent at night not far from the arena.

On the fourth day, a bed of sage would be placed beneath this "tree of life" and the dancer would be taken to this spot and be pierced in the chest by the Sun Dance Chief, the intercessor for the ceremony. A pair of small slits would be made in the man's skin and a wooden peg would be skewered through; in and under the skin. The end of a rope would be brought down from the tree, and it would be attached to the wooden peg by a buckskin thong. The other end of the long rope would be attached toward the top of the tree. The dancer would rise after he was attached and would slowly dance backward, away from the tree's base to the end of his rope. Other dancers would be pierced and after all were pierced the piercing song would be sung and the dancers would dance inward toward the base of the tree to beseech strongly to the Great Spirit whom we believed to be looking on. After the dancers touched the tree, they would go back, away from the center to the end of their ropes. Four times, this beseechment would take place. The on-looking tribe would be in very serious prayer, with very little distraction. The tribe praying together in a concerted effort was considered to be far more powerful and beneficial than the drama of the Sun Dancers. This was the main focus of the Sun Dance — the tribe praying as a unit, praying together — an annual tribal Thanksgiving to Creator, Wakan Tanka.

The drama of the piercing assures an unbroken, non-distracted spiritual focus. After the fourth beseechment, the dancers would be free to lean back and break themselves free by putting their weight upon their tether to the tree of life placed into Mother Earth. The rope is their spiritual umbilical. When the peg would break through, their sun dance vow would be fulfilled. The tribal Thanksgiving would be over.

Such is a description of the Sun Dance as the way we experienced it and which is a personal and a freely chosen self-sacrifice. No one is required to Sun Dance and the majority of tribal members do not actually become pledgers or Sun Dancers. Some variations of the piercing have now entered the later sun dances in contrast to our time. I still think that those poor Oklahoma 'Indians' who may be driving around in fancy cars and some with swimming pooled patio homes, sure did give up a whole lot of real, Natural based spiritual depth when they rejected the old ways of their ancestors. Their choice, however; our land is a democracy! I abhor proselytizing, but I have to admit that at least an interest on the behalf of those 'of blood and tribal status' would be pleasing if they, at least, would look back in respect at the positive spiritual attributes of their ancestors and not brand them as 'pagan' or 'heathen'; which we are not! For what you are about to read next, bears some powerful indication, that a Benevolent Creator, yet a Mystery, still watches over mere two-legged. My opinion.

The Lone Cloud Sun Dance

At a Sun Dance in the late 1960's, a lone cloud appeared far to the south on the final day when eight dancers waited to be pierced.

Chief Eagle Feather and I were the first to be pierced. The large Sichangu Sioux stood next to me urging me to watch what was happening to the south. A distant growing puff of white cloud seemed to be approaching. It was a vast western sky with no other clouds visible. The hot August Bad Lands air was still, yet it kept moving toward us. I could feel a dull throb in my chest as I held my rope's weight off of the pain. After a few minutes the slight weight of the rope changed to numbness and I eased my grip on it and let it hang freely. We watched each dancer lie on the bed of sage face upward at the base of the sun dance tree and be pierced by the sun dance Intercessor. Chief Fools Crow would push his sharp awl in and through the chest skin and back out again, then insert a smooth wooden peg into the first cut and tunneling under the skin he would push the tip back out. Onto this hardwood skewer he would tie the pledger's rope to the peg with a leather thong. The other end of the rope was attached to the tree implanted at the center of the arena.

"It's coming closer," I remember Eagle Feather's awed tone. The cloud about half the size of a football field approached slowly. I should have been in dead earnest awe but I was so weak and tired from four days fasting. I have to be honest. I simply wanted the ceremony to be over. I was now pierced and all would be over in a matter of minutes.

Fools Crow came toward me after the last dancer was pierced. "Hau, Nephew." Bill Eagle Feather expressed. "That cloud is coming right at us!" The cloud was approaching the edge of the campground full of teepees, tents, and trailers surrounding the circular Sun Dance arena with its lone cottonwood tree decorated with colored cloths at its center. The drums were throbbing seeming to speed their hypnotic crescendo; that pulsating, haunting tone which one hears only at a Sun Dance. As a Sun Dancer you will hear it for an eternity. It is so powerful; the pain in your chest seems to be carried away with its soothing, magical tone. Fools Crow took me by my sage gauntlet tied around my wrist and walked me inward toward the tree. All the dancers came inward, dancing a slow shuffling gait to the heavy rhythm of the drums, blowing their eagle bone whistles. We touched the tree and blew our shrill whistles. The tree shrilled back!

We danced backward to the end of our ropes. The ropes tightened and our thongs held firm. The drums throbbed as if we were standing before a gigantic waterfall. Fools Crow signaled with a nod and we all danced back toward the tree, our eagle bones shrilly singing. Again the tree sang back! Four times in all we would dance inward. After the fourth touching of the tree we would dance slowly outward and then lean backward at the end of our ropes. The silent on-looking crowd would send up their prayers to Wakan Tanka, the Great Spirit whom we assumed was watching from somewhere.

The cloud was directly above as we touched the tree for the final time. It sent down soothing, light rain on the dancers and the praying crowd. We went back to the end of our ropes. Some sun dancers would have visions as they leaned back against their bond. Eventually all would break free and the ceremony would be over.

I have little doubt that similar happenings took place at the Sun Dances that Chief Crazy Horse and Chief Red Cloud observed or took a direct part in. Was Creator watching over their ceremonies? I would think probably more so, given their almost pure form of Natural Living. I do not feel that this is a bit unorthodox manner of teaching, dear reader just because the many books on the two famous chiefs do not follow or allow so to speak such a manner of communicating. Now, dear reader, you know much more of the Sioux culture, much more than other readers. That is all I care for, basically as an author: That my readers understand more fully and it certainly helps to have experienced what one is writing about in many cases. The power of the Lone Cloud certainly could not have been conveyed had I not been directly beneath it. This is why direct observation and/or experience is important.

I look back now at Chief Fools Crow and Eagle Feather. I firmly believe their participation in the Vision Quest, Sweat Lodge, and Sun Dance highly enhanced their spiritual gifts. Both holy men were awesome encouragement that I had found a better path for myself. Ceremony can strongly hone many gifts. A happening like the Lone Cloud will certainly afford one far more confidence in the Spiritual. Bear in mind that we are dealing with Mystery. Some may not arrive at what I would like to explain. I realize I have limitations but hope by presenting what I have observed; many will understand another culture more fully. By all means keep your own religion and now go on. As I have often said, 'Like the Jewish people, we do not proselytize!'

Thunder Valley Sun Dance

Participation in Vision Quest, Sweat Lodge and Sun Dance recently affected my nephew. He was always a respected person from my point of view but I saw a profound integration of newfound confidence and pride when I conversed with him after he finished his Vision Quest and Sun Dance under the tutelage of a Sioux medicine man. I also have another nephew who hasn't touched alcohol for years because of his many Sun Dances and related ceremonies. A grandnephew who had once used drugs had the same blessed reaction. All have highly honed their intuition and are much better prepared for life. The ordinary quarrels and pettiness of life have no meaning to them. They have higher goals. They walk with an exhibited pride! This transformation has definitely honed their intuitive abilities. They were not sitting and listening in some workshop or prayer gathering. They were out upon Mother Earth in all three ceremonies, Sweat Lodge, Vision Quest, and Sun Dance. Physically they were immersed in a totally different medium than what Dominant Society experiences. I stood in the arena during the breaking time, holding my nephew's pipe. The drumbeat was mesmerizing, powerful, haunting. The dancers, mostly young men, went in to touch the tree four times, as I had done decades before. Under that vast western sky, many memories returned, of the old sun dances past. Young men of generations ago also had participated in the same ceremonials, four long arduous days of prayer and beseechment; honing their minds for life's challenges and trials. In those days the Sun Dancer would go from the ceremony out onto the Great Plains into the teeth of battle. Mine was the reverse. I returned from the teeth of combat and then on into the powerful ceremony.

Sacred Places

Many non-Indians are now vision questing out in isolated places of Mother Earth. Many ancients did so who walked the earth. I understand that Christ did go out into isolation and 'vision quest' to his Higher Power. Did not Moses seek isolation up on the mountain to commune spiritually? No one owns vision quest obviously. At this point, if you are not tribally enrolled, I reiterate that you do not vision quest at Bear Butte Mountain in the Black Hills. Be polite. Stay away from places the Indian people deem sacred. They are going back to their once-banned religion now and Bear Butte gets very crowded in the spring and summer. I used to Vision Quest on Bear Butte and was the only person up there at night but now there is a tremendous upsurge in Native people returning to the old ways. There are plenty of other distant peaks and mountains and Badlands buttes, and all very isolated too. All over America, even in the east, mountain and hill tops remain vacant — go there. Remember, this is a ceremony just between you and your concept of God (Creator). It is owned by no one or any tribe. It is a universal ceremony but I believe the native people should be given some allowance since the Christian dominated government wrongfully banned us from ceremonial participation up until 1978 when the Freedom of Religion Bill was created by Act of Congress.

1874

It was during this time that most believe Black Elk had his vision. It was the time of Crazy Horse and Sitting Bull. Many believe Black Elk's parents were camped among Chief Crazy Horse's followers for they were far to the west in what was Montana territory. Chief Crazy Horse was not one to get close to the wahshichus. Chief Red Cloud had pledged to keep his word not to 'take up the sword' in order that the Treaty he had won would remain honored. The whites would have surely broken the treaty had he fought anymore, was what he believed. He remained close to the reservation with occasional hunts off and away from the agency which bore his name to supplement his food with wild meat mostly.

Larry McMurtry states in his book, *Crazy Horse*, that "historians often chide the writers — Mari Sandoz, Evan S. Connell Jr., and John G. Neihardt — for producing good writing but bad history."[9] I may agree on his first two examples, especially Sandoz but to include Neihardt with her is a bit in error, my opinion. John Neihardt spent days on end with his source, face to face, with the old man's son as interpreter and the confirming presence of Black Elk's life long friend, Standing Bear, verifying every word. There exists too much exculpating proof on the contrary. Neihardt repeatedly returned, as well, to visit his source as did the interpreter, Ben, visit him occasionally. Sandoz, however never had a minute with her source and greatly expanded upon what little information she did arrive at from those who knew Crazy Horse and of course, did not speak her language. Neihardt's 'problem' was that he put down too clearly, the Indian's version, loyally projected by Ben the son. The Lakota language, especially when shifted to serious revelation in ultra serious discourse, becomes spiritually poetic, an ingredient lacking in the white man's vernacular and therefore foreign and hence Euro-centrically branded as suspect.

Now before we proceed onward from our side step into what I would consider a very important view of these two men's Spiritual prospectus, I wish to make one brief projection into the study, primarily of Chief Crazy Horse, as expressed from the author of *Lonesome Dove*: Mr. Larry McMurtry.

"It is as well as to say firmly at the outset that any study of Crazy Horse will be, of necessity, an exercise in assumption, conjecture, and surmise. We have more verifiable facts about another young warrior, Alexander, called the Great, who lived more than two thousand years earlier than Crazy Horse and whose career is also richly encrusted with legend, than we do about the strange man of the Oglalas (to adopt Mari Sandoz's phrase)…For most of his life he [Crazy Horse] not only avoided white people, he avoided people, spending many days alone on the prairies, dreaming, drifting, hunting. According to Short Buffalo, a fellow Sioux who knew him well, he was "not very tall and not very short, neither broad nor thin. His hair was very light…Crazy Horse had a very light complexion, much lighter than other Indians. His face was not broad, and he had a high, sharp nose. He had black eyes that hardly ever looked straight at a man, but they didn't miss much that was going on, all the same…"[10]

"He came into Fort Robinson, in northwestern Nebraska, with the nine hundred people who, in desperation, had chosen to follow him, only four months before he was killed, and those four months were the only period in his life when he was in contact with the record keeping, letter writing whites; and even then, he camped six miles from the fort, rather than the prescribed three, and saw whites only when he could not avoid them. For almost the whole of his life he did avoid all parleys, councils, treaty sessions, and any meeting of an administrative or political nature, not merely with whites but with his own people as well."[11]

"He was a loner — now, in many respects, he is a blank. Professional writers and amateur historians, professional historians and amateur writers, have all written about him extensively and have not scrupled to put words in his mouth and even to report his dreams — or, at least, one dream that was of great significance in shaping the way he lived his life."[12]

"If the word "record" is to mean anything, one would have to say that for much of Crazy Horse's life- there is no record."[13]

In my time, the best way to convince wahshichus, was to rely on another white man if you could find one who agreed with you. That is just the way it was after Dominant Society set our Indian world in motion once my tribe 'came in.' I did not make the rules. It appears that a pre-set Academia has masked much truth in regards to Native peoples, their leaders and their culture. Too many, purposely avoided a vastly different Spiritual far more connected to Creator's Nature or made sugar coating attempts to mollify as did some of the writers mentioned. Thankfully, there are the Neihardts, Brydes, McMurtrys, Weatherfords, Browns, and uncompromising others who did not bend their findings. I guess I could sum it all up by: 'If you do not know how a people believe, how do you know the people?'

* * * *

Crazy Horse

A story of Crazy Horse – Mystic Warrior of the Tetons – John Owl, Oglala – 1920's

In the heart of America there lived a Mystic Warrior. Ohuzhea Wichastah. (Oh hoo zheay wee chah stah) (Mystic Warrior). I remember him and other great warriors but my memories, and like life itself, are beginning to fade like the sunset that I see beyond this mission window. Westward are the beautiful mountains that I still call home. These mountains remain sacred to my tribe and I suspect to quite a few white men as well.

Several generations have passed since these belonged to us and we fought for them with the passion that men have when fighting for the women of their desires. It is said that from these mountains came the first pair of buffalo, elk, deer, and possibly man himself.

Before the Downfall, our world was an endless cycle of life, of four seasons, four directions, Mother Earth and Father Sky. We forever lived on faith, moving with the seasons, moving with the game that we hunted; the game that sustained us. Our people were forever moving into the unknown. Some say we have always moved and that once, before anyone can remember, we lived in the lands far to the southeast near the great salt water that is called the Atlantic. God told us through the Spirits that God controls or allows to watch over us that danger was coming. These Spirits come into our ceremonies and warned us to move west, always towards the sunset. The ancients were forewarned by God that our survival depended on it; this much we are certain of and so we moved and our lives became of constant change, each man, each family adapting to ever changing surroundings, tools and neighbors. Our focus was survival. Those that survived quickly became the new leaders whom replaced the fallen. Those whom were unfit did not survive. All were free men and together we fought for our nation, for honor, dominance, and for the right to hunt, to live on and to die on the land of our choice. We adapted to the ways of the horse and our lands became the Plains, the center of which is the special place that we call Paha Sapa. Here in this land we encountered the White man and here we made a stand; some say our 'final stand' but this is not true for many young warriors in our tribe continued to fight in the Great War in the lands called Europe.

I was once a warrior too and am proud to have served Crazy Horse as a soldier. I fought on horse back with a stone club, was a skilled archer, and became an expert marksman with the white man's gun. But that was a very long time ago.

Today I am a humble, slow-moving handy man employed at the Holy Rosary Mission. I serve Father Patrick Costigan who keeps me on primarily because of my abilities to make and repair things — skills that served me well during the fighting years; and again later as an actor in Buffalo Bill's Show. I worked beside the famous chief, Sitting Bull in that show. Yes I even went to England and Germany. We did a show for a little fat lady called Queen Elizabeth; she had a Grandson who came on his own in a fancy coach. Englishmen swooned and some even fainted when she spoke to them. We had a hard time from giggling and laughing at that but she was good to us and said kind things about us.

I am happy, at times, to be honest, here at the mission and enjoy my position. There is food and a roof over my head. I have what many consider a paid job; most of my race are not so lucky and many have died over years through disease, exposure, poor nutrition, or perhaps from simply losing the will to live. I work on my English and this also makes the priests happy. I like new words but always find some that are hard for me to remember. I survived for unknown reasons and give thanks to the Great Spirit for my employment at this remote mission which gives me purpose in life during my twilight years.

Father Patrick recently sent one of my braided buckskin saddles for display at the great Vatican Council in Rome as proof of the industry and good deeds done by this Jesuit brotherhood. I was not able to sign my work as the saddle was a gift from the entire boarding school to the Holy Mother Church but I am happy to have my work honored in this way.

Father Patrick relies on me to also heal the broken, homesick students at our boarding school. Not because he feels any of their pain and anguish nor respects my methods but because the pitiful children are less likely to run away after I have befriended them.

Runaway's sometimes cause problems and Father Patrick has little patience for those whom do not readily accept the teachings of the Church. The Church is their legal guardian and is therefore responsible for their proper religious and academic education. The mission educates in English and teaches about the greater things: the ways of civilized life, industry, Jesus, the Great Holy man 'Pope Benedict,' and his one True, Apostolic Church. I have tried hard to master this English. Father William says I am doing very well with my words but many of the hard ones I forget.

Many at the mission believe that the Old Ways were barbaric and that these memories are best forgotten. Soon they shall get their wish; the great warriors are gone now as are most of those who are old enough to remember. The great Red Cloud died a while back, and he is the last of the 'old ones,' 'those chiefs,' as they say. And so it is…the memories of the Old Ways, of the Resistance, and the years of warfare, grow weak like the grey coals of yesterday's fire. Red Cloud lies resting but a few arrow shots from the tiny room I am allowed, not far from the graveyard and equidistant from the cattle sheds farther back from the main road that passes by the cemetery. I spend much good time with the cattle and horses besides this foolish sweeping I have to constantly do.

I am old now and am preoccupied with making peace with myself and attempting, through prayer and fasting, to make peace with those that I killed, yes…in combat…during the fighting years. I was never a great warrior like Charging Shield, Eagle Horse, Gall, Spotted Tail, Sitting Bull, Crazy Horse, and Chief Red Cloud. They were immortal in battle, never flinching, never losing their resolve, showing no fear; I saw my share but I was truly afraid so many times and I often showed it. Like I say, they were immortal; I was human. In the utter heat of battle, their conduct was infectious, their manner, composure; everything. I saw all of this often from you to me, it is strange to say but they were more beautiful than the most fair of all at those moments, than any beautiful woman I have seen and a man that lives among our people sees many. I am no winkteay (different one) mind you; I saw every one I speak of in that manner, even Red Cloud who had as many scalps as Crazy Horse. The older warriors often told how fierce he could fight. Both Red Cloud and Spotted Tail had each killed another chief in earlier times. Red Cloud had little choice but to avenge against Bull Bear who would have done in Red Cloud's chief, Old Smoke. This caused quite a rift between the Bull Bear people and the Bad Faces of the Smoke people and it was Chief Red Cloud who finally united the two factions back together when he took on the U.S. Army. Spotted Tail killed Big Mouth in a duel, they say. Later Spotted Tail was killed by Crow Dog.

At the end of our fighting, after the Army was beaten and had to burn their forts down, Chief Red Cloud and Chief Spotted Tail quit fighting, once the treaty which the Brules and the Oglalas won under Red Cloud was signed. They fought hard and often to win that treaty.

We were younger and eight years after the treaty I was under Crazy Horse at what the whites call the Little Big Horn. Combat is such a strange world, like the sun dance not every man experiences it. It is maybe foolish to talk about it in a keyed up manner for so few have been such privileged to understand it, let alone believe your feelings about it.

But death…I am now told I must now have a conscience if I am to be civilized and of course to receive our Lord's reward in heaven. I am not supposed to think that there is any honor in bringing death to another. I am constantly told that even the counting of coup…must be…had to be wrong. It seems among these priest men, brothers too, a tiny tribe in a way; among themselves; everything must be weighed against their Jesus God. If it is not of him, then according to them, it has to be wrong. My primary desire is to move on to Nagi Makah, the Spirit World; a place which some say is Heaven. I have to forget that past especially we old ones like to think…that glory…it is over.

I would like to believe that Nagi Makah and Heaven both refer to the same place. Father Patrick says 'No, Nagi Makah is a place of evil. There is only one true God who lives in Heaven,' but another priest, Father William says that Nagi Makah and Heaven are the same place. I believe Father William, not only is he very good to me but we have become close like brothers despite the fact that he is young enough to be my grandson. It just feels better, how he says things, like when you mount a certain horse and the way it feels beneath you, the horses gait as you gain full speed, some do feel better than other horses.

After the Downfall I choose to adopt the white man's ways as did most of the tribe. Too many soldiers gave us little choice. Father William however appears to be going an opposite direction; adapting the ways of the Indian. He has been at the mission for less than three years. During this time he has learned to speak Lakota, hunt deer, antelope, and prairie chicken. He's become knowledgeable in buckskin tanning and leatherwork; and has even broken horses in our corral. Father's latest endeavor is to record our language in a book that he calls a 'Dictionary' and says that this is very important but no one, not even Father Patrick can understand why an Indian Dictionary is important. Those of us who work here tease Father William, saying that we will soon need to give him an Indian name; this is something he is likely expecting from us.

After mass this morning, Father William joined the students and me in the stables, lending a hand to help repair several worn leather halters that I had braided years ago. He sat working intently for a fashion and then, quietly putting down his leather awl, he sat and observed us in our work.

"The world has much to learn from the Indian way of life. Your Teton culture is as rich as any known in the world and yours remains a noble race," he said reflectively.

"We remain proud Father," I grunted while pulling wet leather fast against the iron halter ring, even though our halters break allowing our horses to run wild. And run wild they do for it seems that the mission horses are forever running away also. When the horses run, Brother Schilling tracks them down often as far as the remote buttes north of the mission in an area known as 'Makah Sheecha' or Bad Lands. Brother Schilling seems to enjoy this work so much that we tease him also; we say he secretly lets the horses out so he can later track them down.

"John, do you remember the days when the horses ran free?" Father William asked in Lakota, as he inspected my tightly braided leatherwork. "It is said that you were quite a horseman when you were my age," he added.

"I remember pain and suffering Father," I replied, uneasy and back in covering English with the presence of several young impressionable students. "I remember the constant struggle for survival."

He watched me struggle to tie a knot in the thick leather with my weathered hands and took over the task after offering to do so. I am eager so see him master these skills as he may very well pass these on to the new generation of children that will surely come here. As he bit the leather halter ends to further soften prior to setting one final knot I confided to the Father, "I remember those days...long ago and far away. Yes, I can remember when the horses ran free," being careful to not say more.

After the students had left Father William was more direct. "It is said you rode with Crazy Horse and even carried his battle standard," he said handing me the completed halter for approval.

"Father, people say all kinds of things," I answered flatly as he inspected my face while I in turn inspected his leatherwork. I was unable to find an imperfection and therefore a polite means to close the conversation so I left the question hang.

Father William's fondness for the Indian does not sit well with Father Patrick the Senior Jesuit. Talk of the old days is not tolerated nor is the Lakota language except in mass given to the elders whom speak no other language. The worst offense of all are the sacred pipes, medicine bundles, and eagle feathers which Father Patrick has decreed are from Satan and therefore must be burned.

The younger priest is tolerated only because of his wealthy family and other connections that help sustain him and therefore this mission. Last year he was able to raise funds for a large gymnasium that is being planned. "God willing we will begin the gymnasium this spring and learn to play a new game from the east called Basket Ball," he said, 'Basket Ball is more fun than almost any game known except for maybe Inktomi,' which when properly played, is played on horseback. Father William is smart and sees the future. He says some day when we receive better mail service he has a plan to use the children to write 'Solis ahtun'(solicitation) letters back east. These kind of letters he explained will bring us much money from people, mostly in the east who like Indians.

I agree with Father William when he boldly said that the Indian race has wisdom and therefore is of benefit to mankind, however, if the world is to learn from us then it must learn quickly for our race is caught up in a relentless push to be re-educated in the white man's ways. Relentless in no small part due to men such as Father Patrick who says the Indian is much too slow to let go of his history, culture, and religion and is therefore destined to suffer God's wrath. He is the head and like the white man's sheep, we have to follow obediently. We are constantly told we have to be obedient. We have to follow, they say. When things do not go as they want with us they always warn that we will suffer God's wrath. Obedience, sin, hellfire, damnation are words that echo around here. God must come out at night and tell them this.

The Jesuits have toiled at the mission for almost a half century since the Battle of Greasy Grass and yet, sadly, the Jesuits have little to show for their efforts to change the stubborn resistance of the Lakota. The buildings and even the land holdings grow year by year and we now even have a graveled road all the way into the town not far away but this is not the lack of progress the Jesuits grumble over in their private conversations which sooner or later I come to hear. Father Patrick says it is our fault and even many Lakota are beginning to share the view that the world is best served through the discipline and education that the Church provides. Indeed this is our focus at Holy Rosary for here, the Church surrounds us. All of these men are so dedicated that they even deny themselves a woman. Some Sisters of Mercy do come here in the summer. They have so many shrouds and long skirts on you can hardly see them. The young nuns like to talk to the brothers but the old sisters are like watch dogs, there is no chance that any priest or a brother will ever break their vows over the friendly, younger ones. Even so, the priests and brothers look forward to the summer visits and the better food they prepare even though no one touches each other. They are very dedicated and religious.

I was brought up a military man. I am no stranger to discipline. I acknowledge the need to educate, to adapt...yet...I have quietly held on, for decades now, to all I can remember of the old way of life. I hold on as if this is sacred but do not know why, now that I come to be here in this new place. At first I was mainly curious but now I have all kinds of quarreling thoughts in my head. 'Perhaps a warrior's battles shape him in ways that only the Great Spirit understands,' is becoming my major solace.

In my youth I had the honor of fighting for the Lakota cause and fought along side many of the great warriors. These were the best days of my life if I can but shed this haunting so-called 'conscience' as my confessor calls it. 'Those were bad days' his words echo as I stumble guiltily out of the confessional. It is only the following morning after I pay my penance through the night looking back and desperately trying to erase the past that I seem to get some comfort. My agony seems to last until I receive my communion with their God, but then through the following days I regress back into my past and happier thoughts just seem to come. I guess I am supposed to fight those 'happier' thoughts but now with the friendship of this new priest I guess I am in sort of a quandary. I shrug now and simply wait. We Sioux always could adapt. It was our trademark. We could even re-adapt. A larger tribe could stop us or we would have to wait before heading on westward and then we would adapt. But then the Sichangus (Brules) would come along and support us as they always did and maybe some Yanktons or Yanktonais who were always squabbling with their leaders and would come over and fill our ranks more and bringing some horses and the guns- yes the guns, and then on we would go and chase out those who had earlier chased us out. I guess that is re-adapting. Anyway, that is where I am at. I am starting to like that old past again but I must be careful. Father 'Bill' as I now privately call him, he must be careful also.

Yes, Crazy Horse was from my tribe. I was younger than Crazy Horse, a few years but we were of the same blood; I looked up to him all my life. We are both Oglala and he is part Sichangu from his mother. I am Wayzhazha Oglala. He and Red Cloud were perhaps the saviors of the Teton Nation. Yes, and Sitting Bull as well. I knew Crazy Horse as a tribal brother, horseman, warlord…as a Lakota. A combatant in the field is a much different way of knowing, you shall see.

He lived a short life and yet much has been written about him, I have come to discover now as I grow older and hear these writers talk about our history. Some say he was born on the banks of Rapid Creek, the heaviest flowing creek out of the Black Hills which empties on into the Cheyenne. Others claim he was born by the Republican River in 1844. Even his age raises a few arguments so all I will say is that he was close to his mid thirties when he was stabbed by a soldier in September of the year following the rubbing out of Yellow Hair.

Crazy Horse led us to believe that we fought for freedom, honor, traditional values and for a superior way of life. We believed that these were the highest values and were worth dying for. Sharing, Generosity, Giving Away, ahh this was Crazy Horse, Tahshuunka Witko: Bravery and Courage too: Courage enough to face what confronts you and bravery to make the charge and go through with it. The highest mettle of a man is what he does in the face of real combat. I knew Chief Red Cloud too. Ahhh the stories of him when he was a dangerous, fearless warrior! He lived a long time, right here on our reservation. The other chiefs died early; too early for them. Poor Red Cloud, he had to live on into a life completely different from back when he was free and was a fighting war chief. I know much of what he must have felt. He could no longer make many decisions. My life is the same, still, one gets to make a few. He could stand up and explain things his way, especially when he would go back to the nation's capitol and he did go quite a few times. Once he went there before we fought the Battle of the Greasy Grass; Spotted Tail too. The agent hated that, especially Agent McGillycuddy who finally lost out after ridiculing our once great chief. I would dare not complain about Father Patrick, yet I still make my own decision whether I will tell Father William of the past. Chief Red Cloud was, as I heard a white man say it, and it seems to fit, 'One hell of a warrior, in his day.' I heard that right here at the mission by some fancy historians who stayed here for a while and wrote books. Some others disagreed and they almost had a fight over the past they never saw. The old chief used to go to church here, but like me, I think he was laying low no different than I must do. It is not a good thing to say certain things, now that I have to become like the white man. It would be wrong for me to give into what seems to whisper now and then in my head. The dead ones had the better life because they got to leave early and keep all their thoughts. I dare not mention that reasoning to the priests, except, possibly, Father William.

I have to be honest for my memories will all be judged by my peers in that Spirit World beyond in case the white man is not exactly right with the way he says it. Anyway, among us Indians we think differently even when it comes to the Spirit World. This 'conscience' I am supposed to have keeps telling me that it makes more sense the way we see it. I think I am almost living in two worlds but let me get on with my admiration of my great Chief Crazy Horse. I mentioned Chief Red Cloud too, but again I have to be honest, I did not fight for him directly because of my close connection to Chief Crazy Horse, but he was no less a warrior in my eyes. Red Cloud stopped fighting because of the great treaty, otherwise I could have been in his ranks as a more experienced warrior had he taken the field again. Curly as some say, fought for him and that was where he got his start. It was said the older chief saw much into Crazy Horse or Light Hair as we called him. Red Cloud depended on Crazy Horse for the more important decoy missions which were dangerous and Curly or Light Hair always did them well. With the Army it mostly started with that brash Lieutenant and his soldiers who killed Conquering Bear and in turn got the wiping out they deserved.

Red Cloud was the first to win against the wahshichus and their Asaka-toe akicita (blue coated soldiers) along with their mounted ones. Paksah hanska is what we called the cavalry, the long knives. He had to be a fighting chief to win the famous Treaty of 1868. Sitting Bull didn't win it and stayed up north. Crazy Horse was too young then. It was all Chief Red Cloud and his warriors which Crazy Horse was one of them. Who else was there to win it? Spotted Tail did his part. He was a fighter in his day and got wounded several times, ugly wounds. Crazy Horse too but his wounds were mostly from Indians earlier. Crazy Horse was close to the Brules as Spotted Tail was his uncle, they say, on his Mother's side.

When I came of age to become a full-fledged warrior, my people were beginning to follow Crazy Horse even though he was yet young. His exploits were such that warriors wanted to be with him. Reputation in the field reaped followers. A rapidly growing reputation like Crazy Horse displayed ignored the regular custom that a leader had to be older. In those times, many an older leader's term was suddenly cut short by a rifle ball or those later 'catter-geses' (cartridges). Heavy combat saw many casualties and rank rose swiftly for some. There was a time when all we heard was of Red Cloud and his successful exploits and challenges but I was never selected for his war parties not through avoidance of my services but I remained continually at the services of Crazy Horse and I am sure the older chief appreciated my few talents back in those days. In 1868, the chief of the Oglalas had signed the treaty and would not fight no more. Chief Spotted Tail by then also gave up the path of war. They said that both men became quite convinced that there were just too many people back east to fight them all. And there were people back there, they said, that liked Indians and those were the ones who kept the white man from coming out and killing us all with his entire army after they had quit fighting each other. That war gave them a conscience, it was said. The Hahsahpas (Negroes) were free, so; many wahshichus started to think about us in better ways. The Army did not always get its way any more and we started to get the 'peace commissions' even before that big wahshichu war with each other was over with. Of course, we had our share of hot heads that wanted the entire Army to come out and fight us. 'We would show them a thing or two about combat,' they crowed, but it was Red Cloud who had the most sense in the end unless you want to think it is better off for all of us to be dead. The Ghost Dance proved that Wakan Tanka did not have any miracles waiting for us!

After a while, both chiefs fell out with each other. General Crook named Spotted Tail head chief of the Sioux, thus humiliating Red Cloud. Spotted Tail moved to a new agency which was named after him. When our war leader, Crazy Horse, surrendered to the military, about a year after the Big Fight, he went down to that new agency to take his sick wife and had words with Spotted Tail for signing away the freedom of his people. I was with him. Spotted Tail sent him back and that was when he was killed by the soldier and he had his arms pinned by an Indian when it was done. From the point of view of the Custer fighters, the diplomatic chief was a traitor; and many of the Sioux have since tried to implicate him in the conspiracy against Crazy Horse which led to his assassination, but many do not hold up this charge. What did Spotted Tail sign away? The whites had already made up their minds to break the treaty for the Black Hills, one way or another when Custer wrongfully went in there and found gold. "Zizi maza, lelah witko-ko lah!" (The yellow iron, it made them crazy!) It was foolish for Indians to blame Indians, were my thoughts but I was not a great warrior and it is our custom, that only an equally experienced warrior can criticize one who has been brave in many battles.

Speaking out about my past and about what I believe in is strictly forbidden. I have learned that telling my stories often brings hardship…to myself and to those who listen, but I am considering telling Father William these stories because he is a good strong man. Father William would make a fine warrior.

It was old Eagle Feather who taught me to braid and then some. The priests will never know what other things of the Spirit he passed on to me for it was I who would haul his water up from the creek in a stiffened buffalo paunch turned to raw hide until I traded for a big pot with an iron handle from my furs. It was a prize for the wise medicine man. He was Hunkpapa/Mandan sized, larger and heavier boned with a bulbous nose to match his body and like the Mandans, light complexioned. He leaned forward with an elephant's shuffling gait, such an animal I saw in an English circus. No Flay took that chore away from me for he wanted to become a medicine man, someday. Together we were privileged to listen to the medicine man between doing other tasks to fulfill his needs. No Flay's name was from a trader but like a night guard dog 'Puppy,' we once had that kept his name on through the years, it simply stuck to the part Arikara. One Bull, the band's main horse trainer, said it meant, 'No Flesh' in some trader language not English or maybe just made up, no one knows. No Flay was gaunt and skinny, an orphan who was taken in, now he lives on his own, so he filled his name and never seemed to mind. No one taunted him because he would just ignore you anyway. He was always focused upon the medicine man, where he would take his meals and could care less about bows, guns and horses. The Sioux way was that you did what you wanted to do as long as you were of some benefit in some way and of course did not endanger or harm anyone.

I carried Eagle Feather's water long past the age when boys who have served on the warpath do this duty along with gathering firewood but No Flay took over that chore as well. I had even counted my first coup when I still made sure of the aging man's water. I think I was chopping a hole through the ice when he came up to me with No Flay, "Nephew, you cannot be carrying my water anymore," he spoke sternly. It is unthinkable to argue with a holy man, especially a powerful one like Eagle Feather was. I just backed away and handed the axe, the one which I took from a group of gold miners we had tracked for days. As I was handing the axe to No Flay, Eagle Feather gripped my wrist firmly, we stood there in a long silence. "You can't be doing these things for me anymore." He repeated different words but they held the same meaning. It was like a harsh command and it startled me. He seemed angry because it was change, an orthodoxy of code, which he usually distained, but had to respect, regardless. Tribal code is always the most binding over any individual, even over a very powerful, proven medicine man. No one told him so but it was like the stories I have heard from Father Bill about faraway England where I had been with the Buffalo Bill show. They too had codes, knight's codes and their Kings had to have these codes respected. Like a good dog who has never, never needed to be hit or kicked, it was a startling blow to me. "You are a wichastah, (warrior). Wee chah –stahhh he pronounced deeply." He paused and the words sunk in. "My ways and your ways are two different roads now." His eyes meant I could no longer sit or socially come to his lodge: Only if I was wounded or in ceremony. Maybe in later days but he would be gone by then. I was the eaglet, grown now and nudged harshly to fly out of the nest. It took a long time for me but one night I just woke up and understood it. The young warriors could never become distracted once they started on the war parties. Distraction killed many a would-be warrior. Apparently Eagle Feather well knew what he was doing for I knew he cared deeply for me and for a while I was even thinking of becoming a medicine man.

I looked down at the axe and handing it on, I remembered killing two more miners with that axe. I had liked killing them. One thing with the white man, you never tried doing coup while they were alive as you would do a Pawnee in my father's day or a Cree back in grandfather's time…You killed them quickly and absolutely gave them no quarter for they were deadly as rattlesnakes. Light Hair led that raid. We waited for them to start their drinking. They built a fire and fixed us a real good meal. A couple more miners showed up with several jugs of whiskey…More whiskey and the bigger and brighter and foolish their fire. He gave the signal to attack by touching that Wotai stone, flickering behind his ear. It was easy. Our leader poured the whiskey over the gold diggers. He hated it for what it had done to the hang around the forts and he hated the gold seekers wrongfully coming into our land. This was a time after Red Cloud and Spotted Tail had quit fighting but there were many bands who refused to come in and we were at war with anyone who dared come into our territory which the treaty had specified. I remember crossing the pond away from the camp. No one would see the tears in my eyes as the holy man's words echoed.

> *Sound asleep under a soft and warm pile of buffalo robes*
> *I awoke to a noontime nudge from Kayesha, my Cheyenne mother.*
> *"Wake up my little black-face Charging Owl,*
> *the little one who fancies himself a warrior."*
> *Siouxs do not kiss, like the white man does.*
> *They do a sort of nudge with their cheek or lips.*

'Let me sleep Ina,' I said wiping my face. As a night watchman, I had earned the right to sleep till noon. I had been so proud when the chief announced at council, it was time for me to be sort of like an assistant guard to watch the camp at night. It was not that I had suddenly in my mid-teens been elevated to the status of a full-fledged battle warrior. Furthermore, since I had my first real duty, I had also earned the right no longer to be so-called kissed by my mother.

'Little Maaannnn…we have visitors in our lodge, aren't you going to say hello." I gradually pushed out of the buffalo robes and rubbed the sleep out of my eyes. Coming into focus, I saw, Light Hair, my new

Sundance friend smiling at me. At first I was unable to speak in part due to being overly conscience of the gentle nudge from Ina.

I stared at the Lakota with still blurry eyes. He seemed suddenly much bigger and stronger than before. I could not help but think 'wasn't it just last year that we had been playing Inktomi, the game that all the Wayzhazha kids and I made up and played so hard?' Light Hair was clearly one of the best players as it involved a lot of speed and fearlessness; skill that the older boys seemed to excel at. The young warrior in front of me was more like a man this spring. He was only a little older than me yet he was no boy for Light Hair wore the colors that no boy could wear. Like my father, he was Oglala, yet his white buckskin war shirt indicated he was a warrior with this Brule band who, like ours, was part of the Teton alliance. In the Lakota tradition we were loosely related in that Light Hair's father and my father grew up together and had been close friends. This was sufficient for one to be considered traditional "family" and therefore anyone in this family was considered a welcome guest.

For the first time in many, many months, a heavy warrior's shield had been reverently hung outside our lodge. And out of respect someone had placed a tripod taller than a tall man opposite the tipi door for the sole purpose of honorably displaying this symbol of strength. The shield and accompanying battle lance indicated to all in the camp that a warrior was now present.

The shield was obviously new. It had never been seen by anyone in the tribe nor, as many curious onlookers noted, had this elegantly painted shield been scarred in battle. A lighting bolt was displayed down its middle.

"Powerful," Eagle Feather said approvingly upon his inspection. The rest of the tribe had concluded as much. For now there would be no talking to its young owner for he was resting as were most of the accompanying war party. They had traveled throughout the night to avoid detection by other war parties and by enemy scouts. "Later," Eagle Feather said to the onlookers, "we will have plenty of opportunity to talk to this young warrior."

Throughout the camp a dozen other additional shields were hung in the sunshine and were similarly inspected by the curious. Most were quite familiar, each shield was highly intricate, unique to its owner, and each was Lakota in design and spirit. By midmorning all of the shields were hung and nearby the visiting warriors ate, rested and napped.

Some of the younger warriors were understandably too wound up to nap and instead spent the morning visiting with relatives and laughing at the antics of the excited little children who made up a share of the warm hospitality of the Lakota camp.

I had slept thru their arrival but was wide-awake upon Light Hair's noontime greeting. As I grabbed my moccasins my mom teased, "Charging Owl, Light Hair snuck in last night…right past you."

"That better not be true," I said hoping that this was indeed was not the case.

"No," Light Hair reassured, adding, "but I would have if I had known you were on watch." The three of us made small talk while Light Hair ate the lunch that Ina had prepared. Afterwards I politely stepped out and let the important visitor sleep in the peaceful calm inside our tipi.

Outside in the bright sunshine I noticed Light Hair's lighting bolt symbol on his shield and learned several facts about the war party from my friend Two Wolfs. This was a small war party; about fifteen warriors; there had been several border fights and the men were being called in to engage the enemy; they had traveled horse back all night pushing nearly fifty miles from sundown to sunrise; all had traveled continuously over a five day period; one of the warriors was a powerful woman named 'Kills-the-Bull' who had lost her husband and therefore chose to fight; everyone thought this was honorable.

The Brule war party originated from the Black Hills, and was being led by a powerful warrior named Spotted Tail, Light Hair's Uncle from his Mother's side. He was well liked, well built, his broad face and wide mouth made him fierce looking. He was widely known even then. Our band was not asked to nor would it be contributing warriors as was customary; the issue had been discussed upon their arrival and was politely concluded in short order.

The rest was unknown to Two Wolfs and I so we made ourselves content to wait until the council met later in the evening. Our band had a tradition of producing fine warriors and that we had customarily offered warriors to accompany any war party within the alliance. This not only served the individual warrior whom was eager to join but also served to strengthen the alliance by forming bonds between influential men. This day however there were none to offer; many of our warriors were moving in the southern plains, hunting as well and none that remained could be safely spared to join this party.

"Spotted Tail, in this area we need to have a minimum of a dozen good fighting men in camp at all times," Our chief politely reminded yet he kept the subject open if there was a strong need. 'Thank you but we have all the men we need and this time would like to remain a light and fast fighting force.' With a mutual nod the subject was closed. Except not closed for the older boys who did not want to hear that they were not ready to join a war party. Amongst the younger ones a false rumor was quickly passed around that the war party may need extra warriors to help scout, this was followed by word that all the young boys in our band were strictly forbidden to join up with this war party. Word then circulated that some of the older boys were going to sneak out and join anyway. By late afternoon strict orders were given that all boys, young and old, were to be locked up, in the council lodge if necessary, as none were ready for combat despite the fact that many were foolish enough to try to prove the council wrong.

In truth this war party did not come for additional warriors but for a short rest en route and more importantly for the cleansing, purification, and spiritual guidance that one of our elders could offer.

Eagle Feather was one of the most powerful senior holy men in the Lakota territory and loved the never-ending job of healing, mending, fixing broken hearts, purifying, presiding over weddings and funerals. Helping young people, parents, and grandparents transition as must be done. In his old age he realized this work was his passion. Not that he had been a pacifist, in his youth he had been repeatedly proven in battle. He acknowledged the need that all warriors had for combat but yet gave beautiful sermons on the need for harmony and balance. He taught that individual combat was necessary, intertribal warfare was almost always unnecessary. Mostly he taught the need for love and respect.

Those within the Lakota alliance who sought him out respected him greatly. As a former warrior he felt the same power and mystery shared by those that were called to become warriors, the elite class of man, and sometimes, as was evident today, with so many deaths of their men and the ease one could shoot a rifle, the elite class of woman. It was for the warriors that he reserved his finest oratory and ceremonial energies. In his career he came to realize that the warrior needed divine reassurance, blessings, and ceremony in order to confidently go off into battle. Equally important was the same treatment on his return, for the tribe needed a warrior to return as a complete man.

This small Brule band had come to our camp for but one day's worth of rest. They were undoubtedly well prepared for battle in the physical sense and Eagle Feather would ensure that they were equally prepared in the emotional and spiritual.

Eagle Feather was a true believer, sanctified by Creator, humble, faithful, driven to cleanse all of the evil from the Lakota lands and any unclean thoughts from his followers. He knew the history of the land and that of most of the various bands that were Lakota. He had sworn to uphold the time-honored traditions of our grandfathers and lived up to this burden. Amongst the famous medicine men he stood out as distinguished and it was believed that he could work miracles in matters of both sickness and injury; he could help the faithful interpret their private visions; steer good people away from evil and chaos; embolden warriors; and foretell failure as well as success in battle. All of this he was, but most importantly, as a medicine man, the Spirits, under Creator…chose to work closely with him.

Eagle Feather lived the life of a true truthful man and gave the people a sense of strength and comfort. He taught that one must respect all of the Great Spirits creatures, even the enemy, for all had a purpose in the Circle of Life, and all things are considered sacred.

At the edge of camp while two dozen Brule horses were being tended by one who knew their needs, while dogs slept with one or both ears straight up, while Brule warriors rested with full stomachs that were soon to be even more full, Eagle Feather prepared his sweat lodge, and his fire.

The war party's wish for purification was granted and by sunset a sweat lodge waited for their guests. Fresh sage had been picked and was spread upon the floor of the sweat lodge to be used as a healing herb for rubbing sore muscles and serving also as a pleasant smelling ground cover. Cedar smoke drifted up from the mature coals of a fire that raged an hour earlier. Below the coals lay a large fire pit filled with dozens of round, red hot rocks each ready to carry their intense heat into the lodge. From this fire soft drum beats moved outward through the valley calling some to come, 'come immediately' it said, and announcing to others 'soon it will be time for the ceremonial feast.'

The drumming was heard by the great flocks of birds that settled into their nearby nests, these too were invited but most choose to stay put as they had been too busy raising their young; one small flock did hear the invite, these dipped into the valley, and flew over in landing formation, passing noisily overhead as if wishing the war party a safe return. This was seen as a good omen. A great feast simmered on campfires and could be smelled by numerous fox and coyote; they too wished to join the circle.

In darkness I grabbed my weapons for the long night ahead. 'There will be no wild horses visiting tonight,' Little Hawk said to both Two Stars and me and the three of us laughed at the thought and then moved out towards the far perimeter. The wild horses often came to visit our herds and to entice them to leave but the dimming lodge fire would keep them away. I was keeping watch as usual and for once wished I had my old carefree and responsibility free lifestyle back. I wanted to be part of the ceremony but was unable and could only briefly watch from a distance. I did manage to get one of the men to agree to take my post long enough for me to temporarily join the circle.

That day, No Flay and Eagle Feather were busy building their sweat lodge out of willow saplings. A circular 'igloo' type of structure was built with the willow saplings a bit larger than a man's thumb in thickness which could easily bend. Both men simply peeled the pliant willow bark in strips for tying the crossing willow together. A door opening was created and the people brought their more worn buffalo hides for covering. A depression was made in the middle of the lodge and a fire built outside where musk melon sized rocks from the creek were heated. A pair of elk horns were near the rock heating fire and a smaller pair of deer horns were located by the pit within the darkened lodge.

Toward evening after Eagle Feather smudged all present, onlookers and participants, with sage and cedar, he conducted a brief Pipe offering using the pleasant smelling red willow bark 'tobacco.' The war party warriors clad only in a breech cloth stood ready to go within. 'Puppy,' one of our big guard dogs came to visit and stood, tail wagging, sniffing the enclosure, looking out of place, and breaking the deep seriousness or image of the ceremony about to begin.

No Flay had the old medicine man's paunch bucket filled with water and a buffalo horn which was dropped into the water as a make-shift dipper sitting at the entry way. When the dog attempted to drink some of the water, No Flay cuffed him gently and shooed him away. A borrowed metal pot was also filled with water and would fulfill a contingency use if more water was needed to thoroughly steam up the lodge. Eagle Feather would use the 'dipper' to splash steam-making water onto the red hot rocks rolled in with the elk horn by the fire keeper to No Flay who would be waiting inside with the pair of deer horns. Each of the first four stones would be adjusted clockwise in the pit, to each of the four directions, North, East, South and West. Eagle Feather would enter after all warriors had entered. Some discussion as to the warrior woman taking part in the all male lodge was quickly snuffed out when Eagle Feather waved her inward with a look of indignation at any would-be protestors. Unlike the warriors she was covered with a trader's cloth dress. The warrior code preceded all other codes as to Eagle Feather and no one was about to argue with him. Warriors about to go off away took part in ceremony and she was a warrior. All were bare footed including the holy man, and No Flay. The flap was lifted and the woman and warriors all entered. All cried out

'Mitakuye Oyasin,' (For all my relatives, for all my relations) on their knees just as they entered. No one dared question Eagle Feathers authority which strongly supported the Creator's obvious balance.

"Ho- wah nahgi ya ta" was always the medicine man's customary beginning. (We're going to the land of Spirits!) The deer hide flap was closed over the door opening and all was dark within the lodge. Outside of the lodge, the fire man lightly tapped two giggling, noisy children sitting not far from the fire at this moment and they both jumped up running, "Eee yah," they squealed for the fire man forgot that the horn tip was still hot from picking out the rocks from the fire. Everyone else present outside the lodge became suddenly quiet. It was dark by now. Stars began to wink.

The lodge leader called out in the darkened interior; calling on the West Power. It is the first endurance; the first of four endurances which will be beseeched to the Four Directions; the entities of life which bring different things. Mother Earth is present. You are sitting upon her. Father Sky is present. The Sun's heat is within the glowing stones and bringing forth your lifeblood, your sweat, to mix with the lifeblood of the world — the water within the bucket beside the lodge leader. All within the lodge are introduced to the on-looking Spirit World beginning first through the West Power. Each person called out his or her name and a respectful greeting to the Spirits who were now in that lodge.

A simple beginner's song was sung first, for all are beginners at some stage. The song was accompanied by No Flays lodge drum.

> "Wiyopeyata hehhhhhh, hehhhhh. (Oh West Power).
> Wee yohhh-peee-yahhh tahh hehhhhhh.
> "Wiyopeyata kiya etunwin na cekiya yo hey
> Cekiya yo yo hena nitakuye yo hey"

Look to the West and pray to them
Pray to them because those people are your relatives.

Each Direction was in turn called upon and the warriors prayed individually. Light Hair was instructed by Eagle Feather. "You must Vision Quest when you return from this battle. There was silence. Eagle Feather spoke in a different voice. "I see you all returning. Some horses. Light Hair..." and there was silence for Eagle Feather was seeing a preview of a vision but he kept it to himself. He saw a man who would throw dust on his horse before battle, he wore a stone, and he would be told to keep nothing for himself. He would dress plainly and never wear a war bonnet. And when his arms would be held by one of his own people he would be in grave danger. A zigzag would become lightning and several painted dots would be hail or snow. These dots would be added to his shield. Was this his face or would it be upon a shield? Maybe both. The question remained unanswered. Steam filled the room and all became clean. When the flap door was opened and new rocks were brought in, the steam billowed out and upward. Their sweat was mixed in with the steam and was carried outward to the universe. After four beseechments, one to each direction, the ceremony was over and the warriors wiped themselves with the soft fragrant sage which No Flay had placed in a pile for them. They ate briefly and slept like babies after the medicine man's usual powerful lodge. The war party left late the following day. Against clear orders, I joined them

I led my horse to the shadows and slipped away. I rode north to the where the valley opened to grassland and then eastward in the direction of where Little Hawk said there surely was trouble. Within a white man's hour I was riding over Brule tracks and began closing in. I was only about a sunrise to mid-day in horseback time behind the party. I was fresh, well rested, as was my horse and was in no real hurry to join up with them just yet. My plan was to stay tight, solo, out of sight, and later but unsure as to when, I would offer my assistance sometime prior to battle. Or so, I had hoped.

On the night of the ceremony, Two Stars asked "You don't have any intent on joining this war party do you?" I sidestepped the question by saying, "I don't feel like I am ready to fight the Omaha." Which was true but even more true was the fact that I didn't want to be left home either. I didn't feel ready to face a full-grown warrior but I wanted to help, at least in some small way. At mid teens, I was considered well trained and had been in training for most of my life. Recently I had mastered many of the advanced combat tactics and began training daily. I had proven myself as a capable student and felt ready to move forward. By thirteen I had practiced with the bow more than most and could put several arrows in flight at the same time with telling accuracy. Lately I had been practicing with my uncle's war bow. His widow said I would own it in due time. I was pretty comfortable with it as well, on horse back. I could even handle a heavy war shield just not as well as the bigger men. A shield I could not own because I was too young. A shield carrier was one who had been formally initiated into the warrior class; and not everyone was so initiated. There was a good reason for not giving boys shields. The council did its best to discourage the boys from foolishness as was necessary until one had lengthy and rigorous combat training. Not having a shield didn't bother me I was as fast and as quick as a weasel and in venturing east I was confident that this would compensate.

All of the Lakota boys were rigorously trained to a great degree. We were playing War since we were four or five years of age. We threw rocks and shot one another with blunt arrows, some even had scars from these youthful battles and in latter life these youthful epics were replayed at campfires with great humor as if they were real battles. A favorite game of War involved the formation of mounted battle lines whereby boys aged 8 or 9 and up raced into battle on horseback and then knocked one another to the ground; once on the ground you were considered dead and the other team got a point. The game would often result in someone getting hurt but was great fun with frantic yelling, dust, ganging-up, and with horses rearing and bucking and sometimes running off to the deep woods.

By noon the next day I had the resting war party in sight. I stayed low, hobbled my horse so it could fill its belly, and slept away the afternoon in the brush of a heavily wooded backwater off the Loup River. At dusk that evening I rode in and formally joined them. Spotted Tail just shook his head and laughed. To my surprise the other warriors did not seem to mind, several had known my father, and while I was too inexperienced to be of much use they sensed that I belonged. Two of the youngest in the camp smiled gleefully. My presence would free at least one up from the horse holding duty and consequently that one would be closer to the battle and at least see more.

We stayed at the Upper Loup camp for several hours past sunset and ate lightly with no fire. Late in the evening we rode on. "At all times you will do exactly what I tell you," Spotted Tail commanded. This was like the voice of God and I couldn't imagine crossing him in any way, I only wanted to belong and to follow orders.

We were led down an ancient game trail that went southeast and parallel to the Loup. Initially our war party moved quickly pushing hard for the first couple of hours and then later we settled into a slow, quiet, single file formation. Occasionally, we would stop and give the horses a brief rest, other times we would stop for no other reason than to gauge our surroundings and to take note of where we were; everyone took the time to take in the surroundings. We would be returning this way at full speed in less than 12 hours either way, in victory or defeat. It was important to have horse holders who would not panic. The riders would return as the white man says, 'hell bent for leather.' Fresh escape horses could not be staked or hobbled with the enemy closing behind. Eagle Horse was our forward scout in this territory, and except for an occasional whisper between him and Spotted Tail talking was strictly forbidden. Throughout the night I proved myself useful and managed the spare horses for these two men; they in turn rode more freely and remained well ahead of the main party for much of the night. I rode in back and as the night wore on got the sense that everybody was putting themselves in the spirit for battle.

For many months there had been border skirmishes between the Lakota and the Omaha. Several warriors had been killed by Omaha guns and there were hard feelings that did not mend. Feelings remained strong enough to justify a war party. For this reason we rode. At daybreak Spotted Tail gave us the hand signal that the enemy had been sighted.

Many days earlier a plan had been laid out, a plan that went into effect the moment this hand signal spoke its command. Each individual warrior quickly and carefully prepared for battle. Each had his own individual manner, uniform, and style. Colorful war shirts were removed from special protective cases and at last worn proudly by their owners, battle lances were inspected one final time, fresh horses readied, war shield-strapped onto muscular arms, bows were strung, prayers were said, arrows were notched and then…we waited. As each man calmly waited, another signal was given.

We paired up and quietly advanced toward the enemy camp, the whole time staying off the trail and within the shadows of the heavy wood surrounding the mixed meadow countryside. I was given the signal to halt and hold four of the spare horses on a patch of wooded ground, a quick hard ride and upstream from the camp. Eagle Horse and Two Stabs, two of the more experienced warriors, cut to the left to engage an Omaha warrior that had been watering the horse herd; he was quickly taken by surprise. But not without a fight and with his yell the Omaha camp roared into a frenzy of activity. Spotted Tail and Kills-the-Bull rode directly into the village and began counting coup and batting stunned people about with the sides of their bows. All was chaos and for several hilarious moments the village people ran confused in stark fear when a warrior would smack them hard with a bow turning them in another direction, indeed it was a hilarious sight until my own fear made me realize the situation of surprise would be short-lived.

Before long the camp was armed and Spotted Tail and Kills-the-Bull pulled out as the arrows began flying but not before cutting some tied horses loose with their knives and slapping them hard across their rumps.

They then rejoined the main Brule group that was waiting on high ground in full battle formation.

Two Stabs did not rejoin. He left the battlefield, as planned, and was riding fast up-river with six of the best Omaha horses. Eagle Horse whipped the rest of the herd to efficiently scatter them into the woods, river bottoms, and meadow land. Backtracking towards me he motioned for me to come forward where I would be more exposed and casually asked, "Charging Owl, are you alright?" I nodded yes, choosing not to reply. "Stay here and do not move, is that clear?"

"Yes," I answered. As he turned back towards the battlefield I could tell that he had been wounded and was ignoring the heavy bleeding that came from his leg.

Within minutes a dozen mounted Omaha warriors formed an opposing battle line and were riding their best war horses that had been kept tied to the tipi at night for this very reason. I could now see from a better position and realized I was not yet a real warrior and wondered if I could ever be.

For several tense moments the battlefield came into military order. Most were bare-chested. There was no time for the Omaha to dress in their fine clothes but they came forward for it truly did not matter what they wore. They were completely intent on answering the challenge that our formation posed.

I watched from my safe distance, and remained content to keep the spare horses out of harm and therefore ensure a safe withdrawal out of enemy country but the battlefield moved toward me. Warriors are too often independent and one of the Omahas, spying my horses turned from engaging our formation and came full speed toward my position. As he came on, I ran toward a thorn tree. An old branch jutted outward from a scrub oak beyond. I dropped the rawhide ring that held the horse's hackamore ropes together over a broken branch tip and moved it securely toward the trunk. Pulling at my quiver I faced my enemy and moved back to the low thorn tree. I drew two arrows, placing one into the ground and the other I notched. I and the broad thorn tree were between my horses and the charging Omaha. Behind the horses, the land dropped toward the creek bottom.

There is a sound warriors make prior to charging into battle. It is more than just a yell. It is a timeless, universal chorus shared by all whom choose to line up amongst two opposing battle formations. To the warrior this is a sound almost like music; a powerful spiritual music that calls you forward; or perhaps commands you to step back. A rich sound that honors this brief moment of camaraderie, and simultaneously speaks of possibilities: promises to improve life, create life, and draw from life as if tapping into a mysterious primal energy. Rarely heard outside of battle and of no concern to disconnected fighting men, the sound I speak of is a joyful sound; a sound of celebration, a fantastic, mystical sound, an energizing cry of life.

It is heard and unheard for the battlefield song continues, strangely, with an equally profound silence. A silence heard by all, each man's eyes filling the battlefield with a silent chorus of shared thoughts, dreams, and ancestry. A long silence is observed to acknowledge the gift of the mysterious sound that few will ever hear, to honor the place, the past, to pay respect to all who witness the present, and to honor the future memories of this day.

The sound has not been heard on the plains for well over some years now but it shall return someday as it must. Warfare is sustained by the myth that one race is superior to another; this much is unanimous. So warfare will continue.

Hand-to-hand combat was therefore a glorious moment, a time for honor and courage, a time for victory or sometimes a time for incredible bravery against certain defeat. This style of warfare allowed the warrior to triumph; a means to triumph over the enemy, over the mundane, over his past mistakes, over hopelessness, a broken heart, or a future of doubt.

The returning warrior was given resources, a wife, acknowledgement, membership in society and in social groups. Successful warriors would choose, thru exclusive invitation, whom they wished to accompany them in battle.

Often an outbound warrior may be a young man setting out to temper his character. At other times he was a troublemaker ordered by the Chief to go out on the warpath; if his past mistakes were serious he would be ordered out alone, usually against all odds, for if he were to survive he would surely then have something in which to take pride; if he were to fail then so be it, this was a land that had no prisons.

Favorite battlefield opponents were strong fighters who knew the rules: challenge, engage, and withdraw; either in defeat or in victory. Courage and honor were the lofty goals and both parties desired to bring back rich stories that could be replayed and embellished and staged like a great work of storytelling. All this was craved by the little ones, especially at night when they needed to be scared by some monster people that lived far away and were larger than life. Without this type of combat life was boring.

One went down the "warpath" to fight, to bring honor, to demonstrate character, to heal, to live. One did not go down the "kill path," those who chose this path turned to stone and lost the ability to live. Dishonorable killing guaranteed a cycle of revenge raids and therefore was avoided. Great warriors knew that combat that resulted in a humiliated enemy was preferred to combat that resulted in slaughter. One style was remembered and praised as honorable; the other was sickening, shameful and while best forgotten it was like a sore that was whispered about for generations.

To the young impressionable warrior, the call to battle was an irresistible, delightful, and patriotic duty. For some it was more: warfare was sacred and god-ordained. In times of great stress warfare got ugly and conservative leaders of the day made it very clear that the future of their native traditions were sometimes at stake. In times of stress entire villages were wiped out or driven back.

Curiously warriors often took in the women and children of their adversaries, adopting them and marrying them into the tribe. Clearly the enemy bloodline was not what was necessarily despised, only the way of life for which the enemy fought.

The battle of Six Horses raged for 20 minutes. Spotted Tail rode first and met the full charge of the Omaha war chief. Both men fought first with lances and then finally with stone clubs and war shields still circling one another in a tight spinning pattern. For a moment it looked as if the Omaha was losing his balance and with this the entire force of Omaha advanced and onward the Brule rode in defense of Spotted Tail. It was a glorious sight no doubt but I could not view it for my time was being taken by that Omaha bearing down on me.

In the background, through his dust I could see one more peeling off. These were good horses I had been holding and from as close as we were they could tell I was easy prey. I pulled one more arrow from my quiver and stuck that down into the soft earth for I was not far from the creek by now which was heavy with brush, thorned plum, buffalo berry and the taller thorn apple with its knife like spikes. He came at a dead run. I could see his teeth clearly now. He carried a single shot muzzle loader, as they all were, no bow, axe at his center and long knife in a scabbard at his side. It was said that the Omahas were beginning to scout for the Army as were the Pawnee. Maybe that was why we encountered these army guns in this battle. He was laughing for I had to be a pitiful sight, drawing back on the man's bow. No fear showed on his heavy face. He was the size of Light Hair but broader and held a snarl. I saw that face often in my dreams. He must have been the bully for his age group is what he looked like in my memory. Up came his gun but he fired too quickly and failed to slow his horse for a better shot. He should have waited for there was little space for me to run except the creek at my back. When he fired, in fear I let my arrow fly. I felt as though it was aimed true at his torso but just before the moment he fired his horse shied at the on coming thorn tree, rising up and back to prevent itself from crashing onward into misery. The horse must have had a regrettable experience or two in its past for his action threw off his riders aim. The gun shot went high above me into the tree branches sending puckered thorn apples raining down. My arrow came under the rising horse's neck. My fear gave me a man's pull. The horse came crashing down sending its rider on into the tree, impaling him in the thick of the lower branches. The horse rose and crashed on across the creek.

The second rider came thundering in and stopped as I grabbed for my second arrow and had me in his sights dead center. It was to be all over in an eyewink. I was dead the inkling of movement I displayed. I held my bow pointed downward wondering when he would fire. One will prolong his life no matter the circumstances such as this. But a few more seconds I would live if I did not move. The Omaha laughed long and loud, lowering his gun as if taunting me to attempt an arrow. Then he raised his weapon slowly to fire and the laughter turned to a sneer. Something caught the corner of his eye however, and he fired quickly to his right bringing a bellowed snort from the charging horse and its rider. His sneer erased to a look of fear as Light Hair's horse came crashing into him knocking him from his mount. Light Hair was onto him in a flash, clubbing him back down with the Omahas own muzzle loader as he attempted to rise with his axe. Within seconds the man was scalped and then Light Hair turned to me with several steps. He jerked me forward with my bow still firmly in my grip. He pulled me toward the suspended Omaha attached to the thorn apple tree. He pushed my bow onto the bleeding Omaha's legs. I had counted my first coup albeit with help. Light Hair then touched the Omaha with the flat of his knife. A groan emitted from the Omaha but a louder one came from behind us. We watched in horror as Light Hair's battle mount sank to the ground, blood streaming from its nostrils. The Omaha ball had smashed its windpipe and that big blood vessel next to it. "Get back to your horses," Light Hair yelled without emotion. He grabbed the Omaha's powder and ball, and to my surprise began loading the weapon. He then ran after the Omaha horse which was ambling down stream back toward the camp area. It was disappearing over a slight rise with Light Hair in fast pursuit. I ran for the horses and heard a shot then saw Light Hair emerge over the rise astride the Omaha horse just as Spotted Tail came toward me from the opposite direction for a change of mount.

All fought well, but truthfully it ended too quickly, Someone had fired a gun, several from both sides were down, rescue attempts were in progress and the Omaha were beginning to mount additional warriors on the horses that were being rounded up. We withdrew and rode hard for hours, running uphill along side of our horses to keep them strong. We had scattered their horses well for they did not have enough mounts to safely pursue us. By late afternoon we were given the chance to rest. It had been a great day, for some.

Light Hair was unsettled on the long ride home, this was an early battle and though he had performed well, drew a scalp, he had killed an Omaha woman. Something moved in the brush as he was mounting his new horse or possibly she was coming at him. No one really knows. He was yet young and did not take a chance on identification and there were guns among these Omahas. It was all at the height of excitement anyway. Even the most experienced could have done the same. Light Hair was feeling sick about this. I did not know how to console him and let him be quiet with his thoughts. It was an unfortunate event. Perhaps it was an omen; I still do not know.

The ride home was uneventful and we rode hard all day and night stopping only for water, walking when the horses were tired, riding when possible all the while caring for the wounded so that they would return home safely. In time both men healed under Eagle Feather's care.

When I arrived in camp I was stripped of my duties as a night watchman and was assigned as punishment; babysitting duties in charge of those so young they had yet to ride their first horse. For a while at least my warrior days were over.

Two Stars so furious with me he picked me up by my shirt and screamed at me like a raging buffalo, later he would not even speak to me but eventually all was forgiven and much later he secretly told me that he thought I had done a very brave but still foolish act.

Light Hair stayed in our camp for the weeks needed for the two wounded warriors to regain their strength. This was a great time and we enjoyed the beauty and hunting that the surrounding valleys had to offer. He was quiet and probably for his experience but then he was always quiet. During this time Eagle Feather said "That one has a powerful vision...watch him Charging Owl he is the one to watch." Eagle Feather did not seem to be disturbed about the death of the woman. He was not the kind of medicine man that speculated in omens. What he saw in his ceremonial visions he did not attach speculation to. He called them as he observed them but he did have a foretelling sense that Light Hair's future would be heavy in battle and he would ride hard and not receive many wounds not even when facing the white man's Army which too soon replaced the other tribes in our future battles. He would be shot by an Indian but it would not kill him. Another in the party would also see the white man up close and would live on but would be also shot by an Indian. The holy man confided to me. Once both warriors were strong, the remaining Brules pulled out and returned to their camp far to the South. No one asked why an Oglala, Light Hair had chosen to ride or had come to ride with the Brules. Such was the Way of the Lakota. One did not ask what was unimportant. Crazy Horse as Light Hair or Curly came to be known, was Spotted Tail's nephew thru his Mother's side. I may have mentioned that. For those who like to wonder, maybe that could be part of the reason or maybe some sort of connection. To true Lakotas, however, it is unimportant. Puppy continued to help guard the camp.

Well, that was a long story. I told it finally to Father Bill on a long buggy ride over to the Brule mission, St. Francis. No Flay was our passenger and added in now and then from the back. Father Bill asked if he could write it down and if I would go over it again after we had stayed a few days and were heading back without No Flay. I asked him to wait awhile. "Right now, Father, I couldn't be ready to tell it again." I spoke with hesitation and sensed his disappointment but I had just had a scare. No Flay was going on to the Canton Hiawatha Insane Asylum at Canton, way across the state where federal people escorted him from St. Francis mission. I did not know that on the way over and after talking to the Brules at St. Francis they explained to me what such a place was for, at least their interpretation. The Indian 'grape vine' shared much information. They said it even had a graveyard. Father Patrick and the Oglala agent didn't like No Flay because he wouldn't give up the old Way or any of old Eagle Feather's teachings. It made a lot of trouble for him. Both missionary and Indian agents were powerful over our lives. I wondered how much trouble I would be getting myself in for if I continued to talk about these old ways. If it got wrote down, then they would have evidence against me. I would hate to wind up there.

* * * *

Crazy Horse and the Little Big Horn

*"Much of the fun of studying the Battle of the Little Big Horn
is the free rein it offers to the imagination."*
— Stephen Ambrose[1]

Language

Dr. John Bryde had the advantage of the language when interviewing many knowledgeable Oglala back in the forties. His study was not a hurry up, come-to-the-reservation, hire-an-interpreter and find-some-Indians venture. As an energetic Jesuit surrounded by Teton Oglala, and conversing in their language; he had no need for hurry or imagination. The language allowed him to talk to Two Hawks whose Uncle was at the Reno site, and then over to Stabbed because he did not leave a scene early and then Swift Hawk came over to the discussion and added his view; and all in Lakota. Dewey Beard made a special visit the next day or the following week and remarked about what his friends had to say.

The famous treaty of 1868 was the result of the Red Cloud War. It is the later changing (breaking) of this treaty that, more than any other treaty, irks the Sioux living today. This is the treaty that provided that all of the state of South Dakota west of the Missouri, as well as the Powder River country in Wyoming shall be Indian land 'as long as the grass shall grow and the waters flow and our dead lie buried.' This territory, of course, included the Black Hills. The Homestake mining company has finally shut down and moved on, after taking billions in gold and leaving behind Cyanide Creek. Another provision of the treaty was that agencies should be established along the Missouri River. The government, on its part, regarded the agreement to agencies on the Missouri as binding. The government wanted the agencies there because it would avoid the great expense and time involved in freighting rations and material across the plains. It was quicker, cheaper, and less time consuming to ship rations up the Missouri and have the Indians come in there to pick them up. The

Indians, on their part, as it developed later, regarded the establishment of agencies on the Missouri as optional. This was to lead to subsequent quarrels and finally compromise.

Red Cloud Agency

In only a few years following the treaty of 1868, the main agencies were changed several times. The first Red Cloud agency was quite satisfactory to the Oglalas, but the government was determined to establish the agencies farther East. A second Red Cloud agency was established in 1874 at Fort Robinson, near the present town of Crawford, Nebraska. Finally, the government simply moved the agency to the Missouri and told the Oglalas that, if they wanted their rations and equipment, they would simply have to go to the Missouri to get them. The Oglalas spent one miserable year around the Missouri, but they were so unhappy and made so much trouble that the government finally gave in and moved it back to the Pine Ridge country in 1879 where it has remained to this day.

This is the treaty which, if it would have been observed, would have been ideal for both sides. The Indians would have had their lands and would have been left in peace. The government had the southern and northern railroads built, and emigrants and other travelers could go to California without bothering the Indians.

Gold and Settlers

As it turned out, two main factors eventually caused the final major clash and further modifications of the treaty. These two factors were the discovery of gold in the Black Hills and the increasing number of white settlers whom the government could not hold back.

Six years is nothing in the life of an Indian nation. It was in 1874, only six years after the signing of the treaty of 1868, that the Sioux were again stirred up like a swarm of angry bees. Word got around immediately to the bands that a large group of soldiers, complete with a brass band, was headed straight for their sacred grounds, the Black Hills, and led by the notorious Pehin Zizi or Yellow Hair, the name that the Sioux used for Custer as well as Long Hair. Whenever the Indians heard of soldiers in their country, it meant only one thing: trouble and fighting. The fighting might not come tomorrow or next month, but it would come. The Sioux began to prepare in their minds for another major encounter with the military.

In the meantime, since the signing of the treaty of 1868, two other factors were happening that were steering the Indians toward another show down. Because of the agencies and the established reservation areas, the government was insisting more and more that the bands stay within the area assigned them. At the same time, rations were frequently not enough and the Indians solved this by simply leaving the assigned area or reservation and going off to hunt in order to add to their food supply. This wandering off to hunt became more frequent until the government finally laid down the law — that any time they were off their areas out of the assigned hunting times, they would be regarded as hostile, and the soldiers would be sent out after them to bring them in by fighting and force.

Drifting to Hunt

Thus it was that toward the end of 1875, a number of bands had left their reservation areas and had drifted north to hunt. On December 3, 1875, the government, therefore; issued an order to all Sioux out of their areas that, unless they returned by January 31, 1876, they would be regarded as hostile, and that military force would be used on them. We have already referred to this and we have seen that it was impossible for the Indians to comply with the order. First of all, with the bands spread out as they were, getting word to them by messengers was almost impossible. Secondly, even if the bands had gotten the word, winter traveling conditions made it impossible to get back by the assigned time. On February 7, 1876, therefore, the Secretary of the Interior ordered the military against what they regarded as the hostile Sioux. One of the commanders assigned was Lt. Colonel George Custer, who was about to make his last military trip. Custer had been a Major General during the Civil War but, like most of the officers with wartime promotions, had been reduced in rank after the war.

Three Pronged Plan

A common mistake that many people make in thinking of this campaign is that Lt. Col. Custer alone was sent out to bring in the Sioux. The truth is that two generals and a full Colonel were sent out — General Terry, General Crook and Colonel Gibbon and that Custer was a lieutenant colonel under the command of Terry.

In this final campaign against the Sioux, the army knew
two things:
a) This was the largest concentration of fighting Indians
   since Red Cloud's war.
b) They knew approximately where they were.

They knew that these whole bands that had been disappearing from
the reservations would be in the last great hunting area of the Sioux which
meant Red Cloud's old country around the Powder River area. Here alone,
in the last great hunting grounds, would they have enough game to
support such a large concentration of people. Since the army knew approximately where they were and that they were there in large numbers, they
decided to approach them from three different directions at once.

This was to be a massive operation. Thousands of men would be
involved, and they would have to travel hundreds of miles moving toward
the same spot, the Powder River country, and arriving precisely at the same
time from three different directions. General Crook would come up from the
South, from Fort Laramie territory with which we are already familiar. From
up in Montana, Col. Gibbon would come down from Fort Shaw. From near
the present location of Bismarck, North Dakota, General Terry would come
down from Fort Lincoln with Colonel Custer in his command.

All three of these small armies wanted to set out as soon as possible.
They wanted to find the Indians in the spring or early summer, so that if
they had to chase them, they would have the entire summer to do so.
General Crook was the first one to set out. He left from Fort Laramie in
early March 1876. Since General Terry, in Bismarck, and Col. John Gibbon,
in Fort Shaw, Montana, were situated so much farther north, the winter
weather held them up. These generals didn't get away until later,
Col. Gibbon in April and General Terry and Custer in May. In the
meantime, General Crook was going to have his hands full as a result of
his early start.

General Crook

When General Crook set out from Fort Laramie early in March, the
weather was bitterly cold, sometimes reaching thirty below zero. After
traveling slowly for a couple of weeks, his scouts brought back word of the
first sign of Indians on March 16. This was at Clear Creek, a branch of the
Powder River. The village was identified as that of Crazy Horse's and
some Cheyenne allies consisting of about a hundred lodges. This meant
that there were about six to seven hundred people and, among these,

about two hundred warriors. They seemed unaware of Crook's presence, and he decided to surprise them with an attack at dawn.

The surprise was a complete success. One military group was assigned to run off the horse herd, another group to attack and a third group to cut off any escape. About to run off the pony herd, the soldiers ran into a fifteen year old boy who was taking the horses to water. The boy was too startled to move. An officer drew his revolver, aimed it at the boy, and found that he couldn't get himself to pull the trigger. Later, the officer wrote, "He wrapped his blanket about him and stood like a statute of bronze, waiting for the fatal shot — his features as immobile as cut stone." When the fatal shot did not come, the boy let out a loud war whoop, and the battle was on.

Crook had about 1,400 soldiers, and the Indians had about 200 warriors. The village erupted in fear, and everyone fled except the warriors who gathered to fight. Gathering around Crazy Horse, they launched a furious counter attack from the rocks outside the village. As the battle raged on furiously, Colonel Reynolds, who was commanding the attack, was slowly beaten down. The battle carried on all day and, despite their superior number, Colonel Reynolds and his men were driven several miles back down the valley. Finally, in a desperate effort, the Indians retrieved their scattered herd of ponies that night and rode off shouting taunts at the soldiers. I have read a few history books that claim the Indians had bows and arrows mostly. These authors were obviously reluctant to admit that the Army lost a considerable amount of their logistics, namely ammunition and rifles to the Sioux who had the better horses; conditioned horses and able riders. If Col. Reynolds was beaten back it was not by bows and arrows.

When General Crook found out how badly his men had been beaten, he was so angry that he had Colonel Reynolds and several other officers court-martialed. If the Colonel was not beaten back then why was he court-martialed? Crook had to go all the way back to Fort Laramie to get his command back in shape again. For this reason it was not until late in May that he finally got his column moving again to keep his meeting date in the Powder River country with the other two columns coming down from the northwest and the northeast. Crook had 1,200 soldiers, 86 Shoshones, and 176 Crows in his group — a total of 1,462 men.

NOTE: It has always been desired by successful battle commanders before the days of armed mechanization, that a cavalry's horses would achieve top condition and develop stamina for continual performance in a test of battle; to wit; in excess of what their counterparts on the opposite side received from their mounts. It is like a winning hockey team that thoroughly practices repeatedly and builds lasting stamina and not just precisely passing the puck. Hockey is such a game, unlike football wherein the players expend a tremendous amount of energy when on the ice and have to be constantly spelled by a briefly rested line. The Sioux had the advantage of their families in the field which included as many young riders as there were battle tested warriors. Sioux horses were constantly mounted by the youth when the camp was in garrison (not on the move) and the superbly conditioned horses could easily outlast, outclass cavalry horses especially for endurance, combat performance; let alone over all speed when needed.

Weather was also a factor. An army on the move in early spring could find some desperate conditions; bitter cold and snowed over grass can fatigue the horses as well as fatiguing the men who have to do their share of walking to get through it. 'Torrid heat and arctic cold' is a common term for the Great Plains weather. I know; I have lived there a good share of my life. Several accounts hold that Crook had to eat his horses to get back out of the severe weather and looking back in fear that Crazy Horse would attack.

The Mounted Horsemen of the Plains

I left out the Sioux rider who guided his horse by his knees and weight shifting when in combat. On the trail he guided the horse by one rope, a light hackamore arrangement. The cavalry horse was directed by bit and reins, requiring one arm for the horse and the other arm free to carry a weapon but one would have to also aim that weapon with one hand. Try this on a moving horse and see how accurate you are, especially with a heavy, old fashion military rifle. Try fighting an opponent who is coming at you with both hands bearing a rifle or a shield and a weapon, arms free. Maybe it is understandable how two hundred mounted can defeat 1,000. An American army in the field back then did not field all its men as well, not unlike the combat unit of today. Among the Sioux, 200 warriors were just that, all in the field, mounted on superb personally trained horses and no one held back as a support unit, unless on a small raid planned to scout or a quick attack on a camped tribe wherein younger warriors were often held back to handle the escape horses brought along for quick evacuation.

Vietnam Revisited!

The cavalryman's horse was always loaded down as well with plenty of ammunition, water and even food on a heavy saddle. An oft used ploy which worked over and over, not unlike the disappearing strategy of the Vietcong and the NVA back into their tunnels throughout the Vietnam War which the Americans never seemed to get wise to; the Sioux would decoy out a baiting troop of warriors before a stockade or fort. Bored Army commanders would often give chase once they had loaded down their mounts that had often remained within the stockades for too long; **unexercised**. Barely out of rifle range, the warriors would tantalize and wait. Finally charging from the opened gates, bugles blaring and the garrison cheering, the fearless cavalry would give chase. The Red Clouds, Crazy Horses and Sitting Bulls would be waiting in force, back beyond hidden buttes, winding, wooded dry creeks, cedar river breaks, concealing nature. It worked over and over. Even bows and arrows were effective at close range once the Army's horse would become winded. Is it no small wonder why the Sioux had so many guns and ammunition after an encounter? This information has been mentioned before. It is worth repeating.

How could a small force hold its own against such as what Crooks had in the field? The primary answer is in — the **Horses!** And of course the attitude, experience, belief and command of the smaller force. Again I say, 'give credit where credit is due.' Chief Red Cloud started these tactics when he came upon an enemy who distained the word — 'Coup.' It was no longer a game of chivalry the old style warrior hood adhered to when fighting the enemy tribes. Oddly, as it was, American reaction to a so-called 'inferior enemy' was repeated to a degree in Vietnam. The military commanders ignored or just did not realize what was basically — common sense tactics.

Tongue River

Later, Crook again ran into Crazy Horse. This time it was on the east bank of the Tongue River on June 9. A lone Indian appeared on the other side of the Tongue with a message from Crazy Horse: Don't cross the Tongue, or we will fight. Crook sent back word that he was going to cross the Tongue.

That evening, even before Crook could cross the Tongue, gunfire broke out across the river from the Indian side. The soldiers fought back, but when they tried to attack the Sioux, the latter faded away.

They had made their point, and Crook saw it, because he didn't move from the spot for four days. He spent the time drilling his men and preparing for the invasion across the Tongue. He had 200 mules from the pack train broken to saddle and 200 of the infantry broken to riding the mules in order that they could have as many men as possible traveling as fast as possible.

On June 16, he crossed the river and camped on the Rosebud Creek that night. The next day, at the lower end of the Rosebud Valley, he ran into Crazy Horse and his Cheyenne Allies. The battle was on and it continued throughout most of the day, the conflict alternating in favor between both sides. Even General Crook had a horse shot out from under him. In a desperate effort to force the Indians back to their camp, General Crook sent Capt. Anson Mills to circle the map and to find and capture Crazy Horse's village. Captain Mills was only five minutes from the village when he received word from General Crook to return immediately or his entire command would be doomed. Captain Mills returned in time to help save the command from complete defeat. At dark, the battle ended, both sides withdrew, and Crook camped under triple guard right on the battlefield. The next day, Crook was so weakened that he had to turn back. Thus it was that the southern thrust of the three pronged approach to the Indians was beaten back and would not make its meeting with the other two columns coming down from the northwest and the northeast.

Another Account

"On June 17, scouts came in and reported the advance of a large body of troops under General Crook. The council sent Crazy Horse with seven hundred men to meet and attack him. These were nearly all young men, many of them under twenty, the flower of the hostile Sioux. They set out at night so as to steal a march upon the enemy, but within three or four miles of his camp they came unexpectedly upon some of his Crow scouts. There was a hurried exchange of shots; the Crows fled back to Crook's camp, pursued by the Sioux. The soldiers had their warning, and it was impossible to enter the well-protected camp. Again and again Crazy Horse charged with his bravest men, in the attempt to bring the troops into the open, but he succeeded only in drawing their fire. Toward afternoon he withdrew, and returned to camp disappointed. His scouts remained to watch Crook's movements, and later brought word that he had retreated to Goose Creek and seemed to have no further disposition to disturb the Sioux."[2]

As was mentioned earlier, Colonel Gibbon had started down from Fort Shaw in April in order to meet General Terry and Custer at the spot where the Rosebud Creek flowed into the Yellowstone River. General Terry and Lt. Col. Custer set out from Fort Lincoln in May, and the forces of Gibbon and Terry finally met at the Rosebud and Yellowstone. Here they made a simple plan. Colonel Gibbon would go back and march up the Big Horn River (it flows north), and then, if he didn't find the Indians, come back and march up the Little Big Horn. At the same time, Custer would march up the Rosebud Creek also looking for the Indians. The plan was simply to get the Indians between them (between the Big Horn and the Rosebud Creek), close in on them from both sides, and overcome them. If the Indians tried to run south, General Crook would be there with his 1,462 men to catch them — they thought. They did not know that just five days earlier on June 16, Crook had already met some of the Indians and had been sent packing south himself. The closing in date was June 26. Since the timing was important this is an important date to remember, because Custer met his fate on the 25th.

Gibbon's force started out on June 21, and Custer's force started out on June 22. During the very days that Custer and Gibbon were moving southward, Crazy Horse and his Cheyenne allies, after whipping Crook, were moving up north to join the main body of all the gathered bands and tribes, and what a gathering it was. Today, it is impossible to know exactly how many Indians were gathered together in the valley between the Little Big Horn and the Rosebud Creek toward which Gibbon and Custer were moving. Most books say that between 12,000 to 15,000 Indians were there, and about 5,000 of them were warriors. Actually, no one really knows for sure as to the real number of Indians there and guesses range from 2,500 to 15,000. The huge camp extended for three miles along the west bank of the Little Big Horn. Each band was camped in a circle. On the south end of the camp were the Hunkpapas with Chiefs Sitting Bull, Gall, and Black Moon. On the north end of the camp were the northern Cheyennes under chiefs Two Moon and White Bull. In between, each in its circle, were Minicoujous under Chief Hump, Sans Arcs under Chief Spotted Eagle, and Oglalas under Chiefs Crazy Horse, Low Dog, and Big Road. Bands of Brule and Blackfoot Sioux were there, along with some Arapahoes. It was toward this huge gathering that Custer was confidently making his way. Of the three military groups moving toward the Indians, Crook was out of action. Gibbon was not even going to get into it, and since Custer was the only one who was going to make contact, it is on him that we focus our attention.

Custer

As we said, Custer started slowly up the Rosebud on June 22. He had about 600 soldiers, 44 Indian scouts — mostly Crows, and 20 or more packers, guides, and civilians. On June 24, the scouts reported the tracks of a large Indian group moving west toward the Little Big Horn valley. Custer didn't know it, but he was only about eight miles from where Crazy Horse had beaten General Crook on June 17. Custer rested awhile and decided to follow the trail at night in order to be as close as possible to the Indians at dawn.

At daybreak on June 25, the smoke from many Indian lodges could be seen in the Little Big Horn Valley, and Custer knew when he had found his Indians. He itched for action. From this point on, accounts differ as to why Custer went into action so fast. For many years, the explanation given was that a report received by Custer mentioned that the presence of the troops had been discovered by the Indians, and that Custer thought if he didn't move right in (even though it was a day early for the planned attack from both sides) the Indians would escape; therefore, he thought he should act at once to prevent such an escape.

Most of the recent historians, however, hold a different version of why Custer didn't wait another day and attack as planned with Colonel Gibbon hitting from the other side on the 26th. The more recent researchers point out that Custer was fundamentally a "glory hound" and wanted to grab all the credit for himself; that he was simply following his long habit of acting suddenly without sufficient planning. They critically point out that he didn't even bother to scout ahead of time to find out just how many Indians he was about to engage and that, if he had, he most certainly would have waited until the next day when Colonel Gibbon would be in position. Custer was also a Fetterman. He could ride through a thousand Indians if chance could ever place that many in his way. It did! He had long been the most aggressive general in the army since Grant- but Grant also had brains and could plan, think it over and hit at the right time. Not so, Long Hair. He also did not believe in relying on assistance. Not even a Gatling gun, which he turned down for this particular expedition. It, 'would slow him down getting there.' Someone else to assist may get some of the glory as well. An author named Evan Connel, *Son of the Morning Star*, suggested that Custer had dreams of becoming president and that his 'victory' was all he needed. Sandoz, though writing 'fiction' holds the same view. As to the real reason, however, why Custer did not wait, no one really knows for sure.

All Night March

At any rate, Custer decided to move at once after an all night march. He divided his tired men (600) into three groups, one under Major Reno, another under Captain Benteen, and the third group was to go in with him. A fourth group was not to fight, but to guard the pack train and follow as closely as possible. Custer's last movements began as he stood with his group on a high spot facing west toward the Little Big Horn camp. He was about 12 miles from the huge Indian camp which was on the other side of the river from him. As he moved westward toward the camp, he sent Captain Benteen's group about two miles south to make a scout in that direction and to cover any Indian movements in that area. Custer himself and Reno moved directly toward the Indian camp, each group on opposite sides of the small creek that flowed toward the Little Big Horn and the Indian camp.

When Custer and Reno came within about two miles of the Little Big Horn, they could see part of the huge village across the river. If they had been able to see the whole village, they most certainly would not have charged it. At any rate, on seeing the village, Custer ordered Reno to continue moving straight ahead, across the river, and to attack the village. Custer himself decided to swing north and catch the village at one end. In this way, he apparently hoped that, by starting at one end of the village, he could drive everyone who ran right into the hands of Reno and Benteen, since Benteen was even farther south than Reno.

Three Distinct Fights

A popular misunderstanding of the battle of the Little Big Horn is that Custer alone rushed in and was defeated by the Indians. The truth of the matter is that there were three distinct fights and, for a clear understanding of the whole day's activity, it is necessary to understand the sequence of the fights which is as follows: Reno was hit first, then Custer was downed, and then the attack swung back to Reno, who by now had been joined by Benteen.

Reno did just as he was told. At about 2:30 p.m., he advanced straight toward that part of the village he could see and crossed the river. It was only then that his blood froze, as he saw for the first time the huge size of the Indians gathering. Up to this time, the bluffs along the river and the trees along the banks had hidden the complete village from view. Reno knew that he was in for it. As soon as Reno turned north into the village, the Indian warriors swarmed into view. So outnumbered was he, that a cavalry charge was out of the question. He ordered his men to dismount, dig in, and fight from cover. This sharp shooting defense slowed the Indians down at first, but after about a half an hour of this, so many more

Indians kept appearing and moving in, that Reno ordered his men to get back across the river that they had just crossed. Across the river, there were higher bluffs from which they could defend themselves better, if they could reach them. The retreat across the river became almost a rout. It was every man for himself, and Reno lost about one third of his men in the retreat. Once they crossed the river, the Indians stopped attacking and turned their attention to the north and to Custer. In the meantime, Reno's men reached the bluffs and dug in for their lives, expecting the Indians to return at any moment. As a matter of fact, they were going to return, after they directed their attention to George Armstrong Custer who, at this moment, was about five miles to the north of Reno.

Custer's Final Hour

You will recall that, as Reno crossed the river to attack the part of the village that he could see, Custer swung north to catch the village at its northern end. Just as Reno was meeting the Indian charge for the first time, Custer was seen on the bluffs from his northern position, waving his hat to Reno in encouragement right before he swung down from the bluffs to invade the river bottom and catch the Indians at the northern end of their village.

Just as Reno had gotten the surprise of his life when he saw the size of the village for the first time, so now Custer was to get the surprise of his life. Instead of coming out on the north end of the village where there would be nothing, Custer rode down from the bluffs right into the main part of the Indian village. It was on this northern end, you will recall, that the northern Cheyennes were camped, and right next to them were the Oglalas under Crazy Horse, Low Dog and Big Road. This is one of the reasons supporting the fact that the Cheyennes had such a prominent part in Custer's disaster.

Unlike Reno, Custer didn't even get a chance to cross the river. As soon as he was sighted by the Indians, they came boiling across the river after him. Custer had about 225 men, and the number of Indian warriors then present is an estimated 5,000. So mixed up by now were the various bands, that the first warriors to hit Custer were the Hunkpapas led by Chief Gall, who originally had been camped on the southern end of the large village. From the first contact, however, all the bands merged together and, like a huge, never ending wave, they moved in on Custer. Custer's men were spread out over a battle line of about three quarters of a mile on the first considerable ridge back to the river. A few hundred yards from this line on the ridge was another, lower ridge, and it was from behind this ridge that Crazy Horse, along with other bands appeared, cutting off Custer from any possible retreat. It was on this upper ridge that one of the bloodiest battles in the history of the west was fought.

Fighting on horseback was impossible due to the large number of Indians. Many of the soldiers had to leap from their horses and shoot them in order to make a breastwork against the bullets and arrows of the Sioux and Cheyennes who were creeping steadily forward. Most of the battle was fought on foot by both sides. Custer tried to gain a little higher ground, turning left toward the village and fighting on foot. The soldiers were increasingly spreading out as they sought higher ground and gullies for protection, but the Indians were appearing and pressing forward, not only from down below the ridges, but over the top of them as well.

No one knows exactly how long the battle lasted, but many estimate its length to have been about an hour. The horses which were not shot for protection were stampeded by the Indians and many were caught by the Indian women in the village. Without horses as a means of escape, it was only a matter of time as the superior number of Indians pressed forward in a concerted charge that could not be stopped. There was not, as one sees in the movies, the final, dramatic charge with the soldiers finally standing up and swinging their empty rifles. There was just the steady creeping forward and firing by the Indians, with the firing from the soldiers becoming less and less, until it suddenly occurred to the Indians that they were the only ones doing any shooting. Not one of the original 225 soldiers was left alive.

At what point Custer was killed, no one knows. Later on, Custer's body was found and, although it was stripped of its clothing as were most of the soldiers, he had not been scalped nor mutilated. He had been struck twice by bullets, either one of which could have been fatal. Although perhaps reckless, this much must be said about Custer: he was, unlike Fetterman in this respect, did not kill himself when he saw that his end was near. He went down fighting.

It was complete annihilation, and not one soldier remained alive after the battle. The only living thing left after the battle was Captain Keogh's horse, a well built bay named Comanche. The horse had strayed from the battle and had not been discovered by the Indians in the roundup of the other horses. Eventually, the horse strayed back to the scene of the battle, and when found, it was noted he had suffered seven wounds. He was taken back to Fort Lincoln, nursed back to health, and put on the retired list. Every time the regiment paraded, the horse was saddled, bridled, and led in the parade, but no one was ever allowed to ride him again. He died at the age of thirty years and was mounted and placed in the museum at the University of Kansas, where he can be seen to this very day.

Major Reno

Let us now return to Major Reno. We left him after he had retreated back across the river to the higher bluffs on the east side, at which point, the Indians withdrew and gave their attention to Custer. Digging in on the eastern bluffs, Reno had 40 men left, three officers, and a few civilians. He had started out with 140 men. Although he could hear the firing of the Custer engagement in the distance, he did not dare venture out of his position, because he thought the Indians might come back at any moment and finish off his weakened command.

In the meantime, Captain Benteen had been scouting farther south, as Custer had ordered him. He had seen no action, of course, and when he found the bluffs farther south were almost impassable, he swung back north again to find Custer for new orders. As he was making his way north again, still about eight miles from where Custer was last seen, he met a messenger from Custer with a hastily scrawled note which said, "Benteen — come on — Big Village — Be quick — Bring packs. P.S. Bring packs." It was signed by W.W. Cooke, Custer's adjutant. Since this was about 3:30 in the afternoon, Custer was probably already dead when Benteen got his message for help.

Benteen pushed north at a rapid rate, looking for Custer. He found Reno dug in on the eastern bluffs with over two thirds of his men gone and expecting another attack at any moment. Benteen, Reno and the other officers conferred for a while as to what to do. They couldn't decide whether to dig in with Reno and thereby have a strong defensive position, or to go on up and relieve Custer. Finally, it was decided to send Captain Weir with one company of soldiers, and Captain Benteen was to follow them. When Captain Weir came to a high spot about several miles where they thought Custer was, they could see Indians moving around and looking at the ground. Because of the distance, they could not make things out clearly, but this scene took place just after the battle when Custer and all of his men were already dead.

Holding Out

As soon as the Indians saw the soldiers, however, they swarmed up at them in order to cut them off. The soldiers dismounted to fight on foot, and this they did for a while. "When they saw how many Indians there were and the impossibility of holding their present line, they decided to go back to Reno's original defensive position in order to have a more fortified place from which to defend themselves and also to form a single concentration of men. No sooner had they dug themselves in at Reno's old position than Indians appeared from everywhere. It looked like Custer all over again, and the heavy fighting continued until dark when the Indians withdrew to their camp for the night.

All during the night, the soldiers of Benteen and Reno dug rifle pits and trenches with shovels, knives, tin cups, and mess kits, anything to make holes big enough to protect themselves. Ammunition cases and hardtack boxes were pilled up for barricades. Meanwhile, down in the huge village, the sounds of a wild celebration could be heard. Great fires lighted the sky, and the sounds of singing and dancing could be heard most of the night.

At dawn of the next day, the fighting resumed in earnest. The Indians were back in force. Together, Reno and Benteen's men made up a force of about 360. They had dug in well during the night and, unlike Custer, they had all the ammunition from the pack train. The battle continued all morning and into the afternoon, but from their strong defense position, the soldiers were able to hold off the Indians. It was about the middle of the afternoon that the Indians began to withdraw, leaving only a small force to keep up occasional firing to force the soldiers to remain in their place. Gall and his men held the survivors there until word from scouts reported the approach of another army, compelling the Sioux to break camp and scatter in different directions.

Late that afternoon, the Indians set fires to the grass in the valley, and when the clouds of smoke finally lifted the soldiers could see in the distance the departure of the entire Indian village. This long, slow procession of ponies and travels headed mainly toward the west, and before darkness set in, not an Indian was in sight. It was the 26th, and Colonel Gibbon was coming south along the Little Big Horn, right on time, and yet, too late.

It was the next day, the 27th, that Colonel Gibbon's men discovered Custer and his command. All the bodies, including Custer's, were buried on the battlefield where they fell. Markers were set to indicate where they were buried. A year later, Company One of Custer's old Seventh Cavalry returned to the battlefield. Custer's body was exhumed and sent to the post cemetery at West Point, the United States Military Academy. The bodies of every officer except one and two civilians were exhumed and sent to the homes of their relatives for reburial. The remaining bodies of the fallen soldiers, those who 'had fallen into camp' of Chief Sitting Bull's vision were exhumed and reburied in one large grave on the top of what is now known as Custer Hill, where they remain to this day.

After this momentous battle, the huge camp broke up and the various bands made off in different directions. Most of them went right back to their fall schedules, gathering lodge poles here, hunting there, and occasionally brushing with the military. Scattered as they were, the army could not bring about effective strikes, but they were a bother to the Indians. Some, on encountering the army, quietly gave up and went back to their reservations, while others kept dodging the soldiers and remained free for another year or two. Sitting Bull and many of his Hunkpapas finally ended up in Canada in 1877, but they were very unhappy there. The Canadian Mounted Police (the red coats) watched them too closely and, in 1881, after four years there, Sitting Bull decided to return to his reservation. Crazy Horse, after dodging around in the north country and finding his people starving due to the absence of game and buffalo, was finally compelled to return. The last great resistance was over, and life on the reservation was about to begin.

Coming In

In July 1877, Chief Crazy Horse was finally prevailed upon to come in to Fort Robinson, Nebraska, with his band. Most say less than a thousand. General Crook had now proclaimed Spotted Tail, who had rendered service to the army, 'Head Chief of the Sioux,' which was resented by many, and of course Chief Red Cloud.

"The attention paid Crazy Horse was offensive to Spotted Tail and the Indian scouts, who planned a conspiracy against him. They reported to General Crook that the young chief would murder him at the next council, and stampede the Sioux into another war. He was urged not to attend the council and did not, but sent another officer to represent him. Meanwhile the friends of Crazy Horse discovered the plot and told him of it. His reply was, "Only cowards are murderers."

"His wife was critically ill at the time, and he decided to take her to her parents at Spotted Tail agency, whereupon his enemies circulated the story that he had fled, and a party of scouts was sent after him. They overtook him riding with his wife and one other but did not undertake to arrest him, and after he had left the sick woman with her people he went to call on Captain Lee, the agent for the Brules, accompanied by all the warriors of the Minneconwoju (Minicoujou) band. This volunteer escort made an imposing appearance on horseback, shouting and singing, and in the words of Captain Lee himself and the missionary, the Reverend Mr. Cleveland, the situation was extremely critical. Indeed, the scouts who had followed Crazy Horse from Red Cloud agency were advised not to show themselves, as some of the warriors had urged that they be taken out and horsewhipped publicly. Under these circumstances Crazy Horse again showed his masterful spirit by holding these young men in check. He said to them in his quiet way: "It is well to be brave in the field of battle; it is cowardly to display bravery against one's own tribesmen. These scouts have been compelled to do what they did; they are no better than servants of the white officers. I came here on a peaceful errand.

"The Captain, (Agent of the Brules — Spotted Tail agency) urged him to report at army headquarters to explain himself and correct false rumors, and on his giving consent, furnished him with a wagon and escort. It has been said that he went back under arrest, but this is untrue. Indians have boasted that they had a hand in bringing him in, but their stories are without foundation. He went of his own accord, either suspecting no treachery or determined to defy it. When he reached the military camp, Little Big Man walked arm-in-arm with him, and his cousin and friend, Touch-the-Cloud, was just in advance. After they passed the sentinel, an officer approached them and walked on his other side. He was unarmed but for the knife which is carried for ordinary uses by women as well as men. Unsuspectingly he walked toward the guardhouse; when Touch-the-Cloud suddenly turned back exclaiming: "Cousin, they will put you in prison!"

"Another white man's trick! Let me go! Let me die fighting!" cried Crazy Horse. He stopped and tried to free himself and draw his knife, but both arms were held fast by Little Big Man and the officer. While he struggled thus, a soldier thrust him through with his bayonet from behind. The wound was mortal, and he died in the course of that night, his old father singing the death song over him and afterward carrying away the body, which they said must not be further polluted by the touch of a white man. They hid it somewhere in the Bad Lands, his resting place to this day."[2]

I, myself, have a fairly reliable idea where that resting place is at. It is a far different location than the idea of way off in the Bad Lands. But I will never reveal my knowledge in this respect because of the desires of his parents for privacy.

* * * *

8

Ghost Dance

In 1870, Red Cloud and other Lakota leaders went to Washington, D.C. for an audience with President Grant. Snorting, whistling train engines, clattery bridges and one big city after another would have frightened some people who had not seen any of it before. Red Cloud found that the "white father" was under pressure from his people to take the land of the Sioux people. The white people who wanted the land wanted the Indian people to give it up quickly. So they hoped to frighten the Lakota leaders by showing them the many big buildings and great numbers of people. They even had Marines parade and a show of arms to demonstrate the power of the white armies.

The white people hoped the Lakota would take the leftover land without saying a word. Red Cloud had been willing to give his life in battle to defend the good life of his people. Now he had vowed not to go to war, and he kept his word. For such a combat leader, it had to be a difficult thing to do. If he broke his word and went to war then he believed, the whites would have a perfect excuse to break the Treaty of 1868. For such a warrior, this vow and the weight that it carried was a worse fate than being a penned wolf or mountain lion.

What a strange place for this first big skirmish of the new battle — Washington, D.C. — a battle of words. Red Cloud had left his people in the circle of tipis on their homeland which got smaller every year. Still Chief of his people he now looked at Washington, D.C. and clearly saw that the white man's cities were not built around the circle of the people. They were built in squares. Red Cloud must have thought of the Lakota leaders who never took the center of the circle for themselves. *Itanca*, or leader, was a part of the circle, a part of the people. Red Cloud saw no circle of a people all part of one another here. No, he saw one square of people after another.

Some of the squares that people lived in had big, beautiful houses. Some of the squares had poor, rundown houses and these were the majority of the houses once you rode farther away from the leader. Right in the middle of the bigger houses was a really big house. This is where the leader of the white people lived, Red Cloud was told. He was expected to be very impressed, but he would wait and decide for himself.

This also was something new, to see a big house of an important man living in the middle of the people who had less than he had. The only one who lived in the center of the circle of the Lakota was the holy tree during the days of the Sun Dance which symbolized the Creator, the 'Tree of Life.' Red Cloud could have thought of this as he looked at these people who were so proud of their cities and bridges and cannons. Their churches were even big buildings to show off. He saw a large square building in the middle of many square blocks that made up the city. This building stuck out from the rest. The "biggest man in the country lived there," Red Cloud was told. When Red Cloud did see him he looked deep into this man, the 'Great White Father,' He looked at him as his people looked at their leaders — deep inside. The man spoke. After polite greetings and peripheral talk, President Grant stunned the Teton Chief. He told Red Cloud that he wanted the Sioux to move to, 'Indian Territory' (Oklahoma).

So Red Cloud answered back. With the deep talk of a man for his people, he told of the new life that was killing his people like sheep. He told of the men the Great White Father sent to look after the supplies meant for the Lakota. He spoke of these agents who "filled their own pockets." Very clearly, Red Cloud spoke. But for years he would hear the first words almost, out of President Grant's mouth; "move to Indian Territory" (Oklahoma) and other threats if he did not comply.

He shook hands with the officials with seriousness and said, "I came from where the sun sets. You were raised on a chair; I want to sit where the sun sets." He then sat down on the floor and delivered his reply.

"I have offered my prayers to the Great Spirit so I could come here safe. Look at me. I was a warrior on this land where the sun rises, now I come from where the sun sets. Whose voice was first sounded on this land — the red people with bows and arrows. The Great Father (the President) says he is good and kind to us. I can't see it. I am good to his white people. From the word sent me I have come all the way to this house. My face is red, yours is white. The Great Spirit taught you to read and write but not me. I have not learned. I came here to tell my Great Father what I do not like in my country. The men he sends there have no sense, no heart. What has been done in my country, I do not want, do not ask for it: White people going through my country. Father, have you or any of your friends here got children? Do you want to raise them? Look at me. I come here with all these young men. All are married, have children, and want to raise them.

"The white children have surrounded me and have left me nothing but an island. When we first had this land we were strong, now we are melting like snow on the hillside while you are growing like spring grass.

"Now I have come to my Great Father's house, see if I leave any blood in his land when I leave. Tell the Great Father to move Fort Fetterman away and we will have no more troubles. I have two mountains in that country (Black Hills and Big Horn Mountains). I want Great Father to make no roads through them.

"I have told these things three times now. I have come here to tell them the fourth time.

I don't want my reservation on the Missouri. This is the fourth time I have said no. Here are some people from Missouri now. Our children are dying off like sheep. The country does not suit them…

"The railroad passing through my country now. I have received no pay for the land…"

Among Red Cloud's demands were that he choose where, on the reservation land, the agency would be. At the agency the supplies, which his people had given up much life giving hunting ground to receive, were given out. And he had a continual fight to keep pinch-penny Congresses from decreasing the treaty supply amounts. And Red Cloud asked to name an agent from the people he knew and trusted. But these kinds of demands had to be made over and over. His alert ears must have found it almost too much to have to listen to threats of removal to Indian Territory (Oklahoma). It was a continual and bitter fight. The battles were enough to crush a lesser leader. The old man's candor and fame won out however for he earned strong supporters and the once solidly backed idea championed by Grant himself was finally shelved. The Sioux people must always thank the great chief for his stubborn refusal to move south to the federally created, Indian Country Oklahoma, where the tribes succumbed en masse to the white man's religion and almost all abandoned what their forefathers believed in. If that was their free, uninhibited choice; so be it in a Democracy. They may well have had a differing spirituality or religion than the Tetons.

I personally harbor my own conclusion. Like the determined Masada Jews, Jewish people are not Jewish, according to them, unless you believe as did your forefathers. They seem to have held that opinion for some thousands years and goodness knows they even refused to deny their position in the teeth of German liquidation camps. It will be interesting to see if the other tribes have similar mettle as the future rolls on. If history is an example, **I do believe** a significant number of Tetons will return, the way the Sun Dance is reviving. I also realize proudly that; Tetons are Tetons! Something is there. They seldom 'bahh' like the white man's sheep!

In my mere mind, you are not truly an Indian, especially a real Sioux, a Teton Lakota and/or their supportive allies of the past, (a real Yankton, a real Cheyenne, etc.), unless you believe as your forefathers! It matters little, to me, whether you are a full blood, a breed, even down to 1/8th or so. Again, the Jews do not look at blood quantum tracing back to some ancient Hebrew tribes. If they do, their certainly is quite a mix of various ethnicity in these modern times. We Indians have proven our American patriotism, especially in WWII, Korea and Vietnam so Dominant Society should not criticize us. We are very, very patriotic and know how to honor our returning modern warriors. For those who wish to criticize us, I ask, 'Where is your Track Record of patriotism to this great land before you are so qualified to criticize us for returning to our forefather's belief?'

In the old days only a combat warrior would be allowed to criticize another who had fought for his people. The way that the Jews identify themselves makes the most sense to me. It is a personal belief and not meant for any startling propaganda, survey or movement. Besides, who is about to listen this deeply, coming from a getting-older Indian author? I often mention Truth. It seems to be a truthful thought- this way that the Jewish people believe. It is something, simply, deep inside....and it will stay there, refusing to leave me. It is where I am at. Others can speak freely for themselves. The results of the tribes in Oklahoma, however, are proof enough to at least wonder as to the contention. What would have happened to our Sioux Spirituality had we joined those tribes following President Grant's desires? No previous writings credit Chief Red Cloud for keeping our Sioux tribes out of Oklahoma and yet it was one of his crowning achievements.

The skins from the last buffalo hunts were worn now and the supplies issued for shelter were little protection against South Dakota winters. The proud Lakota were used to living well and eating much good meat when they were free to hunt. Now they were confined like prisoners. Mistrust resulted and many ridiculed Red Cloud. Many left the reservations to Sioux bands still holding out. But the white army was increasing its forces against them. The white men were determined to confine all the proud Lakota people to the reservations. Gold was discovered under the Black Hills. That fact alone resulted in the breaking of the Treaty of 1868. Then came the seeds, plows, and overalls. The few who would use them saw their plants burned by drought or eaten by grasshoppers.

The churches did not stop and learn of the Lakota union that is deeply religious. It is union with each other, with rock, tree, water, the Great Spirit. The churches moved into the reservations and soon began to destroy the spiritual leadership of a deeply religious people. They said the Indian must change to their religion: Now. But the old spiritual traditionals **unlike** most of the other non-Teton tribes, stubbornly refused to budge nor would they give up their language and there were many which held onto their Lakota/Dakota which is spoken to this day. It is Lakota sweat lodge songs now being sung across America when this ceremony is being conducted by many non-Tetons.

By public demand, after Washington, D.C., Red Cloud went on to York City before returning home. Again he spoke of the Treaty of 1868. New York newspapers, made something very clear. 'Avoiding telling the truth to the Indians doesn't work. Trying to jolly them or scare them doesn't work. Officials had better begin to talk straight.' Red Cloud spoke in New York.

"We came to Washington to see our Great Father that peace might be continued. The Great Spirit that made us both wishes peace to be kept; we want to keep peace. Will you help us? In 1868, men came out and brought papers. We could not read them, and they did not tell us truly what was in them. We thought the treaty was to remove the forts, and that we should then cease from fighting. But they wanted to send us traders on the Missouri River. We did not want to go to the Missouri, but wanted traders where we were.

"When I reached Washington the Great Father explained to me what the treaty was, and showed me that the interpreters had deceived me. All I want is right and just. I have tried to get from the Great Father what is right and just. I have not altogether succeeded...We do not want riches, but we want to train our children right. Riches would do us no good...The riches that we have in this world, Secretary Cox said truly, we cannot take with us to the next world.

"Then I wish to know why the Commissioners are sent out to us who do nothing but rob us and get the riches of this world away from us? I was brought up among the traders, and those who came out there in the early times treated me well and I had a good time with them. But, by and by, the Great Father sent out a different kind of men; men who cheated and drank whisky; men who were so bad that the Great Father could not keep them at home and so sent them out there.

"I have sent a great many words to the Great Father but they never reached him. They were drowned on the way, and I was afraid the words I spoke lately to the Great Father would not reach you, so I came to speak to you myself; and now I am going away to my home."

The crowd applauded after almost every sentence and at the end the clapping thundered for some time. As he went home he had won his first skirmish of battle by wit and word. He held a big key to peace or war, to life or death. He had not staggered under the load.

On returning to his people, Red Cloud found the problems the same: Hunger, cold, sickness. Tuberculosis, the 'coughing sickness' began its toll. While Red Cloud's eyes were watching all of this, Red Cloud's heard that the Lakota were losing the Black Hills. They were told they must lose them because white men who were never to enter Indian land had entered: And found gold. Gold was the real God of far too many white men.

Ghost Dance – Wovoka

It had been fourteen years since the defeat of Custer. After Custer, the various Sioux bands returned to their reservations and tried to settle down, but these were restless and unhappy years. Most of the people knew that further fighting was useless because of the superior number of the non-Indian soldiers; yet, the desire to wander and follow the buffalo was like a burning hunger pang in them, even though they knew that there were no more buffalo to follow. Of all the reservation years, these were the hardest, because these were the people who were fresh from the plains and who had grown up in the old way. The next generations to follow, although they would find it hard, would not find it nearly as hard as these who first came off the plains to live on the reservations. Up and coming young warriors who were seventeen and eighteen years old at the time of Custer were now in their early thirties and just reaching their prime as fighters, but they could not fight. The very things they had lived for and had been trained for were removed from them, and they lived in constant frustration.

In their despair and frustration, they were willing to turn to and to believe in anything that would offer them the slightest hope of returning to their old way of life. As we saw in an earlier chapter, the Sioux were a naturally and deeply religious people. In their despair, they prayed and prayed and sought visions from God for guidance and deliverance. They were willing to listen to anyone who claimed to have information from God for a way out of the agony of their frustration. It was at this point that a Paiute Indian by the name of Wovoka entered the scene. No one can understand Wounded Knee without understanding what Wovoka offered for deliverance and how eagerly all the tribes on the plains seized his advice. What Wovoka had to offer was the Ghost Dance, and it was primarily this ghost dance that became the force that shaped Wounded Knee. Many people think that Wounded Knee was simply this: a bunch of soldiers went out to meet some Indians. They surrounded them and tried to take their guns away. When a shot rang out, the soldiers shot most of the Indians down. This is not the complete story of Wounded Knee at all. One has to understand the causes leading up to Wounded Knee and the causes that brought about the fight that very morning. One has to understand all these factors in order to have a true picture of Wounded Knee.

The influence of Wovoka began in 1889, not long before Wounded Knee and many miles from it. Wovoka, as we said, was a Paiute Indian, and he lived in Nevada. His father, Tavibo, had claimed for twenty years to have had visions from God in which he was told that there was a great earthquake coming which all the non-Indians would be swallowed up, leaving only the believing Indians, who would then be able to go back to their old way of life. Very few, even among the Paiutes, believed Wovoka's father.

After the death of his father, Wovoka lived with a non-Indian family who were very religious people, and he read the Bible every day. Wovoka himself was very religious and listened eagerly to the stories of the Old Testament. He was especially moved by the deeds and prophecies of the prophets of the Old Testament. The family with whom he lived was named Wilson, and Wovoka even took their name and went sometimes by the name of Jack Wilson.

On January 1, 1889, there occurred an eclipse of the sun which terrified all the Paiutes because, like the Incas of old, they were sun worshippers and they regarded the eclipse as an attack on their God. After the eclipse, Wovoka told the people that God wanted the Indian people to do a certain dance. He told them that on the day the sun died (the eclipse) that he, Wovoka, was taken up into the other world of heaven where he saw God and all the Indian people who had died in the past. Here they were happy, had plenty of game, and enjoyed all their old time sports and joys. God told him that he must go back and tell the Indian people the following:

a) They must not quarrel with one another, nor quarrel with the non-Indians, but live in peace with everyone;

b) They must work and not lie or steal;

c) They must be good and love one another;

d) They must do away with any thought of going to war again, neither with other Indian tribes nor with the non-Indians;

e) They must do a sacred dance which he, Wovoka, would teach them;

f) If they did all these things, they would be united with all their dead friends and relatives in heaven when they died.

This sacred dance would be the Ghost Dance. Since the Indians believed that Wovoka had brought this information from God, they began to regard him as a Messiah, as Jesus was a Messiah — an Anointed One of God. Wovoka himself fell into this and even referred to himself as the Messiah. For this reason, the reaction this had on the other tribes was called the Messiah Craze.

It must be noted clearly that what Wovoka taught the Indian people had nothing of war in it at all. In fact, his teachings were explicitly against war and forbade it. The main hope that Wovoka held out to the people, if they followed his teachings, was that they would be reunited in heaven with all their dead relatives and friends when they died. We shall see that the Sioux added something to the original teachings that was going to cause them much anguish, trouble, and sorrow.

The Ghost Shirt

News of the vision and Wovoka's teachings spread through the tribes of the plains like a prairie fire. In just a few months, tribes from the Indian territories of Oklahoma, and practically all of the Western tribes sent delegations to Wovoka to get his teachings first hand. The Sioux first heard of Wovoka's teachings through the Cheyennes. The Sioux, as we saw, were naturally religious and over eager to adapt new religious ideas to their own religion. This natural religious bond, plus their own frustration at losing their way of life, made them seize upon Wovoka's ideas as a starving man would seize offered food.

When the Pine Ridge Sioux learned about Wovoka late in the summer of 1889, they immediately held a great council at Pine Ridge and selected a delegation to go to Wovoka and learn his teachings first hand. The delegation consisted of Yellow Breast, Flat Iron, Good Thunder, and Broken Arm of the Pine Ridge Reservation as well as Kicking Bear from the Cheyenne Agency Reservation. They traveled for five days by train in order to reach Wovoka at Walker Lake, Nevada. On returning, another great council was held to hear their report.

It was from this meeting that a dangerous addition to Wovoka's original teachings was made. It was most likely the Sioux who added the idea of the ghost shirt. Most likely it was Short Bull and Kicking Bear who came up with this idea. The Sioux were told by Kicking Bear and Short Bull that, if they wore this certain shirt called the ghost shirt, it would stop bullets and they would be safe from any attacks by the non-Indians and non-Indian soldiers. By now, there were 30 to 35 tribes containing over 60,000 Indians practicing the Ghost Dance, and the Sioux were the only ones to add the idea of the ghost shirt. This dangerous idea that bullets couldn't hurt them was going to make some of the Sioux eager to fight and it was going to be a provoking factor in causing the outbreak to follow.

After the report of the delegation that had gone to see Wovoka, many of the Pine Ridge Sioux took up the Ghost Dance with enthusiasm. All over the reservation, dances would go on for hours and even days. Some groups were small and other groups were large, but to the non-Indian people on and near the reservation, Indians dancing meant only one thing: a war dance. Few non-Indian people knew that the Indians had all kinds of dances such as religious dances, social dances, and many others, and that to the Indians a war dance was only one of many dances. But, as we said, the non-Indians didn't know this, and when they saw dancing Indians, to them it meant that trouble was coming. They did not know that the Ghost Dance was a religious "prayer dance" and that in dancing the Ghost Dance, the Sioux were actually praying for peace and deliverance, not war.

Indian Agent

At this time, there was a brand new agent on the reservation, Daniel Royer, who had only been in office for a few weeks and who was not at all familiar with Indians. Dancing Indians, to him, meant trouble and as he looked out over the Pine Ridge Reservation, he was terrified at all the dancing that was going on. In a panic, he did a very foolish thing: he sent for soldiers. He sent the following telegram to his superiors, "Indians are dancing in the snow and are wild and crazy. We need protection, and we need it now. The leaders should be arrested and confined in some military post until the matter is quieted, and this should be done at once." Thus it was that the two fears fed each other: fear of dancing Indians caused the soldiers to come in and prepare for trouble; fear of the soldiers caused the Indians, to prepare for trouble.

General Brooke

There were already a few soldiers regularly stationed in Pine Ridge, but on November 20, 1890, General John R. Brooke arrived with a huge number of troops consisting of five companies of infantry and three troops of cavalry equipped with one Hotchkiss and one Gatling gun. The stage was set on the Pine Ridge Reservation. Almost three weeks later, something was to happen that would put the events in motion toward the Wounded Knee tragedy. The event, which took place about 250 miles to the northwest of Pine Ridge and which put the northern forces in motion toward Wounded Knee, was the death of Sitting Bull which occurred on December 15, 1890. The death of Sitting Bull frightened a peaceful old chief named Big Foot, and he and his Minicoujou people left their Cheyenne Reservation to camp on the south fork of the Cheyenne River.

The army regarded this leaving as a hostile act and sent orders to Col. Sumner to bring Big Foot back to the Cheyenne Reservation. Col. Sumner had been watching Big Foot for months and knew he was perfectly peaceful but, following orders, he sent an interpreter out to Big Foot's camp to tell him to come back. During the night, however, some of the young warriors talked to Big Foot and told him that, if he went back, the same thing might happen to him that happened to Sitting Bull. They persuaded him to slip away and head for Pine Ridge. Big Foot also had another reason for going to Pine Ridge. His Minicoujou people had been practicing the Ghost Dance, and the fact that some of the Indians who had been killed with Sitting Bull were wearing ghost shirts at that time shook his faith in the ghost dance. He wanted to go to Pine Ridge to talk to Red Cloud about the Ghost Dance and the ghost shirts and to get his advice. The moment he slipped away, he was declared hostile, and the soldiers on the Pine Ridge end were alerted to his coming. Red Cloud, at this time, was beginning to be quite dubious as to the merits of the 'bullet proof' claim and the frenzied attention it was drawing.

When General Brooke in Pine Ridge received this news of the probable arrival of Big Foot and his band at Pine Ridge he sent out Major Whiteside with a force of soldiers to find Big Foot before he could reach Pine Ridge. The authorities on the Pine Ridge end, thinking that Big Foot was hostile, didn't want any hostile group coming and stirring up the Pine Ridge Sioux. As it was, the Pine Ridge Sioux were stirred up enough by the Ghost Dance movement, and the army feared that any hostile group coming in might be the spark that would set off the powder keg. It was the plan of the army, therefore, to find Big Foot, take his guns away, and hustle him back to his home base before his group could get together with any of the Pine Ridge groups.

Major Whiteside

Heading out from Pine Ridge in a northeasterly direction, Major Whiteside sent scouts out ahead to find Big Foot's band, promising twenty-five dollars to the first scout who found them. The scouts did not find Big Foot's band; on the contrary, Whiteside's scouts were watering their horses in a stream north of Porcupine when they suddenly found themselves surrounded by Minicoujou scouts. The Minicoujous took the scouts to Big Foot who had become very ill from pneumonia during the trip and who was traveling in a wagon. From these scouts, Big Foot learned that Major Whiteside was camped near Wounded Knee Creek and he told the scouts to go back and tell Whiteside that he was coming in to see him and that he wanted no trouble.

When the scouts returned and told this to Whiteside, he took his 225 men and 10 officers and rode up to meet Big Foot's band that was now slowly moving toward Wounded Knee Creek. At a big hill called Porcupine Butte, he met the band slowly coming toward him with the warriors in the lead. Taking no chances, Whiteside fanned his men out in battle formation in front of the band and ran his two cannons out in front of the line. The Minicoujous kept coming, and the warriors spread out in a skirmish line. Some of the warriors got off their horses and tied up the tails of their ponies in preparation for a fight. Others of the Minicoujou warriors raced back and forth, waving their rifles and giving their war cries. It was a tense moment, and fighting could have broken out at any moment if anyone on either side had made a false move. Behind the Minicoujou warriors came Big Foot's wagon with a white flag attached to it.

Whiteside's orders were to disarm the band and to bring them in as soon as possible. He had originally planned to do that as soon as he saw the band. Now, however, with the warriors riding up and down ready to go into action at the slightest provocation, his scouts pointed out to him that this was impossible right now. He just could not send word to those heated up warriors to put down those guns, get off their horses, give them up, and come walking along behind him. Whiteside rode up to Big Foot's wagon and told the chief that he wanted him and his band to go with him to Wounded Knee Creek and to camp there for the night. Big Foot said that that was exactly what he had planned to do anyway, and so the Minicoujous surrounded by the soldiers made their way slowly to Wounded Knee Creek where they camped for the night. The soldiers surrounded the Indian camp so closely that no Indian could slip out and escape. The army set up a special, large tent with a stove in it for the ailing Big Foot, and Whiteside sent a doctor to treat him.

Forsyth

The next morning Col. James W. Forsyth arrived with more soldiers and took command of the military operation to disarm the Minicoujous. Altogether, he had about 500 soldiers, and the Minicoujous, men, women, and children, numbered about 350 to 400, with about 100 to 150 of them warriors. Since they so greatly outnumbered the Minicoujous, Forsyth did not think they would try any fighting, but he was taking no chances. On the hill overlooking Wounded Knee Valley, four Hotchkiss guns had been mounted. These were small, cannon-like guns which could rapidly shoot shells that weighed two pounds and ten ounces and which exploded on hitting. They could shoot effectively for a distance close to a mile. Most of the Indians knew that any kind of resistance was impossible, but they hadn't reckoned on some very die hard ghost shirt wearers who had their shirts on under their blankets and who still believed that the shirts would stop the bullets.

On the morning of December 29, 1890, after both sides had eaten breakfast, Colonel Forsyth sent Major Whiteside into the Indian camp to get down to the business of disarming the Minicoujous. The Eyapaha or camp crier, named Wounded Hand, was sent throughout the Indian camp to announce that all the men were to assemble in front of Big Foot's tent for a council. When the men had come together, it was explained to them that they must go get their guns and put them into a pile by Big Foot's tent. The soldiers remembered clearly all the gleaming rifles that they had seen the day before when they first met the Minicoujou warriors drawn up in battle formation in front of the rest of their band. Also, the testimony of many of the Indians after the massacre indicates that, though many carried very old guns that weren't much good, there were also many who had Winchester repeating rifles and carbines. Most rifles, especially the older models, came from the Army, in the first place. More than one skirmish or contest had been won by the Sioux who mostly out horsed the soldiers on their sturdier and better conditioned mounts. Soldiers on spent, winded mounts, soon lost their weapons. Sioux horses were not kept in confining stockades. They were used to being ridden and often. Even the children played their part in keeping the Sioux mounts superbly conditioned.

NOTE: The Winchester: In 1858, a Winchester Arms Company rifle mechanic, named Henry devised a new rifle with a 15 cartridge magazine. The gun was operated by moving the trigger lever down and back to its original position. This extracted the spent cartridge, carried a fresh shell from the spring-activated tubular magazine into the chamber, and cocked the hammer ready for firing.

The rifle sold well and in 1866 the Winchester Repeating Arms Company was established at New Haven, Connecticut. Soon afterwards an improved version of the 'Henry' rifle was produced. It was however the 1873 model that was the most successful Winchester. Over the next 40 years the company sold 720,610 of these rifles. That would be about 144 of these rifles per Teton warrior; and there are those idiots who expected the Sioux to keep on fighting and hence condemned Chief Red Cloud.

When the warriors were told to get their rifles and pile them up, they began talking among themselves as to what they should do. They finally decided to send two men in to talk to Big Foot and ask him what they should do about giving up their guns. Big Foot, after thinking a minute, instructed them to give up only their bad guns. These guns were used for hunting. Without them the people would have a hard time subsisting for there was still much game, mainly deer and antelope upon the plains. In the creeks and river breaks, mule deer and white tail were yet numerous. One of Forsyth's interpreters who had gone along with the two men understood what Big Foot had said and he advised them to give up the good guns too. "You can buy guns," the interpreter said, "but if you lose a man, you cannot replace him." Big Foot answered, "No, we will keep the good guns."

The two men went back and told the others what the chief had said. Instead of sending all the men at once back to their camp, Forsyth sent them back to get their guns in groups of twenty. The first twenty to come back brought back two broken and very old rifles and laid them down. In regard to the surrendered guns, an observer later said, "They were long used, no doubt, as toys are by children, but they formed no part of the splendid

Winchesters owned by the warriors." As each group of twenty came back, similar old rifles were put on the pile, and the soldiers could see that they were getting nowhere.

Forsyth had Big Foot carried out to tell the warriors to give up their good guns. This was a huge mistake on the part of Forsyth. Big Foot said that they had no more guns, as they had been seized by the soldiers when they were back at the Cheyenne River Agency. Forsyth then asked Big Foot where all those guns were that the soldiers saw the day before when they first met the Minicoujous by Porcupine Butte. Big Foot just repeated that the guns that his warriors surrendered were all the guns that they had.

Finally, Forsyth saw that the only thing he could do was to search the camp, as well as the men and women in it, most of who were covered with blankets under which it would be quite easy to conceal a rifle. It wasn't long before the good guns began to show up. Warriors who had not wanted to take any chances on losing their guns had left them with their women to hide. The women tried every trick they could think of. Some sat on the ground with their wide skirts spread out over the guns. One elderly grand-mother was lying on the ground apparently quite sick as she indicated by her moaning. Under her was found a Winchester repeater. Some guns were found inside wall pockets of the tipis, while others were found packed in the wagons for the trip to Pine Ridge. To avoid any accusations of indeli-cacies involving the Indian women, enlisted men were not permitted to go inside the tipis; only officers were allowed to do this.

Yellow Bird

It was during this tipi to tipi search, which took considerable time, which the first mistake was made on the Indian side. The one responsible for this mistake was the old medicine man, Yellow Bird. He was a firm believer in the Ghost Dance and the bullet stopping power of the ghost shirt. As both men and women grew restless during the search for guns, Yellow Bird began dancing around the warriors, singing and occasionally picking up a handful of dust and throwing it into the air in the direction of the soldiers. He kept yelling at the warriors, apparently urging them to do something. Yellow Bird kept this up during the long search for weapons, and the warriors grew increasingly more restless. Finally, one of the army interpreters told Col. Forsyth what Yellow Bird was trying to do and what he was saying to the warriors. "Don't be afraid," he kept telling them. "Let your hearts be strong to meet what is before you. "We all know that there are lots of soldiers around us and they have lots of bullets, but I have received assurance That Their Bullets Cannot Penetrate Us. The prairie is large and the bullets will not go toward you. The bullets will not penetrate you." Forsyth gave orders to an interpreter to tell Yellow Bird to sit down and keep quiet, and, after Yellow Bird had completed his latest circle around the warriors, he sat down and lapsed into silence.

In the meantime, the tipi to tipi search was coming to an end. The search had turned up 38 rifles, but most of them were old and not much good. Only a few of the rifles that had been found were Winchester repeaters. The rest of the rifles that the soldiers had clearly seen the day before on first meeting Big Foot's band remained to be found. Since the whole camp and all the women had been searched, there was only one place left where those repeating rifles could be, and that was under the blankets of the warriors themselves. Through an interpreter, Forsyth told the warriors that he did not want to conduct a personal search, but wanted each warrior to come forth like a man, remove his blanket, and put any concealed gun on the ground. About twenty of the older men said, "Hau," got up, and moved toward the Colonel. The younger warriors made no move to comply and Yellow Bird jumped up and began yelling at them again, whirling around and throwing dust into the air. After the older men had passed between the soldiers, removing their blankets and revealing no weapons, Major Whiteside and Lt. Varnum started passing the young men between them. From the very first three who went past, they found two rifles and a quantity of ammunition. At this, Yellow Bird became more excited, and Philip Wells, one of the interpreters, got Big Foot's brother-in-law to try to calm him down, but with no success.

Black Coyote

At this moment, one of the Minicoujous named Black Coyote, seeing that his rifle was going to be discovered, 'took it out from under his blanket and began to wave it around over his head.' Turning Hawk, one of the survivors, explained later that Black Coyote was a "crazy man, a young man of very bad influence and, in fact, a "nobody." Joseph Horn Cloud and Dewey Beard also explained later that he was also deaf. Black Coyote kept yelling that the rifle belonged to him, that he had paid much money for it, and that he wasn't going to give it up unless he was paid for it. Two soldiers approached and tried to take it away from him. In this struggle, the gun went off in the air. At this moment, Yellow Bird leaped to his feet, let out a fearful yell, and threw a handful of dirt into the air. Immediately, the camp was in an uproar as the soldiers instinctively returned fire. Bullets of the soldiers that missed Indians hit other soldiers, and bullets fired by Indians at the soldiers hit other Indians. Wild confusion followed with smoke and dust making it hard to see who was who. Big Foot was killed in one of the first volleys. In the beginning, the soldiers who had been surrounding the

Indians were afraid to fire because many of their own men were still mixed up with the Minicoujous. Captain Gapron, one of the officers commanding the Hotchkiss guns, noticed that one of the gunners was so nervous that he was afraid the man would fire out of sheer excitement. He ordered the friction primer removed from the gun so that it couldn't be fired at the troops. As the groups separated, though, the surrounding soldiers opened fire, and the Hotchkiss guns on the hill did enormous damage. In the smoke, dust and confusion, old men, women, and children were killed and wounded. Since many of the Indian men and women were wrapped in blankets, it was difficult to tell the men from the women in the confusion of the fight. When a warrior went down, the one nearest to him, man or woman, would seize his rifle and begin to fire back. The soldiers, seeing only the flash of the rifle and a blanket covered figure through the dust and smoke, fired back, and a number of women were killed in this manner. Dewey Beard, an Indian survivor, remembered later only the glint of brass buttons through the murk of the confused fighting.

Smoke and Dust

The fight with Minicoujous and the soldiers all mixed up together in the smoke and dust lasted about five minutes and, to this day, it is impossible to tell who killed whom. During this time, soldiers very likely killed as many soldiers as Indians killed Indians. After this first five minutes, the Indians broke for cover, joined by their women and children, and the soldiers, who had been in the camp, headed for their original positions outside the camp. Later on, an officer said that he admired the way in which the Indians handled their Winchesters. These apparently were the good guns that Big Foot told his people to save.

The cannons silenced the fire from the camp shortly after both sides ran for cover. Only a few Indians, who had taken refuge in the tipis and fighting from there, had remained. Yellow Bird was one of these, and he had sought shelter in one of the Sibley tents that had belonged to the scouts. From here, by slitting a hole in the canvas wall, he shot several soldiers before someone noticed where the fire was coming from. Cavalrymen riddled the tent with bullets and a Hotchkiss gun fired two shells directly into it. Later, Yellow Bird's charred body was found within the remains of the tent. The main and final action now moved down to the dry creek where most of the warriors had followed the women and children for shelter. A Hotchkiss gun was moved down from the hill to zero in on the gulch because "bullets were coming like hail from the Indians' Winchesters," as Corporal Paul Weinert was to recall later. "The wheels of my Hotchkiss gun were bored full of holes and our clothing was marked in several places. Once a cartridge (weighing two pounds) was knocked out of my hand just as I was about to put it in the gun, and it's a wonder it didn't explode. I kept going farther, and pretty soon everything was quiet at the other end of the line."

With the main fighting over, one by one, wounded people started coming out of the dry creek and, helped by the soldiers, made their way to the hospital area set up north of the cavalry camp. Phillip Wells was one of those who went down to the village to see how many wounded could be helped. About a dozen people were badly wounded, but still alive. One of the wounded survivors named Frog was being helped from the village area when he saw a burned Indian body lying within what had once been an army tent. Looking around for someone who could speak Indian, he saw Phillip Wells, one of the interpreters. He called Wells over and asked, "Who is the man lying burned there?" Wells told him that it was Yellow Bird. Later, Wells related that Frog raised himself up a little higher, raised his closed fist, pointing it in the direction of the dead Indian, shot out his fingers (which among the Indians is a deadly insult meaning I could kill you and not be satisfied doing it. I am sorry that I could do no more to you), and then used words trembling which I could not catch. But he said this, which I did hear, speaking as though to the dead man: "If I could be taken to you, I would stab you," and then turning to me he said, "He is our murderer; only for inciting our young men, we would have all been alive and happy."

The disarming of the Indians was the main mistake though in that type of situation. Later, an Army General, General Miles would have sense enough not to attempt the same as Forsyth in a related situation. They had always had their arms for hunting and to give up your hunting rifle, especially a coveted Winchester was a difficult thing to do especially for a hungry people who needed to contingently supply other rations from what game still remained. To give up your source for food procurement especially to one who constantly lied to you and whom you could not trust, yes, would be a difficult thing to do. Had Major Whiteside been in command, from his actions the day before; refusing to demand the Minicoujous guns, quite possibly he may have used wiser protocol on the fateful morning compared to Forsyth's mistake.

The fighting had lasted a little over an hour and when it was over, 146 Minicoujous were counted dead and were later buried. The dead included 84 men and boys, 44 women, and 18 children. These were not the total Indian dead and wounded, because many others were carried off by surviving Indian relatives and friends. It was, therefore, impossible to make a count of these. Fifty-one wounded Indians were taken to the Pine Ridge hospital and, of these, at least seven died later, mainly because, out of fear, they would not let the army doctors treat them. Thus, the total known Minicoujou dead numbered 153. Very few of Big Foot's people escaped death or at least injury. Among the non-Indians, there were twenty five dead and thirty nine wounded.

In asking the question, "What caused Wounded Knee?" one would like to be able to point his finger at one single thing and say "This caused it, or that caused it." In the case of Wounded Knee, this is impossible, because there were a number of things causing it, and each one of these things could not have caused it alone. Each one of the factors involved, leading up to the final tragedy, depended on one or several other factors.

All the Factors

Therefore, one cannot point to any one thing and say that it was the cause. To explain Wounded Knee fully, one has to point to all the factors involved and to note their connections.

Wounded Knee was brought about by:
a) Wovoka.
b) Kicking Bear's and Short Bull's invention of the Ghost Shirt protection.
c) **Forsyth's attempt to disarm** the Sioux of their weapons and hunting rifles. Why did the Army have to have the Indians hunting rifles? No soldier had been killed, at least in any significant numbers since the Custer battle, 14 long years earlier, wherein most every one will or should agree that Custer deserved his fate. Because Indians are doing a superstitious dance is the reason to disarm them? Even an Army General wisely would not carry through with this request under similar circumstances less than a month later.
d) Yellow Bird's obsessed, blind faith in Wovoka, Kicking Bird and Short Bull and the 'bullet proof' power of the Ghost shirts and hence stirring up the young braves.
e) Federal Indian Policy of not honoring their Treaties. This Policy of Greed culminated in the frustration of the people for the preceding 14 years which, in turn, goaded them to strike out at almost any provocation, plus Yellow Bird's inciting the warriors, plus the presence of the soldiers.
f) All these factors working together and influencing one another caused Wounded Knee, and one does not have a true picture of the tragedy unless he sees all these connections.

Wipe Out Potential

Very few people have noticed the fact that, right after Wounded Knee, there was such a gathering of Indian warriors that there very well could have been a wipeout similar to that of the Custer battle or, at least, a smashing retaliatory blow on the part of the Sioux. It happened as follows.

The firing of the guns at Wounded Knee could be heard at the Pine Ridge Agency. Many Indians, friendly and semi-hostile, were camped around the agency, and, at the sound of the guns, they took down their tipis, packed everything they had and left in a northerly direction. One outcome of the conflict was an almost immediate investigation of the battle scene by 150 Brule warriors; originally from Rosebud, they were followers of the aged and uncompromising Brule chief, Two Strike. As soon as they heard the distant gunfire from Wounded Knee, the Brules, painted for warfare, hastened toward the sound of battle ready for a fight. When they dejectedly returned to Pine Ridge, their news of the slaughter provoked many heretofore peaceful Lakotas to open fire on the unsuspecting buildings at the agency. General Brooke, however, refused to be panicked and denied his troopers permission to use their Hotchkiss gun against the restless Sioux, many of whom had gathered near Red Cloud's house.

In the midst of this chaos, Two Strike decided to take his Brule band and flee northward along White Clay Creek; a number of prominent Oglalas joined his hasty migration. Notwithstanding General Brooke's forbearance, this party, which was part of a great exodus involving four thousand Lakotas, rendezvoused with those two high priests of the Ghost Dance, Short Bull and Kicking Bear, who, after much soul searching, were returning to make peace. When that troubled duo heard what had happened at Wounded Knee, however, they and their followers united with Two Strike and his band to travel to an abandoned camp some seventeen miles downriver. There they were joined by many survivors of Wounded Knee, some of whom were wounded but all of whom were ominously bitter.

"Among the disenchanted Oglalas to join Two Strike willingly were Little Wound, No Water, and Big Road. Young-Man-Afraid-of-His- Horses, probably the most steadfast progressive among the Oglalas, was in Wyoming at the time on a hunting trip. But the most surprising new members of Two Strike's band were Red Cloud and his family. Two Strike, who apparently resented Red Cloud's peace efforts, decided to abduct the old chief against his will. As the once great Sioux warrior described this humiliating episode in a letter to Dr. Thomas Bland, "the Brules forced me to go with them. I being in danger of my life between two fires I had to go with them and follow my family. Some would shoot their guns around me and make me go faster.

"This episode was probably the lowest point in Red Cloud's life. The thought of the Oglalas' renowned chief being taunted in this fashion would have been impossible to envision a quarter of a century earlier, when Red Cloud forced the federal government to close the Powder River Road. Notwithstanding his mortification, there were still those who questioned his motivation, implying that he willingly conspired with his abductors. Ethnologist James Mooney from the Smithsonian Institution, whose history of the Ghost Dance period was the standard for many years, wrote historian Doane Robinson on February 20, 1904, that Red Cloud was probably not held against his will. How could such a respected leader, he asked, be denied freedom by his "own followers?" Of course the best rebuttal to this argument was that these kidnappers were not Red Cloud's "followers." Instead, they were exceptionally hard line Brules who had left Rosebud for Pine Ridge because most of the Ghost Dance activity was centered on the latter reservation."[1]

Strong Hold

By the next day, more than 4,000 people, including 800 to 1,000 warriors, were all gathered together about 15 miles north of Pine Ridge in an area known as the Strong Hold. There was much mourning, singing of death songs, and evidence of anger and hostility. The leaders went into council and they decided that no one should go back to the agency and they "should die together." This was death talk and death, to a Sioux, came honorably only by fighting. With a warrior force this size, they could have, with organization and leadership, either wiped out or driven the soldiers from the Pine Ridge Reservation. Without a stronger leadership, however, they were unable to get together and to return the tremendous blow that they might otherwise have mustered.

After awhile, the whole group went farther north and camped on the edge of the Bad Lands where they continued their dancing, mourning, and talking. They were so hostile, that not even friendly Oglalas could get near them. General Brooke tried sending scouts out to talk to them, but the scouts could not even get close to the camp. "The able commander (General Miles) knew the Sioux well enough to exploit the divisions among the camp's progressives and non-progressives. At the same time, he skillfully used his troops to surround the defiant adherents of the Ghost Dance. He addressed a letter to the still formidable holdouts, telling them that if they would make peace, there would be no trouble. Significantly, the captive holdout, Red Cloud, found his name at the top of the General's list of chiefs, which included Little Wound, Two Strike, Short Bull, Kicking Bear, Crow Dog, Big Road, and "all Indians away from their Agencies." Even though

Red Cloud was being ostracized by civilian authorities and was in disgrace, Miles sent him another note, acknowledging his abduction by Two Strike's band and assuring him that it was the Indian Police, not the army, who fired on his house before those embittered Ghost Dancers had left Pine Ridge. This latter reference was to a widely held belief that Red Cloud had left because his home was shelled. Apparently still feeling that the old chief's support was necessary to end the impasse, Miles promised to return any personal belongings taken from Red Cloud or to compensate him for any possessions irretrievably lost."[2]

"For two weeks the intense standoff persisted. Yet participants on both sides did exchange some surprising communications. For example, the obstinate Lakota holdouts, the majority of whom continued to intimidate the minority with threats of injury or death, insisted on a personal dialogue with Secretary of the Interior Noble and Commissioner of Indian Affairs Morgan. The strong willed Miles responded to these insurgents in yet another letter, telling them that they had to deal with him first. Red Cloud implored General Miles to remove the troops who were aggressively circling the large and desperate Sioux encampment. Miles refused, telling Red Cloud that men were only protecting the reservation and safeguarding welfare of those Sioux who had remained friendly. He did promise those still intransigent Sioux leaders that if they would come to terms promptly, he would arrange a conference with President Harrison as well as Secretary of the Interior Noble. As a result of these strong assurances, a meeting was held with Miles the next day, January 5, 1891, which involved such important Lakota leaders as He Dog, Big Road, Little Hawk, and Red Cloud's son. Jack.

"General Miles's optimism soon began to wane, however when he realized how divided his adversaries were. But the stalemate could not continue forever. On January 9 an important break occurred. Red Cloud, He Dog, White Hawk, and their families made a dramatic late night escape from the sleeping Sioux camp, where they had been virtually captives. According to one version of this episode, one of Red Clouds daughters courageously led her almost blind and helpless father through a severe blizzard in order to reach the agency. Red Cloud's explanation for the flight was fairly simple: "I tried my best for them to let me go back, but they would not let me go; and said if I went they would kill me."[3]

"Despite Red Cloud's disturbing loss of prestige, his surrender undoubtedly had an important effect on those Sioux who still resisted Miles and his forces. How strong could their cause be if such a prominent leader as Red Cloud felt compelled to seek the protection of the U.S. Army?

"The growing menace from Miles's troopers also threatened the resolve of such leaders as Big Strike, Short Bull, and Kicking Bear who had vowed to "die together" rather than surrender. But Miles was also able to undermine the confidence of these insurgents in two ways. He kept his promise to all those Lakotas who had surrendered earlier by giving them food and warm clothing and he had used his influence to remove the inept Agent Royer, temporarily replacing him with the popular army officer Captain F.E. Pierce. Indeed, a general housecleaning at all the Lakota reservations by the spoils oriented Harrison administration was one result of this Ghost Dance fiasco.

"When the defiant Sioux encampment finally surrendered on January 16, the once feared general mixed his characteristic sternness with a willingness to accommodate, an approach probably necessary to get the Lakota hardliners to capitulate. He insisted that Short Bull, Kicking Bear, and twenty of their more fanatical adherents be arrested and sent to Fort Sheridan, Illinois, until all the Ghost Dance troubles had subsided; interestingly enough, many of them were eventually sent to Europe as part of Buffalo Bill's Wild West show. Miles avoided Colonel Forsyth's tragic mistake; although he disarmed the zealous Ghost Dancers, **he did not thoroughly search them for guns**, even knowing that many had not complied with his order.

"General Miles also kept his promise to allow a Sioux delegation to visit Washington for a conference with the president and his secretary of the interior. The delegation, which actually did represent several shades of opinion, was headed by the reliable Young-Man-Afraid-of-His-Horses, who was joined by such ordinarily friendly Lakota Sioux as American Horse, High Hawk, Big Road, and He Dog. Yet chiefs like Little Wound and Two Strike, despite their strong identification with the Ghost Dance movement, were also represented.

"Significantly omitted from the delegation was Red Cloud; the old chief, who had been the voice of the Lakota Sioux for twenty-five years, had not been forgiven by Secretary Noble and the other civilian officials, for refusing to sign off on the treaty breaking taking of the Black Hills, despite the deference shown him by some high ranking members of the military. Red Cloud was obviously disheartened, rationalizing his omission on the basis of his failing eyesight: "Owing to the condition of my eyes, I was unable to accompany them." Yet he begged the moralistic and self-satisfied commissioner of Indian affairs, Thomas J. Morgan to permit him to come to Washington when his eyes were better so he could give his side of what had actually transpired at Pine Ridge.

But Commissioner Morgan, who was socially and geographically from the same eastern establishment that had welcomed Red Cloud to Washington in 1870, apparently felt that the old chief was no longer useful. Morgan's cynical rejection was recorded on Red Cloud's January 26 request for a visit to Washington. It was a simple one-word response: "File." This terse dismissal of a once indispensable leader prompted historian James C. Olson to remark that while the careers of Crazy Horse, Sitting Bull, and Spotted Tail ended in violence, if not martyrdom: Red Cloud's was lost in a government file. The end of the bloody Ghost Dance troubles had truly marked the end of Red Cloud's great career as far as the U.S. government was concerned."[4]

Sun Set

"Consequently, although Red Cloud did not seek martyrdom through hopeless military resistance, he did use his abilities as a negotiator to oppose every federal policy that he regarded as being against his people's best interest. His ability to stall, deviate from the subject, and filibuster often made him appear as an obstructionist to government negotiators, but it was through these tactics that he gained as much time for his people as possible."[5]

One is constantly reminded that Red Cloud, did not join Crazy Horse and Sitting Bull in resisting the federal government during the Great Sioux War. Red Cloud maintained always that he had given his word; this unfortunate duty to maintain the Treaty, regardless of penalizing honor; added to his loss of esteem. His numerous trips to Washington made him realize the futility of warring against an opponent with a population of 36 million, while there were probably fewer than 25,000 Lakota Sioux on the Northern Plains. In 1880, the population was close to 50 million. That is a 2,000 to one edge. Did Sandoz and the other lamenting writers expect the Sioux to carry on against such suicidal odds? Chief Red Cloud extended to Crazy Horse several invitations to go with him to Washington. No doubt, he believed the trip would have been a convincing eye opener.

Jealousy

Red Cloud has been accused of often being jealous of his major rivals, especially, Sitting Bull, Crazy Horse and Spotted Tail, all of whom died not too long after the Battle of the Little Big Horn. But to be honest, jealousy is almost a custom among the tribes that I have experienced. Maybe that is why the Great Spirit allowed the wahshichu (white man) to come over here in the first place. Maybe they were rewarded for being less jealous! The Ultimate no doubt got tired of our constant jealousies, despite the great Eden' we had all to our selves. Maybe the Great Provider just got sick and tired' so to speak of our not fully appreciating our great fortune! The rivalries among the Oglalas would continue long after Red Cloud's and Crazy Horse's demise. Red Cloud's feud with the progressive-minded Young-Man-Afraid-of-His-Horses divided many Oglalas at Pine Ridge during the 1880s until the departure of Agent McGillycuddy brought about their reconciliation. The long lived rivalry between the people of Bull Bear and Old Smoke's Bad Faces lasted for decades even into reservation days. This would be a minor blemish in my mind however compared to all that the chief stood for. Maybe Crazy Horse and Sitting Bull had a few jealousies as well. There certainly existed a jealousy and animosity between Chief Spotted Tail of the Sichangus and Crow Dog which led to the death of one of them.

Oklahoma Territory

During the federal government's drive to acquire the Black Hills in 1875, Red Cloud stalled the Black Hills cession until it was forced upon the Lakotas as a result of their defeat in the Great Sioux War, mainly between 1869 and 1877. When that conflict ended, he effectively opposed Washington's plan to remove the Sioux to the banks of the Missouri and President Grant's specific intention to remove the Sioux to Indian Territory in present-day Oklahoma. Red Cloud, on his own volition, ended his people's migration to the Missouri about eighty miles short of their proposed reservation there and successfully lobbied against Grant's dead set intentions. I shudder to think that at one time, my people could have been sent to Oklahoma and I shudder again when I think that our Way could have died there as it has within so many Oklahoma tribes who are under the sway of the wahshichu evangelism. Their choice, however; this country's Democracy must be so honored. Much Thanks to those friends of Red Cloud in the East who could moderate issues considered crucial for the Sioux. When I enter the Spirit World, I shall make it a point to honor them.

Preserving the Culture

Red Cloud struggled with Agent McGillycuddy during the 1880's to preserve such Sioux customs and traditions as the Sun Dance. In 1882, when he was 60 years, a bit old to take part in the demanding event which was mostly pledged by the much younger men, Red Cloud took part. His stubborn resolve to continue the tribe's all-important legacy is now echoed by the present resurgence of modern Siouxs back to their traditional religion. With a Pilamiya (Thank you) to the old chief, again it is the Teton Oglalas who lead this resurgence. Another 'Pilamiya' to the Religious

Freedom Act 1978 and thanks to the initial endeavors of Dr. Martin Luther King who made America come to their senses regarding Human Rights. Numerous Sun Dances are now held all over the Dakota reservations and most are on the Oglala reservation, followed closely by their ever present allies the Sichangu (Brules). The positive results of these Sun Dances changes the participants lives forever; yes, — positively forever! Nothing that the white man has to offer can be as positively powerful as the Sun Dance especially for the younger Indians. Young men take four year vows to not imbibe in alcohol or drugs during their four year sojourn under the guidance and counsel of Sioux medicine people. Most continue on with their abstinence. Not just a few embark upon this spiritual voyage but literally hundreds and in the recent years, thousands have pledged their lives due to the tremendous growth of the spiritual thanksgiving and ultimate expression of Sioux gratitude to Wakan Tanka. The Track Record of the participants as compared to non-participants speaks for itself. The white man's religion was not wholly embraced by his (Red Cloud's) championing of the Sun Dance, therefore, unbeknown to him, he would risk the ire of many writers who would readily condemn any other religion but their own. Was this a major reason why Mari Sandoz had such animosity for a truly great chief?

Mari Sandoz

Robert Larson, a modern historian has this insight to offer. "Crazy Horse's biographer, Mari Sandoz, was as much responsible for Red Cloud's bad image as Crazy Horse's chief nemesis as anyone else; she tended to contrast every heroic trait of Crazy Horse with an ignoble one for Red Cloud."[6]

My opinion of Sandoz is that she verifies an old Sioux statement, "Watch out when they admit something good about you for they will turn and look for something bad." With that, it is often added, "It is hard for them to hold us in much high regard, and if so, it won't be for long." We are often, yes, very often immediately asked, 'Why are you so angry?' If we ever criticize or innocently question the wahshichus religion regardless of what they say about ours. Dominant Society will think or claim that we are just feeling sorry for ourselves. As I have said all along. We Sioux, base our lives on what we observe but that also may include what we hear, especially repeatedly. We are simply stating our experiences and what we have heard about ourselves innumerable times.

Legacy

Red Cloud was one of the most talented and one of the most tenacious of all the old Indian leaders. He was not a magician or a Messiah. Is anyone? Was he supposed to come up with some miraculous strategy that would pit 25,000 Sioux victoriously over 36 million Americans, mostly in the East? As I mentioned, soon these odds in one decade would rise 2,000 to 1. By 1890, they would increase to 2,500 to 1. Is this what he was to perform to be finally acclaimed by nattering, nit-picking white writers as a truly great leader? Five years after Chief Red Cloud died, the Winchester Rifle Company would produce its 720,000th Model '73' repeating rifle. Giving the Tetons a generous 35,000 people for that time, we would now have almost 21 repeating rifles per Teton, mostly women and children and not combat warriors. If the Tetons could field 5,000 able warriors, it would be almost 145 Winchester rifles per warrior. And that is what the romanticist Red Cloud criticizers would have loved for us to set out against? He was clearly, a man, forced by circumstances to fight a rear guard action, and who did contest every federal policy to alter the Treaty of Fort Laramie and for which his warriors had laid down their arms. At a Washington church reception in 1889, Chief Red Cloud had this to say. "When I fought the whites, I fought with all my might. When I made a treaty of peace in 1869 — I meant it, and risked my life in keeping my covenant."

No one collected more arms, ammunition and horses than did his warriors under his command. This weaponry and battle strategy helped the collection of more weaponry and ammunition from the Army. His horses began the increase of the horse herds found at the Little Big Horn. His role in the Fetterman and Wagon Box fights should never be forgotten, nor should his reputation as the most feared Oglala warrior before Crazy Horse. He was a man of honor. He kept his word and shrewdly, by so doing did not give an inch toward the government's treachery and greed as portrayed by those in Washington who specifically wanted the Black Hills gold and the Bozeman Trail for more gold. They now have it and the Homestake mine in the Black Hills has finally played out. It was once the largest in North America. It is the one resource; our country surely will not miss!

His Track Record, starting out as a renowned warrior and the one needed Chief to bring solidarity in a difficult, intense time and then down through a thankless political life is pure, admirable fact. Both lives made him a great warrior and a rear guard fighting statesman despite being initially out numbered 1440 to 1.

He was not 'bought off' either with materialism, as we see so many of the leaders of mostly third world nations today, especially those who have resources that our country covets and desperately needs. This land was once so abundant in Natural Resources that news reels would proclaim it as the 'Land of Unlimited Resources!' During my high school years I was preached that. But over-exploitation of the land, materialism gone wild, unlimited immigration, and mainly not learning or respecting the values of the American Indian, as those we have just finished studying; their life upon the Great Plains; their respectful frugality and using only what they needed to live; this gross denial will become a once great nation's undoing unless we realize and change our overly consuming ways. The most important move the White man can make in this time of Environmental Warning is to start learning from the Red man- but he won't do it until it will become disastrously too late! It is up to you dear reader to start teaching him now, what you have managed to learn so far. It will be a worthy goal for the sake of your own progeny. Mother Earth will teach in time to come, and the whole world will wake up but it will be a harsh teaching.

Education

Wounded Knee was the last so-called 'armed' conflict between the Sioux, as a group, and the government. The Sioux learned that resistance was useless and they turned their faces fearfully toward the future and that new, strange way of making a living which so puzzled them. They saw that, in order to live in that uncertain future, they would have to make their living in the same way that these non-Indians made their living. They had been overcome by sheer force of numbers and they saw that there was no shame in that. They had gone down fighting. Now, in order to cope with that new way of making a living, they saw, as Red Cloud had come to understand; they would need the "wahshichu woonspe" the white man's learning. The first generation found this very hard, but each generation has found it a little easier.

The knowledge his people had used to make their living (hunting the buffalo) would no longer be needed. His people would have to have new knowledge for this new way of making a living and, for this reason, Red Cloud asked for teachers for his people. The Boarding Schools, however, in which Indian youth were separated from their parents for nine months out of the year, failed miserably for quite some time to offer an adequate education. It was only when Indian parents were allowed to have their own school boards and school buses converted the boarding schools into day schools was progress achieved. It was natural for the youth to be at home at night with their parents. White folks practice it all the time! Educational results made a dramatic upswing and now many students go on to college.

POST RED CLOUD AND CRAZY HORSE

Science vs Spirituality

From an educational perspective, the Sioux are deeply spiritual but unlike many white people who are deeply religious or what some say 'over-zealously,' the Sioux are not adverse to Science. Fortunately, most of Dominant Society still has a high respect for Science. To an Indian, Science is simply — Direct Observation. There is nothing wrong with studying what the Great Mystery creates. If it works, then Creator obviously has designed it for a use or many uses, otherwise it would not have these capabilities is our reasoning. Something not observable in some form or way, like a scientific instrument that helps us to so-called 'see' or understand, is however OK with us. An x-ray can 'see' our bones and helps fix them. Radar can see other ships through blinding fog. Obviously, the Benevolent Creator wants us to have such an entity to help us is our line of reasoning. Something that the white man has dreamt' up, however just to scare us, and then to control us is not OK with us especially if there exists no scientific proof. We do not have to believe such a thing exists. But yet we are liberal, in this regard. The white man can keep this belief because he seems to be quite comfortable with it. Maybe he likes to be afraid of these things. Maybe he wants to be a follower and does not want to admit that a Creator did make all life that surrounds us and therefore we can learn from it directly. Maybe for some, his mind is no longer a rational God given mind that is just not capable of understanding the depth of what we are saying. His choice, not ours. Maybe generations of materialistic thinking just closes up the mind like an alcoholic loses his reasoning in his constant quest for the stimulant. Often there is a big difference in being an Indian!

It appears that some of us — Indians...are now studying the wahshichu. Why not, for centuries he has been studying us!

Military's Role

Too many historians are not conducive to recognizing the American military as a soul enhancing occupation but in all practicality, which modern academics cannot understand, even the Indian academics, is that the Sioux did find plenty of opportunity to become warriors in the American military. Most Academics avoid the military and bitterly criticize our American Soldiers, Sailors and Marines on many occasions. This has been my observation but in all truth, the entering into the service has changed many an Oglala's life and usually for the better. The majority enter either the Marine Corps or the Army's more elite organizations such as paratroopers, Rangers or Airborne units. The tribal military flag bearing units of former veterans for pow wows and memorial services will prove this point. World War II saw an almost 100% enlistment from Sioux reservations. These men were years often, sharing foxholes, ship berths or troopship space with G.I.'s from all over the 48 states at that time. Many never returned. Some earned Medals of Honor. Most would 'take the point' more so than others. The warrior spirit has always been there and unfortunately, our country had plenty of wars wherein they needed capable warriors. It was good and bad so to speak but Indians were never allowed to make military or national political policy, so despite having the highest ratio of any nationality or ethnic group,* they cannot be held responsible for starting or entering the wars. The wars have gone on and Sioux men still enlist readily. It is just the way it is and many of these men stay in the service for a full retirement. Reservations are barren of jobs and it is a means to live for many. It is also a means to get G.I. Bills for education. I used two G.I. Bills, one from Korean service for under graduate and the Vietnam G.I. Bill I used for Law School. Indian parents can hardly afford to send their children on to college. * *Senator Inouye Study.*

Honoring Warriors

Many white Vietnam veterans were insulted when they returned home. Our returning Sioux warriors came back to the reservations where they were highly honored, however. When I returned I was given an eagle feather by my tribal chairman, Enos Poor Bear, a relative and had to speak before many tribal members at our Sioux Sun Dance. I even had to fly a flag 'over the enemy' as the tribal stationery so read when they sent the flag to my squadron. Like the Marine Corps, the Sioux deeply honor their warriors and always go back after their dead. Or at least make every reasonable effort to do so. I personally object to the way many academics portray our military men and women. There is great honor, in my opinion, when you fight against those who would take away God given freedoms. Why is freedom, 'God given?' Simple. Our animal brothers and sisters, the Wamaskaskan — all are born with God's, Creator's inherent Freedom. It is contrary to Creator's ultimate plan to take away or deny basic freedom, our opinion and based on what we observe! Red Cloud and Crazy Horse fought against the U S Army for their own freedom especially after continual false promises were made and broken. I fought in the Marines against Communism. Where is Communism now? Whatever, thousands of Sioux have served in the military and thousands have seen repeated combat in the units they volunteered for. It is an undeniable fact. See Honoring at the Wall for an elaboration on honoring of warriors.[7] Highly recommended for Vietnam veterans.

* * * *

9

Spirit Ceremony

I was reluctant to include this chapter but then I considered that it would be, in an Indian sense of the word, a lie, if I did not include it. To withhold knowledge is not a good thing to do according to some of the traditional values regardless if a bit of bravery or courage is required. What is knowledge? Well, for one example, I believe knowledge can come from what one experiences. If it happened, then, why wouldn't some knowledge come from what one observed. Millions of books have been written on observations or what one 'thought' had happened. If what you are about to read is too much for you to comprehend from an Indian point of view then by all means simply state that it is all preposterous and could not have happened and we can both go on our way. I certainly am not going to insist that you can perceive and understand from my point of view. Maybe we come from just too extreme of differences in our backgrounds. I abhor arguments and do appreciate that you have come this far in this presentation. We can simply let it go at that and at least, by now, you do know much more about our Indian past and values. Together we can still go on and defend this great country we are so fortunate to live in. I will not ridicule you and hopefully you will not ridicule me.

For the benefit of those readers who could or would appreciate its added value, I will go ahead and include it and also to relieve the nagging question I offered at the beginning of the book. 'For what other reason would the Sioux, up and leave what appeared to be a lush paradise (Carolinas)?' Once mentioned, I would consider it a disservice to my loyal readers who have cultivated a more progressive understanding had I cowardly omitted what to me is related knowledge.

I primarily offer it in an attempt to help those to understand more fully, the mind of the two leaders we have studied who were, no doubt, familiar with such a ceremony and who no doubt held it in great respect. The reader always has the option to state quite simply — 'Pure Poppycock!' and go on with...hopefully, at least some form of new knowledge stemming from the rest of the previous pages. By all means, feel free to do so.

It, no doubt, will be considered an impossible ceremony, by many especially by the over zealous and narrow minded and even harvest a few accusations. Such is the mind set of modern society, that I can hardly object to such reaction. All that I can offer for verification is that many such ceremonies are held and have been held down through time at least by members of my tribe and other tribes of related ceremony. I cannot change history to satisfy what seems to be a growing multitude.

Dr. Wm. K. Powers, a noted anthropologist has even written several books on the subject. I am not into convincing anyone, however, but I **do not** shy away from actual observation and real life experience. Doubters and skeptics are free to look me up in the Spirit World. By now, I think that most readers will be convinced that I actually think one exists. Again, I **do not** insist that you necessarily have to believe as I do. Like the 'Lone Cloud' which mysteriously came over our Sun Dance, this happening was another of my mystery projecting experiences and was certainly observed with a host of other interested people. The participants in this particular situation, the following, were all University related and some sporting some rather high degrees academically along with accomplished Track Records from an academic point of view. Dr. Bryde still lives and he will certainly verify as to this happening as will Lula Red Cloud, the great, great granddaughter of Chief Red Cloud. Without further distraction let us continue.

University of South Dakota

At the request of the University Administration, Chief Eagle Feather came to the University of South Dakota to conduct a revealing Yuwipi ceremony.

At this ceremony, in the late 1960's, many so-called "credible" people from the white man's view attended, as previously mentioned. These were university professors with graduate degrees. (Therefore, I guess, a detractor would almost have to assume that they were maybe more "credible" than most ordinary folks.) This ceremony was for the benefit of non-Indian people and was held at the University of South Dakota to find five students and their pilot/professor who crashed somewhere in the cold, remote, snow-covered region called the Nebraska Sand Hills. They were returning from Denver to Sioux Falls, South Dakota, and encountered a blizzard. The pilot developed vertigo and it was presumed the plane had crashed on the windswept Nebraska Sand Hills and was covered by snow. An all-out search began — even the Nebraska National Guard was used — but after a while it was too expensive and futile to continue. The search was called off. At that point the University of South

Dakota Indian Studies program, where I worked, had connections with Sioux holy men and none other than the President of the school called upon them for help. At the ceremony, I sat next to his beautiful blonde wife, Connie Bowen.

Bill Eagle Feather asked for a map. He specified that he wanted "the airplane kind of map (WAC chart) and not the ordinary road map." A line was drawn from Denver to Sioux Falls, the plane's intended destination and Eagle Feather proceeded to study it before the scheduled evening's ceremony in the basement of the school's museum.

The ceremony began with Eagle Feather's peace pipe being offered to the Ultimate Powers under one Benevolent and All Providing Creator. Lula Red Cloud, a university student held the pipe after the opening. Chief Eagle Feather was bound and covered with a lightly wrapped blanket. We then lowered the huge man face first to the rug provided for some comfort over the hard floor. After the tobacco offerings were spread out and the lights turned off, the ceremony began.

The singer boomed out the calling song, and after a few minutes the Spirit People entered, flourishing in the form of blue-green lights. The calling song to the spirits finished. A brief discussion seemed to occur between Eagle Feather's muffled voice and some other entity. A song was called for and once it began, the electrical-appearing lights seemed to exit through the wall. Eagle Feather called for the song of Chief Gall of the Hunkpapas. The singer sang out, and at the conclusion Grey Weasel, Eagle Feather's spirit helper, came forth.

A purring sound filled the room. The patter of small feet was accompanied by the excited chattering of a weasel. Eagle Feather began to talk in Sioux to the animal, and the visitor chattered and purred as the holy man spoke. They continued to converse for a period until finally the animal no longer chattered but purred slowly.

Then Eagle Feather called for the same song. A woman sang. When her song finished, a loud crack came from the center of the floor and something slid toward the keeper of the pipe. I felt it impact into my feet with a sharp jab. I actually leaped sideways and into the lap of Connie Bowen. Sheepishly, I remarked that something had hit me.

Predictions

Once the song ended, Eagle Feather called out: "Ho, Grey Weasel has made seven predictions:

1. The airplane crashed in a storm not far from a town that has two creeks with almost the same name. We should send an airplane out to look for it. A man and woman will fly that airplane.
2. The animals will point to where we should go.
3. If we fly where the animals point and head past the town with two creeks, we will fly over the plane, but it is pretty well covered with snow.
4. The plane sent out will have to land but everyone will walk away from it. Do not worry, the pilots will be smiling as they look back.
5. In the next day or two some people who are not looking for the plane will be led to it by an animal.
6. Only five will be found. One of the six will be missing. She landed away from the others, but she will not be too far away.
7. Her face will be upon an ice colored rock. She has a Chinese (pageboy) hairdo and wore big glasses.

"Those are the seven predictions. Now also, a rock that looks like ice has entered the room. It will have these signs I spoke of. Ho, Nephew (meaning me). Reach out in front of you and pick up the rock. Hold it until the final song. You are of the rock clan, and you should welcome your rock brother, not be afraid of it." Somewhat skeptical, or else still in a degree of remaining fear from the encounter, I readily handed the rock to Connie, who asked for it.

Before the final song and the lights turned on, Eagle Feather said "the two who fly like the winged ones," meaning my companion and I (both pilots) would hopefully find the crashed plane by flying and using the stone as a map. As it turned out, we followed the deer which seemed to be foretold on the stone because deer images were inscribed on it. We passed over the small town of Arnold, Nebraska. We figured out that the cloudy, unclear sign on the stone represented fog, as we were starting to notice the clouds getting lower to the ground. So, we had to reverse course and land back where we started from.

But the next day, close to where we had reversed the plane's course, two coyote hunters followed the tracks of a coyote. The animal's tracks led them to the wreckage of the Cherokee Six airplane. The tail of the doomed plane was exposed due to the rising temperature from the fog. They reported the position and soon rescue vehicles converged on the scene. All of Eagle Feather's (actually Grey Weasel's) predictions proved true.

Summary

Well, there you have a ceremony that the preachers, popes, cardinals, and mullahs can never do. While other religions have their own ceremonies, there are a hundred clues as to the beyond in a powerful ceremony. Nature's Path is truly the world's most powerful religion if prediction and spiritual communication is the standard. It is also the result of the sheer truth and dedication of the intercessor and, of course, the sincerity of the audience that allows or makes a pleasing atmosphere for the spirits to come in or want to come in. Various tribes had this ceremony as well but called it different names. I imagine the preparation and sincerity of the old Celtic bards produced similar ceremony. It is all an allowance of the Ultimate power, however; our point of view.

Without harmony and undiluted truth, however, nothing will happen. It is nice to believe that the Spirit World will truly be a truthful and sincere place where earthly lies and manipulation will not in the slightest be allowed or condoned. Nothing but pure truth will be the total mental (or thought-wise) atmosphere. Again, our observation of God's Nature readily displays, God's (Creator's) Nature is always truthful. Should not Creator's Spirit World be like wise? Makes one wonder why we long to stay here!

"Life is but a mere shadow on the wall compared to the complete reality that lies beyond."[1] I reflect upon Plato's meaning in his "Allegory of the Cave." What we experience here, observe here, can and no doubt will be reflected to a related degree in the Beyond.

It is obvious that the spirit is able to go back into time and discern what took place. The girl who was thrown out of the plane had her seat belt come unsnapped no doubt by flying debris from a high G force, spinning airplane. Extreme centrifugal force ejected her through the plane casting her out away from the others. This prediction would be impossible to conjure. The spirit guide obviously has the ability to revisit this happening back in time to be able to report specifically as to the findings. "One of the six will be missing. She landed out away from the others." I find that statement impossible to conjure unless one had 'non-earthly' help.

Carolina Influence

This ceremony, in my mind, could quite possibly have influenced the Carolina Dakota as to what danger was about to cross over the Atlantic. It is my mere supposition. Both of our main subjects in this writing quite possibly knew of this ceremony and may possibly have depended upon it to some degree, who knows? I find that it has certainly influenced my journey.

What about the alleged power or manipulation of the white man's 'Devil' or 'Satan?' Well, first, the Traditional Sioux do not believe in such things. They (Man conceived Devils, Satans, Spooky Goblins, Incubi, Werewolves etc.) do seem fairly preposterous. (Malleus Maleficarum-Pope Innocent VIII, declares it heresy to deny the existence of Werewolves.) Recently Pope John Paul II sanctioned classes on the clergy to perfect their means to exorcise this white man's devil. It was all on the internet news showing many young priests attending classes on the subject. For them, Satan abounds and must be dealt with. Traditional respecting Sioux reasoning is that a Benevolent Creator has no need to allow such things nor would they (Spooky Devils included) be in the 'so-called mind' of such a powerful Force. **Where in God-given Nature is there such evidence?** We Sioux have never seen or observed such things and do not expect to. If you have such an entity, why is it **we** can never observe it?

So far I have kept Sioux Contraries out of this work which is difficult to do for a Sioux writer. My last work, *Nature's Way,* has its set of Contraries who actually proved quite valuable, my opinion. We call them Iktomis or some relate to them as Heyokahs. These are our own little mythological creations spawned somewhere back in our history but we readily admit they are just that: **Mythology**, pure and simple. Our Iktomis and Heyokahs are simply mischief makers, tricksters and are material for humorous antics and stories which entertained many a long winter night. I could inject, in Sioux humor, which one of my contraries (self-created of course) is clamoring that this Satan guy is prejudiced, since that he obviously prefers to spook white folks only and ignores us. "We'll have to turn him over to that Civil Rights board," would be typical Iktomi advice since Contraries are always loaded with questionable/humorous 'knowledge.' Well, so much for Contraries which I remain bound and determined to keep out of this work.

Odd, that so many non-Indian readers will sincerely believe that the above innocent beseechment, the Yuwipi, intended to bring closure for the bereaved families, which was a direct observation, and even generously intended to help their own kind, will be considered preposterous and thus will have to invoke some sort of 'Evil' to it! Not long ago we would have all been drawn and quartered or burned at a stake for simply wanting to find the six victims. Thankfully, we now have the protection of the clause: Separation of Church and State.

By now we are drawing close to the end of this work and I have to add that Mari Sandoz probably more than any writer spewed much academic racism in her works — my opinion. She had absolutely no reason to project the constant negativism against a proven warrior — Red Cloud and did great damage to the real depth of the Teton Sioux. I look forward to meeting her in the Spirit World as I am sure Chief Red Cloud will also. We both can listen to what she has to say. It will happen regardless of what we say down here. I have initially included my view on Ted Turner's Red Cloud/Crazy Horse documentary. I appreciate that you have taken the time to look at another side contrary to Ted Turner's.

Lastly, I must lament, that it is very difficult to be an Indian writer, especially one of Sioux lineage and of course, writing from experience and access to the old timers. How I have wished over and over that I would have continued on with my Marine career and did another combat tour. I was discharged a Major in the Marine Reserves but had I stayed in and gone back, and probably a third time, which I probably would have, I am quite sure I could have gained a few more ranks, besides of course, the added adventure. Check my record book. I had some very positive fitness reports. What a more comfortable life I would have had providing I would have survived Vietnam. It was not just the security but the expanded comradeship of the warriors whom I am fortunate to still have contact with despite having only one combat tour, albeit it was fairly heavy with combat. But life was not to be so. I am in great debt to Doctor John Bryde for my 'reach-back,' and so many others that I met and have known by 'getting out.' Knowing Chief Fools Crow, Bill Eagle Feather and Ben Black Elk in such close rapport and the mission we had before us was an avenue that many would have chosen over another combat tour or two, I know. I have to also add in, Jack Weatherford, Hilda Neihardt and John Bryde as great influencers on a personal level, as well. As I recall someone saying what Stephen Ambrose had to say once he found he was fatally ill, "The good part is that you don't give a damn about what the critics have to say about how you write anymore!" So far I do not know if I am fatally ill or not but I am getting older. I echo his words.

* * * *

10

The Mountain

Although he became most famous as a mountain carver, Korczak Ziolkowski was a noted studio sculptor and member of the National Sculpture Society before he came west. Crazy Horse represents only the second half of his life, and he said it was the collective experience of the difficult first half of his life which prepared him for Crazy Horse and which enabled him to prevail over the decades of financial hardship and racial prejudice he encountered trying to create an Indian memorial in the Black Hills.

I never met Korczak, although almost every one in the Black Hills knew of him and about the mountain he proposed to carve. 'Kore Jock Jewel Cuff Ski' was a big bear of a man. My sisters, Eldean and LaVerne met him and Eldean (Chick) supported his project at a meeting with some Indians present. I guess she lit into some who were playing that old Academic game, questioning this and questioning that. "The white man has his mountain. Why shouldn't the Indian have theirs?" was her reasoning. Besides an older Indian had specifically asked Korzcak and he was a relative of Crazy Horse. Overly questioning Academics can't get around that one. She always hated the name Eldean and went by 'Chick.' She was a very forceful and dominant woman as many Sioux women are. Once I saw her knock some wise guy clear down the stairs at the VFW club. It was a long steep flight of stairs too and he wound up just laying there sort of dazed. LaVerne is my crippled sister who was there also. She grabbed LaVerne's crutch and really whacked him. She was an attractive woman as was LaVerne, but Chick was also quite strong and could hit hard, especially swinging a crutch. Few people ever insulted her the second time. That is a very stupid myth that Indian women are always cowering piteously behind their men, at least not Sioux women. Maybe when the tribe was on the move, a man was out in front with a ready bow in case game would be scared up. But to think that Sioux women are reticent, weak wall flower, walk-behind types is like ignorantly reaching in and grabbing a hold of a healthy and angry wolverine or a mountain lion. If you ever marry one, you'll soon find out. My mother was very dominant as well. My father never said much and my mother did all the disciplining which you quickly learned how to avoid. Such crazy ideas so many white people have about us keeps we few Indian authors extra busy. Often their conceptions are the exact opposite of the real truth.

'Chicky' or 'Sister Chick' as I always called her and got away with it, said that she was either the first or one of the first Indian women on the mountain. I want to be accurate with that statement as I cannot exactly recall but it was one or the other. After the meeting, Korczak thanked her and in appreciation, took her up to the top of the mountain. Detractors and naysayers are often present when you have a good idea, and in my experience, most simply want to mouth off negatively to get some sort of attention for themselves, since most of these types would never conceive of an original idea. His project was going to be even larger than the famous Mt. Rushmore which we all thought as children was the main reason why any tourist would come all the way out to the western end of South Dakota. My mother cleaned house for a very wealthy lady whose businessman husband had a lot to do with Mt. Rushmore. He even had a picture of himself in their living room that depicted him standing next to the President of the United States. President Eisenhower, as I remember. He also had his picture with a famous South Dakota Senator and one with Congressman Ben Riefel, who was a Sioux Indian. They were all shaking hands type pictures and looking at the camera. At the time, I thought that this Mr. Boland must be a very powerful man with pictures like that. He even had a life size carved bust of himself in their spacious living room. Now, that, proved he was a powerful man, my impressionistic young mind told me at the time. Both he and his wife, who I remember as very pretty, were good to my mother. They had an older son named John, Jr. and I received his younger clothes which were often fairly fancy. I dressed pretty well for school, thanks to this older-than-me only child. He never seemed to wear his clothes out much like mine were before my Mom started cleaning houses. He even had his name, printed on a little cloth tag, stitched on the inside of his pants as I think he was always away to some fancy school. I never saw him until he was much older and in fact was with my sister Chick. Well enough digressing. Korczak's carving was going to have Chief Crazy Horse's face alone, larger than the four faces on Mt. Rushmore. As a young Indian, I remember thinking proudly when someone told me that. I didn't know that the head alone was going to be 90 feet high. His arm was going to be 263 feet long. That is close to the length of a football field if you need a comparison. The horse's head will be 219 feet high.

Early Korczak

Born in Boston of Polish descent, Korczak was orphaned at age one and grew up in a series of foster homes. As a boy he was badly mistreated, but he learned to work very hard. He also gained heavy construction and other skills helping his tough foster father. On his own at 16, he took odd jobs to put himself through Rindge Technical School in Cambridge, after which he became an apprentice patternmaker in the shipyards on the rough Boston waterfront.

He experimented with woodworking, making beautiful furniture. At age 18, he made a grandfather's clock hand-crafted from 55 pieces of Santa Domingo mahogany. Although he never took a lesson in art or sculpture, he studied the masters and began creating plaster and clay studies. In 1932, he used a coal chisel to carve his first portrait, a marble tribute to Judge Frederick Pickering Cabot, the famous Boston juvenile judge who had befriended and encouraged the gifted boy and introduced him to the world of fine arts. Judge Cabot was an exceptionally kind and caring man. His personal interest in the boy had young Korczak attending the Boston Symphony and other cultural activities. He met people in the arts, music, sculpture and literature. As an orphan growing up, he never had these opportunities; this cultivating stimulation to develop and hone his inborn gifts. Judge Cabot, indeed, had a profound influence on the young and impressive Korczak.

Moving to West Hartford, Conn. Korczak launched a successful studio career doing commissioned sculpture throughout New England, Boston and New York. His Carrara marble portrait, PADEREWSKI, Study of an Immortal, won first prize by popular vote at the 1939 New York World's Fair.

Gutzon Borglum

A childhood dream came true when he was asked to assist Gutzon Borglum at Mt. Rushmore. The two sculptors became close friends during the summer of 1939, when Korczak was Mr. Borglum's assistant at Mt. Rushmore.

Back in Connecticut he spent two years carving his 13 1/2-foot *Noah Webster Statue* as a gift to West Hartford. The work drew national attention but embroiled the community and the sculptor in controversy, foreshadowing what was to come at Crazy Horse. At age 34, he volunteered for service in World War II. He landed on Omaha Beach and, later, was wounded.

At war's end he was invited to make government war memorials in Europe but he had decided to accept an Indians' invitation to carve a statue of the famous Indian leader and to dedicate the rest of his life to Crazy Horse Memorial.

During nearly 36 years he refused to take any salary at Crazy Horse Memorial, on which he worked until his death October 20, 1982 at age 74. He is buried in the tomb he and his sons blasted from a rock outcropping near which the permanent Indian museum will rise at the foot of the mountain carving. For the tomb door he wrote his own epitaph and cut it from three-quarter inch steel plate. It reads:

KORCZAK
Storyteller in Stone
May His Remains Be Left Unknown

In 1998, after the face of Crazy Horse was dedicated, Korczak's sons switched gears from highly detailed finish work to blocking out the horse's head, which requires moving much more rock at a time when lighter charges are used as the closer to the finished surface the workers progress.

A jet finishing torch is used for the final finishing of the surface of the mountain carving. The jet removes drill marks and smooths the final surface. The torch runs on diesel fuel and compressed air. The 3,300 degree F. jet flame causes tiny fragments of rock to flake off as the result of heat expansion, leaving a polished surface. The variety of minerals in the pegmatite granite makes torching a challenge because each mineral reacts to the heat differently.

Crazy Horse Memorial has received many generous gifts of construction equipment and materials over the years. Such equipment has served the Memorial well, but the crew faces a constant challenge of replacing aging equipment. The mountain crew is still using donated equipment that is quite old. The primary source of funding for the work of carving Crazy Horse comes from visitor admission fees, souvenir sales and generous contributions and donations of equipment from corporations which provide critical additional resources to make continued work on the mountain carving possible.

Without Korczak there would never have been a Crazy Horse Memorial. Its history always will revolve around his own extraordinary story, which is reflected in his log studio-home, workshop and sculptural galleries at Crazy Horse. His life and work are an inspiration to many, especially to young people.

Standing Bear's Invitation

"Why am I carving Crazy Horse? That's a very good question. The answer is a very rather unusual story." Korczak stroked his beard slowly and looked at a young boy — a boy scout with narrowed eyes.

"The story began in 1939 — way before you were born. That was the year that marble portrait of Paderewski won first prize by popular vote at the New York World's Fair. Nobody was more surprised than I was."

"The head you carved in five days?"asked Tom.

"Five and one-half days. In my basement under a 60-watt light bulb. It was done in a fury. I didn't even make a clay study for it. I never met Paderewski so that portrait was made from photographs. I had a chance to meet him once 'He asked for me to come visit him,' but I said, 'no.' I was very young then. What did I have to say to such a great man as that? Later, I always wished I had gone He was so remarkable.

"That same year, 1939, I made my first trip to the Black Hills. In early summer I worked briefly as assistant sculptor to Gutzon Borglum at Mt. Rushmore Oh, Mr. Borglum was a great man. I could talk about him all day. We were both members of the National Sculpture Society. But, that's another story. I will say one thing: if it hadn't been for Gutzon Borglum's work at Mt. Rushmore I never could have moved one piece of rock to build a memorial to the Indians in the Black Hills.

"It was ironic that I should come out here to work with him. You see, when I was 13 years old, I had read about Mr. Borglum's plans to carve a mountain in Georgia. I thought carving a mountain was something I would like very much to do when I grew up. I wanted to be a sculptor. Wasn't it unusual that 18 years later I would have the chance to work with Mr. Borglum on a mountain carving?

"I didn't get to work on it for long. Only about two and one-half months. It seems I got into a pretty bad fight with Mr. Borglum's son, and Mr. Borglum had to fire me. I'm very proud of Mr. Borglum's letter where he 'fired' me. He said some very fine things. In fact, I've had an enlarged copy made of it, and it hangs in my room.

"A short time later, out of the blue, I got a curious letter from a person name Chief Henry Standing Bear. He lived on the Pine Ridge Reservation here in South Dakota. He said he understood I'd won the first prize at the World's Fair, to wit: Paderewski, and I guess he knew I'd worked at Mt. Rushmore. Standing Bear said the Indians wanted a mountain carving to honor one of their great chiefs, Crazy Horse. He asked if I'd be interested in carving such a memorial for them.

"Well, Tom, I'd never heard of this Standing Bear. To carve a mountain is not a small thing, so I just thought someone must be playing a practical joke. I'm not sure I even answered that first letter. But, pretty soon Standing Bear wrote another letter, again asking me to carve a mountain. In that second letter he wrote, 'My Fellow Chiefs and I would like the White Man to know the Red Man had great heroes, too.'

"Tom, you must admit, that's an interesting sentence. Very interesting. Mind you, at the time I knew nothing whatsoever about Indians. In fact, I thought they were all gone — like the dodo bird. His second letter made me curious though — especially that one line. I answered Standing Bear that I was thinking about it, and asked him for more details. In the meantime, I went to the library to see what I could find out about Indians. I always loved to go to a library.

"I looked up Crazy Horse in the encyclopedia. There wasn't much information, but what I found was very interesting. It said he was an unusual leader, and that he was one of the Sioux chiefs who defeated Custer at the Battle of Little Big Horn. Of course, I'd heard of that famous battle, but it was news to me Crazy Horse had anything to do with it. I thought it was all Sitting Bull.

"In the encyclopedia it told how the Indians called Crazy Horse their 'strange one,' and how they respected and followed him. It also said as a boy his name was Curly because his hair was long and wavy. It was much lighter in color than other Indians. It was his father who was called Crazy Horse, but he was so proud of Curly, the father took the name, Worm. He gave his own name, Crazy Horse, to his son.

"Don't you think that's rather an unusual thing, Tom?" asked Korczak, his voice very emotional. "To give away his own name!"

Tom replied, "Curly must have done something very special for his father to do that, to take a name like Worm."

Exactly," said Korczak. "I was intrigued. So, I took some books about Indians home with me. Was I in for a surprise. Tom, what Boy Scout Troop are you in?

"I'm in Troop 15."

"There you are! Do you know what you learn in the Scouts? Indian lore! The old Indian tradition is what scouting is all about. Living in the wilderness, tracking, cooking, observing Nature. I had been a Scoutmaster in Boston, and almost everything we studied in scouting came from the Indians."

"I guess that's right," said Tom. "We learned to make a bow and arrow when I was a Cub Scout. And, how to fish with a spear. We tried to make some things like I saw in your Indian Museum."

"Well, those books told how the Indians made and used all those things centuries before we white men came to this country. I also learned the Indians made great contributions to our way of life. Do you know where we got corn, potatoes, squash, turnips, and tobacco? From the Indians. They had all those things before we came here, and they gave them to the white man. Willingly. When the Pilgrims landed here, it was the Indians who saved them from starving. Brought them all kinds of food the white man never knew before. Even wild turkeys, which is why we still eat turkey on Thanksgiving. Ben Franklin wanted the turkey to be our national bird.

"Those books I was studying also told how the federal government had made treaties with the various Indian tribes, and then systematically broke each treaty. It was the first time I learned about that famous Treaty of 1868. In that treaty the President of the United States said, 'As long as rivers run and grass grows and trees bear leaves, Paha Sapa — the Black Hills of Dakota — will forever be the sacred land of the Sioux Indians.'

"But, Tom, after gold was discovered in the Black Hills, just a few miles from where we're sitting now, the white men came and took the Black Hills. I was surprised to learn there was a real gold rush here in 1874 to 1876, and thousands of white men came to get rich. Settlements and towns sprang up everywhere, and the government did nothing to stop them. It broke its treaty with the Indians, who were, sent to reservations. They were lands the white man didn't want.

"Of course the Indians tried to defend themselves in every way they could. The Indian always had lived off the land, but with the taking of his land and the slaughter of the buffalo, it was the end of the trail for the Indian. It was just a matter of time.

"I read about all these things, and I didn't know what to think. Tom, I'm a storyteller in stone. That's all I am, and this story of the American Indian had begun to interest me more than a little. And, there seemed to be a bit of a mystery about this fellow, Crazy Horse. Ever since I was 13, I had wanted to carve a mountain. I started to give the invitation from this Indian more serious thought.

"Standing Bear and I had been exchanging letters, and in the spring of 1940, I decided to come back to South Dakota to meet him to find out more about the Indian Memorial he kept asking me to carve from a mountain."

"Gasoline only cost about eight or nine cents a gallon then, and I decided to drive out. I arrived on the Pine Ridge Reservation in March 1940. It was about the most desolate, lonely place I'd ever seen. There weren't any hotels or motels. Just one brick building where the government agent lived. The rest were a few wooden buildings, pretty dilapidated. There wasn't any snow and it wasn't cold, but the wind blew all the time. It didn't look like anything would grow. The dirt and dust were terrible. I thought it looked like the end of the world. I asked myself, 'Is this where we put the Indians?' I couldn't believe it.

"Standing Bear and his lovely wife lived in a rather neat tiny white house back a little off the main street. There wasn't any room for me, so I slept in my car. I was on the Pine Ridge for three weeks, and I slept in my car the whole time."

"Had you ever met an Indian before?" asked Tom.

"No. Really, I didn't know sickum' from come here about Indians. All I knew was what little bit I'd read. I wasn't quite sure they still existed. That was one the things I wanted to learn by coming to Pine Ridge. Also, I was very curious about this mysterious Crazy Horse. I kept thinking about what Standing Bear had written, 'My Fellow Chiefs and I would like the White Man to know the Red Man had great heroes, too.' What a story line that is."

"Was Standing Bear a real Indian?" asked the boy.

"Oh, yes. Indeed. He was a full blooded Sioux Indian. His skin was a rich full blooded mahogany color, very shiny. An interesting color."

"Did he speak in Sioux?" Tom asked.

"Yes. He spoke Lakota. That's the proper word. Sioux is a French word. Henry spoke Lakota, but also spoke English very well. He gestured a lot and spoke very slowly. He would apologize for his English, but he didn't need to. Henry was a well-educated man. He graduated from Carlisle University. His brother, Luther Standing Bear, had graduated from the first class at Carlisle. Luther had become quite famous in Hollywood. He wrote books about Indian life that were translated into several languages. He illustrated many of them himself. In one of his books he mentions the idea for an Indian memorial similar to what we're doing here.

"When Henry spoke about Crazy Horse, it was with great reverence. Henry was a direct descendent of Crazy Horse, a distant cousin. Although Crazy Horse had no children who lived to maturity, Henry was descended from one of Crazy Horse's uncles. When Henry told me this, he also told me of an Indian tradition that had a great influence on my decision to carve that mountain.

"Standing Bear explained that the Indian has a concept of honoring their great that's totally different from the white man's. It was difficult for me to understand at first. It seems with the Indians only a relative of a great man has the right to honor that man or build a memorial to him. Other people who are not relatives have no right to honor that great man because those people might have evil motives, want to get something out of it.

"It is a rather beautiful way. We white people do it the opposite. Relatives do not seek to build a memorial to a great man. We get a group of citizens together and have them do it. We go through the back door. The Indian uses the direct approach. He says: 'that man was my ancestor, and he was a great man. We should honor him — I would not lie or cheat because I am his blood.'

"You know, Tom, I bought that. Isn't that the right way? No politics."

"So Standing Bear could ask to honor Crazy Horse because he was related to him?" said Tom with a serious expression.

"That's it. Oh, that had a lot of impact on me. I always had been a sucker for a left, but something about that concept of honoring your own hit home to me."

"Did Standing Bear know Crazy Horse?" Tom asked.

"No, but Standing Bear's father had known Crazy Horse. Thus Henry knew a great deal about his great ancestor, Tashuunka Witko. That's Crazy Horse's name in Lakota. I remember him telling me how the Indians called Crazy Horse the 'silent one' or 'strange one' because Crazy Horse was a very quiet man. He never said much. He didn't participate in camp activities or the councils. He always wanted to stay apart by himself.

"As Standing Bear described him, he wasn't a very tall man. Only about 5 feet 7 inches or 5 feet 8 inches, rather slight. He only weighed about 160 pounds. Sioux Indians were usually much larger in stature. As I told you, he was lighter than most Indians and was called Curly because of his wavy hair. Well, it seemed this boy, Curly would distinguish himself in everything he would do. Hunting, fishing and all the things Indian boys did.

"Standing Bear confirmed the story I'd read in the encyclopedia about Crazy Horse's father giving the son his own name. He told the story with great conviction.

"When he was older, Crazy Horse always could go out and bring back food for his tribe in the winter when no one else could find food. He could always get deer or a buffalo. He always would go out alone, but often others would follow. This was how he became a chief, although he was very young.

"As Standing Bear explained it, a chief was not elected as we pick our leaders. A man became a chief if he was the most skilled at whatever he did. If you were the best hunter or the best warrior or the best medicine man, others would follow you. As long as you could produce for the tribe, you would be chief. You see, the Plains Indians were nomads. They didn't live in one place, but they roamed the plains following the food and water supplies and the seasons. They lived from day to day, and those who could provide for them were their leaders.

"Crazy Horse was so skilled at so many things, he became a chief even though he didn't want to be one. He was just a natural leader, and the other Indians wanted to follow him. Since he was such a young man, I don't suppose some of the older Indians much liked the idea of following someone his age, but he was the most skilled, so his people wanted to follow him.

"He was not a council chief, but a war chief. Crazy Horse was a natural military leader. Standing Bear told how he would plan military strategy using decoys to lure his enemies into a trap where he could take them by surprise. Crazy Horse is the first Indian we know of to use the decoy system. It was very successful, although Standing Bear didn't talk much about the battles. He and the others would never mention the Battle of the Little Big Horn, I guess because they won the battle but lost the war.

"He talked with great admiration about Crazy Horse's bravery. He would be at the front of his warriors and enter battle crying, Hoke a heyyy! 'It's a good day to die.' It was a curious thing, but he never wore a war bonnet; Didn't own one; Only a single feather in his hair. He did become a hair shirt warrior, the Indians' highest honor, but it was taken from him.

"Crazy Horse had another brilliant military idea. He never wanted warriors over about the age of 22 years. From about 15 years to 22 years was perfect. They would obey orders without question. Older men had their own ideas.

"Also, Crazy Horse never abandoned his wounded.

"Standing Bear talked so much about Crazy Horse's great military abilities I could hardly believe my ears, Tom. Remember this was a whole new world to me in 1940 on Pine Ridge. Years later I read that President Dwight Eisenhower, a five-star general, said Crazy Horse was the greatest cavalry leader since the Greeks. That's what they teach at the West Point Military Academy. Since the Greeks! That's something for Eisenhower to say.

"During those weeks I was in Pine Ridge, Standing Bear told me this story in bits and pieces. As I mentioned, he spoke very slowly and deliberately. There would be long pauses when he seemed to be in a trance. I would wait and wait. Finally, he would continue. We would talk day after day, and besides telling about Crazy Horse he talked about the traditional Indian way of life.

"He spoke very reverently about the Great Spirit, although I didn't understand much about that concept at the time. He did say all Indians everywhere in this nation worshiped the Great Spirit, and he said there never had been a religious war among the Indian tribes.

"To the Indian, the Earth was the Mother, and the sun, moon and stars — all relatives. Everything was a circle. A circle of life. He told how the Indians took care of Nature, taking from it only what was needed for their existence. One thing I remember so well was his telling about the buffalo. Without the buffalo the Plains Indians could not live. Of course, when the white man came, he slaughtered all the buffalo. Buffalo Bill alone killed about 2,800 in one eight-month period.

"The Indian killed only what buffalo he needed. Standing Bear told how when the Indian took a buffalo, he would turn its head to the east and thank the buffalo for its meat. Every part of the animal was used. Nothing was wasted. The meat was for food, the bones for utensils, jewelry and weapons, the hide was for shelter and clothing. Some parts were for medicine.

"Standing Bear also talked about the craftsmanship of the Indians. How they made the beautiful things you saw in that museum out there: Wonderfully beaded and quilled clothing and moccasins, intricately woven baskets and blankets: Tools and practical items for the household: So many things: All by hand: All from Nature.

"Henry spoke passionately about the Paha Sapa, the Black Hills. They were sacred to the Sioux Indians. To them the Hills were like a cathedral, a sanctuary, their sacred ground. They never lived in the Hills, but would come here only to worship, to hunt and gather berries and edible plants or to get tipi poles.

"Standing Bear grew very angry when he spoke of the broken treaty of 1868. That was the one I'd read about in which the President promised the Black Hills would belong to the Indians forever. I remember how his old eyes flashed out of that dark mahogany face, then he would shake his head and fall silent for a long while.

"After a couple of weeks, I understood why Crazy Horse was a heroic figure to Standing Bear and the others. He had fought valiantly to defend his people and their way of life in the only manner he knew. He never surrendered, never signed a treaty, he had never gone on the reservation. I realized, also, Crazy Horse was a symbol of everything the Indian had stood for and lost, his whole way of life. Most of it was already gone in 1939. Oh, you wouldn't believe how desolate the reservation was: Poverty stricken in every way. It hasn't changed much in these years since.

"Of all the stories Standing Bear told me, one seemed to sum up the whole character of this remarkable man called Crazy Horse: the year after the Battle of Little Big Horn and after all his followers had gone on the reservation, Crazy Horse remained free. The soldiers were searching for him everywhere, but they couldn't catch him.

"One day on the prairie Crazy Horse met a white trader who spoke Lakota. This trader mocked Crazy Horse and made fun of him, saying, 'Where are your lands now, Crazy Horse? All your people are captured and put on reservations. Where are your lands you fought for?' Korczak's voice grew much softer and very emotional.

"It was a beautiful September morning. The sun wasn't too high in a clear sky. It was still and rather warm, just a touch of autumn in the air. Crazy Horse sitting on his pony, said nothing for awhile. He just stared at this white trader. Then, he slowly raised his arm and pointed out over his horse's head to the east, and said proudly, "My lands are where my dead lie buried."

Korczak's voice broke. A small tear slid down his furrowed cheek and trickled into his beard. He continued very softly, "I can hardly tell that story. I get all choked up. Every time. What a story that is!"

"That's why he's pointing over the horse's head?"

"That's why he's pointing. To his lands. Of course, they were all taken when he said that, but as far as you could see in every direction those had been the lands of the Indians. 'My lands are where my dead lie buried,' that's the tragic story of the American Indian in one sentence. It marked the end of Crazy Horse and the end of a beautiful way of life for a proud race of people that had lived here for untold centuries.

"That same day Crazy Horse went to Fort Robinson in Nebraska under a flag of truce to talk about provisions for his people. He was stabbed in the back by a white soldier, and he died early the next morning, September 6, 1877. Crazy Horse was only 33 or 34 years old."

THE MOUNTAIN
Postlude

The mountain portrays a great man who shunned publicity and the camera's eye. He was a man who avoided the limelight. He was a warrior, a superbly courageous one and he was deeply spiritual. He wore the wotai stone, as we have read, a special stone behind his ear when he entered battle. For who made the stone? For who makes all stones especially the protective wotawe; (woe tah way) one's powerful stone which comes to one in a powerful way? Upon these stones are special images or maybe just one significant image placed there whenever they were formed by you know who. The image alone proves the power, the closeness of man to the stone's Creator and the required respect the warrior must carry, if he is to live. The stone is millions of years, how old are we? The warrior who wears a wotai or a wotawe is indeed dependent upon the Spirits when he is in the midst of combat. It is Sioux culture, belief, the Way. One almost needs to wear such a stone and experience the utter ecstasy, confidence, sureness, yes even a occasional sereneness at times, when in the heat of battle for one to truly understand. I do know this: one cannot convey its inner essence to another without having been there. Confidence before battle was just as important as the event for often one needed to plan ones move with a clear head and devoid of panic, even in those last mini-seconds when ballistics, shells, arrows, lance heads, axes, tomahawks were on their way. It is indeed a special gift the Spirit World can grant a warrior and in my opinion, Chief Crazy Horse had it. Red Cloud and Sitting Bull too, among so many Sioux warriors.

Ohhuzhea Wichastah (Oh hoo zhey we chah stah) is a Mystic Warrior. One who follows the Way and most generally carry a special stone or else an ingredient of Creator's Created Nature such as an eagle's or a hawk's claw for example which also are directly made by the Ultimate. Even an eagle feather can have special images. Take a long deep look at one, especially the tail feathers. Every image will be dissimilar. I wore a special wotai in repeated combat. I can only speak from my own observation. It can even slow down time, the rising fire, coming up to dissolve you; these can be seen, and…this can be all bent away by your calm, steady action for the moment. My combat stone had but one significant image. My next one which came to me after my first Sun Dance piercing has many images – many. I respectfully request all of those who have never worn a wotai and have never experienced combat, sheer direct combat, to hold their tongues until they have reached the Spirit World and then they can question such a belief for indeed it is a profound mystery. If you have ever possessed such a gift it is difficult not to be moved deeply when you speak of it.

The great chief wore a stone and now
he is cast in a huge stone —
the Mountain.

* * * *

Notes

Contributors
1. Larry McMurtry, *Crazy Horse* (New York: Penguin, Inc., 1999), p. 11.

Foreword
1. George Catlin, *Episodes From Life Among the Indians* (Norman: University of Oklahoma Press, 1959), p. xxv.

Introduction
1. Larry McMurtry, *Crazy Horse* (New York: Penguin, Inc., 1999), p. 10.
2. Ibid.
3. Jack Weatherford, *Indian Givers* (New York: Crown, 1988), p. 123.
4. Dr. Dale Stover, Eurocentrism and Native Americans: www.aril.org/booksf97.htm Review of Clyde Holler's Sun Dance Books and related commentary on other writers.

Chapter 1 Carolinas
1. Joseph Bruchac, *American Indian Museum* (New York: National Geographic Volume 206, no.3, September, 2004), Supplement.
2. Louie Volpe, *The Pilgrims* (Levittown, NY: Holidays on the Net, 1995) www.holidays.net
3. Dr. Bea Medicine, *Learning to be an Anthropologist and Remaining "Native"* (Urbana and Chicago: University of Chicago Press, 2001), p. 188.

Chapter 4 Red Cloud's War
1. George Hyde, *Red Cloud's Folk* (Norman: University of Oklahoma, 1937).

Chapter 5 Black Elk's Vision
1. Larry McMurtry, *Crazy Horse* (New York: Penguin, Inc., 1999), p. 12.
2. Thor Heyerdahl, *Fatu-Hiva, Back to Nature* (New York: Doubleday and Company, 1974), pp. 198-202.
3. Bill Moyers, *Global Environmental Citizen Award speech* (Boston: Center for Health and the Global Environment at Harvard Medical School, 2004)

4. John Neihardt, *Black Elk Speaks* (Lincoln: University of Nebraska Press, 1961).
5. Ed McGaa, *Nature's Way* (San Francisco: Harper/Collins, 2005), pp. 74-77.
6. www.hiawatha.historicasylums.com
7. Raymond DeMallie, *The Sixth Grandfather* (Lincoln: University of Nebraska Press, 1984) pp. 12-14.
8. Dr. Dale Stover, Eurocentrism and Native Americans: www.aril.org/booksf97.htm Review of Clyde Holler's Sun Dance Books and related commentary on other writers.
9. Larry McMurtry, *Crazy Horse* (New York: Penguin, Inc., 1999), p. 13.
10. Ibid., pp. 7, 8.
11. Ibid., p. 8.
12. Ibid., p. 9.
13. Ibid., p.10.

Chapter 7 Crazy Horse and the Little Big Horn

1. Larry McMurtry, *Crazy Horse* (New York: Penguin, Inc., 1999), p. 91.
2. www.Indians.org

Chapter 8 Ghost Dance

1. Larson, Robert W., *Red Cloud, Warrior - Statesman of the Lakota Sioux* (Norman: University of Oklahoma Press, 1997), p. 280.
2. Ibid., p. 281.
3. Ibid., pp. 281, 282.
4. Ibid., p. 282-285.
5. Ibid., p. 301.
6. Ibid., p. 293.
7. McGaa, Ed, *Rainbow Tribe* (San Francisco: Harper/Collins, 1992), Chapter 10.

Chapter 9 Spirit Ceremony

1. John M. Cooper, *Plato's Complete Works - Plato's Republic* (Indianapolis, IN: Hackett Publishing Co. 1997), pp. 1132-1134.

Chapter 10 The Mountain

1. Robb DeWall, *Crazy Horse and Korczak - The story of an epic mountain carving.* (Crazy Horse, SD: Korczaks Heritage, Inc., 1982), pp. 49-60.

Other Books written by Ed McGaa

Mother Earth Spirituality:
Healing Ourselves and Our World

Rainbow Tribe:
Ordinary People Journeying on the Red Road

Native Wisdom:
Perceptions of the Natural Way

Eagle Vision:
A Sioux Novel of a Tribe's Return

Nature's Way:
Native Wisdom for Living in Balance with the Earth

$15 plus $2 for mailing

For autographed copies of the above publications
send check or money order only, in U.S. currency to:

Four Directions Publishing
1117 Silver Street
Rapid City, SD 57701

Correspondence:
Eagleman4@aol.com or Pahaeagle@rap.midco.net